ANY FAIR INTERFERENCE

A PRIDE & PREJUDICE VARIATION

NAN HARRISON

This is a work of fiction. Names, characters, businesses, places, events, locales, and incidents are either the products of the author's imagination or used in a fictitious manner. Any resemblance to actual persons, living or dead, or actual events is purely coincidental.

Edited by Debra Anne Watson and Regina McCaughey-Silvia

Cover Design by Beetiful Book Covers

ISBN: 978-1-956613-12-4 (ebook) and 978-1-956613-13-1 (paperback)

To Tom, for all our laughter-filled adventures

CHAPTER 1

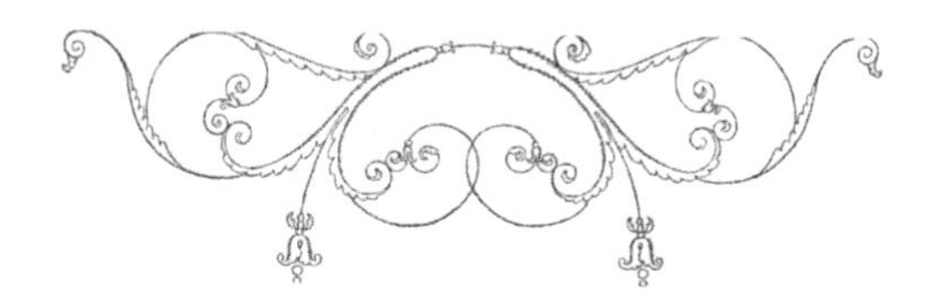

Netherfield Ball, 26 November 1811

Fitzwilliam Darcy had dressed with special care, though neither the occasion nor the company merited such distinction. He could not satisfactorily explain the compulsion, even to himself. He would not dance, of course, despite some broad hints from Miss Bingley about the opening set. If forced, he would sooner dance with Mrs Hurst, a sweet, reticent lady who was shamefully ignored by her husband, but he could not dance with her without dancing with her sister. In any event, Mrs Hurst would be preoccupied with the details of a hostess, having, he suspected, shouldered the burdens of planning the ball while Miss Bingley claimed the credit.

No, he would not dance. That would be publicly singling out any lady he chose to ask, causing gossip. He would not do that here. There was no lady worthy of his attentions. Certainly not.

Amid a sudden cacophony of loud greetings and shrill clamours of delight, a low, melodic gurgle of laughter caught his ear, causing his head to whip around reflexively. The Bennets had arrived and were gathered in the receiving line. Good God, *all* of them, even Mr Bennet himself. How on earth had they all fit in the carriage? That stout, sweating parson must have taken up most of one seat.

Miss Elizabeth Bennet, under cover of the noisy confusion, had slipped away from her family to greet Miss Lucas, her particular friend. The two ladies laughed and chatted merrily. Elizabeth's smile was dazzling, and her marvellous eyes sparkled with anticipation as they roved the brightly lit, beautifully appointed ballroom. Her gown would never pass muster in town, of course, but it clung delightfully in all the right places. Her unruly curls, no matter how they were styled, always seemed as if they might tumble about her shoulders at any moment, even with the pearl hairpins she was wearing.

Frowning, Darcy belatedly stepped back into an ill lit corner so as not to draw notice. He watched as Elizabeth seemingly searched the crowd. Was she seeking him? She *had* seemed to flirt with him while she stayed at Netherfield. Though it had not exactly been the same coquettish behaviour of the ladies of the *ton*, that was what it had to be. All ladies flirted with him. He saw the excitement on her radiant countenance fade into disappointment. Miss Lucas, one brow arched, said something in her ear. An expression of vexation flitted across Elizabeth's face, her lips thinned, but she rolled her eyes and said something back to Miss Lucas, and both ladies laughed.

Perhaps one dance…

Quis custodiet ipsos custodes? Who watches the watcher? mused Gilbert Hurst, as he observed the great and powerful Fitzwilliam Darcy half-hiding in a corner, staring at Miss Elizabeth Bennet. *Apparently,* I *do*.

He had wandered away from the receiving line early, to his wife's dismay. He should have stayed, he knew that. He had disappointed Louisa. Again. She had worked so hard to put together the ball that the youngest Miss Bennets had demanded of Charles, but Hurst had had more than enough of Caroline's airs.

He relaxed against the orange silk upholstery of an impractically delicate ballroom chair near the punch bowl, enjoying his third glass. Conversation droned around him. He had already conversed with garrulous, kind-hearted Sir William Lucas, and was anticipating a pleasant verbal joust with the intelligent though self-absorbed patriarch of the Bennet family as well.

The ball proceeded apace, and his vision began to blur a bit under the influence of the punch. And the glasses of wine he had drunk before the guests arrived. And the ale he had enjoyed in the late afternoon. Bingley and Miss Bennet seemed to be in a world of their own, with only Caroline to forcefully remind her brother to dance with other young ladies occasionally. Mrs Bennet's voice arced from one end of the ballroom to the other. Miss Elizabeth's lovely smile was less and less in evidence, her easy grace a striking contrast to Mr Collins's ponderous clumsiness. She was soon restored to her usual cheer by a dance with one of the officers.

Darcy, on the other hand, had been reduced to an elegant shadow, slowly pacing along the wall, observing the dancers, and periodically being forced to converse awkwardly with the most persistent of the locals. As Hurst watched, he straightened his shoulders, seeming to arrive at some sort of decision, and strode across the floor towards Miss Elizabeth. He stopped in front of her, made a slight bow, and spoke briefly, startling her. She stared up at him, wide-eyed, her lips parted in surprise, then nodded slightly. Darcy stalked away, and the look of consternation that crossed her features made Miss Lucas laugh heartily.

What is this? Had Darcy asked Miss Elizabeth for a dance? Caroline would not be happy. Miss Elizabeth did not look happy either. *Interesting.* Other young ladies, when solicited for a dance by such a man, would instantly disappear into the ladies' retiring room to fix their hair, bite their lips, and pinch their cheeks into rosiness. Not this girl.

She does not like him! Hurst realised. Memories slowly took shape in his soporific brain. When Miss Elizabeth had stayed at Netherfield, Darcy had uncharacteristically engaged her in conversation on the few occasions she had joined their company. Their verbal exchanges had been uneven: he seemingly transfixed, she obviously vexed. Caroline had inserted herself into their conversations, endeavouring to flatter Darcy and shine an unfavourable light on Miss Elizabeth. Darcy had even asked her to dance a reel, and she had refused! She had done it with grace and humour, but it was a refusal. *She is a spirited one.* Or perhaps foolhardy, if what was rumoured about her prospects was true. *How would this play out?*

Soon enough, Darcy was leading Miss Elizabeth out onto the floor. Hurst sat up in his chair, intrigued, wondering what he might witness. Darcy moved with his usual stateliness, while she seemed slightly tense, almost glaring at him. Hurst could see them begin to speak as they moved gracefully together through the complicated steps. Seemingly, their conversation intensified; they focused on each other to the exclusion of all else. Miss Elizabeth's complexion flushed, a beautiful pale rose tint moving slowly up her bosom to her neck and her face. Darcy was staring at her wide-eyed, first his cheeks, then his entire countenance shading scarlet. The music ended, and for a long moment, they stood silently, facing each other, trapped in each other's gaze. Darcy broke the spell, bowing jerkily; Miss Elizabeth offered a perfunctory curtsey. They both turned on their heels and walked off the dance floor in opposite directions.

Well! What could they have been discussing? After witnessing that little scene, Hurst was alert; the lassitude brought on by the accumulation of alcohol in his system was gone. Had anyone else noticed? The odd pairing of Darcy and Miss Elizabeth most likely had been observed, but the talk was predominantly of Miss Bennet and Bingley. Sir William Lucas could be overheard declaiming something about a 'certain desirable event', and others were nodding, imagining future balls at Netherfield. Bingley was oblivious, Caroline was fuming, Darcy was sulking in a corner, and poor Louisa looked exhausted.

Hurst rose from his chair. Enough idleness. He needed to show some concern for his wife. He would take her in to supper and then see if she would dance with him.

TWO DAYS LATER, pale morning sunbeams slipped briefly through the leaden clouds, so low in the eastern sky they were nearly horizontal. Their light poured fleetingly over the Hertfordshire landscape and through the carriage window, vexing and inconveniencing Mr Hurst. He was feigning sleep, leaning his head against the side wall of the carriage with his eyes screwed tightly shut. If only he had had a brandy or two, or maybe three, before leaving, he could have had the escape of actual slumber. But it had been too early in the day, even for him.

Too early, as well, to be stuck in a carriage with Louisa and Caroline. The latter was in a state of near euphoria, having convinced Darcy that their party urgently needed to leave Netherfield and join Bingley in London, where he had journeyed on business only the day before.

Hurst cursed himself for having ridden in the carriage, instead of following Darcy's example and riding horseback. Now he was forced to listen to Caroline crow all the way to town. She was in rare form. There were not enough words, or volume, to disparage the vulgarity and shabbiness of the country neighbourhood, in particular the Bennet family, and more in particular, the two eldest Miss Bennets. He surreptitiously cracked open one eye and peered through the window at Darcy, riding beside the carriage. Darcy's posture was tense, his face seeming carved in stone. The man did not look any happier than Hurst felt, though he and Caroline had won the debate over returning to town. *Perhaps it is just as well to ride in the carriage.*

Louisa sat next to her husband, unable to escape her sister's soliloquy, replying in monosyllables, her fingers unconsciously twisting the charms on her bracelet.

Hurst felt the slightest twinge, but absolved himself, leaving her to contend with Caroline alone. *She is used to it, old man.* Finally Louisa, too, pretended weariness, which quickly turned into fitful sleep.

Hours later, the carriage rolled into London, and its exhausted occupants recovered in the faded comfort of the Hursts' town house on Grosvenor Square. Hurst sought out the soothing relief of a bottle of wine in his study, while Louisa retired to her rooms.

Darcy rode on to his club, where Bingley, meaning to return to Netherfield within days, was staying. He retrieved his baffled friend and returned with him to the town house. Caroline was waiting to receive them. She had asked Louisa and Hurst to be a part of the family confab, but they both refused, pleading exhaustion. Louisa genuinely did look tired and unhappy, but Hurst had simply wanted no part of what was to come. Caroline and Darcy were going to tell Charles that the lovely young woman he had lost his heart to did not return his regard.

After a short time, he perceived raised voices, particularly Caroline's, coming from the drawing room. Then the doors burst open, and Charles walked quickly, almost running, out of the room and down the stairs to the front door. His friend was right behind him. The two gentlemen left immediately for Darcy House; Bingley's overheated, red countenance showing obvious distress, Darcy's face a pale, rigid mask.

ENSCONCED IN A SAGGING armchair with his feet comfortably propped on a threadbare footstool, Hurst sipped his wine, reflecting on the previous weeks. He was glad to be back in town, but he had not thought Hertfordshire so bad. Surprising, since he generally was not inclined towards country life. His family had an estate in Northamptonshire, but Hurst left the management of that to his younger brother and handled the family's business interests in London.

Hurst had not considered the residents of Meryton as beneath him, as Caroline did, even though his own family ranked quite above the Bingleys. Certainly he had seen examples of behaviour that could be considered vulgar and gauche, but he could see that in town too, among the ranks of the nobility. If Mrs Bennet was avaricious, loud, and crass, so were dozens of fashionable mothers of the *ton*. He had discovered that Mr Bennet had a sly sense of humour, and had enjoyed a pleasantly satirical conversation with him at the ball until the older gentleman had been called away to prevent Miss Mary Bennet from monopolising the pianoforte. He had enjoyed meeting Miss Bennet and felt that Louisa had relaxed a bit around her. Louisa had smiled more often in Miss Bennet's gentle company, and her habit of nervous fidgeting had stilled.

Hurst was certain Bingley was utterly in love with Miss Bennet. He had seen him in love several times before, but this time it was different. There was something in the air when they were together, as they had been to an indecent extent during the ball.

Could Darcy have truly not seen any evidence of Miss Bennet's regard for Bingley?

Perhaps Darcy has never been in love himself, or perhaps his experiences with the *ton* had made him cynical. Hurst snorted. The marriage mart of the *ton* would make Cupid himself cynical. And Caroline, of course, never noticed anyone, unless she thought they might be advantageous to know. She fumed at the possibility of her brother forming a connexion with the Bennets, and had long had her sights on Darcy as her own future husband. The prestige of such a match would surely, finally, bring her acceptance among the *haute ton*, banishing at last any taint of trade.

While it was the nascent attachment between the two young people that had precipitated their abrupt departure, Hurst had discovered himself to be envious of their budding love. As he had danced with his wife that evening, he had been unable to put it out of his mind.

DARCY AND BINGLEY drew up in front of the Darcy town house on Brook Street. Bingley had not spoken since leaving the Hursts'. Flushed and agitated, his unseeing eyes stared straight ahead, his lips were set in a grim line. They handed their horses off to a pair of grooms and Bingley followed his friend into the house. He had taken up Darcy's offer of hospitality when he had understood their reason for quitting Netherfield. Darcy guiltily had no wish to exacerbate his profound disappointment by forcing him to be in proximity to his sister and had pressed his friend to stay with him.

Darcy broke the long silence, "Your things have been sent to your usual chamber, Bingley."

"Thank you," Bingley said in a low voice, not meeting his eyes, "and thank you for your hospitality. I am going to my rooms now," and without another word climbed the stairs.

Uncharacteristically ill at ease, Darcy needed time to collect himself after the distasteful scene he had just been party to. He stood, wool-gathering, at the bottom of the staircase for some moments and then, shaking himself, retreated to his study for a drink.

It had been a ghastly day. During the hours-long journey from Hertfordshire, he had ridden alongside the carriage, trying to ignore the muffled sounds of Caroline's vocal exertions through the walls of the conveyance. He was glad, even relieved, to be leaving the small society of Meryton behind. So relieved, in fact, he had fought the urge to gallop all the way to town.

To be sure, the Netherfield estate was satisfactory, and upon improvement could be excellent. His friend's infatuation with a young lady from a neighbouring estate had changed the situation.

Darcy had observed the beautiful and serene Miss Jane Bennet over the course of their stay, and though her eyes lingered on Bingley's face and her smile was warm, he convinced himself that she did not reciprocate the depth of Bingley's regard. He felt compassion for Bingley, who had reacted with shocked distress to the truth they had just revealed to him, but Darcy believed that his friend's natural cheerfulness would quickly reassert itself. No doubt he was doing a great service, discouraging him from pursuing a woman whose family was inferior and mercenary. It was his duty, and he knew that someday Bingley would thank him.

Uninvited, a lovely, laughing face with sparkling eyes rose before his mind's eye. He squeezed his eyes shut and dismissed the vision. If she had had a larger fortune or better connexions, he might have been in some danger, but that was not the case. *A minor distraction. I will acquire a suitable wife in town this Season, and that will be the end of it.*

WITHIN THE HOUR, the butler knocked on the door and announced his cousin. Colonel Richard Fitzwilliam walked into the room with his usual good-humoured air, but checked his step when he caught sight of the glower on his cousin's face. "Darcy! Back from Hertfordshire already? Mother saw you riding in Grosvenor Square today, and told me that you were in town. I had not expected your return so soon."

The frown on Darcy's face deepened. "It became necessary to remove from Hertfordshire earlier than planned," he said. "Bingley was on the verge of making an imprudent alliance. A young lady from a small estate, with no fortune, an indecorous family, and objectionable connexions, including relatives in trade."

He stifled his annoyance when his cousin rolled his eyes. Though the son of an earl, Fitzwilliam was a military man with a wide acquaintance who delighted in chaffing his punctilious cousin with his more relaxed views on social rank.

"Be that as it may, that still makes the young lady a gentleman's daughter. I fail to understand how she is so ineligible. I also fail to understand why Bingley should not make these decisions for himself."

"Bingley needs to marry to enhance his family's prestige. His heart is easily engaged, so he needs guidance and advice from someone who has experience navigating the *ton*," replied Darcy his countenance and tone both hardening defensively.

Smirking, Fitzwilliam retorted, "So you, dear cousin, *you*, who despises the *ton* and the Season and everything about it, are going to guide your friend through society? You do not even like coming to town!"

"That is true. However, I am renewing my efforts to find an appropriate wife," said Darcy. "I have been remiss in my responsibilities. Pemberley needs a mistress, and we both know Georgiana needs more female companionship."

He felt Fitzwilliam's curious, assessing gaze, and would not meet his eye. It was difficult to hide his emotions from his cousin, and behind his superior expression, Darcy felt unsettled. He could only imagine the interrogation Fitzwilliam was likely to launch.

CHAPTER 2

A few days after settling back into their home, Hurst received a letter from his business agent, a Mr Henderson, requesting a meeting to discuss an investment opportunity. He readily agreed, and returned the message, not wishing to spend any more time listening to his sister-in-law pontificate about society. His conscience niggled at leaving Louisa alone with Caroline, but any efforts on his part to separate the sisters in the past had come to naught, and he was resigned.

Their marriage had been a business proposition. The Hursts were an ancient family, fallen on hard times. He and his younger brother, Arthur, had been working to rebuild the family fortunes, which had suffered from the profligate behaviour and disastrous investments of their father. Louisa had brought her twenty thousand pounds to the marriage, and Hurst had brought his old and distinguished family name. It had been an important step towards the Bingley family objective of recasting themselves as gentlefolk. The marriage had been one of the last arrangements made by old Mr Bingley before he died.

In his youth, Hurst had thought himself in love with a flaxen-haired girl from an adjoining estate. He and Marianne Winstone had spent sunlit days playing in the woods and meadows between the two manor houses. Their mothers would sit picnicking in the grass as they rambled around the gardens, little Arthur trying to keep up. After his mother died, kind Mrs Winstone had tried to assuage their grief, inviting to the boys to their home again and again, but in due course, the families grew apart. His father went into an alcohol-fuelled decline, frittering away the family's assets, though the boys were unaware of any changes other than fewer servants and the increasing dilapidation of the manor house and outbuildings.

Over time, Hurst's feelings towards his playfellow turned to young love, and he thought she loved him in return. He wrote to her from university. Eventually, her replies became less frequent, changing in tone from familiar enthusiasm to stilted politeness. Still, when he was home on holiday from Cambridge, he asked Winstone's permission to court Marianne. His request was refused on the grounds of his lack of fortune and his family's declining reputation.

Marianne forgot about him, and Gilbert found that drink sometimes dulled his loneliness. Hurst went back to university and redoubled his efforts, both in the classroom and in society. He attended dances and parties, and even spent a Season in the family's now-shabby town house, hoping he might find a young lady to share his future hopes and dreams with—but the status of his fortune had preceded him to London. The young ladies he met there were civil, but not welcoming. His thin, handsome face took on a hard, cynical look, his expression sour. He almost always had a drink in his hand, never drinking to the point of intoxication, though he had dozed off on more than one elegant settee. He began to find the habit of small talk annoying and hypocritical, and so spoke little. By his twenty-fifth year, he had gained the reputation of being cross as crabs. Hurst contemplated not marrying at all, but for the sake of the estate, he needed to marry for money. Following a chain of rumours and gossip, he met the elder Mr Bingley, and a deal was struck.

After their marriage, he began to admire Louisa. She had lovely fair skin and large expressive grey eyes. She rarely smiled, but when she did, it was beautiful. She was a graceful dancer. She played the pianoforte beautifully and expressively.

Even though they had been married for almost three years, she did not reveal much of herself around him. She was an enigma. Moreover, her quiet ways intrigued him. They spent nights together when Hurst requested it, but Louisa gave him no indication of real affection. She was respectful, did her duty as a wife, but otherwise did not seek him out.

What he had not known at the time of his marriage was that his wife came with her sister, and it seemed they were inseparable. Moreover, he discovered that when Louisa was around Caroline, she seemed to disappear. Caroline dominated the conversation and Louisa concurred with her out of long habit, often while staring out the window.

Upon their marriage, Hurst had determined they would have a wedding trip; a holiday to get to know one other. Louisa was pretty and pleasant, if perhaps diffident, and he had great hopes for their marriage. New brides were often accompanied by a female relative, so he had not thought it unusual when her sister had accompanied them. He had determined not to spend any of Louisa's dowry on a lavish trip. That money was for their estate and their future together. He had rented a modest cottage by the sea in Blackpool, only for a week.

The first inkling of the imminent ordeal occurred shortly after they had embarked, and escalated from there. The carriage was not as comfortable as their father's. The inns were not up to their standards. Why could they not also hire a private dining room? Blackpool was out of fashion, why were they not going to Brighton? The shops were execrable. The cottage was too small, it was damp, and why was it not directly on the esplanade? Caroline had spent the entire week complaining. Just thinking about it made Hurst pour himself another drink.

HURST WOULD HAVE NEVER SUSPECTED that he intrigued Louisa as much as she intrigued him. She did not dislike him. Indeed, she was greatly relieved not to have been married to her father's other choice for her, a portly, pocked-faced baronet in his forties. Her husband was never rude to her, but he often ignored her. He was a tall, slender man who hid behind a habitual scowl, and often as well behind a glass of some fiery liquid.

On their nights together, he was always gentle and oddly formal. He usually retired to his own room after he had finished, sometimes with a quiet thank you, but a few times he had fallen asleep in her bed beside her. She had lain next to him, watching him breathe. When he was relaxed, his face was so handsome. Once he had smiled in his sleep, and it had touched something inside her. She had touched his face gently, but he had stirred, and she immediately feigned sleep.

CAROLINE BINGLEY WAS AN INDIFFERENT CORRESPONDENT. She took no enjoyment from writing or receiving letters as other young ladies did; she had no bosom friends with whom to exchange long, cosy missives. The joy of settling into a chair to rejoice in happy news or commiserate with the lamentations of a loved one was beyond her understanding. Upon leaving Netherfield, she had suggested a correspondence with Miss Jane Bennet merely as a convention. She had no real intention of furthering her acquaintance with anyone from Longbourn.

Only a few days into December, a missive from Miss Bennet appeared on a stack of letters in the study. Caroline snatched it up, fearing Charles or Louisa might see it. She held the letter in one hand, tapping it against the other while considering what to do. Her gaze swept over to the fire. She rolled her eyes when she realised that even if she disposed of it, Miss Bennet would most likely write another. Caroline went to her writing desk and skimmed Jane's letter. *How dull! As if any of us would be interested in their pathetic drab lives.*

Smirking, Caroline sat down to write. She described loftily to Miss Bennet how exceedingly busy they all were; how they hardly had a moment to draw breath for all their social obligations. She mentioned more than once that unfortunately she herself really had almost no time for correspondence. She also mentioned that Miss Darcy, a particular favourite of theirs, would be in town soon (*Well, she might*, reasoned Caroline), and that she and Charles would be much in company with each other. Caroline's object, to shame Miss Bennet into epistolary silence, succeeded. There were no more letters from Longbourn.

Welcoming the opportunity to get out of the house, the two eldest Bennet sisters walked to Meryton with some commissions from their mother. The early December day was unusually fine. Elizabeth loved the pale golden light and crisp, clear air. She had not taken time to appreciate the late autumn beauty around her. She had been preoccupied with the inmates of Netherfield for the past several weeks: her sister's growing attachment to Mr Bingley, her mother's public behaviour, Mr Darcy's dark, forbidding stares. She felt a tingly shiver run up her spine and shook it off. The sisters went in and out of the shops, stopping to chat with acquaintances along the way.

Elizabeth half expected to encounter Mr Wickham in the village. She had hoped some conversation with him would lighten her mood, but he was not to be seen.

As the girls turned to make their way back to Longbourn, they saw their Uncle Philips standing outside his offices, taking a moment to bask in the lukewarm sunshine. He greeted them affectionately, teasing Elizabeth, "Looking for a handsome officer, Lizzy?" Elizabeth blushed faintly, but laughed at her uncle's gentle jest. Jane smiled, but it did not reach her eyes.

Their uncle, a great friendly bear of a man, regarded his nieces with compassion. Exchanging a commiserating glance with Elizabeth, he gently chucked Jane under the chin before they started for home, just as he had done when she was a little girl. Elizabeth had perceived other pitying looks covertly cast their way as they passed through the town. While Netherfield had been occupied, the local residents had expected any day to hear an announcement pertaining to Jane and Mr Bingley. When the Bingley party suddenly withdrew from the neighbourhood, the general feeling was that Jane, who was quite a favourite in Meryton, had been ill-used.

Elizabeth concurred. She had been keeping a close eye on

her eldest sister since Jane had received Miss Bingley's note apprising her of their departure from Netherfield. Elizabeth distrusted the rather too effusive protestations of friendship in her letter. On the surface, Jane seemed to be her usual composed self, her appearance of tranquillity hiding her hurt and confusion from everyone but her sister. Elizabeth remembered Charlotte's warning that Jane's natural reserve might fool Mr Bingley into believing that she did not care deeply for him. She firmly believed that Mr Bingley had not been allowed to make that decision for himself.

As Jane continued to make excuses for Mr Bingley's unceremonious disappearance from her life, Elizabeth was fuming. Miss Bingley's subsequent letter made it clear that her objective was to keep Bingley away from Jane and push him into the path of Miss Darcy. She did not know whether it was Miss Bingley or Mr Darcy who had engineered the destruction of her sister's happiness, but suspected that together they had conspired to keep Bingley from making a misalliance.

Of course, Miss Bingley was pursuing her own ambitions. If she could get her brother married to Miss Darcy, it would increase her own chances of trapping Mr Darcy. If she had not been so vexed, Elizabeth might have found some amusement in Miss Bingley's hopeless designs. Apparently, that lady was unaware her ambitions were doomed to failure, and that Mr Darcy was expected by his family to marry his cousin; Mr Collins had told them all about it. Elizabeth smirked. From Mr Collins's grandiloquent and appalling description of Lady Catherine, Mr Darcy deserved to be her son-in-law.

A more immediate problem was their mother. Mrs Bennet remained callously insensitive to Jane's sorrow and humiliation, constantly reminding her eldest daughter of what she had lost when Mr Bingley left Netherfield without a word. Her habitually tactless comments were made worse by the disappointment of her hopes of having two daughters engaged: Jane to Mr Bingley and Elizabeth to Mr Collins. She simply could not leave the subject alone. While she tactlessly pestered Jane with speculation about Mr Bingley's departure, she angrily castigated Elizabeth for having refused Mr Collins.

As THE SISTERS retraced their steps towards Longbourn, the stiffening breeze dropped a piece of fabric right at Elizabeth's feet. She bent to pick it up and found she was holding a man's large handkerchief made of fine lawn material. It had been made into a handkerchief dolly, the middle tied into a head and two corners tied into knots approximating hands. It was smudged and dirty, and had a sticky spot of jam on it. Someone had crudely stitched a smiling face on the head with yarn, but of greater interest were the initials *FD,* expertly and exquisitely embroidered on a corner in a complicated entwining design. It was the most beautiful silk thread she had ever seen; even through the dirt, it glowed in the pale afternoon light.

"Miss Lizzy! That's my dolly!"

They turned to see a small girl running towards them. "That's *my* dolly!" the child repeated. It was Meggy Elkins, the blacksmith's daughter.

"How fortunate that we found it, Meggy! Your dolly was going on an adventure with the wind." Elizabeth knelt down and placed the handkerchief into the little girl's hands. "Wherever did you get such a pretty dolly?"

"A man made it for me," the little girl said solemnly. "He had a big black horse that threw a shoe. We were supposed to go home for supper, but Papa had to stay and fix the shoe. I wanted to go home; I was so hungry! So the man took out his handkerchief and made a dolly for me so I wouldn't cry. He said he made dollies for his little sister when she couldn't sit still in church." She beamed proudly, touching the yarn stitching. "When we got home, my mam made the face."

"I wonder who the man was," said Jane.

"Did he tell you his name?" asked Elizabeth.

"No." The child thought for a minute. "Papa said he had a very fine horse, though." She scampered away, and the sisters tried to think of anyone they knew with the initials FD. Mr Denny's Christian name was Horace, so it could not be he.

"Perhaps it was Mr Darcy?" ventured Jane.

Elizabeth had to laugh. "Can you imagine Mr Darcy sitting with a blacksmith's child and making her a dolly?"

Jane smiled noncommittally and pulled her sister back to the path to Longbourn.

THE SUN WAS low in the sky as the sisters neared the house, and the chilly breeze had strengthened. Jane and Elizabeth entered the house through the kitchen door. As they came through the hall, they could hear their parents' voices in conversation, discussing the upcoming reprise of their cousin's visit.

"Only think, Mr Bennet, that we are again forced to offer our hospitality to Mr Collins! He and Charlotte Lucas will be continually talking of when they can turn us all out! I cannot bear to think that they should have our home! How vexing to think that Lizzy might have been Mr Collins's wife! And Jane might have been Mr Bingley's! They say in Meryton that Mr Bingley is not coming back."

"I would not have Lizzy marry Mr Collins, and as for Jane, next to being married, a girl likes to be crossed in love a little now and then. It gives her something to think of and lends her a sort of distinction among her companions," replied Mr Bennet with his usual dry tone.

Jane froze, her face stricken, and then recovering herself, said, "I am going upstairs to rest, Lizzy. I am afraid our walk tired me out."

Elizabeth was speechless. Did not her parents understand how deeply they hurt Jane, each in their own way? She stepped back outside to escape the sound of their voices. Looking to the west in the waning light, she watched a line of ragged dark clouds in the far distance and felt the chill wind gain strength. A line from a sonnet appeared in her mind, '*How like a winter hath my absence been from thee, the pleasure of the fleeting year! What freezings have I felt, what dark days seen! What old December's bareness every where!*' She shivered and went into the house.

ON THE APPOINTED DAY, Hurst sat down warily in Henderson's office; the man beamed at him.

"Mr Hurst, I have an investment opportunity for you. Now that the Somerleigh estate is beginning to show a profit again, diversifying your investments will make you and your family less vulnerable to crop failures and variations in grain prices."

"I have met a businessman," Henderson continued, "a Mr Edward Gardiner, who has extensive holdings in imports, shipping, and warehouses, and he is looking for investors in all aspects of his operations. He has enjoyed great prosperity, and now needs investors to help his company expand."

Hurst pricked up his ears, his posture suddenly erect, his eyes meeting Henderson's. *This sounds promising.*

"I have been making enquiries," continued Mr Henderson, "and have found nothing amiss, or I would not have brought it to your attention. His finances are sound. He has been in business these eighteen years, beginning with one warehouse and gradually expanding. He is a shrewd and careful entrepreneur. His father was a respectable country solicitor, and he studied law and attended university before he chose a career in commerce."

"Why is he looking for investors, then?"

"His shipping line is in need of expansion to meet demand. He could afford to finance the expansion himself, but does not wish to leave his warehouses underfunded."

"Well, by all means, let us become acquainted with this paragon," said Hurst. "Perhaps I will be able to steal some thunder from my brother Bingley, or even his friend Darcy."

THE NOTE CAME from Henderson within hours. Would it be possible to meet Thursday morning at his offices? Hurst sent a note in agreement, then sat down to pen a letter to his brother to notify him of the upcoming meeting and describe what he knew of the possible investment. He knew Arthur's reply would not arrive before his meeting, but the brothers always discussed their ventures with each other; his brother's letters always describing in detail the ongoing improvements to the house and grounds of their estate. Hurst had begun to feel pangs of jealousy when he read them. Arthur was actively working towards the physical improvement of their old family seat, while he was in London handling business affairs and unfortunately, hobnobbing with people he cared nothing about. Hurst was beginning to feel oppressed by the hauteur and indolence of the *ton*. When he and Arthur had devised their plan to raise their family fortunes, he was happy to leave the crumbling farm. Lately, with his marriage, and gaining in maturity, happy childhood memories of rambling about the old estate began to creep into his head. *Silly,* he thought, shaking his head. The envy, however slight, that he felt for Arthur left him unsettled.

His thoughts strayed to Louisa. A marriage of convenience for both sides. His family gained money to invest in the estate and her family gained in social rank. Suddenly, surprisingly, he wished it were more. He had come to admire her quiet grace and elegant manners. And she had a good mind, that girl. He poured himself another glass of wine. Could he somehow show Louisa his growing regard? He took a sip reflectively. In order to find out, something had to be done about Caroline.

THE DAYS SLIPPED BY, and Jane, all protestations to the contrary, did not recover her spirits. Charlotte was immersed in wedding preparations, so Elizabeth could not confide in her, and she simply could not speak of her concern to her parents. Her mother would have one of her spasms and her father would make sport of it.

Desperate to talk to someone, Elizabeth thought of her Aunt Gardiner, her closest confidante save Charlotte and Jane. She sat down at the little writing desk in her room, took out paper and ink, and carefully considered what to say. As she went over the events in her mind, she realised that the Bingleys had only quit Netherfield a little less than two weeks previous. Despite Miss Bingley's letter implying that they would never come back, Elizabeth wondered if that was true. A fortnight was not a long time.

What if Mr Bingley did return, and wished to court Jane? If this happened, she did not want their admired aunt to think poorly of him. After some further thought, she decided not to name the members of the Netherfield party, but to refer to them by initials. She set to work on her letter, describing the events of the Netherfield party's visit: their words, their behaviour, and their personalities.

After a few days, her aunt's reply arrived. Mrs Gardiner sympathised with her nieces. She pointed out that though Elizabeth's account was certainly not impartial, from what she had been told, Mr Bingley's sister had probably talked him out of returning to Netherfield any time soon.

She disagreed with Elizabeth over Mr Darcy's role in the matter, however. Elizabeth bristled as she read her aunt's opinion that Mr Darcy may have been attracted to *her*, in which case he certainly could not have wished to leave Netherfield.

Where had her aunt gotten that idea? Charlotte had reached the same conclusion, and Elizabeth had scoffed. She and Mr Darcy had disliked each other on sight. In every encounter, they argued with and vexed one another. Aunt Gardiner had some strange notions about what constituted attraction.

When Mrs Gardiner went on to suggest that Jane spend a few weeks with them in London when they returned to town after Festive Season, Elizabeth rejoiced. The invitation was just what she had been hoping for.

CHAPTER 3

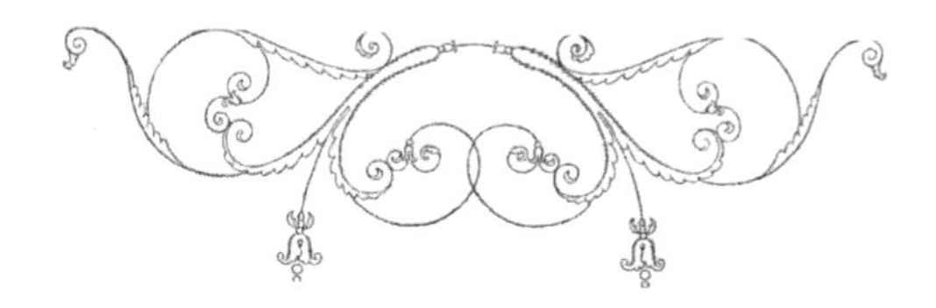

On the following Thursday, Hurst, grouchy and irritable, was up before the sun, riding to his damnably early business meeting while trying to ignore his usual morning headache. Upon arrival at Henderson's office, however, the aroma of roasted coffee beans enveloped him, and he began to feel curiously optimistic. The feeling was reinforced when he stepped into Henderson's meeting room and met Mr Edward Gardiner.

The elegantly dressed man with the intelligent expression looked him in the eye and shook his hand heartily as Henderson performed the introductions. Gardiner brought his own man of business, a Mr Haggerston, to assist him in describing his business holdings and his future plans. They produced account documents, ship registers, and bills of lading, answering questions with candour and thoroughness. Hurst could not have felt more comfortable if he had been in his own breakfast room. The discussion flowed until Gardiner looked at his watch. "Drat, I shall have to leave you gentlemen. One of our ships is docking today, and I wish to meet with the captain."

A glance and a nod passed between Hurst and his solicitor. "I believe we have come to an agreement, sir. I will draw up the contract," said Mr Henderson. "When can we meet again?"

Mr Gardiner opened a small leather-bound calendar, frowning over it. "My schedule is rather inflexible next week, and for some days after." He raised his eyes to Hurst. "I have an opening tomorrow morning. Would that be too soon?" he asked.

"Can you have the documents drawn up by tomorrow, Henderson?" asked Hurst.

Henderson nodded. "Of course, sir. They will be ready."

"Then I will take your leave until tomorrow, gentlemen. It has been my great pleasure," said Mr Gardiner.

"Mr Gardiner, I assure you, the pleasure has been mine," said Hurst.

He hurried to fetch his horse, eager to tell...who? Would Louisa want to listen to this? Probably not, and she was probably out making those interminable calls with Caroline. He wished he could share his good news with someone besides Arthur. A letter was not as rewarding as a face-to-face conversation. He thought of Bingley and determined to have a nice chat with his brother. Accordingly, he turned his horse in the direction of Darcy House.

Upon arrival, Hurst knocked at the door, and was received by the butler. He was informed that Darcy was out, but that Bingley was in the parlour. When he was announced, Bingley rose to meet him. It became apparent that he was not his buoyant, enthusiastic self, but subdued and abstracted.

They sat down and Hurst described his morning meeting to his brother. Ordinarily Bingley would have attended to his narrative, but his attention was wandering, his eyes were clouding over, and his chin slumped into his hand. Hurst sighed with irritation. "Have you heard a word I have said?"

Bingley started, and sheepishly sat up straight. "I am sorry. I own I am somewhat preoccupied," he replied with an unconvincing smile.

Hurst looked at him closely. Bingley's countenance was pale and there were shadows under his eyes. "Charles, what is the matter?"

Bingley's eyes dropped to the floor. "Well, it is not an easy thing to discover how stupid I have been."

"I would never call you stupid. In fact, I would say you are one of the most intelligent men I know, not to mention your great heart and kind manner."

"I am afraid it is my heart that is the problem now."

"Is this about Miss Bennet?" asked Hurst, finally catching on.

"Yes, I am afraid so," sighed Bingley. "She is everything I could ever want in a woman, but…I learned that I was making a fool of myself. I have fortunately been saved from further embarrassment by Caroline and Darcy. They have convinced me that Ja…um, Miss Bennet, did not return my feelings, but considered me merely a friendly acquaintance. It is..." His face worked. "Most disappointing."

"I am truly sorry—"

"Oh," hastened Bingley, pinning a lopsided smile on his face, "Do not concern yourself! No doubt I will have forgotten all about her within a week. Caroline did me the favour of reminding me how many times I have fallen in and out of love before."

Hurst could not think of a thing to say, vexed at the insensitivity with which Charles had been treated. Caroline, his own sister, and Darcy, who professed to be his friend, had not respected him enough to allow him to form his own opinions about something so important, and then had had the appalling callousness to tell him he would soon forget about it.

"Bingley," he said urgently, "do not punish yourself. I cannot say that I agree with Caroline or Darcy about what Miss Bennet's feelings may be. Perhaps take a while to give it some thought and try to distract yourself. If, after some time, you find that you are still so affected by her, you should follow your instincts."

"That is by far the kindest thing anyone has said to me on this subject," said Bingley ruefully, "I will certainly keep it in mind."

"Pray, do not repeat my advice to either of your sisters or to Darcy." Hurst raised an eyebrow meaningfully. "Keep it to yourself, man! It would not do for me to damage my misanthropic, wine-soaked, jaundiced reputation!"

Bingley guffawed his first genuine laugh in days. Darcy, entering the room at just that moment, patted himself on the back for his astute judgment of his young friend's character. He was forgetting the girl already.

Hurst stayed just long enough to describe again his meeting with Mr Gardiner. Both Bingley and Darcy listened attentively, asked many questions, and requested that Hurst keep them informed, so that they might also consider investing with Gardiner.

On his way home, Hurst thought of Charles. He genuinely liked his brother-in-law. He felt that Charles deserved a chance to court a young lady without the scrutiny and opining of his sister or his haughty friend. Then a thought crossed his mind that startled him.

He had never truly courted a young lady. He had instead agreed to a convenient marriage for his family honour and Louisa's dowry. When he had met her, he had been prepared for a plain or ill-bred girl, but had been pleasantly surprised. Louisa Bingley was handsome, intelligent, and pleasant to be around; she was a woman who deserved to be courted. She still did, he suddenly realised.

CURLED UP IN A DEEP, comfortable chair, Elizabeth opened her book. She had been desirous of finishing it for weeks, but between Mr Collins's proposal and Jane's melancholy, she had been distracted. Their mother's lamentations had driven Jane to their bedchamber and, since the day had turned cold and stormy, Elizabeth could not go outdoors, so instead entered her father's sanctum. Her father smirked and silently raised his glass of wine to her as she entered, but otherwise left her in peace. She was grateful for it, as her patience with everyone was wearing thin. Even Jane's stoic sorrow had begun to offend her. Elizabeth wanted to strike someone, preferably Mr Bingley, or Mr Darcy, or both. She did have two fists after all. She let her eyes rove over the cosy room, with books and papers everywhere. What a contrast to the almost bare shelves of Netherfield! How glad she was to be home, despite her mother!

She had been so weary of Netherfield and its inmates those last days. Miss Bingley's idiotic promenade about the room and the ensuing pointless debate over personal defects had pushed her over the edge. She had written to her mother, begging the use of the carriage to convey them back home. The footman had returned with her unfavourable answer: the carriage could not possibly be spared till Tuesday next. Her fist had closed about the note, crumpling it into a ball.

Perhaps, in hindsight, she should have applied to her father. She gazed at her papa over the top of her book. He was, as usual, settled deeply in his chair by the fire with his wine and books. On his desk was a stack of overdue correspondence. She heaved a sigh. He would not have even taken the trouble to read it.

She had gone to Mr Bingley and requested the use of his carriage. He had at first objected, insisting Miss Bennet was not well enough, but she had been firm. Then, in need of some calming solitude, she had taken herself to Netherfield's library. Her wish had been in vain; Mr Darcy was already there. His nose in a book, he had not even raised his eyes, nor made the slightest acknowledgement of her presence. It had both vexed and relieved her. The maids had been busy in her room, and Miss Bingley was holding court in the saloon. With it unpleasantly drizzly outdoors, it had had to be the library. Either that or the scullery.

She had found a seat near the window and opened her own book. Almost immediately, she had experienced a tingling sensation, as if something had skittered across her face. She had reflexively looked at her accidental companion, but he still adhered to his reading, his admittedly striking profile resolute. Was it yet another example of his disdain, or had he been immersed in the prose? Elizabeth had readily understood; one of the great pleasures in life was losing oneself completely in a book. Still, she had wondered if there was a comfortable chair in the scullery.

AT DARCY HOUSE, Bingley had retired early again, still uncharacteristically sombre. Darcy found himself at loose ends. Perhaps his friend was correct, he truly was an awful object when he had nothing to do. He went to his library, his favourite place to step away from the world and relax. There was a small stack of books on a table next to his chair by the fire. They were his most treasured tomes, the ones he most often packed when travelling. He picked up the one on top and recognised it as a title he had been reading at Netherfield.

He had been unsettled over the general tone on one of the last evenings *she* was there, when Miss Bingley had inadvertently made him so conscious of Elizabeth's enticing form as they walked about. The ensuing discussion had veered uncomfortably into the personal. He had wondered, then, when they would leave? Surely Miss Bennet was well enough for a three-mile ride in a carriage.

The next morning, he had found much needed quiet in the library. When Elizabeth had entered the room, he had cringed. *Blast it, why her?* Likely because none of the Bingleys can read apparently, and she also seeks sanctuary. He had hoped she would take a book from the paltry collection and leave, but she had brought her own book, and taken a seat by the window. Determined not to engage her in conversation, he had allowed himself a glance out of the corner of his eyes. Oh, how the auburn highlights in her glorious hair caught the light from the window! She moved slightly, and he had instantly snapped his eyes back to the pages, then sensed that he was being examined closely. He clutched the book more tightly and riveted his eyes to the text for almost two minutes before succumbing to curiosity once more and peeking at the lady.

For a full half an hour, the eyes of the unknowing, unsuspecting combatants had feinted and dodged, performing a little *pas de deux* of avoidance. Heart rates had quickened, eyelids twitched, lips tightened in annoyance, but neither gave any ground. Finally, a maid had arrived and requested Elizabeth's attendance on her sister. She rose and left the library without speaking a word. Darcy, exasperated with himself and annoyed with her for reasons he could not explain, had thrown down his book, leapt to his feet and begun pacing in agitation. He could no longer even sit, much less read. With a deep breath, he had taken himself off to seek male company, joining Hurst in the billiard room.

And here I am, weeks later, again unable to concentrate on a book. He wished to deny that it was once again Elizabeth Bennet's fault, but could not.

THE CONTRACTS WERE SIGNED when the men met at Gardiner's offices near his warehouses. Hurst and his brother, along with Mr Henderson, had decided on how much to invest and, while it was perhaps not as much as some of his acquaintance could put into a business venture, Hurst was happy with the amount. Mr Gardiner was pleased to have them as partners, and again they spent a few rewarding hours learning about the plans for expansion.

As the afternoon drew to a close, Gardiner wished them all happy Christmas. "I expect I shall not see you until some time in the new year, Mr Hurst, Mr Henderson; so I will wish you a very happy Christmas now. In a little more than a fortnight, my family and I will be off to my brother's estate to greet the Festive Season," he laughed, "and my nieces can give my wife some rest by attending to our noisy children!"

"Your children, Gardiner, will require the vigilance of all five of your nieces!" laughed Mr Haggerston. Hurst and Henderson also chuckled at this and wished him merry.

DECEMBER CONTINUED and the pace of London social life quickened. Even though it was almost Christmastide, some families came in from their country estates to celebrate in London before Parliament convened in January. Though the Season would not truly begin for weeks, there were still plays, concerts, and parties to attend.

Caroline came into some intelligence that many of society's most fashionable would be attending a performance of *The Rivals*. It would be a splendid opportunity to attract notice before the theatres became more crowded. She insisted that her brother procure tickets, but Darcy took pity on his friend and offered his box. The Hursts, Bingleys, and Darcy would ride to the theatre and attend together.

The evening at last arrived. Caroline wore a richly decorated gown with layers of flounces. Her hair was intricately styled and embellished with feathers. The beaded, beribboned bodice was not performing its office, exposing a shocking expanse of bosom. It was clear to Louisa that her sister was intent on dazzling the *ton*. She was determined to entice Mr Darcy, and shine for the other personages who would be assembled there. Caroline even confided that she thought she could secure Mr Darcy's addresses for herself before the Season had even begun. *And pigs might fly*. Louisa smiled prettily but gave her sister no false hope.

When she descended the stairs, enchanting in her own elegant, subtle way, her husband smiled his admiration and looked into her eyes. "You look lovely, my dear," he said, with a level of feeling in his voice that neither of them expected.

Louisa blushed and wondered. Gilbert seemed so sincere at times. She did not know whether to accept his compliment as genuine or assume that he was merely creating a prelude to a conjugal visit. She impulsively decided to give him the benefit of the doubt. He took her hand and wound it through his arm, giving it a little squeeze. Louisa's eyes widened slightly in surprise, but her instincts were telling her to trust him, so she did. Caroline had others to pay attention to her tonight, and Louisa was weary of her sister's company. She smiled slightly to herself, content to stay next to her husband, unaware that he had avoided the liquor cabinet all afternoon, so he could gaze at her, not to mention stay awake through the play.

ONCE THE CURTAIN HAD RISEN, the Hursts busied themselves with quiet observations on the play. They sat with their chairs close to each other, their heads bent together. It was an unusual sight, thought Darcy, from his seat on the other side of the box. He wondered at their conversation, shifting uncomfortably as Miss Bingley leaned in from her seat to titter at her sister and her husband. She was sitting a little too close to him, her hand always on his arm. Darcy's mouth was so grimly pursed, he looked as if he were eating lemons, and his ears ached from Miss Bingley's voice, unceasing in its comments and slightly unmodulated, for she was playing to the crowd just as surely as any of the actors. She was at the play to be seen, and to be seen close to him. His stomach clenched as she flirted and simpered and remarked upon high-ranking persons in the audience. "There is Miss Beauchamp! Such an accomplished girl, but that squint! Oh, and there is Lord Ashbury! Oh, I think he is waving!"

As Darcy retreated further and further behind his mask of hauteur, he counted the seconds to the interval. He tried catching Bingley's eye, in the hopes of directing some of the lady's attention away from himself. Bingley, however, had retreated into preoccupied gloom again, his chin on his hand, taking no notice either of the play or of his company.

The interval came at last, and the gentlemen left the box to procure refreshments for the ladies. Darcy watched Hurst's usually bland expression break into a delighted smile as he spied a fashionable couple strolling past. Suddenly Hurst stepped towards them and called out a greeting.

"Mr Hurst!" said the gentleman. "What a pleasant surprise

to be sure! I did not expect to see you until after Twelfth Night. May I take this opportunity to present my wife?"

Darcy and Bingley could not help but listen to the exchange, including the lady's perceptive remarks on the play, and they stepped over to join the group. Hurst made the introductions and the conversation touched on the performance and other works by Mr Sheridan and then veered briefly into Mr Gardiner's business. The waiter brought their drinks, and it seemed no time at all had passed before the bell rang, and they returned to their seats. Darcy was impressed with Hurst's new partner, and with his charming, well-spoken wife; *truly, who would think they come from trade*? He hoped his surprise at Hurst's newfound enthusiasm for business—and for Mrs Hurst's company – was not obvious.

The second act was dramatically performed, both on the stage and in their box. Again, the Hursts sat quietly together while Caroline held court over the rest of their party, and anybody else within earshot. Darcy's already pale countenance progressed from cold to frigid to glacial as the play wore on. Some part of his brain cried out in pain, and looking down, he discovered that he was gripping the arms of his chair so tightly that his fingers were white. He could hear titters of amusement coming from nearby boxes. He had never been so mortified in his life.

THERE WAS one particularly interested observer of Caroline Bingley's behaviour. A stunningly dressed and coiffured woman sat in the next box, acutely observing every detail of Caroline's performance. At first, she had been merely entertained by the lady's strenuous efforts and by her companions' embarrassment, but at some point, the wheels began to turn, and she realised that this social climber was known to her, and that renewing their acquaintance could be useful.

Sophronia, Baroness Riverton—rich, titled, and beautiful—was slightly older than Caroline, but far advanced in sophistication and cynicism.

When they had been together at school, Caroline had doggedly pursued her and other girls from noble families. She had unabashedly wrangled invitations to balls and house parties. Veiled insults, icy glares, and whispered gossip never seemed to penetrate Caroline's armour; they merely made her more determined.

Turning her attention away, Sophronia smiled fondly at her husband, an elderly baron, dozing in the seat next to hers. She leaned over and took his hand. Her eyes then drifted across the theatre to a handsome young man in a box opposite hers. She caught his eye and gave him a smouldering look. He smirked, made an exaggerated wink, and then turned his attention back to the young lady at his side.

THE EVENING'S entertainment at an end, the theatre-goers went out into the night. The temperature had plummeted, and a crisp smell of snow freshened the city air. When the Darcy carriage rolled up to the Hurst's town house, its owner withstood Miss Bingley's teasing or pouting, and neither he nor her brother could be persuaded to come inside,

Later, as the clock chimed two, Darcy sat slouched in his darkened study, brandy in hand, staring at the banked coals of the fire. He reproached himself for ever having partnered with Caroline. When they had hatched their plan to remove Charles from Netherfield, he had not realised how much she would infer that they were now bound together. In addition to that, visions of interminable balls, parties, introductions, and the calculating stares of mothers and daughters made him wonder why he had ever thought he could spend the winter in town.

Most of all, the unshakeable memory of a pair of fine eyes and a burbling laugh completely destroyed his equilibrium. The grating simper of Caroline Bingley's voice and her imposition on him had angered and shamed him. Elizabeth Bennet's arch sweetness and informed observations would have been welcome tonight in their box. She would have watched the play, not the audience; she would have wished to discuss the plot and the performances, not the gowns and faults of those in their company. But it was not to be.

I am altogether sick of duty and expectation. Would that I could seek only happiness!

Sweeping a hand through his disordered hair, Darcy's unhappy thoughts went to his sister. *But I cannot fail her again! Not in my choice of a wife!* He rebuked himself for neglecting her, and recognising both his need to see Georgiana and his desire to escape London, his decision was made. He wrote a note to Bingley, and another to Colonel Fitzwilliam. A light snow was falling in the weak predawn light when Darcy climbed into his carriage and struck out for Pemberley.

CHAPTER 4

Winter intensified at Longbourn. Several inches of snow were already on the ground, unusual for mid-December. The morning chill had a bite to it, though not enough to keep Elizabeth from her perambulations around the countryside.

She stepped inside, just in time for breakfast after a long walk. Her hands and feet were numb with cold. Her rambles had taken her in the direction of Netherfield before she realised it, and she had taken a long look at the darkened manor house from a distance. Mr Darcy's face appeared before her, his dark eyes focused unswervingly on her. She had, at her first sight of him, thought him exceedingly handsome, until he had opened his mouth. But handsome is as handsome does, and that impression had been quickly discarded. She shivered, and a tingle went up her spine. She hated to admit, even to herself, how unnerving that had been.

Mary was sitting with Jane at the breakfast table, watching

as Jane unfolded a piece of paper. Reading it, Jane blinked rapidly for a moment, then smiled at Mary, reaching to touch her arm.

"Thank you. I will cherish it."

"Lizzy, see what Mary has made for me." Jane passed her the paper, decorated with small drawings of birds and flowers, and with a verse from the Bible that read, *'And we know that all things work together for good to them who love God, to them who are the called according to his purpose'*. Jane rose, taking the paper back from Elizabeth. She wrapped an arm around Mary's shoulders and gave her a squeeze, and then left the room. Mary stiffened slightly and looked down at her breakfast. Her prim, affected countenance was coloured by a faint blush.

"Jane has been trying to hide her sadness, but I could tell. I hoped to lift her spirits a little," Mary said, sounding faintly defensive.

"That was very kind of you," Elizabeth said gently.

"Dear Jane! I wish I could do more for her," sighed Mary. Elizabeth had not thought anyone else had noticed Jane's distress but herself. She patted Mary's hand, and both sisters rose to start the day.

CAROLINE BINGLEY HAD NOT WAITED a full day after the theatre outing before she sent an invitation to dine over to the denizens of Darcy House. That evening, when Charles was the only gentleman to enter the saloon, she was furious to learn that not only had Mr Darcy not come to dine, he had removed himself from her presence for the rest of the winter.

The moods of two Bingleys made the next days difficult for the Hursts. Charles had retreated to Darcy House, where his host had left a note prevailing upon him to stay through the winter. Caroline prowled moodily about the Hurst town house, too vexed even to make her morning calls. Hurst took refuge in visits to his club or hid in his study, in the chair next to the liquor cabinet. When Louisa, almost overnight, appeared harassed and desperate, he realised guiltily that he needed to come to her aid. If he was going to court his wife, he needed to do a better job of it.

The next morning, he told the ladies that he was at their disposal, and would happily escort them to the shops. Louisa threw him a grateful look, and as soon as cloaks and wraps were found, and the carriage called, they were out the door. As they walked up the street and stepped in and out of milliners, jewellers, and drapers, Caroline began to regain her spirits. Louisa, too, enjoyed the family outing. Hurst surreptitiously watched his wife as she admired an emerald necklace and earbobs. That gave him an idea, and as the ladies left the jeweller's shop, he quietly stepped around to look at the necklace.

It was a short time later in their shopping excursion, as they stepped back out on the street from a fashionable milliner, that Caroline heard someone call her name.

"Goodness me, is that Caroline Bingley?" called a honeyed contralto voice behind them. The three turned to see a luxurious carriage embellished with a family crest pulling up alongside them. The smiling face of a beautiful woman leaned out through the window. Caroline did a double take. "Lady Riverton!" she gasped, hardly believing her luck. She had always admired and envied her high-ranking former schoolmate, and here she was, glad to see her! Calling out her name! In a public street! Next to her, the Hursts stood stock still, exchanging startled glances.

"Why Caroline, I was just thinking about you the other day, and here you are!"

"You were thinking of *me*?" repeated Caroline, flushed with excitement.

"But of course," said the baroness. "My particular friend, Lady Drayton—you remember Annabelle, of course—mentioned you not long ago. She had seen a gown of a particular blue, and she said the colour reminded her of a gown you had when we were in school."

Caroline, overwhelmed by such notice, could not know that there was but a tiny element of truth in Lady Riverton's comment. The gown had indeed been mentioned—but only to remark upon its excess of lace.

More pleasantries were exchanged, and at length, Lady Riverton made a request. "Caroline, would you care to call at Riverton House? I have some friends whom I would like you to meet."

"Why, yes…yes, I would enjoy chatting with you again!" Caroline answered, struggling to gather her wits about her, "We have so much catching up to do!"

"That would be lovely. I will be at home tomorrow morning."

So, it was agreed, and the elegant carriage rolled away. Caroline turned quickly to her sister and brother-in-law, her eyes ablaze with calculation.

"Louisa," she proclaimed urgently, "we must return to Madame Justine's shop. I will have that peach silk gown we admired earlier. And the pearl earrings! And the lace shawl!" So back they went, wending their way again to the shops, as Caroline plotted her entrance into the highest circles. *If only Mr Darcy could see me now!*

ELIZABETH SAT near her Aunt Philips, pouring coffee and tea for her aunt's guests as they enjoyed after dinner cakes and sweetmeats. As she poured and chatted with her neighbours, her eyes alighted on Mr Wickham. Across the room, he held the attention of a small group of Meryton ladies, his hand over his heart, reciting once again with a martyred yet noble expression his tale of persecution at the hands of Mr Darcy. Elizabeth concentrated on being attentive to her aunt's guests, but her mouth tightened and her eyelids flicked in annoyance. She enjoyed the dashing officer's company, but could he not be aware of how inappropriate it was to recount his story again and again to persons he hardly knew? What had happened to the sentiments he had expressed so prettily early in their acquaintance, that he could never expose Mr Darcy to disgrace while he still had kind thoughts of his father? She now understood that Mr Wickham's desire to be the centre of admiration and sympathy outweighed his discretion. Mr Darcy's disgust of Wickham came to mind, and Elizabeth felt a glimmer of understanding.

Within a few minutes, Kitty sat next to her. "Would you care for some coffee?" asked Elizabeth.

Kitty grimaced. "I thank you, but no. You know I do not care for the taste of coffee. It is too bitter! I just came to sit over here away from Mr Wickham's stories. I have already heard them a dozen times. Lizzy, I know you are fond of Mr Wickham, and that Mr Darcy is unpleasant and disagreeable, but he is gone now. Do you not think it is wrong for him to say those things about Mr Darcy when he is not here to defend himself? Why does he still go on about it?"

Elizabeth smiled at her younger sister. "I had the same thought. That is most perceptive of you! I am glad that you are considering what kind of behaviour is appropriate in society," she said kindly.

Kitty squirmed uncomfortably and frowned, her eyes fixed on the floor. "To tell you the truth, ever since the ball at Netherfield, I have been feeling ashamed of my behaviour at parties," she said. "Mr Bingley's sister…"

Elizabeth narrowed her eyes. "Did Miss Bingley say something to you?" she asked sharply, her hackles rising.

"No, it was not Miss Bingley, it was the other one...Mrs Hurst. And she did not say anything. I saw her watching me. Oh, it is hard to explain...as if she pitied me!" Kitty said. "I have scarcely even spoken to her, but I do not think she is like Miss Bingley. She rarely speaks, but her eyes are kind. It made me think of how I must appear to other people. I want to be admired, not have them look down on me!"

Elizabeth sent a silent thank you to Mrs Hurst. "That is a mature point of view, Kitty. I admire you already!" she said as she squeezed her sister's hand.

They heard a commotion from the other side of the room. Two officers were laughing uproariously at Lydia, who had one of their hats precariously perched on her blonde ringlets. Their youngest sister, a gifted and aggravating mimic, was also laughing, too loud for politeness, and they could see by her movements that her tall shapely figure was engaged in a little performance for the officers' benefit. It quickly became apparent that she was imitating their commanding officer.

Elizabeth's wide eyes quickly searched the room. "Do not worry," whispered Kitty. "Colonel Forster left earlier. He is not here."

"Thank heaven for that!" answered Elizabeth, turning her eyes back to Lydia, just in time to see one of the officers winking at the other one, and handing over a shilling.

"I HAVE no doubt she will be here as early as is permissible," said Lady Riverton to her dearest friend, Lady Drayton.

Annabelle laughed. "I daresay this will seem to her to be the entrée to the *ton* that she has always waited for," she said in agreement, then added, "I declare, Sophy, I almost feel sorry for her!"

The baroness scoffed, "Oh, it is not as if we are going to hurt her in any way! She will enjoy our society and all the benefits afforded to her of it, and of course she will never know of her role as a diversion in our little intrigue! I would go so far as to declare that she will have the best time of her life!"

"But surely at some point she will realise that she is being used most shamelessly!"

"I do not believe she will. All she will notice is that she is moving in the first circles," said Sophronia matter-of-factly. "She has always been exceptionally conscious of her own consequence. She will not notice anything that goes on around her unless it relates to her own status directly."

A SHORT TIME LATER, Caroline arrived at Riverton House and was ushered in by the butler. She was shown through a magnificent hall to a large and sumptuously appointed morning room. Other visitors were already there. The baroness rose and crossed the room to greet her.

"Caroline! I am so glad you are here! We shall all spend a lovely morning together. Let me present you to my dear husband." Lady Riverton took her arm and led her to an elderly man sitting in an armchair. "Miss Bingley, may I present my husband, Baron Riverton of Abbotsford Park. My darling Rupert, may I present Miss Caroline Bingley."

Old Baron Riverton, smiling dimly, slowly stood while

Caroline made a deep curtsey. The old man somewhat shakily bowed over Caroline's hand. "Pleasure, m'dear" he mumbled, and almost fell back into his chair.

Lady Riverton fussed over him for a few moments, then straightened to take Caroline around the room for introductions, linking their arms companionably together. "My dear friend Broughton, this is the lady I was telling you about. Miss Caroline Bingley, may I present Lord Alfred Broughton."

Another deep curtsey from Caroline. "It is an honour, my lord."

"Why, Sophy, she is even lovelier than you promised!" drawled the tall blond man.

Caroline blushed and an uneven high-pitched titter escaped her mouth. She gurgled, "Thank you, my lord, you are too kind," and held out her hand to him. He took her hand and bowed over it, pressing it warmly.

"Here, Broughton, do not be greedy," huffed another well-dressed man walking over to them. "Miss Bingley," drawled Lord Broughton, "this poor specimen is our friend Lord Norling."

"Delighted to meet you, Miss Bingley! Lady Riverton has described you as quite lovely, and I can see that she has not exaggerated," smiled the viscount.

For an instant, Caroline stopped talking, her jaw going slack. Recovering herself, she purred, "Dear Lady Riverton, we have known each other for such a long time. We are quite old friends!"

At that point Lady Drayton bustled across the room holding out both hands to Caroline. "Lady Drayton!" said Caroline, curtseying again.

"Just call me Bella, dear. We have known each other too long for formalities," cooed Annabelle.

Caroline could have pinched herself. This was not a

dream. It was truly happening, at long last! She was going to be counted among the Quality!

The morning flew by. There were *so* many introductions. Judith Spurlock, Countess of Deerhurst, estate in Gloucestershire; her sister Cornelia Markham, betrothed to a viscount; Lord Jonathan Mortimer, third son of a marquess; Sir Magnus Wareham, baronet, estate in Lincolnshire; and on and on.

At last, Sophronia ushered Caroline to the door. "Caro, it has been such a pleasure to have you here this morning. We are having a little musical evening tomorrow, just a small group of intimate friends to enjoy dinner and then play and sing together. Pray do join us, dear. We would love to hear you play the pianoforte. Oh, do please say you have not given it up!" said the baroness.

Caroline arranged her gleeful features in what she hoped was a modest expression. "Thank you, Lady Riverton. I simply adore music! I would be most happy to oblige you!"

"Until tomorrow evening then? We will look forward to it," said Sophronia.

CAROLINE FLOATED home with visions of bowling over the assembled company with her musical talents. She was met by her sister in the saloon. "How did your morning go?"

"Wonderfully, my dear Louisa! I have made the acquaintance of many august persons today. They were particularly welcoming to me, and Lady Riverton has insisted that I be her guest at a musical evening tomorrow and sing and play for her friends. This is what I have been waiting for! Sophronia remembers me from school and wishes me to be her intimate friend!" crowed Caroline.

Louisa's eyes sharpened at her sister's use of the baroness's given name. "Should you be so familiar with Lady

Riverton? I do not remember that she was ever a friend to you at school."

"Silly schoolgirl rivalries are all forgotten now," trilled Caroline. "We have met again, and she wishes me to be part of her circle. Her titled and noble friends have all been most cordial and welcoming. Now I must look over my music and choose what pieces to play!"

She gleefully hurried from the room. Louisa watched her go, misgiving written all over her face.

ELIZABETH GLANCED across the room at Mr Wickham. He was sitting next to Mary King, a sweet, cow-eyed girl with a round freckled face, flirting with her and making her giggle. Jane sat down next to her, eyeing the mismatched couple.

"Do Mr Wickham's attentions to Miss King disappoint you?" Jane asked quietly.

Elizabeth's mouth quirked up at one side. "No, my watchful sister! Mr Wickham has always been plain about his need to marry for money. To be sure, I find that I am relieved. This may sound like sour grapes, but I have been tiring of Mr Wickham for some time now. Yes, he is charming and handsome, but he has only one topic of conversation, and that is himself. I suppose I was never in love with him," she concluded, making a mock-tragic face at her sister.

Jane smiled and took her hand. "Then I am relieved too."

Charlotte's wedding had been a few days previous, and all the neighbours at Mrs Long's card party were still talking of it. Elizabeth missed her already. With Charlotte gone, and Mr Wickham turning into such a bore, she wondered who she would have left to converse with, besides Jane and Papa?

At Riverton House, the elegant dining room glowed with the light of dozens of candles. Caroline, dressed in an elaborate new gown with matching headdress, entered the dining room on the arm of Viscount Norling. Every dish was delicious, and the wine flowed. The conversation was convivial. Caroline hungrily soaked it up. She sat near Lady Drayton, with Norling on her right and Broughton on her left. After the last dishes were cleared, the gentlemen sat for a short interval with cigars, while the ladies settled themselves in the music room. When the gentlemen joined them, the musicale could begin.

Sophronia invited Lady Drayton to begin. She played a Beethoven sonata and some traditional songs. Lord Broughton turned the pages for her, and then they sang a duet. He had a fine baritone voice, and Caroline determined to herself that she and Broughton would perform together. Two other ladies played, one on the pianoforte and one on the harp. Caroline silently champed at the bit, her music clutched tightly in her hands, bearing an uncanny resemblance to Miss Mary Bennet in her desire to exhibit.

At last, Sophronia turned to her. "I have been so looking forward to hearing you play, if you would please entertain us?"

"I am most happy to oblige, dear Sophronia." Viscount Norling came forward to turn the pages for her at the same time that Broughton also rose with the same idea. The two men glared at each other briefly and then Broughton bowed to Norling and sat down.

To showcase her abilities, Caroline had chosen a particularly demanding piece. She played through it without making a mistake, her technical skills showing to the best advantage. To the assembled company however, it was the absent qualities of Miss Bingley's playing that defined her performance, though they applauded politely. While Caroline could play the most difficult music flawlessly, it was a lack of sensibility and expression in her playing that struck her listeners.

Caroline beamed at the applause, then pulled another piece of music from her collection. It was a traditional air, one which she knew to be well-suited to her vocal range. Again, she achieved technical perfection, but her tone was affected and unnatural. Still, Broughton praised her performance warmly, and later, when the evening came to an end, offered to drive her home in his carriage. A sleepy maid was quickly pressed into service as a chaperone. Caroline was triumphant.

BROUGHTON, after walking Caroline to her door and then leaving Grosvenor Square, rode back to Riverton House and deposited the little maid at the service entrance. After a short interval, he alighted from the carriage and sent it on to his own residence, stepping into the shadows and watching for a moment as it drove away. He then entered through the kitchen himself, taking a narrow back stair up two flights and stepping through a small door into a luxurious bedchamber, darkened except for a candle branch by the side of the enormous bed.

"Alfred," said a low and melodious voice, "you were *marvellous*. Perhaps a career on the stage for you, dearest?"

He laughed, removing his greatcoat and draping it over a chair. Then he approached the bed, sitting on the side closest to Sophronia. "I thought the dispute with Norling over turning the pages was a nice touch," he grinned down at her naked form, illuminated by candlelight. She laughed, then reached up and began untying his cravat.

Over the subsequent days, Caroline spent most of her time with Lady Riverton and her circle, attending balls, routs, card parties, and dinners. Indeed, she was scarcely to be found at the Hursts' town house at all. She was always escorted home by Lord Broughton or Sir Magnus, or one of the other handsome gentlemen who seemed to always be at Riverton House. After one exceptionally late evening, or early morning, Sophronia invited her to stay the night. More and more frequently, Caroline was a guest at the expansive town house on Hanover Square. Finally, one morning, Sophronia invited her to stay at Riverton House for the Season.

Louisa heard Caroline's voice and realised that she must have arrived home from spending yet another night with the baroness. Louisa had barely seen her sister lately, and while she had marvelled at the peace and ease of their home without her, she could not help but wonder at the alacrity with which Lady Riverton had adopted this tradesman's daughter into her circle. It simply did not make sense to her.

She followed the sound to her sister's rooms, finding Caroline grabbing armfuls of clothing from her dressing room and throwing them on her bed. Back and forth she ran between the dressing room and the bed, all the while urgently clamouring for her maid, Bertha, to order her trunks. Louisa stopped dead on the threshold, taking in the scene.

"Caroline, what are you doing?"

Caroline startled, so intent on her purpose that she had not noticed Louisa in the doorway. "Louisa!" she shrieked, her eyes ablaze. "Sophronia has invited me to be her house guest for the Season! I shall be taking all of my clothing and jewellery and my maid with me!" Then she rounded on Bertha, who had returned with footmen carrying the trunks and was folding and smoothing some of the gowns that had been thrown in haste on the bed. "Can you not work any faster?" she cried to the hapless maid.

"Caroline, you must compose yourself! Why are you in such a hurry? Are you afraid that Lady Riverton will rescind her offer?"

Caroline froze for an instant, as if that thought had not occurred to her. She began to work even faster, throwing clothing into the trunks regardless of what condition they would be in upon unpacking. "Make haste, make haste!" she cried to Bertha. Louisa, feeling pity for the maid, was sorry she had said anything.

"Caroline, you are going to ruin your gowns. I will call Clara to help. She and Bertha will be able to pack much more quickly without us in their way."

"Yes," said Caroline, breathing hard, "Yes. I will see if there is any music I would like to bring." She hurriedly left for the music room.

Within a few hours, Caroline's trunks and boxes were packed and loaded onto the carriage, ready to make the trip to Hanover Square. Louisa stood at a drawing room window, watching it drive away. She wondered again at the speed of it all, feeling for the first time a flicker of suspicion. Sighing, she turned and looked around the large, deserted room. "Now what?" she asked aloud to the silence.

WITH CAROLINE GONE, Louisa was left adrift. Hurst saw his chance.

He wished to turn back the clock, to court Louisa as if they had met in a candlelit ballroom, or at a garden party on a summer afternoon; not in her father's offices as terms were debated and contracts signed. He wanted to start over and treat her as the girl she had been: refined, sweet, dutiful, and shy. And innocent. He would woo her, not as a wife, but as a maiden, and not return to her bed until he was sure her heart, not just her body, was his.

He began by spending more time with her during the day. They lingered over the breakfast table, sharing the newspaper, discussing news and gossip. He sat in the music room with her while she practised and complimented her playing. They talked about the books she was reading. They went to the lending library, and Hurst playfully threatened to read her romantic novels aloud to her, as she blushed and turned away to hide her smile. He held her hand on the carriage ride home.

One windy evening, as the sleet pelted down outside, they sat in front of the sitting room fire and played backgammon. Hurst took only one glass of wine, Louisa forgot to fidget, and they caught each other's eyes again and again.

CHAPTER 5

The carriage finally rolled up to Longbourn, having taken almost twice as long as usual to travel there from London. The Gardiners had been shocked at the depth of the snow once they had left the city. Even though Hertfordshire was not a long journey north, it was markedly colder and snowier than in town. The children had slept part of the way, but they were all now awake and unhappily restless. The carriage had been terribly cold inside too. They all heaved a sigh of relief when they turned off the main road and into Meryton. The front door to the old manor house at Longbourn opened and out came Mr and Mrs Bennet to welcome them with open arms. Jane, Elizabeth, and Mary followed and helped hurry the children out of the carriage and into the warm house. Footmen unloaded boxes and portmanteaus, and the carriage was driven over to the stables, the horses unhitched and rubbed down after their long day. The Yuletide celebrations could begin.

After dinner, Mrs Gardiner sat down for a cosy chat with her favourite niece. "So, Lizzy," she said quietly, "How does Jane fare?"

"No better, I fear," replied Elizabeth in low tones, careful that neither her parents nor her sister would overhear. Mrs Gardiner glanced across the drawing room at Jane. She was seated on an embroidered footstool, spinning a brightly painted wooden top for her littlest cousin Henry. She had her usual smile in place, but Mrs Gardiner could see that her eyes lacked their characteristic glow. "Your uncle and I look forward to having her with us in London," Mrs Gardiner said. "It is to be hoped that a change of scenery will do her good."

Elizabeth agreed. There was a slight risk that Jane might encounter Mr Darcy, the Bingleys or the Hursts in London, though highly unlikely. Her aunt and uncle were certainly not of the same society as their former neighbours.

Aunt Gardiner steered the conversation to another topic. "Lizzy," asked her aunt, "Do you still see Mr Wickham? Would I like to meet him?"

One corner of Elizabeth's mouth turned into a wry twist. "Mr Wickham, I am afraid, has become rather tedious," she answered.

Her aunt's eyebrows rose in enquiry.

"He has only one topic of conversation, how he has been wronged and left in poverty by his former patron's son," Elizabeth went on. "Though he can be a charming conversationalist, that subject bores me. He also needs to marry for money. Lately he has developed a sudden *tendre* for Mary King and her ten thousand pounds."

"How do you feel about that?"

Elizabeth reflected, and was confounded that Mr Wickham had begun to compare unfavourably with his nemesis. No matter how proud and disagreeable Mr Darcy was, she was certain he was honourable and would refrain from any public discussion of a private matter. It was a pity really. She had rather enjoyed disliking Mr Darcy.

"I can truthfully say that while I enjoyed Mr Wickham's company for a time, my heart has not been touched. I was not in love with him, Aunt, and I always did know that." She heaved a rueful sigh. "Though he was quite entertaining for a while."

Mrs Gardiner patted her arm. "I am happy to hear that, Lizzy. Perhaps you would like to come down to town later this winter and meet more people your own age. You must miss Charlotte."

"I do," her niece said wistfully. "I wish exceedingly to broaden my acquaintance."

LADY RIVERTON LOVED a peaceful sort of Christmastide. The few memories she had of her beloved mother came to the fore during the festive season, and they gave her a quiet, bitter-sweet joy. This year, she also needed a respite from her houseguest.

Alas, she was not to have it.

"Surely you will wish to spend Christmas with your family, Caro?" she hinted as that lady entered the breakfast room on Christmas morning.

Caroline trilled a laugh and waved her hand dismissively. "Oh, no, they will be doing nothing of consequence, to be sure. Who will we see today? Norling? Broughton? Sir Magnus?"

Sophronia saw her last hopes for a peaceful day slip away, and forced a civil response.

"Our friends are all spending the day with their families,

dear. We will not see any of them until tomorrow at the earliest."

Caroline stared at her in shock. "*No one* will be in attendance today?"

"No," came the dismissive reply. "I myself have a megrim, and will be retiring to my rooms. Do whatever you wish, and be sure to send a message to the kitchens if you wish a cold collation brought to your room later. I have given most of my servants time off for the Christmastide, and no regular meals will be served."

Sophronia rose and left the room, hoping she could salvage something of Christmas cheer in the affectionate company of her husband. That, too, was not to be. She found Lord Riverton in his sitting room, dressed, but already napping in a chair. Over the past months, he had experienced a few short intervals of frailty and confusion, but had always come back to himself. This time seemed different. Sophronia gently stroked his cheek, and, pulling a chair next to his, took his hand in hers.

AFTER ATTENDING church on Christmas Day, Hurst and Bingley sat next to the fire in the music room, sipping hot buttered rum. Louisa had gone to see about luncheon, and the two gentlemen were companionably silent.

Bingley sighed heavily, his eyes fixed on a distant vision. Hurst's quiet, steady voice broke through his thoughts. "Charles," he said gently, "have you given any thought to visiting Netherfield again? I would wager that Miss Bennet would be glad to see you. Perhaps there will be a New Year's Eve assembly in Meryton."

"I never took my leave of her, you know. The last time we spoke I intended to return within a few days. I cannot write to her—well, I did not ask to properly court her, more fool me." He looked at Hurst. "Do you think…?"

"I think you should follow your heart, and to the devil with anyone else."

Later that night, Bingley sat in Darcy's study, an unread newspaper in his hand, staring meditatively into the fire. The ache in his heart persisted. He thought of Hurst's advice. *Listen to your heart,* he had said weeks before, and had repeated it that afternoon. He resolved to go to Netherfield, maybe even tomorrow. Just then, the door opened and in walked Darcy's cousin, who occasionally made his residence at the house. Bingley made to rise, but Colonel Fitzwilliam waved him to remain seated.

"HAPPY CHRISTMAS TO YOU, Bingley! Am I to understand that you have this big house all to yourself?" said Fitzwilliam as he shook Bingley's hand heartily and sat down on a chair next to him. "I have been away and just received Darcy's message declaring his intention to leave town. I came to see for myself."

"Yes, your esteemed cousin sounded the retreat and returned to Pemberley," Bingley laughed. "So far he has not even answered my letters."

"My father has not heard from him either," said Fitzwilliam, "but there is no need for concern. Derbyshire has already had two major snowstorms, even this early in the winter, and I do not think the post is getting in or out. Most of the roads are closed. No sooner do they get them open, than they drift shut again."

"Is that so?" frowned Bingley. "I had just been thinking about riding up to Hertfordshire. What have you heard about travel there?"

"My commanding officer has heard that travel has been hazardous there as well, indeed, anywhere north of town. The roads have drifted shut, and the weather has been so bad that most of the militia has been confined to barracks."

Bingley's face fell, and he stared into the fire again.

Fitzwilliam studied Bingley's face. His mouth turned down, his eyes looked strained and sombre. He would not have believed that such an amiable man could look so melancholy. *I wonder what happened in Hertfordshire?* Whatever it was, Bingley was still feeling the effects, and Fitzwilliam wondered if the same was true of Darcy.

ON BOXING DAY, after a noisy, lively day of merry Christmas celebrations at Longbourn, Mr Bennet lay in his bed, unable to summon the strength to rise; he was feverish and ached all over. His brother-in-law sat with him and played a game of cribbage, which was enough to exhaust him. He remained abed for the next few days, his absence from the dining table and his book room dampening the merriment of the Yuletide season and driving fear into his wife and daughters. Mrs Bennet, who had hoped to have two daughters settled by the new year, swung erratically between shrill outbursts of fear for her future and resentful frustration with the daughter whose stubborn refusal to marry Mr Collins had doomed them all to the hedgerows.

Elizabeth did her best to ignore her mother, for her own concerns centred on Mr Bennet's health. She was heartened on New Year's Eve, when her father dragged himself downstairs and insisted he was on the mend. Mr Gardiner was unconvinced. The time drew near for the Gardiners' return to London. Not only were they uneasy about leaving while Mr Bennet was so ill, but the weather had remained bitter and stormy. More snow had fallen during their visit, and travel was treacherous. However, his thriving business required his presence. As the Gardiners packed to leave, Jane came into their chamber and announced that she would not be traveling with them. "I cannot leave when Papa is so ill. Perhaps I can visit you later this winter."

"Oh, Jane! Are you sure?" asked Mrs Gardiner.

"I am, Aunt. My place is here, with my family."

The next morning, they bid the Gardiner family goodbye, as snow began falling again.

DARCY DID NOT REGRET his decision to leave London. The wind was raw and bitter, the snow was already deep, and it was clear that there would be little if any travel beyond his estate. Delivery of the post had become intermittent and then ceased altogether. He was not bothered in the least, in truth he was relieved. Everyone he cared about most was here, with one exception—and he could not with any propriety further *that* acquaintance. He was grateful to have spent Christmastide with his sister at Pemberley, the main rooms magnificently decorated with holly and evergreen boughs, and the enormous Yule log burning in the drawing room fireplace.

Now, on the last evening of the year, he sat comfortably in the music room, a hot toddy cupped in both hands. He was content to rest at the end of a long day of traveling across his estate checking on his tenants. He and his steward had travelled by sleigh, stopping at every cottage to see that each family had enough food, warm clothing, and fuel. Traveling through the snow had been arduous, and by the end of the afternoon he had been chilled to the bone. Still, he was relieved to know that his tenants were safe and well. Georgiana and Mrs Reynolds had fussed over him and filled him up with hot soup and freshly baked bread. He was looking forward to being entertained with music and smiled warmly at his sister. Georgiana shuffled through her music, considering what piece might please her brother. She played a few introductory chords to an old and sentimental air, but her song did not have the desired effect.

Her brother startled and choked, spilling a little of his drink. He shifted abruptly in his chair and called out to her. She stopped singing, her eyes round with surprise. Fitzwilliam had never interrupted her before.

"Erm, dearest, would you mind playing the Haydn piece you have been practising?"

"Of course, Brother." Flustered, she hastily reached for another sheet of music.

In the matter of seconds, Darcy had gone from relaxation to agitation. Georgiana had begun at first to perform the lovely air that Elizabeth Bennet had sung at Lucas Lodge. And although his sister went on to play her difficult Haydn piece beautifully, he did not hear it. He was no longer at Pemberley, listening to his sister. He was back in Hertfordshire, a vision of Elizabeth rising before him; his mind filling with the sound of her sweet, expressive voice singing an old song of love, her eyes only on him.

WHEN CHRISTMAS HAD NEARED and Louisa had still not heard from Caroline since the day she, her maid, and her trunks had departed, she sent a footman with a note to Riverton House, inviting her sister to return home and celebrate Christmas with them. Louisa could not know that the note was passed from footman to butler to maid to Bertha, who duly delivered it to her mistress. Caroline glanced at the envelope and set it on a salver for later perusal. She needed to prepare for an exclusive soiree.

When two days passed with no response, Louisa understood. *I am unlikely to hear from my sister*, she mused. *Perhaps I should be offended.* But in light of her own happiness at home with her husband, she was not terribly disappointed.

On New Year's morning, Gilbert joined Louisa in the breakfast room and presented her with a small blue velvet box bound with a creamy satin bow. She looked at him curiously as she untied the bow and opened it, and then she gasped, her eyes wide. There, resting on pale satin, was the emerald necklace and earbobs she had silently admired at the jewellers' weeks before. "Gilbert! How did you know?" she asked in breathless amazement.

"I was watching you the day we visited the shops. I saw the look on your face as you gazed at it," he said quietly, "and I thought it was about time you had something new and beautiful to wear."

"Thank you so, so much!" she said in wonderment. "But it looks too expensive!"

"My dear, I have realised that in my desire to restore the family reserves...*our* family reserves," he said, looking pointedly at her, "I had forgotten that we need pleasure and beauty in our lives as well. I hope you will take great pleasure in that necklace, and I will take great pleasure in seeing you wear it." He placed a soft, feather light kiss on her forehead, and left the room.

Louisa stared after him, wide-eyed, clutching the box to her heart, filled with a sense of yearning. *Who is that man?*

CHAPTER 6

Early one morning, a week into the new year, Elizabeth carried a pitcher of water upstairs and saw that the door to her father's chamber stood wide open. Mrs Hill was standing on the threshold and turned to Elizabeth, distress and worry on her countenance.

Her mother was standing by her father's bed, tugging at his arm, exhorting him to rise. "Mr Bennet! You must get up! All will be well! You must get out of your bed and move about. I am sure you will regain your strength if you make the effort to exercise! Oh, you have no consideration for my nerves!"

"Mrs Bennet," said her husband firmly, albeit in a weakened voice. "Do not fuss! All will be well. Just let me rest." He saw his daughter standing in the door. "Lizzy, help your mother to her chamber!"

Elizabeth stepped into the room and set down the pitcher.

"Mama, may I take your arm?" She reached towards her mother as if to put her arm around her shoulders.

Mrs Bennet spun around and glared at her second daughter. "You!" she cried. "Do not touch me! You were of no help when you were needed and can be of no help now! You would not have Mr Collins, and now look at us!" Her wails turned into angry sobs. She turned to her husband. "And you would not make your precious favourite marry him! We will all be starving in the hedgerows!"

"Madam!" Mr Bennet cried, coughing as he sat up. "Go to your chamber until you can calm yourself!"

Mrs Bennet burst into hysterical tears. Jane appeared instantly at her side. "Come, Mama." she said her voice soothing but firm. "You need to rest. You are upsetting Papa." She led her sobbing mother away.

Elizabeth turned. There stood much of the household, including Mrs Hill, two maids, Kitty and Lydia—taking in the scene with wide eyes. She took a deep breath, as much to calm herself as to conceal her mortification and turned to her father. "Papa, you must lie down. Please try and calm yourself and I shall read to you."

As the witnesses dispersed, Elizabeth helped him settle back into his pillows. His body sagged, clearly weakened by his burst of temper.

"Well, Lizzy? And how do you propose to entertain me?" he challenged waspishly. Elizabeth had not planned on that. She looked around and spied a book half under a chair. Grinning slyly, she retrieved the book and held up the copy of Hannah More's *Practical Piety* that Mary had left behind. "Ha!" he barked a laugh. "Well, it will put me to sleep at any rate!"

Elizabeth settled herself in a chair and began to read, the dull pieties and advice indeed lulling her father to sleep and then allowing her own mind to drift to what had occurred moments earlier. Her mother's fears for the future were worsening, and somehow blaming Elizabeth for the situation redirected her grief into anger.

Mrs Bennet's grief, fear, even tattered remnants of love; indeed, all her feelings for her husband were inextricably mixed with anger; for more than twenty years of mockery, for his isolating himself from his family, for not making the most of his income. Both her parents were selfish and incorrigible in their own way.

I could have married Mr Collins and preserved Longbourn, but that responsibility was not mine and I could not accept it. I cannot be a martyr for my mother's sake, so she can live at ease and always be mistress of Longbourn, for that is what would surely happen. Mrs Bennet would never willingly relinquish her position even upon her husband's death; she would instead make the succeeding mistress miserable.

That is not the only sacrifice that was expected of me; the greater sacrifice would have been the surrender of my hopes for a marriage built upon respect, perhaps love. Even disregarding her revulsion towards his person, Mr Collins would never have given Elizabeth respect. She had always hated being talked down to by men who were her intellectual inferiors: the patronising chuckles, the raised eyebrows and smirks, the smooth or not-so-smooth interruptions as she spoke. *Though Mr Darcy listened to me.*

Marriage to her father's heir could only have been her lot or perhaps Mary's. Mrs Bennet would never have wasted Jane on such a man as Mr Collins; Jane was reserved for someone handsome, charming, and rich.

Well, Mama, you got your way. I hope you are happy now, throwing poor Jane at Mr Bingley, only to have him break her heart. No matter how lovely and good she is, our lack of fortune, connexions to trade, and deplorable comportment would keep Jane from the match their mother dreamed of. *Papa would have done better to match us up with shopkeepers and farmers. At least then we would have roofs over our heads and regular meals in our futures.*

SOPHRONIA AND ANNABELLE, having met at Hatchard's, decided to continue their visit secluded in Sophronia's cosy private sitting room, as yet undiscovered by Miss Bingley. They entered Riverton House, but there was no footman in the vestibule to take their wraps. Crossing into the hall, they saw two footmen struggling to carry a rolled carpet up the main staircase. Behind them, another two footmen gingerly carried a large mirror in a gilded frame. The butler, standing next to several large boxes, gravely watched the proceedings.

"Haskell, what is the meaning of this?" asked Sophronia.

"Miss Bingley has purchased several items for her chamber, my lady," he replied, obviously discomposed. "I believe she means to do some redecorating."

Annabelle gasped in astonishment, her hand fluttering to her bosom. Sophronia, in shock, stared at him.

"Redecorating."

"Yes, my lady."

"In my house."

"Yes, my lady." Haskell stared at the floor and cleared his throat. "I did not think it my place to stop her, madam," he added, with an air of mortification.

"I understand. Do not blame yourself. I will speak with her," said Sophronia. With an air of unnatural calm, she climbed the stairs in silence, Annabelle at her heels.

The door to the rooms occupied by Miss Bingley was standing open, the sound of a noisy bustle emanating from within. When they entered, the sight of Caroline in the centre of the bedchamber shrilly directing maids and footmen met their eyes.

Much work had already been done. There were new draperies at the windows and a matching bedspread and tester. The new carpet was being rolled out and the previous carpet, purchased by the baron when he had toured India many years before, carried away. The enormous gilt mirror was being placed next to another, on the wall where an early Gainsborough landscape had previously hung. Elaborate ormolu candelabras with dangling prisms stood on floor-length posts. A larger dressing table had replaced not only the existing dressing table but a small bookcase.

"Caroline." Sophronia's quiet but authoritative voice cut through the noise. "What are you doing, dear?"

"Oh! Sophronia!" Caroline bustled over to the two ladies. "I was shopping yesterday, and I had such an inspiration! I saw the linens," She gestured at the draperies. "And they were so like those in dear Lady Anne's chambers at Pemberley! I have found so many things that complement them nicely!"

Annabelle, her eyes wide, stared at her. "Lady Anne? Do you mean…Mr Darcy's late mother? Her private rooms? Does he not keep those rooms closed?"

Caroline was caught out, but she prevaricated. "I have… had the opportunity to tour those rooms on occasion."

Drawing on a deep well of sangfroid she had not known she possessed, Sophronia kept her voice level. "My dear, this is all lovely, but will not it be a great deal of trouble to move it all to your sister's house when the Season is over? This house will be closed. And will you not be spending a good portion of the summer at Pemberley?"

Her houseguest blinked. Caroline clearly had not thought it

through. "Oh," she said. "Very well, I have what I want for now." She brightened. "I will shop for more in the summer."

"We will leave you now, so you may complete your project." Sophronia caught the eye of a footman. "Stephen, I need you to carry a note for me."

She went out into the corridor, fishing a small notebook out of her reticule. After scribbling a note, she handed it to the young man and gave him the direction.

The two ladies made their way in silence to Sophronia's rooms. It had all happened so quickly, they were still wearing their coats. Her maid assisted in removing them and went for tea. Shortly thereafter, Lord Broughton burst in, slightly breathless, having come up the back stairs.

"I met Stephen on the street and came immediately. What has she done now, Sophy?"

Sophronia threw up her hands. "She is redecorating her rooms, Alfred." She shook her head in disbelief. "Perhaps I should be grateful that she is not charging her purchases to me."

"What?" He looked at Annabelle, who nodded her confirmation. "And spending a fortune on it."

"I have seen encroaching behaviour, but this is beyond… anything," he said in wonder. "Are you well, Sophy? Why are you not in a rage? I certainly would be."

"As would I…as I *am*!" cried Annabelle. "First, she tries to dismiss one of your maids, and then she has the furnishings removed from a room *in your home* and replaces them with hers!"

They paused while the tea tray was set before them. After the maid left, Annabelle laid her hand on Sophronia's arm. "Sophy dear, do you not think it is time to end this charade?"

"Perhaps," she answered. "I often wish to, but…Havering has made it his mission to slander me, even though it was his own cousin who wrote that will, and I was a mere child at the time. Did you see him glowering at Lady Castlereagh's soiree?" She turned to Broughton. "Alfred, you have also had much to bear from my guest. Shall I send her packing?"

Lord Broughton took her hand and met her gaze with his own. "You do understand, my love, that I can bear much for you. I know how much you were hurt last year." He leaned back in his chair and took another sip of his tea. "I can stand it. The Season will end, and Miss Bingley will return to her sister, or perhaps to Derbyshire for their summer visit. It will pass."

Annabelle huffed. "I do not know how Darcy puts up with her. Bingley is pleasant enough company, but there are limits! How do you think she is so familiar with the mistress's suite at Pemberley? Does she bribe a servant to let her in?"

"Darcy's servants are renowned for their loyalty. He treats them well, so that would be surprising," said Broughton. "Poor devil, I do not know how he stands her either."

"I would not put it past Caroline to pick the locks, she is so certain that Pemberley will be her home any day now," mused Sophronia. "Perhaps she has had a key made for herself." She looked at her friend, and at her beloved. "So, shall we press on with my guest?"

"If you are agreeable to that, so we all can be."

ELIZABETH SANK into a chair and stared out the window at the swirling gusts of snow obscuring the much-loved view of Oakham Mount. The New Year had brought no relief from the cold. It only seemed to worsen. Unable to walk any distance through icy paths and snow, she felt the confinement to Longbourn all too well. Sighing, she reached for the letter she had finished writing earlier that day and read it over.

My dear Charlotte,

I do hope this letter finds you well and happy in Hunsford, and that your winter is mild. We are having quite a stormy season already, and we are not even a fortnight into January! I miss being able to walk to Lucas Lodge and chat with you any time I choose, though on a day as cold as this, that would not be possible, even if you were still there.

My aunt and uncle Gardiner and their children were our guests over Christmastide. Our time with them was delightful until my father took ill on Boxing Day. Jane was to join them in London for the winter, but has chosen to stay home and help care for Papa instead. We all keep ourselves indoors, which can be rather a trial.

Uncle Philips braved the elements on Sunday to bring us news and some letters and documents. He tells us that our neighbours in Meryton do not venture out unless it is completely necessary. Even the regiment has been confined to their barracks, except for those on guard duty. This may hinder Mr Wickham in his courtship of Miss King, poor, unfortunate man.

Please keep us in your prayers, my friend. My father tells us that he will soon recover, but Charlotte, I have never seen anyone look as ill as Papa.

With affection,
Your Eliza

Mr Bennet awoke with a start. The darkness was almost

complete; only a bit of light was shed by the guttering candle on the small bedside table. He felt a hollow weakness, and suddenly he knew that he would not recover; this would be his last illness. He reeled and recoiled from the thought. He could almost hear Fanny's voice wailing about the hedgerows, and his stomach turned. He had always ridiculed her fears, and now they would become reality. He was overcome with self-recrimination at not having made more of his income.

His wife and children would be close to destitute, and almost certainly homeless. They would be forced to rely on the charity of others. He should be the one to suffer for his own faults, but instead it would be those for whom he should have been responsible.

He turned his head away from the tiny light and shut his eyes tight against the tears that threatened, his heart sinking even lower. Lizzy was working herself to a frazzle caring for him, managing estate manners, all while withstanding frequent tirades from her mother. He had not done right by his family, and he knew she knew it. His dear girl was keeping herself under tight control, but he did sometimes glimpse the simmering anger she kept hidden away.

A SE'NNIGHT into the new year, Hurst received a note from Mr Gardiner with the news of his return to town. They met again at his offices.

"First, Mr Hurst, I wish you a happy new year."

"Thank you, sir," said Hurst, "How did you enjoy your travels?"

Mr Gardiner's smile faded, and his brows furrowed into an expression of worried abstraction. "We did enjoy seeing our family, but my sister's husband fell ill while we were there, which is worrisome to us all. He tells us he is recovering, but he looks so pale and drawn that that is hard to believe. We had hoped to bring my eldest niece to stay with us, but she remained at home to help care for her father. The weather almost prevented us from returning at all. We barely managed to make our journey before the roads were drifted shut again."

"I am truly sorry to hear that." There was an awkward pause in the conversation.

Mr Gardiner finally drew a breath, "Sir, let us discuss the matters at hand. With the help of your investment, I have been able to purchase and refit a small schooner for short, quick trips to the Continent and back. It is much more economical than a larger ship. Would you care to see the latest cargo we have received?"

The two men spent several hours in the warehouses, and Hurst learned that his investment was already bringing him a profit. He was impressed by the warehouse containing spices and exotic woods, but it was upon surveying bolt upon bolt of fine fabrics, laces, furniture, and decorative ornaments in another building that he exclaimed, "I wish my wife was with me today!"

Mr Gardiner beamed. "You and Mrs Hurst would certainly be free to sample our inventory. You could certainly purchase anything you would like at cost, or take it out of your dividends."

He studied Hurst. "Mrs Gardiner and I greatly enjoyed meeting you at the theatre last month," he said carefully, unsure of Hurst's willingness to mix outside of his class. "Perhaps our wives might form an acquaintance as well? Would you and Mrs Hurst consider honouring us with your company for dinner this week?"

The thought of dining at the home of new acquaintances prompted Hurst to examine his own drawing room later that afternoon. He looked at his wife. "This room has not been refitted since my mother was living. How would you like to redecorate this room?"

Louisa regarded the formerly elegant chamber. Hurst's mother had had exquisite taste, but the walls and fabrics were faded, the furniture was worn and patched, and the colours were out of date. "Of course, but the expense!"

"I have a surprise for you." Hurst grinned and sat down next to her, taking her hand in his. "Not only have our latest investments with Mr Gardiner been doing well, decidedly well, but he has warehouses full of fabrics and furniture. As investors, we may purchase merchandise in the warehouses at cost."

Hurst continued, looking sideways at his wife with one raised eyebrow, "I have accepted an invitation from the Gardiners for dinner this Friday. He is in trade, and he and his family live on Gracechurch Street, my dear. Caroline would be horrified, of course."

He waited a little uneasily for her answer, but his apprehensions were unfounded.

Louisa laughed. "All the more reason we must go."

FRIDAY EVENING ARRIVED, and the Hursts braved the streets of Cheapside. Gracechurch Street proved to be a wide street with newer town houses, not as imposing as Grosvenor Square, but in the recently popular classical style. Mr and Mrs Gardiner greeted them warmly and ushered them into their stylish and comfortable home. They even caught a glimpse of the merry chaos of the Gardiners' children being sent to bed. After dinner, the gentlemen and ladies did not separate, but continued their visit in the pleasant drawing room. The conversation flowed easily between all four, and broadened to subjects including home, family, and books. After Louisa admired Mrs Gardiner's colour scheme, the ladies resolved to visit the warehouse together.

Most of all, Hurst was struck by the respect and equality, the true partnership of the Gardiners' marriage. He vowed to himself that he and Louisa would achieve that somehow. It was late before they said goodnight to their hosts and rode home through the freezing night in companionable silence, sitting close inside the carriage, their hands clasped, their legs pressed together under the heavy lap robes.

At home, they climbed the great stairs together, and Hurst turned to bid Louisa goodnight, when she caught his face in her hands. "Gilbert, my love…could you…would you come to me tonight?" His heart leaped. "My darling," he sighed softly, and whisked her into his arms.

Clara stepped silently into her mistress's bed chamber early the next morning to stoke the fire and lay out her mistress's clothes. With a quiet gasp, she stopped short when she saw the clothing strewn all over the floor. Not just the floor; items had been tossed helter-skelter, pell-mell over furniture and fixtures; coat, waistcoat, neckcloth, gown, slippers, shirt, breeches, smallclothes, everything. One polished leather shoe had landed in the wash basin and toppled the matching ewer. *That will ruin Bixby's morning.* A crumpled chemise was caught on top of the tester. She turned to the bed and was amazed by the picture she saw there, through a gap in the bed-curtains, of Mr and Mrs Hurst, each smiling in their sleep, spooned together under the covers.

Clara, a true romantic herself, sighed with satisfaction. *At last.*

HER EYES ROVING the crowded ballroom at Almack's, Caroline could hardly believe it, beyond excitement at having *finally* gained an entrée. All her attempts in the past had come to nothing. As the particular friend and houseguest of Baroness Riverton, she found herself at the centre of the most elite social circles in London. Every day she met more of the highest-ranking people and was accepted by them because of her friendship with Sophronia. The dashing Lord Broughton could not take his eyes off her. Caroline had always thought herself partial to dark men like Darcy, but Broughton was fair. The other gentlemen were greatly solicitous of her as well. Annabelle, Lady Drayton, treated her as a cosy conspirator.

In her smug delight, Caroline had completely forgotten about how sarcastically condescending they had been to her in school. She and the other ladies of Sophronia's circle sat together talking and laughing, making a running commentary of snide remarks about those outside their clique. She knew that her brother and sister would think her new friends rather wicked, but Caroline did not care. She had arrived. *Would not Mr Darcy want me now?*

She pictured Darcy walking into a crowded ballroom and seeing her laughing with her new friends, a vision of sophistication and breeding. In her imagination, he would walk right over to her to claim a dance, only to find them all taken.

"YOU DO REALISE we tolerate that *arriviste* only at your request, Sophy." The voice came from behind her. Sophronia turned and there was Lady Jersey, one of the patronesses. "And now I come to understand she is living with you? How do you stand it? Or perhaps the greater question is, what are you up to?"

Sophronia's expression did not change, but she flicked her

eyes to Lord Havering, standing a short distance away, conspicuously ignoring her.

Lady Jersey's eyes widened slightly. "Ah, I see." She turned her eyes to Caroline hanging on Broughton's arm. "How long do you think your young man will tolerate her? I hope you know what you're about, my dear."

CHAPTER 7

The fierce cold intensified in Hertfordshire. Layering two shawls tightly around her shoulders, Elizabeth wondered how they would ever keep the house warm. *At least it is not snowing today.* She left her father's room to fetch another blanket to put over him. She took the back stairs, and as she stepped past the kitchen, she heard Mrs Jenks cry, "Six months' wages? But I heard they'd all been let go without an extra farthing!"

"Aye, they were at first!" exclaimed Davy, the youngest footman. "But when Mr Darcy found out that Miss Bingley had dismissed all the Netherfield help without so much as a character, or any wages through the end of the month, he went to Mr Morris and paid all their wages for the next half year! Everyone! All the new house servants hired on and the extra stable boys! *And*, he offered himself as a reference if any of them needed a character!"

"Where did you hear this?" asked Jenks.

"You know what an old gossip Mr Morris is. He told Mr Philips, and I had it from his groom the last time he drove out here to see the master."

"Why, I never heard the like," the cook marvelled. "Now there's a *real* gentleman, not like the Bingleys."

Elizabeth could not believe her ears. It was unsurprising that Miss Bingley had abandoned the Netherfield servants without a second thought, but Mr Darcy had cared enough about another estate's servants to make sure they were provided for? *Mr Darcy*, who had behaved as if the entire neighbourhood was beneath his notice!

Unsettled, Elizabeth wondered. Would such a man truly deny his father's godson his inheritance? Was Wickham's story a lie? Was she a fool in mistaking both men's characters? It would seem so, but it was too upsetting to think about at that moment, and she recalled herself to her purpose. *Six months' wages for a houseful of servants is likely nothing to him!* she told herself stubbornly as she took a blanket from a folded stack of linens.

Retracing her steps, she passed the breakfast room and heard Lydia's familiar whine, which set her even more on edge

Elizabeth tried to tease herself out of perturbation. *Today is your day for eavesdropping it seems, Lizzy.*

"KITTY, I am so bored! I cannot stand it another minute! Let us get Mr Emmons to drive us into Meryton."

"It is too cold! Even if Mama would let us go, nobody would be out!"

"We could go to Aunt Philips's house! Perhaps some of the officers are there!" Lydia persisted.

"You know perfectly well that the entire regiment has been

confined to barracks! Sir William told us just last week!" said Kitty firmly.

Lydia was not used to being scolded by her usually silly and compliant sister. "Kitty, you are just as tiresome as Mary or Lizzy! If only I could go to a party or an assembly! I hate it here!"

Kitty opened her mouth to answer but stopped, her eyes widening, looking beyond her younger sister. Lydia whirled around and was confronted by Elizabeth, standing in the doorway, her eyes on fire in her pale face.

"What makes you think that anyone would wish to see *you*, Lydia?" she asked in a frosty, hard voice. "Our father is grievously ill, and you are, as always, preoccupied with your own selfish concerns. We may soon have no money and no place to live, and you wish only to go to a party and make a fool of yourself in front of the officers for the attention it brings you. Do you think any of those officers would ever consider courting or marrying a girl like you, with no money, no accomplishments, no education, and the manners of a common trollop? I think you had better be quiet for a change and think about how any of us are going to survive when Papa is gone."

Lydia opened her mouth and then shut it again. She was unused to being spoken to so harshly, and suddenly she was afraid of Elizabeth, with her furious blazing eyes and her icy voice that cut like a knife. Elizabeth glared at Lydia for a long moment and then with a swirl of skirts was gone.

Kitty sat frozen, her face pale. "Lizzy is right," she said slowly when she could finally speak.

"How can you say such a thing, you traitor! shrieked Lydia.

"It is not just Lizzy who says that," said Kitty quietly.

"Maria heard some of the officers joke about the ease of tricking you into doing any foolish thing they wished."

Lydia was motionless, her mind furiously scrolling through scenes from dances and parties where she had believed she was the life of the party. Had she instead been the dupe of pranksters? Suddenly she remembered seeing Lieutenant Denny hand Captain Carter a coin at the ball when she had gone down the dance shrieking and laughing, wearing a newspaper folded into a hat. They were placing wagers on her?

Lydia had never known mortification before, but it hit her full force. She bolted upstairs to the room she shared with Kitty, threw herself on her bed and shattered into tears.

ELIZABETH, after covering her father with the blanket, also retired to her room. She stared out the window, horrified at the vitriol she had just unleashed upon Lydia. *Where did that come from?* She sank her head into her shaking hands for a few minutes and then, taking a deep breath, went to apologise to her sister.

She tapped quietly on the door to Kitty and Lydia's bedchamber. After a moment, it was opened a crack by Kitty, who looked at her enquiringly. "I wish to speak to Lydia," Elizabeth said quietly. Kitty wordlessly stood aside and motioned for Elizabeth to enter.

She went over and sat on Lydia's bed. "Lydia, I am sorry for my hurtful words. I know not what came over me," she said, tentatively resting her hand on her sister's shoulder. Lydia flinched at her touch and turned her face into her pillow. Elizabeth quickly snatched her hand away and turned to look at Kitty, who silently motioned her out to the hall, closing the door behind them.

"I never expected her to be so angry with me. I feel terrible about losing my temper with her."

Kitty took Elizabeth's hand. "It was not your anger, but your words that have affected her so deeply—for they have been corroborated from other sources. Maria Lucas found out that many of the officers were mocking Lydia, and goading her into some of her more, erm, flamboyant behaviour. They made wagers against each other, that they could make her do anything they chose."

Elizabeth recalled the coin that had passed between the two officers after Lydia's imitation of Colonel Forster. Aghast and angry, she gasped. "How callous and mean-spirited! I cannot believe an officer, or a gentleman, would do such a malicious thing! Heartless, cruel men!"

The truth of it, Elizabeth knew, was that Lydia should not have been out at all. She was an immature girl of fifteen, a boisterous child with a womanly figure, and she had been thrust, through the inattention and laxity of her father and the exceptionally poor judgment of her mother, into situations with neither the preparation nor the maturity to handle them.

"I will try to talk to her again later. We all need each other now more than we ever did. If Papa dies—" Elizabeth faltered, then swallowed. "If Papa dies, who will take care of us? We need to take care of each other. We cannot depend on Mama, and we cannot expect our uncles and aunts to do everything for us. We must try to plan for our own futures. If our recent experiences are any example, we cannot expect to be rescued."

Elizabeth loved her parents, yet she had always known that they had been neglectful in their duties to their daughters, especially the younger ones. It was as if they had made a half-hearted attempt and then run out of interest in raising children. For probably the thousandth time in her life, Elizabeth wondered if things would have been different if there had been a son.

BY SPENDING hours each day at hard physical labour—feeding livestock, moving heavy snow and ice from overloaded roofs, clearing paths and roadways, attending to his tenants' needs—Darcy kept his mind centred on immediate goals and his body in a state of exhaustion. Thus, most of the time, Darcy could hold his deepening misery at bay until late in the evening. After he and his sister said their goodnights, he would go to his study to read, fending off sleep and the accompanying visions of Elizabeth Bennet that rose before him in his dreams. He drank more than his usual single brandy each night, hoping it would help him achieve a dreamless slumber.

Late one evening, as he sat at his desk, he caught sight of his own reflection in the window. He was jolted back to another time, another place, where he had sat writing before a darkened window.

It was the evening at Netherfield when Elizabeth had joined them in the drawing room after Miss Bennet had fallen asleep. She had smilingly declined joining the ongoing card game, taking up a book, sitting on a chaise longue several feet behind the writing table where he was seated. He had feigned busyness over the writing paper, while gazing at her surreptitiously in the dark reflection.

To his secret delight, Elizabeth had begun nodding off over her book. Her head had fallen back against the chair, her lips slightly parted, her creamy bosom rising and falling to her deep breathing. As she shifted slightly in her doze, her gown had shown signs of slipping off one silken shoulder. He had been riveted to the sight of her, unconsciously holding his breath.

At that instant, his concentration had been shattered by the raised voice of Miss Bingley, who had intuited that even though Mr Darcy was seated with his back to Elizabeth, her rival was still casting some sort of spell over him. Miss Bingley had flounced over to him, rapturously complimented the evenness of his handwriting, and offered to mend his pen. The moment had been destroyed.

Unnoticed by anyone else but Darcy, Elizabeth had quietly startled awake. She had looked about her in embarrassment, a blush rising to her cheeks, as she quickly straightened her gown and set her book on the small table next to the chaise. She bid the others good night and withdrew to her room. The intimacy of the experience had affected him deeply then, and now, months later, the memory was equally powerful. He poured himself another brandy and drank it in one gulp, hoping it would put him out quickly.

Alone in his enormous bed, he was relieved to feel himself drifting off. His slumber deepened, images swirling in his brain. He was again in the drawing room at Netherfield.

He looked up from his writing to see that Elizabeth was still dozing on the chaise longue, her book falling from her hands. Her gown had slipped further, and was lowered considerably over her bosom. Her curls had partially broken free from her hairpins and were falling down over her bare shoulder. The Bingleys and Hursts had vanished, and he and Elizabeth were alone in the room.

He rose from his chair, and in a few strides was beside her, seating himself next to her. She opened her eyes and looked up at him, smiling drowsily. Her arms reached for him as she sighed, "Fitzwilliam."

He bent his head to hers, kissing her lips, then trailing small kisses down her neck and along her collarbone, his hand moving up from her waist to cup...

In the fireplace, a burning lump of coal exploded like gunshot. Suddenly he was awake, sitting upright, sweating and breathing hard, alone in his bed at Pemberley, almost in pain from his arousal.

As the weeks wore on, other fantasies began to infiltrate his dreams; some rooted in memory, others originating in his owned fevered imagination. Finding that the dreams seemed more overwhelming and sensual in his bed, he began to sleep in his study.

JANE AND ELIZABETH stood by the boot room door, bundled up to the point where only their eyes could be seen from underneath layers of cloaks, old coats, shawls, and scarves. "You truly need not come out. What use is it that we should both freeze?" Elizabeth's muffled voice came from behind a huge woollen scarf obscuring most of her face.

"You have been handling the farm business by yourself long enough, Lizzy. Your trips to the barn are exhausting for you. Even if we find that I am useless as a farm labourer, I can at least make sure you get back to the house safe and sound." Jane's eyes crinkled at her sister.

"You have convinced me, but I will excuse you if you wisely choose never to do it again," said Elizabeth dryly. She opened the door, and the two girls stepped out into the cold. After struggling through bitter wind and drifting snow, the great barn was a welcome sight. Elizabeth put all her weight against the thick wooden door and shoved. The two girls stepped into the barn, their eyes adjusting to the dim light and their minds adjusting to the sight before them.

Lydia, clad in a pair of their father's discarded breeches, filthy old boots, and a ragged barn coat, was standing atop a haystack, wielding a large pitchfork, throwing hay into a cattle pen. Their groom, Emmons, his grey, grizzled head looking up at her, was directing her aim. They both turned to look at Jane and Elizabeth, who were standing as if paralysed in the doorway.

"Miss Elizabeth!" scolded the old man. "Close the door if you please! 'Tis cold as a witch's ti…'tis too cold in here already!"

Elizabeth quickly turned, and with an effort, pushed the heavy door shut. Then she tried to make sense of the picture before her.

Although the youngest, Lydia was already the tallest of the Bennet sisters. She was strong and robust, able to dance vigorous country dances all night without tiring in the least. Now she was garbed as a farmhand and talking animatedly to Jane and Emmons. Elizabeth was perversely grateful that the weather kept them from leaving Longbourn and mingling with the neighbourhood. She had a peculiar sense that a disaster had been averted.

"Lizzy!" cried Lydia, as she effortlessly threw another huge forkful of hay over the side, "we have already finished feeding the horses and bedding the cattle. We moved the chickens into the barn as well, so they will be a little warmer than in the coop."

Elizabeth finally found her voice. "Lydia! You are an Amazon!"

Lydia paused, the pitchfork stilled over her head. "A what?"

"Miss Lydia is a force of nature, and no mistake,"

commented Emmons with satisfaction. "She can carry two buckets of oats at once, instead of just one," he continued, pointedly eyeing one of the footmen as he struggled by with a single bucket. "We got most of our work done today in half the time." He rolled his eyes. "She is a chatterbox though. Needs to learn to hold her tongue."

Lydia tossed the pitchfork down and slid quickly down the haystack on her bottom. "And I do not like the idea of young ladies wearing breeches," grumbled Emmons. "But it is more practical, for now."

"I will do my share of the work, Lizzy," said Lydia, walking towards her older sisters. She paused, searching for the words. "I was upset yesterday," she said tentatively, her eyes beginning to moisten once more. Jane stepped to her side and put her arm around her shoulders. In a trembling voice, Lydia continued. "I was angry and embarrassed. But I know that it was my own fault. I think I am glad we are snowed in. I do not want to go to Meryton and feel people staring at me and thinking me a fool!" Her tears came again, leaving crooked little trails in the dirt and dust on her face.

Emmons growled, uncomfortable with watery-eyed females. "That will be all for today, Miss Lydia. I will leave a message at the house if I need assistance. You ladies should get back inside where it is warm." He turned and headed towards the horse stalls.

Minutes later all three girls burst through the back door, stomping their feet and shaking the snow off their garments in the boot room. Lydia went to wash her face and change into a morning gown; Jane and Elizabeth joined Mary and Kitty at the breakfast table and described the scene in the barn to them.

"Papa is asleep," said Kitty. "I was just reading to him. Mama is looking at fashion plates with Mrs Hill. Ever practical as usual," she said wryly.

Lydia soon entered and slid into the chair beside Kitty. "Lizzy," she said pensively, "what is an Amazon?"

Colouring slightly, Elizabeth considered her words, but it was Mary who supplied the information. "The Amazons were a mythical race of female warriors," she said quietly. "They are found in stories from Greek mythology. They were strong and brave and independent of all men. They had their own society with only females and were fiercely warlike. It has been said that they burned off one of their breasts, so they could shoot their arrows more efficiently."

"Eww!" cried Kitty and Lydia, crossing their arms over their chests.

"I like being compared to an Amazon," reflected Lydia a moment later. "Except for the part about their bosoms."

"Well, Lydia, you can be a farm Amazon," said Mary gravely, her face perfectly solemn. "I suspect they were allowed to keep both."

The sisters dispersed to their duties, but Elizabeth reached out to touch Mary's arm before she could rise. "I had no idea that you enjoyed mythology." She had only ever observed her sanctimonious sister reading sermons, improving tracts for young ladies, and the Bible.

Mary looked at Elizabeth with a raised eyebrow. "I suspect that my reading interests have been wider than you think, Lizzy."

Elizabeth blushed fiercely, caught out in her erroneous supposition.

"But only *slightly* wider," Mary admitted. She paused thoughtfully. "We are all, I think, becoming aware of how difficult our lives will be without Papa. It is clear to me that we sisters need to be kinder to one another, and perhaps try to know each other as friends. We stand a better chance of surviving well if we work together." She looked at Elizabeth a little sheepishly. "Perhaps in my case, I can be a little less judgmental, and a little more charitable. Suffice to say, I am working on it."

Elizabeth stared at Mary, then reached over and squeezed her hand. "I will also try to be less judgmental, Mary. I have been much taken lately with exactly how faulty my impressions of others often are. *Usually* are, I fear." She sighed, feeling a wave of self-recrimination. "I was much in the wrong about Lydia, for example."

Jane returned to the breakfast room as Mary replied, "I think Lydia will recover and grow from this experience. Look at how proud of herself she is today. We have to remember that she is young, almost a child."

Elizabeth frowned, her eyes downcast. "Did Kitty tell you what Maria Lucas said? Of the officers placing wagers on what sort of ridiculous escapades they could talk Lydia into? She is so humiliated! It was not completely her fault. She should, of course, have understood that wild behaviour is never acceptable, but she should never have been out! She is an unformed girl with an excess of energy and high spirits."

"I recall another little girl with an excess of energy and high spirits," Jane said with an arched brow, joining the discussion. "But that little girl had her father to take her in hand and help her direct and develop her lively mind and talents, not to mention her prodigious energy. And she had younger sisters to help care for."

Elizabeth looked up, only to find both Jane and Mary looking at her. Understanding of her similarity to Lydia—and her good fortune in having her father's attention—quickly dawned. Lydia had needed, still needed, strong parental guidance and discipline, but all she had ever received was talk of parties, gowns, and officers. *Both* her youngest sisters needed guidance, she realised, though Kitty had discovered that fact herself through the unlikely example of Mrs Hurst.

Elizabeth did not know whether to cry or laugh. Mistaken prejudices and poor judgment indeed!

"We will work together, Lizzy," said Mary once more.

"And we will get through this dark time somehow," added Jane. "This, too, shall pass."

CHAPTER 8

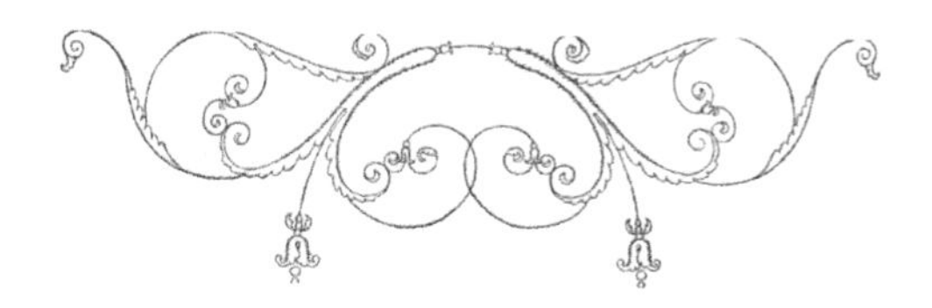

Her self-assurance growing, Louisa decided to make her own morning visits, to see *her* friends instead of using the time to dance attendance on persons Caroline deemed necessary to know.

She ordered a footman to accompany her the following morning, but to her surprise, it was her husband who stood waiting by the door. Bundled up against the cold, they visited neighbours from Northamptonshire, and then proceeded to leave cards at the homes of several old school friends. As the morning waned, they stopped to leave a card at the home of Louisa's oldest friend Lady Ellerby, the former Susan Hammond.

To Louisa's delight, Lady Ellerby was home, and her surprise and pleasure at seeing Louisa—and what is more, seeing Louisa without Caroline, was heartfelt.

"Does your sister still live with you? I believe I heard that she is in town this Season."

Louisa stiffened, wondering what she had heard, but answered the question in full.

Lady Ellerby stared at her for a long moment and then exclaimed, "You are roasting me! Lady Riverton would no more have Caroline as a houseguest than she would marry a tavern keeper!"

Hurst barked out a laugh; Louisa tried to smother a chuckle, and almost succeeded. "I have to admit I agree! I would not believe it myself if my husband and I had not both witnessed the baroness inviting her."

Hurst nodded. "Lady Ellerby, Louisa and I suspect that the baroness has ulterior motives; that is, by her presence Caroline is serving some purpose for her. Try as we may, we cannot puzzle out a reason," he said. "We assume she is happy living with the baroness. She never answers the notes and invitations Louisa has sent her, so we believe that she is content there."

"To be truthful, it is quite pleasant not having her with us. I know how dreadful that sounds," Louisa said quietly.

Lady Ellerby looked at her wryly, raising one eyebrow. "Louisa, you do not have to apologise for your sentiments. Remember that I have known Caroline as long as I have known you. I completely understand."

Settling back in her chair, Lady Ellerby speculated at the baroness's motives. "Now *there* is a mystery. Sophronia was certainly not kind to Caroline in school. Although, as I think about it, she is not *habitually* unkind. She may be inclined to superiority and the mockery of others, but I have never heard of her acting with malice. She is always conscious of her rank. She is from a noble family, you know. She was a young child when her mother died under mysterious circumstances, and her mother's aunt, Lady Havering, brazenly went to her father's estate and stole Sophronia away to live with her in

London. She was raised by Lady Havering, and I know not if she ever saw her father again.

"Lady Havering was a widow, vastly wealthy and completely independent. She was a cousin of my father's--in case you were wondering how I came into the possession of all this gossip!" She smiled slyly at the Hursts. "As a young woman, Lady Havering married a much older man, but after a few years of marriage, her husband died and left her a large fortune. Only the family seat was entailed to his cousin. The family howled but there was nothing to be done. Apparently, she had no desire for children of her own. It is said that she had love affairs even before her husband died, and she raised Sophronia to be just as independent. In fact, among our family, it is believed that she counselled her great-niece to marry an older man, just as she had herself. After Sophronia married Baron Riverton, my father took that as a validation of the rumour."

She looked at Louisa archly. "I cannot say that I agree with him. Lady Havering died when Sophronia was only sixteen and left her entire fortune to her. She did not need to marry for money or marry at all. The baron had no need to marry either. *And*," she added, "Baron Riverton was Lady Havering's long-time lover. He practically lived with her as Sophronia was growing up. Sophronia's first Season out was difficult, to put it mildly. She was besieged, and there were several rather ugly attempts to compromise her. I think he married her to protect her from fortune hunters. He and Sophronia positively dote on each other, but it is platonic."

Hurst said thoughtfully, "Does it not seem strange then, that a wealthy, titled woman like Baroness Riverton would invite my sister-in-law, a social climber whom we know her to have disdained in the past, to be her houseguest. Of what possible benefit could that be to her?"

Lady Ellerby shook her head. "I do not know. I really cannot see, *unless…*"

"What?" cried both the Hursts in unison.

She leaned forward, her eyes bright and speculative. "Rumour has it that Lady Riverton has taken a lover over the last two Seasons. This is not unusual among the *ton*; we all know that, but some still choose to pretend outrage over adultery. Lady Riverton inherited what was once the Havering fortune. There are some in that family who will never forget or forgive that and like to cause trouble for her. Last Season, some vicious gossip caused a lot of troublesome talk, even causing some highly placed persons to publicly cut the baroness. Lady Riverton likes to live her own life, but she likes to do it quietly. Perhaps by having Caroline stay with her, escorted by the gentlemen of her circle, she is trying to throw the rumourmongers off her trail. Honestly, that is the only reason I can think that would cause Lady Riverton to tolerate her!"

"Why would she choose Caroline?" asked Hurst.

"I can answer that," said Louisa. "Caroline is so pleased to be living among such lofty circles, she will not ask questions."

Her hostess nodded. "Did you receive an invitation to the Markhams' ball? I would wager Caroline will be there if you wish to see her. The Markhams are friends with Lady Riverton."

"Yes, we did. I was completely taken by surprise, until Gilbert told me they are some connexion on his mother's side. Perhaps we should go," Louisa added thoughtfully.

After more conjecture and speculation, the Hursts took their leave of Lady Ellerby, happily planning future visits and looking forward to their introduction to her husband, Sir Edmund.

CERTAIN HER FATHER was deeply asleep, Elizabeth closed the door and followed Jane to their chambers. It was late in the evening; snow was again falling outside. They could no longer ignore the fact that their father was failing.

"Oh, Lizzy, what will become of us?"

They sat together on Jane's bed, their arms around each other, silently pondering the future. If the past weeks had been difficult, Elizabeth knew that the months ahead would be far worse. There was no hero to rescue them; no saviour, no white knight, no Mr Bingley to marry Jane, as her sister sometimes dreamt about. Elizabeth knew Mr Bingley still haunted Jane's memory and that her sister suffered guilt over her love for a man who had abandoned her, when she should be thinking about her own father and her family's future.

Elizabeth, equally aware that their lives were soon going to change—and not for the better—struggled with similar escapist thoughts. She tried to push such notions out of her mind, wishing only to focus on what were sure to be the last days and weeks to be with her dear father. She wished to spend every minute with him and burn each memory into her mind so she would have part of him forever. Still, deep in her heart, she desperately needed to be comforted and cared for. To her utter mortification, when she most keenly needed consolation, those thoughts were always accompanied by none other than Mr Darcy! Elizabeth was baffled and displeased that he should have taken up residence in even the smallest corner of her mind.

THE DRAWING ROOM project commenced with no contribution from Caroline Bingley. Wishing to share her excitement over the project with her sister, Louisa had sent a note to Riverton House. The note went from footman to butler to maid to

Bertha, only to nestle, unopened, on the salver amongst its predecessors. Caroline was already late for an appointment with her *couturière.*

Hurst and Bingley were banned from the drawing room for the duration of the renovations, and the three of them spent cosy evenings by the fire in the parlour instead. The subject of Caroline came up during one discussion, and Louisa shared Lady Ellerby's ideas with her brother.

"I have sent several notes to Riverton House for Caroline. I invited her to spend Christmas with us! I have never received the favour of a reply, not once! I can only presume that she is enjoying herself in exalted company and does not wish to be reminded that she has a family!"

Bingley groaned. "I have seen Caroline's bills, and I know for a fact that she is enjoying herself!"

Hurst laughed. "Well, if exorbitant bills are any indication that Caroline is happy living away from home, I would be most pleased to pay half."

A FEW DAYS later found the Hursts, along with Mrs Gardiner, at Mr Gardiner's warehouse. "This is our most recent shipment," said Mr Gardiner, grinning, "and you ladies have first crack at it! We have some silks from France, and laces from Belgium. We have also acquired some fixtures and furnishings from what were some of the loveliest chateaus in France before the recent troubles. I have asked Wilkins here to assist you ladies in looking over whatever takes your fancy. There are some large display tables over there where you can lay out lengths of fabric."

As the ladies admired colours and textures, carpets and furnishings; they established between themselves not only a similarity in tastes but an easy informality. By their third visit to the warehouses, they had established an intimacy enough to permit the use of each other's Christian names.

While the ladies were making Wilkins run up and down the warehouse floor, the men reconvened in Gardiner's meeting room, where he outlined his plans for the next few voyages of the trading ships. Hurst related that Louisa's brother had also expressed an interest in investing, and possibly another friend whom Gardiner had met at the theatre back in December. "My brother is here in town for the winter, but our friend is at his estate in Derbyshire, and from what I understand, they are completely snowed under."

"Yes, it has been a hard winter, but I believe we have been relatively fortunate here in town," answered Gardiner. "Perhaps we can meet with them when the weather is more temperate. I am traveling this week, if the roads are passable, to see my brother who is still ailing. I wish I could say that we are optimistic about his recovery, but there is little hope, and I wish to help him make the best of a dreadful situation. He has five unmarried daughters with no dowries, and his estate is entailed to a distant relative."

"None of them are married? Are there no prospective husbands for them?"

"The eldest girl had formed an attachment to a gentleman in the autumn, but it came to nothing. The elder daughters have decided to seek employment, but I hope to dissuade them from that notion." Mr Gardiner frowned, "My sister's husband is an educated gentleman, but never sensible in running his affairs. My sister, I deeply regret, is no more practical than a child. I need to see what, if anything, I can do to assist the family."

Hurst shook his head. "You have my sincere sympathies. My father was capricious and unstable; never able to handle his financial affairs with any sense. My mother kept him steady, but when she died, his handling of the family finances was irresponsible. He almost lost the family seat before he died. It was my maternal grandfather who stepped in and kept us from losing everything. My brother and I have been trying to rebuild since we came of age."

SOPHRONIA LED the ladies to the music room, leaving the gentlemen at the table. It had been an intimate evening, with just a dozen or so friends gathered together. Certainly enjoyable enough, but with Miss Bingley in constant attendance, this close-knit circle of friends could not truly relax together as they had used to do.

She smiled as graciously as possible through gritted teeth as the ladies settled into chairs, Caroline moving to the instrument with alacrity. So it was to be another evening of exhibition, self-congratulation, and self-promotion from her pretended bosom friend. Annabelle and Judith exchanged a pained glance and Cornelia forced an unconvincing smile as the performance began.

In the dining room, the gentlemen sat together, smoking their cigars and sipping their brandy, companionably quiet. Sir Magnus blew a smoke ring and quipped, "How many feathers do you fellows think Miss Bingley will wear in her hair at the Markhams' ball?"

Mortimer grinned. "I shall put my money on three feathers!" He reached into his pocket and plunked down a guinea on the table.

"Only three?" cried Broughton in mock horror. "I say five feathers!" and he too put his money on the table.

"Four," said Wareham, adding his money to the small but growing pile of coins.

"None," said Drayton, as he reached into his pocket for his money.

"None?" said Norling. "You are joking, man!"

"I say none," repeated Drayton. "I think she will wear that ridiculous headdress affair with the dead bird and dangling fruit." The gentlemen roared.

"Oh, Lord, I had forgotten about that one!" conceded Broughton, "although I think the proper term is *stuffed* bird."

Suddenly five guineas landed on the table. Startled, the gentlemen turned around to see Baron Riverton standing next to them, shakily leaning on his cane. He was grinning slyly. "I say seven feathers!" he cackled uproariously. The gentlemen all laughed, and a few more wagers were placed.

"Gentlemen, shall we join the ladies?" said the baron, and they all rose and filed out of the room, the baron slapping Broughton on the back as they proceeded through the door.

THE SNOW PELTED DOWN so thick and fast they could hear it hitting the windowpanes. Louisa was grateful it was only a short ride for Charles, who after their dinner together had driven off alone into the bitter, frigid night.

"I must insist Charles leave Darcy House and move in with us. I wish to keep an eye on him. He is so lonely," she said pensively She was curled on her husband's lap, nestled in his arms, her head resting on his shoulder.

"I agree," replied Hurst. "I believe he is still heartbroken over Miss Bennet."

Louisa sat up straight and looked intently into her husband's face. "I think so too. Do you think Miss Bennet had feelings for Charles?"

Hurst tightened his hold around Louisa's waist. "I never agreed with Caroline or Darcy about Miss Bennet's feelings.

Shortly after we returned to town, I told Charles that he should listen to his own heart. He should at least seek out Miss Bennet and find out for himself. It is unfortunate that he may have to wait for spring to travel to Hertfordshire."

Louisa sighed. "Caroline was determined to keep Charles away from Miss Bennet. She has no concern for his feelings, nor anyone's for that matter."

"Caroline cares only for rank, as does Darcy. Though in this case, he may have truly been concerned that Miss Bennet did not return Charles's feelings. He does value Charles's friendship." Hurst chuckled wryly. "Frankly, my dear, I wonder if Darcy would even recognise love if he saw it."

His wife looked up at him. "In all fairness to Mr Darcy, Miss Bennet was not at all demonstrative. I, too, believe that she was falling in love with Charles, but the signs were subtle. I liked her exceedingly. I would like my brother to be happy, and I would like to have had Miss Bennet in the family, no matter what Caroline or Mr Darcy had to say about it. In fact, I think Mr Darcy was in some danger of falling for Elizabeth Bennet. He certainly could not take his eyes off her."

"You saw it too? I thought perhaps I was imagining things." Hurst laughed. "The alacrity with which he entered into conversation with her when he is usually so taciturn. His unease? No, rather, his *intensity* in her presence. He could not stay away from her. Did you see him prowling the ballroom at Netherfield, and his blush when he danced with Miss Elizabeth? He danced with no other. Yet I do not think she liked him at all."

Louisa arched a brow. "*Some* of us were too busy receiving our guests that evening to observe who was dancing with whom," she said tartly.

At his penitent expression, she continued. "Whether she liked him or not does not signify. Mr Darcy would never stoop to court her; he will always put his position in society first. He is a good man, but uncommonly proud. Although Caroline would never admit it, for much of society, the Bennets' rank exceeds that of the Bingleys. My father's fortune came from trade, but Mr Bennet is a gentleman."

"True, but as for Darcy, his pride predisposes him to detachment, which is its own kind of loneliness," mused Hurst. "It is rather sad, actually. I pity him."

Louisa laid her head back on her husband's shoulder. "So do I."

CHAPTER 9

In the early morning hours, oblivious to the howling storm outside, Darcy replayed the ball at Netherfield for the thousandth time in his mind. Elizabeth had looked so beautiful, her face glowing with anticipation. They had verbally sparred during their dance, and he had been annoyed with her, but not so upset that he had not noticed the pink flush of her skin and the fire in her eyes. Unable to help himself, he had no sooner seen the blush moving up her neck than a vision of a rosy flush all over her lithesome body had appeared unbidden in his mind as they danced. Immediately, scarlet heat had risen to his own face.

The behaviour of her family had made him wince. Her mother's noisy effusions over Bingley and Miss Bennet, the wild behaviour of the two youngest sisters; Mr Bennet's refusal to exert himself to put a stop to it, had humiliated Elizabeth. He had watched the emotions play over her face. That she could be so mortified by her family, yet remain so caring of them was a credit to her. Caroline Bingley had been inexcusably rude to Elizabeth during their time at Netherfield, but she had responded with grace and even levity. Her wit and resourcefulness, her curiosity and intelligence, her uncommon perspective and sense of humour, and her disinterest in conforming to missish notions made him realise how rare she truly was.

Could he have reacted to embarrassment with as much grace? Passing his hand over his face, he recollected the evening at the theatre before he had left London. The mortification of sitting with Miss Bingley still discomposed him, and he shuddered. Lady Catherine had also caused him considerable embarrassment over the years.

There was a surfeit of ill-mannered and uncouth people in the *ton*, and there were businessmen who were well-educated and genteel. That elegant couple from the theatre that Hurst had introduced, the Gardiners, for example. They had been most impressive, and he already planned to speak with Mr Gardiner when he got back to town. But could he court Miss Elizabeth Bennet and present her to his family and peers? When he asked himself that question, the answer always came back: No.

He fought to extricate himself from such useless reflections. Yet the thoughts and dreams were stubborn, unyielding, returning again and again.

EVEN AS DARCY meditated on his heart's desire, Elizabeth dozed on the chaise longue in her father's chamber, wrapped snugly in a thick quilt. It was almost dawn, and the overcast sky outside the windows began slowly to lighten. Her Uncle

Gardiner's short visit had brought her some small comfort; before he had left Longbourn the day prior, he had advised her and her sisters of the assistance he could bring, disabused her and Jane of any thoughts of seeking employment, and assured Mrs Bennet that the hedgerows would not be her new home. Although her mother remained angry at her actions, Elizabeth had no regrets that she had refused Mr Collins and 'let the man slip into the embrace of the grasping Lucases'.

Poor Charlotte, married to such a man.

She settled deeper into the cushions of the big old chaise longue, half sleeping and half waking. Her hazy dream of a cosy chat with Charlotte in the parlour at Lucas Lodge was interrupted by Mr Darcy suddenly materialising on the sun-faded sofa there. He was gazing at her with the familiar intensity he had throughout his stay in Hertfordshire. Dream Charlotte, her brow arched, ignored him, looking her in the eye and taking her to task. "Do not be so surprised, Lizzy! You *were* the only lady he danced with at the ball, after all."

Elizabeth's eyes flew open and she sat straight up. With a gasp, she wondered if Charlotte and Aunt Gardiner might have been correct. Could Mr Darcy have formed a *tendre* for her? Her hard feelings towards him had mellowed slightly once she realised George Wickham's true character, but she wished Mr Darcy would not appear in her dreams. The hard reality of her situation made such thoughts ridiculous. Would a man of such consequence and pride ever have anything more to do with an impoverished country girl? She groaned and lay back down, pulling the quilt over her head. *Pathetic, thy name is Lizzy!*

DARCY STOOD up slowly and stretched. The weather had been too foul that day to spend more than a few minutes outdoors.

He had been kneeling next to a wooden chest, searching a storage room near his steward's office for old estate records. Even though he and his steward made sure that all residents of Pemberley estate wanted for nothing, he was curious to discover if a similar winter had been recorded, and what previous masters of Pemberley had done. He bent over and pulled out some dusty logbooks, over thirty years old. He recognised the handwriting of old Mr Wickham, his father's steward.

It struck him like a thunderbolt. When he had left Netherfield, the militia was still encamped there. He had left the field open to that scoundrel, George Wickham!

"Good God!" Wickham was a despicable cur, but he knew how to charm his way in society. Elizabeth had already been fooled into thinking Wickham a gentleman when last he had seen her. His imagination reeled at the thought of what damage might have been done since then. The idea that Wickham had somehow succeeded in getting his filthy hands on Elizabeth nauseated him.

He sat down heavily on the floor, put his head in his hands and sent up a fervent prayer that she would be safe. Could an intelligent woman like Elizabeth truly believe that lying fiend for any length of time? He hoped she had finally recognised Wickham's true character, and was safe from him, but the thought left him feeling sick and hollow inside. Unable to contemplate reading any more records, he threw the logbooks back in the chest and slammed the lid shut.

THE NIGHT AIR was so bitter, it was painful to even draw breath, but the glittering ball at the magnificent home of the Markhams was proceeding as planned. The line of carriages waiting to discharge their passengers at the door clogged the street.

Lord Jonathan Mortimer had arrived earlier than his friends and was mingling with the crowd when he spied Baroness Riverton. "Good evening to you, my lady," he said, with a deep bow. He straightened and smirked conspiratorially at her. "So, how many feathers this time?" Sophronia rolled her eyes. "See for yourself." She gestured with her head towards the centre of the room. Mortimer turned his eyes in the direction indicated by the baroness.

Caroline Bingley was resplendent in a gown of orange shimmering material, a beribboned bodice that left little to the imagination, multiple layers of deep lacy flounces, richly bejewelled, all set off by a jewelled turban with no less than nine feathers, in three rows of three.

Lady Drayton and Viscount Norling joined them. Annabelle, her mouth gaping, stared at Caroline. "You know, Sophy, she truly is magnificent in rather a bizarre way. She honestly has no idea, does she?"

"No, Bella, I do not believe she does. No doubt she will hear any number of barely veiled insults about her gown and turban this evening, but she will not even notice. The divine Caroline has the hide of a rhino. I almost admire her," marvelled Sophronia.

THE OBJECT of their attention walked down the centre of the room with her nose in the air, quizzing glasses rising in succession in her wake. Caroline basked in the attention. She could feel dozens, nay, hundreds of admiring eyes upon her. How vexing that Mr Darcy was not there to see!

But she had conquered the *ton* without him. The gentlemen she had met were decidedly attentive and charming, even flattering, unlike the aloof and taciturn master of Pemberley. Still, it was Pemberley that Caroline wanted most. With her newly enhanced prestige and presence, she was certain she would win Mr Darcy before the next Season. She anticipated more than ever her summer sojourn at his estate in Derbyshire.

THE HURSTS, along with Bingley, arrived late, having been caught in the tangle of carriage traffic outside the Markhams' imposing town house. Mrs Markham was delighted to see them. Hurst's mother had been her second cousin, and they had come out together long ago. She introduced the elegant couple to her husband and daughters, but had to let them go due to the press of other guests.

Cornelia Markham whispered in her sister's ear. "*That* is Miss Bingley's sister?" Judith nodded, her eyes following the couple as they made their way down the grand staircase. "Hard to believe, is it not?"

Louisa scanned the crush of people in the capacious ballroom. How would she ever find Caroline? She was unable to see more than five feet away, and between the orchestra and the hundreds of voices straining to be heard over the music, the three of them could hardly hear each other.

"I wonder if Caroline will deign to give us notice."

After another look around the ballroom, Bingley leaned his head closer to his sister. "I will be in the card room. I have no interest in dancing tonight."

She looked at him sympathetically. "I understand, Charles. Perhaps you will see some friends there." She caught sight of a few elaborate headdresses circulating about the room, but the crowd was such that she could not tell who was wearing them.

"There is one with nine feathers," Hurst said. "Any wagers on who that might be?"

"Oh dear, no. I do not think I want to wager on that."

He leaned in to speak in her ear. "May I have this dance?"

"Yes, please," she sighed happily. "Let us just forget about my sister for a while."

"That is just what I wanted to hear, my dear."

They spotted the tall feathers several times as they followed the figures of the dance around the floor. Louisa saw an occasional flash of orange that set her to wondering, but they had danced two complete sets before the crowd shifted enough for them to get a good look at Caroline, ostentatiously dressed to the nines and standing with a tall blond gentleman, whose face was a mask of weary resignation.

Caroline looked their way, her eyes widening in obvious disbelief. Her expression remained frozen, and—the couple realised—distinctly unfriendly. Clearly she had no interest in introducing them to her friends, but more outrageous, even for Caroline Bingley, her stony countenance sent a message of disinterest in greeting them herself.

Louisa lifted her hand to her throat, bringing her sister's attention to the emerald necklace she wore. Caroline's eyes sharpened and she seemed intent on turning in their direction when the man beside her absently towed her away into the next dance.

The Hursts stared after her in disbelief. *The cut direct!*

"Louisa, my dear, this is outrageous! This is beyond anything, even for Caroline..." Hurst broke off in dismay, as he saw his wife shaking with merriment. She clapped her elegantly gloved hands over her mouth to stifle her laughter, shoulders shaking, tears sparkling in her lashes. He, too, began to laugh at the absurdity of the situation.

"Let us find Charles and go home, my dear," said Louisa, finally catching her breath.

"You no longer wish to dance?"

"I would rather be home with you." She looked up into his eyes. "I am sure we can find something else to do, my love," she said mischievously, waggling her eyebrows.

CHAPTER 10

Elizabeth's correspondence with Charlotte became something of a lifeline, if sparse and irregular because of the weather. Hertfordshire suffered from an almost constant onslaught of snow and sleet, while farther south in Kent, there had been occasional snowstorms but mostly steady cold winds and sleet which turned roads into quagmires. She sat in her room writing, having left Mary and Kitty watching over their father.

My dear Charlotte,

I hope this letter finds you safe, warm, and well. I wonder if you have been suffering the same bitter weather at Hunsford that we have been having at Longbourn. We keep to the house, although I still occasionally try to walk outside if I can. I would lose my mind if I could not, although some days I struggle through drifts of snow. Many days it is simply too cold to venture outdoors. Has there ever been such a winter!

I do not doubt that your parents or Maria have described my father's illness to you. He does not improve. Jane and I are dependent upon the advice of our uncles and our dear neighbours, whenever we can receive the rare letter or visit. Our mother keeps to her room, and Jane, Mary, and I are charged with our father's care. Kitty and Lydia, to our great relief, do not complain about their removal from society. Indeed, they have been so helpful and responsible, I have no idea what we would do without them.

The weather also causes the regiment to be mostly confined to barracks, which we have heard has been difficult, especially for Mr Wickham, who we now know to be of low and odious character. Oh, Charlotte!The scales have fallen from our eyes! Gaming and intoxication are the least of his sins. It is said that he is in debt to many of the shopkeepers in Meryton and has debts of honour among his fellow officers as well. There was a rumour that he tried to drag Biddy Sykes into the stables behind the inn, but was stopped by her brother. I confess that I am heartily ashamed to have been so taken in by him, having once believed myself to be a tolerably good judge of character. I am chagrined to find that Mr Darcy, and even worse, Miss Bingley, were in the right about him.

Colonel Forster and Mr Denny have been so kind as to visit with my father occasionally, weather permitting. Uncle Philips and your good father also have attended him as much as they can. Although my mother would strenuously deny it, Jane and I believe this to be our father's final illness. We have been considering what choices we may have in keeping our family together. We can stay with my Aunt Philips temporarily, but as you know their home is small. Jane, Mary, and I have decided that as soon as possible, we will make enquiries into finding positions as governesses, or perhaps companions. Our uncle Gardiner wishes us to postpone our enquiries until details of the estate are settled, but I will feel better if I can bring additional income to my family as soon as possible and cannot in any event imagine any other alternative.

Well, my dear Charlotte, I have wallowed in self-pity long enough. I will finish now and get this letter ready for the post. Uncle Philips is with my father, and he will take it in to Meryton for me.

With affection,
Your Eliza

Elizabeth, mentally and physically exhausted, lay in her bed. Her father had been noticeably worse all day, and she had been up and down the stairs many times fetching for him, as well as wading through deep snowdrifts out to the stables to speak with Emmons. As had come to be her usual reaction to Mr Bennet's bad days, Mrs Bennet had taken out her anxieties on her second daughter. Elizabeth's head throbbed, and her tensed muscles were tied in painful knots from head to toe.

Jane had come into Mr Bennet's room and sent Elizabeth off to bed. She was sitting with their father now, reading to him. Elizabeth was trying to relax enough to fall asleep, to no avail, even though she was bone-weary. Snow was falling thick and fast outside, and in the unnatural quiet she let her mind drift. Before she knew it, into her wool-gathering arrived Mr Darcy. She was too tired to push him out of her mind as she usually did, so he stayed.

He gazed at her seriously, but not in the fierce way that he had at Netherfield. His eyes were soft and his expression gentle. "You are so weary, Miss Elizabeth. I am quite worried about you," he said softly to her in his deep voice.

He sat on the bed next to her and took her hand in both of his. "Let us imagine that we are walking on a warm summer morning," he said, and all at once they were strolling down a lush green path under dappled sunshine, her arm twined with his. As she felt herself relaxing into deep sleep, he smiled down at her, kissed her hand, and let her go.

DARCY, having thrown a dressing gown over his breeches and shirt, slowly and wearily stretched his long legs out before the roaring fire, warming his bare feet. His toes were numb. He was mentally and physically exhausted. In addition to his now chronic sleeplessness, he had worked feverishly in the stables and barns all day alongside the stable hands, moving hay and oats, preparing for another fierce winter storm. His muscles ached and his fatigue was overwhelming. He prayed he might sleep deeply tonight. Darkness had fallen, but he could hear the wind rising and knew that clouds laden with snow were once more poised to bury

Pemberley. Such a winter had not been seen within living memory.

Yet he was glad of it. He need not make excuses for never going out or being in company. He raised a glass of port before the fire's glow and stared into the deep red lights of the wine. Tossing the remains of the liquid back, he set the glass down on the side table and settled deeper into the luxurious leather chair, legs resting straight out before him on the foot-stool. He could feel his tired, aching body sinking into the cushions, and his weary mind sinking into slumber. The soft darkness enveloped him, and he was once again lost in a memory of Netherfield.

He was walking back to the manor house after spending the morning shooting. Bingley had been so anxious to enquire after Miss Bennet's condition that he carelessly left his gun leaning against a tree when he hurried away ahead of the others, instead of handing it to his servant. Darcy, not wishing to be back in Miss Bingley's company quite so soon, took it upon himself to carry it to the gun room at the back of the house. As he passed the open door to the kitchen, he could hear the sounds of conversation and laughter.

A laugh like musical bubbles pricked his ear, and his feet stopped walking of their own volition. He forgot his errand and stepped as quietly as possible towards the wide wooden door. Choosing an angle where he would not be easily discovered, he peered into the large, warm kitchen. There she was, smiling and talking to one of the undercooks. From what he could make out of the conversation, he gathered that the woman was the daughter of one of Mr Bennet's tenants. She appeared to hold Elizabeth in great regard.

He drank in the vision of his sparkling girl, rocking and cuddling the young woman's baby, and talking softly to it. For her efforts, Elizabeth was rewarded by a wide toothless baby smile. The kitchen servants were gathered round, and they all laughed together. Elizabeth's face was suffused with delight. His heart beat faster. He wanted to be next to her, and one foot shifted forward before he recalled himself to the unseemliness of fraternizing with his host's servants.

At that moment, the cook stepped over to Elizabeth, "Here you are, Miss. Some nice broth and bread for Miss Bennet. I am glad to hear she is ready to take some proper food today!" As Elizabeth handed the baby back to its mother, Cook turned to the group, "All right you lot, the party's over! What if Miss Bingley should find us like this!" Everyone laughed, and the group broke up. Elizabeth thanked the cook and left the kitchen with the tray, accompanied by a maid with a pitcher of water.

Darcy stood rooted to the spot a moment longer before he recalled himself and finished his errand.

As the memory transformed into a dream of Elizabeth and himself cuddling their own baby, Darcy slightly shifted position in his sleep. His face relaxed, and a tiny smile teased the corners of his mouth.

In the dark of the study, his valet, Talbot, stood watching over him with concern. He observed that his master was having a pleasant dream that for once had not brought him the passionate night visions from which he awoke, breathing hard, drenched in sweat or worse. No, tonight Mr Darcy would get some desperately needed rest. His valet covered him with a blanket and left the room

FROM THE TIME Sophronia had gone to live with her aunt, she and Baron Riverton had breakfasted together at every opportunity. Her Aunt Augusta preferred to sleep till noon, and over the years Sophy and the baron had built a deep and enduring friendship over kippers and sausages.

Sophronia knocked quietly on the door to her husband's sitting room. "Enter," came the faint reply. She came into the cosy room to find him sitting up with a newspaper in his lap, a twinkle in his eye.

"Rupert!" she exclaimed with delight. "I came to see if you felt up to having breakfast. You look well today! The last few weeks…well, I have missed you, dearest friend."

The baron's smile was rueful. "I am sorry, little Sophy. I miss you too. Of course, there is nothing to be done about it, is there? The fog just seems to take over my old head sometimes. You are stuck with a doddering old hulk."

She moved to his side and put her arms around him. She looked at him with moist eyes. "I am not stuck! I love you dearly, and it is my privilege to care for you. You have always taken such good care of me."

He chuckled. "As if you needed anyone to take care of you. You are a rare one, Sophy, just as Gussie was! I tried to make her marry me, you know. But after Havering died, she did not need or want another husband. Just being her lover was heaven on earth though." He smiled faintly, his eyes focused on a distant vision.

Sophronia regarded him sympathetically. "I understand my aunt's determination to be independent, but in your case, I think she should have given remarriage more thought."

The baron threw back his head and laughed. "So, when I am gone, are you going to marry that handsome young fellow of yours? Do not be coy, girl, I know what is going on! He is a decent man, and he certainly would do anything for you, including squire around that ridiculous Bingley woman. Egad, that chit loves the sound of her own voice, eh? Who are her people, any way? Would I know them?"

"Her family is rather more recent than those of our circle, my dear," smirked Sophronia, sidestepping the marriage question. She rang for breakfast, and they settled in for a chat as they ate. She watched as her husband pushed more food around his plate than he consumed. He smiled and laughed as she related the latest gossip, but he was only half attending to her words.

"My child," he began, "There is something I wish to speak with you about." He paused, and with a twisted smile pointed to his head. "I do seem to be rowing with both oars today, so now is the time."

She steeled herself. She had feared that this was coming.

"Sophy, my child, I feel that I am…well, running down. No, not ill precisely, but…enormously tired, very weary and… I have decided to go home to Abbotsford. My body is beginning to fail me, and I wish to spend my last days there. As soon as possible, though I will wait until it is safe to travel." He looked at her. "Is there any hope that you will come with me? It would, of course, mean leaving town and…"

"Certainly I will come with you! You are my only family. We will go, you and I, as soon as possible."

Charlotte Collins sat in her snug little sitting room and sorted through the newly-arrived post. It was a larger stack than usual, and she supposed some break in the weather in Hertfordshire had allowed letters to finally escape to their destinations. She wrapped her shawl more tightly about her shoulders and began to read. After perusing them all, she sat frowning, staring at the fire for a long time. Finally rousing herself, she went to her little desk and began to write.

My dearest Eliza,

This morning two of your letters came at once, delayed no doubt by the terrible winter Hertfordshire is experiencing. I also had a letter from Papa and two from Maria in the same bundle. The coincidence of all these points of view being expressed to me on the same day, I almost feel as if I were home again.

I have also discovered, dear Eliza, that you have not been describing the half of the sorrow you have been living in. I am deeply grieved to hear that your beloved father will not recover. My own father concurs with your sad news. Papa also tells me that your mother is not only too overwrought to care for your father, but requires care herself. He grieves that he and my mother, and your uncle and aunt Philips are often prevented from assisting you by the deep snow and wretched cold. You did not mention that in addition to caring for your father, you have been trying to manage estate matters with so little assistance. I wish with all my heart that I could be there with you in person.

Since that cannot be, I shall contrive to do what I can for you from here. I have not told Mr Collins of your father's illness, nor has anyone in my family. I will not apprise my husband that anything is amiss until after I am informed of your father's death.

Until then, as future mistress of Longbourn, I insist that you, your mother, and your sisters remove anything you wish to keep from the house before we arrive. I know that you will take all your personal things, but I urge you to pack up any pictures, small furnishings, books, letters, playthings, and other mementos and take them with you to wherever your family will abide. I do not believe my husband will miss them.

When the time comes, I will inform our esteemed patroness, Lady Catherine, that until she can find a new parson to take the place of Mr Collins, we will stay on. That will allow you and your family what I hope will be a generous amount of time, perhaps until summer, to find other lodgings. My thoughts are continually with you. If there is any other way I can assist you, you have only to name it.

May God bless and keep you, my dearest friend.
Fondly,
Charlotte

ELIZABETH DREAMT OF DARCY AGAIN. It had become a habit. She had come to welcome his presence in her dreams. At first, he had only walked with her, her hand tucked into his arm, and listened carefully and seriously to her woes. Then he began to hold her hand, their fingers interlaced, and she could hear his voice as if he were truly standing right next to her. Occasionally he took out his large handkerchief and wiped away her tears. Then one day, her imaginary friend put his arms around her and comforted her, murmuring in a low voice as she laid her head on his strong shoulder.

As the weeks went by, Elizabeth's dream persona became more and more deeply attached to her tall, handsome confidant. Mortified, she found that she had no control over the deepening familiarity between her imaginary self and Mr Darcy. Just last night, she dreamt he had laid his cheek upon her hair! In her waking hours, she blushed to think that she often dreamed of sitting in his lap. Deeply discomfited, she gave silent, fervid thanks that there was no likelihood that she would ever see him again. How would she even look him in the face?

GEORGIANA AND MRS REYNOLDS entered the breakfast room together, discussing the distribution of food to the tenants, to seek Darcy's opinion on moving more provisions around the estate by sledge. Her brother sat at the table with some papers in front of him, obviously exhausted. He appeared not to notice them.

"Fitzwilliam," said Georgiana gently, trying to get his attention without startling him.

"What is it, Elizabeth?" he answered abstractedly, without looking up.

Georgiana and Mrs Reynolds looked at each other in astonishment, and then beat a hasty, if silent, retreat from the room. "This is worrisome," said the housekeeper. "The master has not been himself since he returned to Pemberley before Christmas."

"I confess I have been worried about him for some time," answered Georgiana, "and this is the third time he has called me Elizabeth in the last few weeks."

"Talbot tells me that he sits in his study until late at night, and often spends the night in there, sleeping in his clothes," fretted Mrs Reynolds. Georgiana was silent, her brows furrowed. It was evident that her brother's mysterious behaviour did not relate to her misadventure at Ramsgate the previous summer.

Later that evening, as she prepared for bed, Georgiana was lost in thought. She felt she should recall something about an Elizabeth. It was familiar, but just beyond the reach of her memory. She could not think of any woman with that name who was known to her. Where would her brother have met someone that she had not met? In London?

Her brother never spoke with her about any of the women in his life. Although Georgiana was naively unaware that her brother was considered such a prize in society's avaricious marriage mart that he avoided the company of most women, she assumed that at eight and twenty, he must have met some ladies he admired by now.

Her brow furrowed, she barely noticed as her maid brushed out her hair and helped her into a flannel nightgown. She climbed into her bed, already warmed by hot bricks, and tried to put it out of her mind. She was drifting off, feeling her muscles relax under the thick counterpane when the penny dropped.

Her eyes flew open. She scrambled out of bed and ran to a small cupboard, throwing open the door. She seized a carved wooden box which held all the letters she had received from her brother, and took out the letters he had sent from Hertfordshire. Georgiana wondered why she had not realised it earlier—perhaps because she had been so caught up in her own misery—but Fitzwilliam's letters from Netherfield had been unusual. Her brother, who had never written to her about women, had mentioned one young lady several times in each of his letters from Bingley's estate. With the letters in hand, she scurried back across the cold floor and leapt back into the warm bed. Wrapped snugly in her down comforter, Georgie unfolded the letters, and there she was: Elizabeth Bennet. She raised her face from the pile of letters in her lap, her eyes wide, a smile slowly spreading across her face. *Fitzwilliam is in love!*

IN THE DEPTHS of the night, Jane woke, drowsily aware that someone seemed to be speaking to her. She raised her head from her pillow, her eyes barely open, trying to understand who was talking and what was being said. As her head began to clear, she recognised that she was in her bedroom, and that Lizzy was talking, but not to her. Jane peered through the darkness at her sister, who was herself deep in slumber. Lizzy was murmuring in her sleep, and as Jane pondered whether to wake her or not, she heard the words "Darcy...so kind..." Jane snapped to wide-eyed attention and listened intently. The words were muttered and blurred with sleep, but she came to understand that Lizzy was carrying on a conversation with Mr Darcy, and a most familiar one at that.

Her sister, who had professed a dislike of that gentleman from the beginning of their acquaintance, was dreaming of him, speaking to him in tones that could only be described as warm and cosy. Jane lay her head back down on her pillow, wondering. Mr Bingley esteemed his reserved friend deeply, believing him to be a good, decent man. Could Lizzy have sensed that about him as well? Jane decided not to say anything about it to her sister. Why embarrass her? She herself derived some small comfort from her dreams of Bingley. She could not begrudge similar comfort to her sister. But Mr Darcy? And Lizzy? Together? The very idea made her chuckle. She closed her eyes, snuggled back into the warmth of her blankets, and drifted back to sleep.

CHAPTER 11

By late February, Sophronia was encouraged by a slight easing of the weather, and set the household to packing for the journey to Sussex. She was determined to honour her husband's wishes and take him home to his estate there to enjoy the last weeks or, hopefully, months of his life. Although his estate was only a day's ride from London, Sophronia feared that the journey alone would be enough to put him into a final decline.

Broughton was worried about her, and hated to see her go. "I should like to accompany you, Sophy. I cannot let you deal with Rupert's health alone. Do you think there is any way we can accomplish that without drawing too much attention?"

She threw up her hands in vexation. "I do wish you could accompany us, Alfred, but then we would have to bring Caroline. Her company is always disagreeable, but so much worse at such a time as this!" She sat down and put her head in her hands.

"If some of us came along and put it about that it was merely a house party, perhaps we will not raise suspicion."

So it was decided that Broughton, Lord and Lady Drayton, and Lord and Lady Deerhurst, along with Miss Bingley, would accompany Lord and Lady Riverton to Sussex. Bracing themselves for a treacherous journey, they were pleased to find that the farther south they travelled from London, the easier travel became. At the end of a long day, the small caravan of coaches arrived at Abbotsford Park.

JANE AND ELIZABETH sat at the darkened window in their father's chamber, watching the cold rain make wet trails on the glass. Over the most recent days the sun had finally begun to show its face occasionally and the air had warmed slightly. Hill had even reported hearing birdsong. Mr Bennet had fallen asleep, and Elizabeth set down the book she had been reading aloud. Their silent reverie was interrupted by the sound of his voice, hoarse and weak, but his familiar dry and quizzical tone was intact.

"Girls," he said, beckoning faintly as they both quickly turned to him.

Jane moved to his bedside. "Yes, Papa?"

Mr Bennet patted the edge of the bed for her to sit down beside him. "My firstborn," he said in a cracked voice. "Try not to be so melancholy."

"Oh, Papa," said Jane, almost in a whisper, "Try to save your strength. You must have a sip of water."

Her father did as he was told as Jane held the glass to his lips. "You have taken such good care of me. You will be quite a wonderful mother someday."

Jane shook her head sadly. "I do not see that in my future."

"Of course you will. On this, your mother and I agree; you

cannot be so beautiful for nothing. Your Mr Bingley will find his way back to you," he said, wheezing. "Perhaps the bad weather has been keeping him away. I will tell you this, my child, he was completely in love with you."

"I know it is wrong, but I still dream of him."

"It is not wrong, my girl. You are worthy of love. Get some rest, my dear, and savour your dreams."

"Good night, Papa. Sleep well, and God bless you," Jane kissed his cheek before leaving the room, closing the door quietly behind her.

Elizabeth, her voice strained, snapped, "You should not have teased Jane and given her such assurances. There is no reason to reopen old wounds! You know that Miss Bingley wrote that they would not be returning, and that Mr Bingley is courting Miss Darcy!"

The room was silent for a moment before he replied quietly. "Lizzy, my argumentative child. Of all things, I will be most sorry to leave you."

Leaving her place at the window, Elizabeth walked over to the bed and sat where her sister had been sitting moments before. He reached for her hand, and she took his in hers. It felt hot and dry, and his pulse, though slow and steady, was faint. There was no use in denying how short his time was.

He continued, "I am sorry to leave you to suffer, you have borne much between caring for me and taking over my affairs. I am aware of how much your mother hounds you. She is weak and frightened. Please do not be afraid of what the future will hold for you, my child."

"I do not think I could have married Mr Collins, even under our dire circumstances. Mama might just as well wish that Mr Bingley had not quit Netherfield," said Elizabeth bitterly.

Mr Bennet looked at her seriously. "Not only is it my

belief that Mr Bingley will return, but he will likely bring his tall, proud friend with him."

Elizabeth's eyes widened in surprise, and a deep blush crept up her cheeks. "You have been caught out, my dear. You *have* been thinking of him!" he chuckled, as Elizabeth's cheeks blazed scarlet.

How strange it was to see her father's teasing ways re-emerge in his last hours. It seemed to rally him a little. With an effort, she tried to counter with the raillery she knew he enjoyed.

"Sir, I hardly know Mr Darcy, and you yourself know that he did not recommend himself to me during our extremely brief acquaintance. 'Not handsome enough to tempt me' were, I believe, the words he used." Elizabeth kept her tone carefully light, heartened her father had the strength to tease, but unhappy to be his target.

"I do not recollect telling you that I was observing my daughters carefully that evening at Netherfield. My object was to watch Jane and Mr Bingley, but their feelings were obvious, at least for those of us who know Jane. There was no sport in that. No, Lizzy, my evening's entertainment then rested with you and Mr Darcy. He could not take his eyes off you."

"No doubt he was making notes on our conduct for Miss Bingley's amusement later in the evening." Elizabeth was unable to keep the bitterness out of her voice, "When I recall our family's shameful behaviour, I am relieved that I shall never have to meet him again."

"From my experience, an expression of superiority such as the one Mr Darcy habitually wears is assumed when one is ill at ease in society."

It was startling to think of the austere Mr Darcy as uncomfortable or awkward in society, but she realised that there might be something to that notion. "I believe Mr Darcy was rather entranced with you," her father continued, "I believe that also had something to do with the Netherfield party's precipitous departure."

"I cannot believe that! The Bingleys left because Miss Bingley and Mr Darcy decided that the society of Meryton, and particularly the Bennet sisters, was not up to their standards."

"Do you not think it possible that they left because Miss Bingley was afraid that she had lost both her brother, as well as Mr Darcy, the object of her ambitions, to those said Bennet sisters?"

"I do not think anybody, even Miss Bingley, could have made Mr Darcy leave unless he wanted to." Shocked at the hurt in her own voice, she shut her mouth so abruptly that her teeth clicked.

"Perhaps I will not convince you, but I saw Mr Darcy unable to look at anyone but you."

Elizabeth was incredulous. Her father was weak, near death, but he had summoned the energy to encourage Jane's lost hopes for Mr Bingley and tease her with ridiculous observations about Mr Darcy. If only he had had these reserves, and the interest, to put towards preparing his family and estate for what lay ahead when he was gone!

"What an entertaining character he is," he went on. "I almost pity the man. When actually confronted with a woman worthy of him, he turned tail and ran."

Elizabeth, her distress mounting, could not help but scoff. Her father continued, "Mr Darcy is trapped under the weight of social expectations, just as surely as you and your sisters are. A man who has so much at his command, yet seemingly has no joy? You can bring him laughter, my dear."

"So I am to marry Mr Darcy because he needs a good laugh?"

"You need a man like him too, my girl, and that is why you do not like him," rasped her father. He stopped speaking, momentarily winded.

"Papa!" Elizabeth gasped. "You must save your breath."

But her father continued. "He may be proud, but he is an honourable and intelligent man. You need someone who is your equal; that you can esteem and trust."

His ragged voice took on an increased urgency. "Your lively talents place you in the greatest danger of an unequal marriage. My child, let me not imagine the grief of seeing *you* unable to respect your partner in life."

Elizabeth found herself in a state of agitated disbelief. Here they were, discussing a man with whom they had had the barest acquaintance, when she and her family were on the verge of homelessness and penury. She was pierced by a white-hot bolt of anger, her jaw clenching, her hands contracting white-knuckled into fists. If her father had been more diligent in his responsibilities, if her mother was not a helpless fool, it would not now be incumbent upon their three eldest daughters to keep the family together, find a place to live, and work to provide income. Yet here was her father, using his last breath to tease her about a man she hardly knew, a man who despised them as far beneath his consideration. No sooner had she felt the flash than she suppressed it with an effort and struggled to compose herself. She closed her eyes, forcibly straightened her fingers, and swallowed, hard.

"Papa, I know not why you are going on about Mr Bingley and Mr Darcy. They have nothing more to do with us. Let us just find comfort in the time we have together this moment." She again reached for his hand and held it in both of hers as he sank back into the pillows.

Mr Bennet shut his eyes, and then opened them again.

"Nevertheless, tell your sister that both of your forthcoming nuptials have my blessing."

Elizabeth found that remark neither humorous nor appropriate. She was upset and angry, and did not want their conversation to end this way. She rose abruptly and walked to the window so her father would not see the tears beginning to course down her cheeks. She had sworn not to cry in front of him.

"Lizzy," she heard him say, his voice a gentle breath, "Do not cry, child. My most fervent wish is for you to be happy."

She returned to his bedside and sat next to him. "Oh, Papa," she said in a whisper.

"Remember, Lizzy. Take joy." He managed a weary smile before closing his eyes. All was quiet, the clock ticking on the dressing table.

Elizabeth closed her eyes, fighting to keep herself from slipping into a haze of grief and worry. "Take joy," she repeated to herself absently.

Mr Bennet fell into a deep sleep. The hours passed, and as the moon rose and the melting snow dripped off the roof, he slipped quietly away.

CHAPTER 12

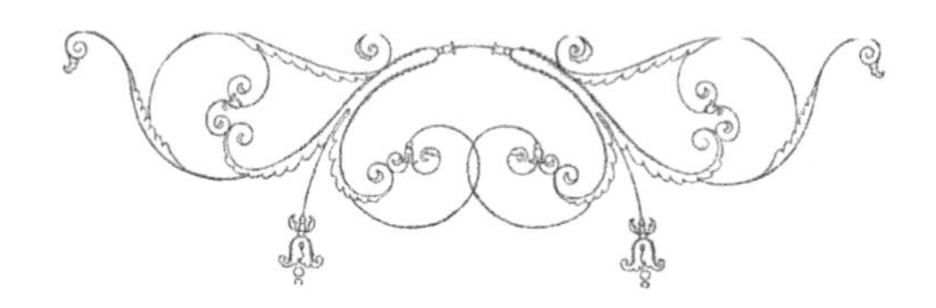

In Derbyshire, the days were growing noticeably longer; the sun, though usually behind clouds, was rising higher in the sky. Darcy and his steward rode sturdy farm horses around the estate, not wishing to risk harming any of the thoroughbreds in the deep and heavy snow, taking note of slight changes in the air. It had been several days since the last storm, although it was still windy and too cold for any snow to melt. Darcy began to consider another attempt to clear the snow from the road leading out of Pemberley. Surely by now the weather would be moderate enough to prevent another inundation of snow, and regular travel could resume. Later that day, plough horses—pulling planks behind them, followed by men with shovels—began the arduous task of clearing the road out of Pemberley.

Hours later, Darcy stood at the window of his study as the clock chimed four times. The night sky was crystal clear for the first time in weeks, and the Milky Way glittered austerely over the white landscape, but his eyes did not take in the stark beauty before him. After another sleepless night, he was casting a hard look at his own life.

Darcy had not minded involuntary confinement over the past few months; in fact, at first, he had welcomed it. As the weeks and months wore on, however, his splendid isolation had become something more like torture, as forced inactivity had led his mind to dwell more and more on what was missing in his life.

He now understood how truly lonely he was. He knew that his long-held plan to marry any tolerable woman of sufficient breeding and fortune to preside over his establishments would never work. After weeks of denial, it had become painfully clear that he had fallen deeply in love with Elizabeth Bennet. No other woman would ever do for him.

The impossibility of their marriage pained him to his core. His family and society would disapprove. His choice was between his duty and his personal happiness.

Many men of his status married for societal expectation and found a mistress for love. Darcy would never even consider having a mistress. Steeped in the belief that duty, obligation, and honour were central, Darcy arrived at the bleak conclusion that he would most likely never marry. Still standing, unseeing, at the window, Darcy pressed his overheated forehead against the frost-rimed glass, wondering how he would ever manage to live without her.

He thought about Bingley, and a corner of his mouth lifted slightly. Even if he was sentenced to a loveless life, it did not mean his friend had to suffer the same. Bingley's fortune and family were new and without the heavy weight of generations of tradition and expectation, providing him more freedom to marry where he chose, his sister's opinion notwithstanding. Truly remorseful, he pictured Bingley as he had looked when last he had seen him, still suffering over Miss Bennet. *Will he forgive me?*

He turned away from the window and went to his desk. Sitting down, he took out a sheet of paper and a pen and began to write. By the time he had finished, he could hear servants beginning to stir. He folded the letter, addressed, and sealed it. He then hurried out to the stables and spoke to the first stable boy he saw.

"Jem, take this letter to the post office in Lambton," he said. "The roads should be improving. Tell them it needs to go out today as an express."

"Yes, sir. I know I can get through as far as Lambton." The boy ran to saddle a sturdy little mare and was soon galloping down the snowy road.

THE AFTERNOON SUN was shining in a blue cloudless sky as Hurst arrived at Gardiner's office for another meeting. The harsh winter was abating. Clear air with the barest hint of warmth added to his uplifted mood. Hurst looked forward to these meetings. As Hurst's relationship with Gardiner had grown from business partner to respected friend, Henderson no longer came with him to every appointment. He swung himself up the stairs and through the door, only to find that Gardiner was not there.

Hurst was nonplussed. Gardiner was so dependable. Something must have happened. He hurried to the house on Gracechurch Street to see if his friend had become ill. Upon arriving there, he raised the knocker, and the door was abruptly opened by an agitated Gardiner standing in the vestibule with his wife.

"Oh, Hurst!" he exclaimed. "I forgot our meeting. My deepest apologies, I meant to send a message to you!"

"Have you received some unhappy news?" asked Hurst, taken aback at his friend's distress.

Mr Gardiner took a breath. "Do you recall that I have spoken of my brother-in-law's illness over the last several weeks?

"I do indeed. Has your brother taken a turn for the worse?"

"It is much worse," said Mrs Gardiner in a shaky voice, "We just received an express. Our brother has died early this morning. We are leaving for Hertfordshire immediately. His widow is not up to the responsibilities of arranging these affairs, and their two eldest daughters have been managing the household and estate themselves. Now their situation is precarious indeed. Their estate is entailed to my brother's distant cousin, and his wife and five daughters will have to leave their home."

Hurst gaped at them, as a bell went off in his head. "Hertfordshire! Where in Hertfordshire? Are the roads passable?"

"It is an estate called Longbourn, not but a mile from the town of Meryton, so we hope to get there before it is too late in the evening."

"Longbourn!" cried Hurst, "I do believe I know of it. I am deeply sorry to hear of your grief and all the difficulties inherent! Is there any way that Louisa and I can be of assistance?"

"That is indeed kind of you," said Mr Gardiner. "I know not what arrangements we will need to make nor how long we will be gone. Once their cousin chooses to take possession of the estate, they have nowhere to go. Their income will not be sufficient, either. Solutions for all these problems must be found." At that moment, the Gardiners' coachman stepped through the door, and the couple boarded the carriage and rode away.

Hurst rode home as quickly as he could, threading his way through the traffic and cursing the crowds. It was the first decent day in months, and everyone was out. After handing the reins to his groom, he ran into the house, taking the stairs in twos, and hurried into the parlour.

Bingley and Louisa stared at him in surprise.

"I have just had some shocking news!" he said, looking from one of them to the other. "I have just discovered that our own Mr Gardiner is uncle to the Bennet sisters of Longbourn! The uncle in Cheapside sneered at by Caroline is Gardiner!"

Louisa stared, open-mouthed, but Hurst had not finished his news. "When Gardiner spoke of his seriously ill brother, it was Mr Bennet to whom he referred! Mr Bennet died early this morning, and the Gardiners are on their way to Longbourn. The estate is entailed away, and Mrs Bennet and her daughters must secure other lodgings. They have nowhere to go, and their resources are limited."

Bingley stared at him in horror. His mouth opened and closed, and then opened and closed again. Then he was on his feet, pacing in agitation, wringing his hands. "And to think that I could have married Jane by now! I could have taken them all to Netherfield!"

Hurst gripped his arm. "You could still do that. You still hold the lease to Netherfield. Gather up your courage and go to Longbourn. Offer your condolences and your assistance. Offer them the use of Netherfield. Or open up the dower house for them. They need you."

"I will. I will! Poor Jane! What they have been through! But what shall I say? How will she receive me? What must they think of me?"

Louisa spoke up. "That does not signify! They are in need, and you may be able to help them as well as assist Mr Gardiner."

"I will order the carriage for the morning and leave at first light," said Bingley, an expression of determination forming on his face.

"I shall send some provisions with you," said Louisa, rising and walking towards the door as she made her plans aloud. "I have some fabric suitable for mourning clothes as well."

Louisa rang for the housekeeper, and the two women gathered up several bolts of black and grey fabric and trimmings that remained from their mourning for old Mr Bingley. A case of wine and one of cider, a box of tea leaves, cheeses, potted meats, and fruit were added to the list.

ALL THREE WERE UP EARLY the next morning. Hurst was standing in front of the house, seeing to the loading of the carriage when a muddy, travel-stained rider pulled up, and dismounting, made for the front door. Hurst stopped him and asked him his business. "I have an express here for Mr Charles Bingley, sir," the messenger said.

"I am he," said Bingley, stepping over to the messenger. The man handed him a letter, collected his fee, and was off again.

Bingley, his mind on his journey, shoved the letter in his pocket and climbed into the carriage. A crack of the driver's whip, and they were off. The recent warm spell had melted the snowpack considerably, but the roads had been severely damaged by the long winter. The carriage was forced to a crawling pace, and there were some stretches that were still almost impassable. On more than one occasion, Bingley, his valet, and the groom had to get out of the carriage and push.

When at last they reached a smoother stretch of road, Bingley sat back against the squabs and let his mind drift. He recalled the express he had stuffed absentmindedly in his pocket early that morning. He pulled it out, and to his surprise, saw that the letter had been sent from Pemberley. He could see then that the handwriting was Darcy's, yet it was not quite the even hand he remembered.

Bingley stared at the letter. Here he was, no sooner going directly against his friend's advice, then he received a missive from him? *Good God, is the man clairvoyant?* He hesitated, afraid that his overbearing friend might be exhorting him to go on without Miss Bennet as he had before he left London.

With an overwhelming sense of the rightness of his decision, Bingley opened the letter. No matter what Darcy had to say, nothing on earth could convince him to give up the chance for future happiness with Jane, should she agree to receive him again. He knew from the centre of his being that he was doing the right thing.

Bingley,

My hope is that this letter makes its way to you expeditiously, and that you will waste no time once you understand its message. My friend, I write to apologise for a great wrong I have done you. When last I saw you in London, I had convinced myself that I had done you a service by telling you that Miss Bennet did not return your regard. I have had time to reflect upon that this winter, and I now condemn myself for the fool that I am, and the pride and conceit which caused me to give such mean and faulty advice to you.

I will not endeavour to explain here but suffice to say that our time spent at Netherfield has been much on my mind as I have been forcibly idled by the violent winter weather we have had. Scenes from our stay there have played out before my mind's eye repeatedly. Your Miss

Bennet was all that is serene and lovely. Even though she was not overtly demonstrative, I should have seen the regard she had for you.

I now believe that at the time she was as much in love with you as you were with her. I was blind to it because of my selfish preoccupation with my own concerns. I fear that by my despicable behaviour, I may have lost your trust and esteem, and while I would deserve that, I most humbly beg your forgiveness, and pray that we can maintain our friendship.

I now understand that few people get the chance to have a life companion whom they can love and be loved by in return. To live a life filled with such intimacy and joy is something to be greatly desired. If you still feel as deeply for Miss Bennet as you did last November, you must go to her immediately, and not let this chance slip through your fingers. When next I see you, I hope to find you courting your lovely Miss Bennet.

May God bless you,
F Darcy

Bingley was astonished. Though he had made up his mind to court Jane regardless of his friend's feelings, he was overwhelmed by the sentiments expressed in the letter. Once his initial anger at Darcy's meddling passed, he was touched by the humility and frankness of his words, and at his heartfelt apology. These feelings mingled with exultation that he himself was pursuing the right course.

Once this wave of emotion had washed over him, Bingley

read the letter again carefully. Certainly something of importance, a life-changing event of some kind must have occurred for his friend. There was an undercurrent of anguish in his words. What could it have been?

Unbidden, an image of Darcy staring intently at Miss Elizabeth in the drawing room at Netherfield appeared in his mind. Though his thoughts had been only of Jane, he remembered vaguely noting how lovely Miss Elizabeth had looked at the ball, and how *overheated* they had both looked when they danced together. *I wonder*. It would explain the grimness of Darcy's aspect and his short temper when they had all removed to London.

It was late afternoon before the carriage rolled through Meryton. Bingley had the carriage stop at Netherfield to order the surprised butler and housekeeper to open up the house and prepare for a stay that could last a few weeks. His valet, groom, and the footman disembarked there. Despite his valet's entreaties, by this time Bingley was too impatient to consider any refreshment of his apparel or appearance. He jumped back into the carriage and was off to Longbourn.

THOUGH WINTER WAS RELENTING, the days were still short, and twilight engulfed the late afternoon. Longbourn manor was so quiet, from where Elizabeth sat, she could hear every clock in the house ticking.

It had been a difficult, busy day. Her father had breathed his last not two days before, and the house had been full of callers for hours. Now all was silent, the family exhausted. The Gardiners and the Philipses had seemingly been everywhere at once, greeting neighbours, directing the servants, soothing Mrs Bennet when she gave way to shrill lamentations.

Elizabeth was numb with sorrow. She recalled how hotly she had argued with her father only hours before he died. Their last conversation had been a quarrel. She had practically snarled at him. She struggled for breath, pacing the room stiffly, her arms wrapped around her own waist as if physically holding herself together.

The unnatural quiet was disturbed by the sound of a carriage approaching at speed. *Oh, no! Who would visit at this hour?*

Jane and Uncle Gardiner had also heard the commotion, and the three of them went through the front door and out into the front garden. A mud-splattered carriage jerked to a stop. The occupant did not wait for the coachman to open the door but sprang out himself. Walking towards them, covered with mud from head to toe, his clothing disarranged, his hair sticking up in untidy clumps, wearing an expression of great agitation, was Charles Bingley.

CHAPTER 13

For a long moment, no one spoke. Jane flushed pink, swayed slightly, and for an instant, Elizabeth feared she might swoon. The eyes of the couple met, and they were immediately lost in each other's gaze.

It was several long seconds before Bingley appeared composed enough to speak to all three of them. "I came as soon as I heard about Mr Bennet. I am so sorry, so deeply grieved for your loss! I came to offer my services to you all!"

Jane and Elizabeth's stupefaction was profound at seeing Mr Bingley, but even greater surprises were to come.

"Mr Bingley?" said Mr Gardiner, "I confess I am surprised to see you. I was not aware that you were acquainted with my brother's family."

"Mr Gardiner, my brother Hurst put two and two together when you told him of your family's grief. He realised that your family was one we became acquainted with last autumn, when I leased a neighbouring estate."

Mr Bingley's gaze again met Jane's. "When we realised who your sorrowing relations were, I knew I must come to offer anything, anything at all I can do to assist! We spent many happy hours in each other's company in November, when Mr Bennet was healthy and his old humorous self. Miss Bennet, Miss Elizabeth, how can I serve you?"

Elizabeth, her eyes moving back and forth between Mr Bingley and her uncle, was struggling to digest the stunning information of their acquaintance. "You…how…how do you know each other?" she finally stammered.

Mr Gardiner, sensing that there was more going on than met the eye, explained. "Mr Bingley and I were introduced by Mr Hurst, who is an investor in my company. I met Mr Hurst in December, when we began doing business together, and have become good friends with him and Mrs Hurst. Mr Hurst introduced us to Mr Bingley and another gentleman when we met quite by accident at the theatre just before Christmastide."

Jane, also struggling to take it all in, let a small smile flit over her face. "How wonderful that Mrs Hurst and Aunt Gardiner are friends."

"The Hursts wish to extend their condolences to your family," said Mr Bingley earnestly, "They are coming to Netherfield as soon as they can manage it to offer their assistance. Louisa has sent some provisions for you. They are here in the carriage."

Mrs Gardiner had by then come out of the house and greeted him cordially. She ordered a footman to help the coachman unload the supplies, and invited Mr Bingley to come inside Longbourn. directing him to the sitting room.

Elizabeth was speechless. She felt that she was in a waking dream. Her dear aunt and uncle were intimate friends with the Hursts? They were friendly acquaintances with Mr Bingley? And who was the 'other gentleman' that her aunt and uncle had enjoyed conversing with at the theatre? Could it have been her nocturnal counsellor, Mr Darcy? Had Papa not teased them only two days ago about this very thing? She imagined she heard her father's dry chuckle from far, far away.

AFTER MOST OF the household had gone to bed, Mr and Mrs Gardiner called Jane and Elizabeth into the parlour.

"Did I sense some undercurrents in our conversation earlier?" asked Uncle Gardiner. "Am I correct in my speculation that there is some sort of history between the Bingleys and the Bennets?"

Elizabeth and Jane exchanged glances. Their aunt studied their faces thoughtfully.

"Lizzy, would Mr Bingley, by chance, be the gentleman who stole our Jane's heart last year? I believe you referred to him in your letter as 'Mr A'?" she asked gently.

"'Mr A'?" said Jane, confused, staring at her sister.

"A for Amiable," admitted Elizabeth resignedly. She looked at Jane. "You were so hurt, and I was so angry. I wanted to ask Aunt Gardiner's advice and describe the entire scenario to her, but I chose not to use his name in case he came back. In case we had misunderstood the whole situation. I did not want it to reflect badly on him. I used initials for each of the persons I described. Mr A stood for amiable, Mr P stood for proud, and Miss C stood for...crab-apple," she said, with a defiant lift of her chin.

The corners of Mr Gardiner's mouth twitched slightly. "Did you have a pseudonym for Mr or Mrs Hurst?" asked Jane.

"No," said Elizabeth. "I did not have a chance to get to know them. I did not think they were party to the decision to leave Netherfield. It does not signify, any way," she shrugged.

"Everything is different now. Being slighted by persons we hardly know seems a most insignificant problem."

WITH THEIR OWN TRUNKS PACKED, the Hursts departed for Netherfield the next morning. Louisa penned a note to Caroline to inform her they would be out of town for a few weeks, and had a footman deliver it to Riverton House. The note travelled from footman to butler to chamber maid, who deposited it on the salver with all the others on Caroline's deserted dressing table. Louisa had no expectation of hearing from her sister, and truth be told, rather hoped she did not. The butler took the knocker off the door, and they were on their way north.

THE FOLLOWING MORNING, Mr Bingley returned to Longbourn as soon as could reasonably be called proper. After he had been ushered in by Hill, he sat down next to Mrs Bennet and, endeavouring to find an unexceptionable topic, engaged her in discussion about the winter weather. "I spent the winter in town, ma'am," he said quietly. "It was so exceedingly cold, the Thames froze over. We heard that it was often stormy here, and even worse to the north."

"Yes, indeed, Mr Bingley," answered Mrs Bennet, still fragile, but rallying to the conversation. "It did snow a great deal, and the roads were often blocked. We received the post only occasionally. There were many days where we were quite confined to the house."

Jane, sitting across the room, trying to concentrate on her embroidery, noticed in the daylight that Mr Bingley seemed to have lost weight. His face was thinner, and there were lines on either side of his mouth and between his brows that she had never seen before. He was smiling, but not the easy wide smile she remembered. It was careful and apprehensive.

Mr Bingley, replying to her mother, said, "I had heard that travel was not possible here. I had hoped to ride up to Netherfield after Christmas, but was told that the roads were impassable." Jane's heart skipped a beat, and her eyes flew up to meet his gaze. He *had* planned to return.

At that moment, Mr Gardiner came into the room. "Ladies, our visitors will soon begin to arrive. It will be necessary to remove to the drawing room. Shall we all go, or do you wish to take turns receiving them?" The sisters agreed to start the day together, and then spell each other over the course of the day.

Mrs Bennet determined she would go to her rooms. Elizabeth, who was sitting closest to her, automatically rose to take her mother's elbow. Mrs Bennet rudely snatched her arm from Elizabeth's hand and turned her back to her, refusing to even look at her second daughter. Kitty gave her sister a sympathetic glance, and quickly took her mother's arm and led her out of the room and up the stairs. Elizabeth, two deep red spots burning in the middle of her drawn white cheeks, ignored Mr Bingley's shocked gaze and walked stiffly out to the back garden.

Again, the house filled with neighbours and old friends, all sombrely dressed, speaking in hushed tones. Mr Bingley proved himself extremely useful, quietly greeting many residents of the neighbourhood who were universally surprised to see him, fetching refreshments and ushering mourners in and out of the drawing room.

As the day drew to a close, the Hursts' carriage pulled up outside Longbourn. The Gardiners met them with welcoming words, handshakes, and embraces. As Bingley escorted the Hursts into the house to greet the Bennets, he saw barely concealed confusion on the faces of the sisters. Their cautious greetings and tentative smiles demonstrated their surprise at the warmth and concern from a couple they had assumed to be as cold and condescending as Caroline. With a flash of insight, he understood. Louisa had been quite reticent during their autumn stay, Hurst had been uncommunicative, and he had been oblivious to anything but Jane. They had all allowed Caroline and Darcy to set the tone for their relations with the neighbourhood. Clearly that mistake would need mending.

As he watched Louisa take Jane's hands in her own and express her condolences, then move to speak with the other girls, Bingley hoped they saw how different his eldest sister was from his social-climbing one. Shortly after the Hursts paid their respects to Mrs Bennet and left for Netherfield, Bingley made to take his leave. He bade goodnight to Mrs Bennet, and then her daughters, saving Jane for last. "I am sorry you have all had another difficult day, Miss Bennet," he said seriously. "If it is not too much to ask, might I visit your family again tomorrow?"

"Mr Bingley, I must thank you for easing our burden," replied Jane quietly.

He then sought out Mr Gardiner, and the two men walked together through the darkness to retrieve his horse from the stable.

"Mr Bingley," said Gardiner wearily, "I know you were taken aback by my sister's treatment of her daughter Elizabeth. Since you are brother to our dear friend Hurst, I feel I can apprise you of that circumstance. Mrs Bennet has taken it into her head that Elizabeth is to blame for their family's current dire straits."

"What? Surely she does not blame Miss Elizabeth for her father's illness!"

"Not exactly, although, because of the entail, my sister always suffered great anxiety over her and her daughters' futures, should something happen to her husband. Last November, Mr Bennet's cousin and heir, a Mr Collins, was received as a guest at Longbourn, and his design was to take one of my nieces for his wife. This prospect was of great satisfaction to my sister, because it precluded any possibility that they would face penury in the case of Mr Bennet's death."

Mr Gardiner eyed Bingley and continued. "Mr Collins's original intention was to offer for Jane, but my sister told him that her affections were already engaged."

Bingley caught his breath as he realised the implication of such a statement.

After a pause, Mr Gardiner continued. "He then settled on Elizabeth as the companion of his future life, but she refused his offer, with her father's approval. Mr Collins then went on to propose marriage to Miss Charlotte Lucas, who accepted him. They were married in December. Since then, my sister has irrationally chosen to vent the totality of her anxiety and anger solely on Elizabeth."

"I am acquainted with that peculiar man. I do not know that I would have let a daughter of mine marry him either! What a terrible way to treat your own child!" Bingley cried, then instantly regretted it. "I do beg your pardon, Mr Gardiner! That was completely inappropriate of me."

Mr Gardiner frowned. "I guess it is then inappropriate for me to confess that I agree with you. Elizabeth was her father's favourite almost from her birth. They shared a bond that I believe my sister came to resent, especially as in his last days, Bennet made it clear he preferred Lizzy's company to that of his wife. These past few months have been extremely difficult for all the family, but particularly grim for our Lizzy."

Gardiner then gave a little shake of his head, as if clearing his mind. "Mr Bingley, it is growing late, and the day has been long. There is another subject that I would like to discuss with you privately, but it can wait for now. I thank you again and again for your kind concern and generous attention to our family. We will look forward to seeing you tomorrow."

"I am at your service, sir."

CHAPTER 14

Darcy, striding from the house to the great barns, slowed his steps, then stopped. He had almost forgotten what warm air felt like. Immediately upon stepping outside, he felt the change: slightly warmer air, with the scent of moist earth instead of snow beguiling his senses. The sky was overcast, but the clouds were lighter and higher in the sky. As he gazed upward, he saw thin places where the sun might actually break through. He inhaled deeply, filling his lungs, smiling at the relief he felt. It had begun to feel like the winter would never end. The roads out of Pemberley had stayed mostly clear since the most recent round of snow removal. There had been a few light snowfalls, but no drifting. The post had not yet begun to arrive, so perhaps the main highways were still closed.

Still, he could most likely travel somewhere if he wished. The prospect was liberating. Where would he go? London, where the Season was probably gathering momentum? Absolutely not. Hertfordshire? A picture of Longbourn manor appeared in his mind. No. He had already had that conversation with himself. No, it would be best if he stayed put at Pemberley, at least until the post started arriving regularly. If the weather stayed warm, he and his cousin would be traveling to Kent in a few weeks' time for their annual visit to Rosings. Darcy continued his walk to the barns, his habitual frown now firmly back in place.

CAROLINE GAZED out of the window of her bedchamber at Abbotsford Park as Bertha laid out her evening clothes. It was a lovely estate, known throughout the kingdom for its great antiquity and history. The house and grounds practically smelt of its ancient heritage and wealth. She had jumped at Sophronia's invitation, even though the Season continued in London. Having cut a dash in society, with Mr Darcy safely tucked away at Pemberley and Charles permanently removed from Hertfordshire, she could afford to relax.

She thought of her brother and a petulant frown warped her pretty face. She wished Charles would make haste and find their family a suitable estate. Netherfield was, of course, out of the question. Perhaps when the weather improved, Charles's agent could earn his wages for a change and find another manor for their family.

She could no longer be content with being plain Miss Bingley. She needed to be Miss Caroline Bingley of some great estate. That was how the highest-ranking ladies were introduced. A thought struck her. Charles had been looking for an estate no more than a days' drive from town. Why did not he look farther north, for an estate in Derbyshire? Then she could be near Darcy, even before they married.

Caroline refocused on the view outside her window. This

was a grand estate, but it was no Pemberley. She thought of her hostess and smirked. When she married Darcy, *her* estate would put Abbotsford Park to shame.

BY THE FOURTH DAY, the number of visitors had dwindled to nothing. The Gardiners, the Philipses, Mrs Bennet and her daughters gathered in the sitting room with the parson.

"The family crypt has been opened," Reverend Blythe reported. "I understand you will be using your own horses and wagon for the funeral procession?" Except for monosyllables, Mrs Bennet was quiet. She seemed to have run out of energy for hysterics, yet had enough spite left to cast a bitter glare at Elizabeth, then deliberately turn her face away.

As the details were concluded, Elizabeth slipped away to the drawing room. Standing by her father's coffin, she whispered her goodbye, and then went out the door for a walk. Frozen in her grief, she could not cry. She did not feel the waxing strength of the sun or smell the warming earth. She trudged through mud and dirty slush, oblivious to her cold, wet feet, or even which direction she was going.

The sound of hoofbeats came to her ears. It was Mr Bingley, on his way to Longbourn. When he saw her, he reined in his horse and dismounted.

"Miss Elizabeth! Where is your cloak!"

Elizabeth looked down and realised that she had left the house without her cloak. Her feet and the hem of her gown were soaked, and she was shivering in the chilly wind.

Mr Bingley quickly took off his greatcoat and wrapped it around her shoulders. "Miss Elizabeth, I am taking you home! You will make yourself ill!"

Without so much as a by-your-leave, he grasped her by the waist and threw her up in the saddle. He trotted rapidly alongside his horse's head as they turned towards Longbourn. When they arrived, he lifted her down from the saddle and walked her into the house.

Jane, Lydia, and Mrs Gardiner met them just inside the door. Mr Bingley, standing behind Elizabeth, met Jane's eyes. "Your sister was out walking, and I am concerned that she may have taken a chill," he said.

Elizabeth protested. "I had not realised that the wind was so cold. I am quite all right, really."

Jane pushed aside her shock and said briskly, "Lizzy, back to bed with you."

Elizabeth, by now ashamed of the attention, quickly acquiesced. She wanted to get away from the worried faces surrounding her. She gave Mr Bingley his coat, along with her thanks, and allowed her youngest sister to bully her upstairs and into a thick flannel nightgown.

Later, curled up under the bedcovers, Elizabeth cringed with embarrassment. Walking outdoors had ever been her remedy for working through emotions and thinking through dilemmas. The paths around Longbourn had always sustained and healed her, but not today. Not only had her walk failed to ease her mind, but she had also frightened her family and made herself foolish in front of Mr Bingley. But even as Elizabeth sternly reminded herself that she was and had always been a rational creature, not given to the fervent outbursts of her mother and younger sisters, and that she needed to control her emotions, a small voice whispered: *time. Give yourself time.* Weariness overtook her, and as the warmth of the quilts replaced the chill in her bones, she fell into a deep sleep, her first in many days.

THEY WERE all sitting together in the parlour when Mr Gardiner came in. "Ah, Bingley," he said, "just who I wished to see. May I take you away from the ladies for a while? I would like to discuss the plans for tomorrow with you."

Bingley rose from his chair, and with a bow to the ladies, followed Mr Gardiner into Mr Bennet's library. Gardiner gestured Bingley to a chair, and they both sat down. "I wished to tell you that the funeral is taking place tomorrow morning. You and Hurst will arrive here by ten o'clock?"

"Yes, of course," answered Bingley, and then went on, "Sir, last evening you mentioned that there was something else you wished to speak about. I think I may know what is on your mind, and I would be happy to answer any questions you may have."

Mr Gardiner smiled. "I appreciate your frankness. Your arrival three days ago surprised the entire family. I think I can say we are all glad to see you, and deeply grateful for the help and comfort you have offered to the Bennet family. However, I would be remiss in my duties to my late brother's family if I did not ask you what your intentions are in regard to my niece Jane."

Bingley straightened and took a deep breath and began carefully. "I think that in order to answer that question, I must tell you the history of my acquaintance with the Bennet family, and with Miss Bennet in particular."

He described his plan to purchase an estate and acquaint himself with the neighbourhood. He talked about the assembly, the great enjoyment he had had and the almost immediate connexion he had felt with Jane, the joy and contentment he had felt in her gentle presence, and then the abrupt and unexpected end to their acquaintance.

Bingley met the older man's gaze. "Sir, my grandfather was the son of a blacksmith in Yorkshire. When he was a young man, he invented a machine for combing wool for the weaving mills. His invention is the foundation of my family's fortune. He and my father built our family business and later diversified and increased our investments. My father's life wish was to see the family elevated to the rank of the gentry.

"Social standing is of great importance to my sister, Caroline, as well, and her feelings on my marital future, and on the Bennet family, were made clear. She urged me away from your niece and I failed to assert myself. Later, when I thought about it, I saw how hypocritical it was for Caroline to condemn Mrs Bennet for wishing her daughters to marry well, as she pushed me to form an alliance with my friend's sister to raise our own family's standing! At the time, however, I was devastated, being told that I was fooling myself about Miss Bennet's feelings, when I had already set my heart on marrying her. I did not know what to do."

Ah, Miss Crab-apple, I presume. Gardiner mused as the younger man paused.

Bingley raised his head to look squarely at Mr Gardiner. "I have been thinking of Miss Bennet all winter, sir. She deserved better from me. By yielding to the opinions of others and not returning to speak directly with her, I caused her substantial pain in an already dreadful situation. I have learned from this to trust my instincts more, and to always ask, never assume. I still wish to marry her…if she will have me."

Mr Gardiner looked at Bingley with compassion. "I believe you to be a respectable man, and through your sister and brother-in-law I know you to be kind, generous, and amiable. I cannot make any promises about my niece's feelings, but let us say that I give my permission for you to call on her, and my blessing for you and Jane to find your own way together."

Bingley visibly relaxed. "I hope to come to an agreement

with Miss Bennet, and I also wish to offer my assistance in arranging for the family to find new living quarters. There is a dower house on the Netherfield estate. I hold the lease through September. Mrs Bennet and her daughters are most welcome to live there until we can find more permanent accommodations for them. I have servants cleaning and airing out the house as we speak. Louisa and Hurst believe they can have it ready the day after tomorrow."

Gardiner sat back in his chair, his eyes wide. "You would seemingly solve the most difficult of all our problems in one stroke. I hope we can soon count you as a member of the family."

THE DAY that Thomas Bennet was laid to rest dawned sunny with a gentle spring breeze, in contrast to the grey, leaden spirits of his family. The old master of Longbourn, the manor where he had been born, lived, and died, was leaving his home for the last time.

The gentlemen mourners gathered in the drawing room and carried the coffin to the wagon parked outside the front door, bedecked in black. Black ostrich plumes had been fastened to the horses' heads. The coffin was loaded carefully in the wagon, and the slow procession to the church began. Two dozen or so men joined the cortege; Longbourn's tenant farmers, neighbours, tradesmen from Meryton, and a few of the officers who had enjoyed the Bennets' hospitality in the past.

The tiny church at Longbourn was an ancient, thick-walled stone building of Saxon origin, with a slightly more recent round Norman tower. The men sat together in the small sanctuary, listening to the time-honoured words of the funeral service. After the service, the men of the village left, leaving the Longbourn party to stay for the committal of Mr Bennet's remains to the family tomb.

Bingley and Hurst were fascinated by the crypt. There had been Bennets at Longbourn for more than four hundred years, many of them distinguished in the military, the natural sciences, philosophy, and religion. Longbourn was a small estate, but the family had a venerable history. Hurst frowned. *If only Caroline could see this, the little snob.*

Late that evening, as Bingley prepared to leave, he turned to Jane. "Would you and Miss Elizabeth consent to accompanying Mr and Mrs Hurst and me on a walk tomorrow? My sister and brother did not see much of the countryside last time we were here."

"I would like that exceedingly, and I think it would be beneficial for Lizzy," she said.

"Is half past nine too early?"

"That would work well, I think," Miss Bennet considered. "A little late for Lizzy, and perhaps a little early for Mr Hurst?"

They laughed together, and he took her hand and kissed it. "I will look forward to it," he said, smiling into her eyes.

CHAPTER 15

The next morning, the Netherfield party arrived at Longbourn as Jane and Elizabeth were finishing breakfast. With their guests, they briefly debated over muddy paths and scenic views. Once a course was agreed upon, the girls found their cloaks and boots, and the walking party set out for Oakham Mount, where the path was on higher ground and relatively dry. The sun shone brightly, the clear air held the promise of warmth, and Mrs Hurst marvelled aloud at the succession of fine spring days after the relentlessly cold and stormy winter. Dirty, ragged snow drifts remained in deep shade, but thin, bright blades of new grass were putting their heads above the soil, and willows were in bloom.

The path was not wide enough for five people to walk together, so they fell naturally into three and two. Jane and Mr Bingley were immediately lost in conversation; neither of them conscious of the scenery, or even of their company. They quickly fell behind.

Mr Hurst grinned slyly at his companions. "Ladies, perhaps we should pick up our pace. In my opinion, Charles and Miss Bennet need as much privacy as propriety will allow."

His wife laughed. "Miss Elizabeth, I must apologise for my husband. If I may be frank, he wishes to nurture a fledgling romance."

Elizabeth had noticed the easy, affectionate interaction between the Hursts since they had returned to Netherfield. She marvelled at the obvious change, but did not know them well enough to enquire. Now, as they walked along, Elizabeth was not up to chatting, and so appreciated their conversation as well as their sense of humour.

"Laugh if you will, my dear, but Charles was most melancholy without Miss Bennet over the winter, and we will be doing him a great favour to let him have her to himself for a while. Do you think you can join us in our plot, Miss Elizabeth?"

Elizabeth, doing her best to enter the spirit of the exchange, arranged her face into a small smile, and quickly glanced at the besotted couple lagging behind. "You can be certain of my assistance, though from the evidence before our eyes, their happiness will depend on our benign neglect rather than our deviousness."

BINGLEY INHALED THE SPRING AIR. It was such a beautiful morning. He watched Jane out of the corner of his eye as they walked, knowing how much she still suffered. *How shall I begin? What shall I say?* These thoughts had kept him awake during the night. He decided to simply say what was in his heart; that was what he wanted her to know.

Taking a deep breath, he reached for her hand and took it,

winding it through his arm. "Miss Bennet, how are your spirits today? The last several days have been so difficult for you, as I am sure the entire winter has been. I wish I had made a greater effort to come to Netherfield sooner. If I had known that your father was ill, I would have moved Heaven and Earth to get here!"

"Thank you," she answered in a soft, slightly trembling voice. "Your presence has made the last few days bearable, not only for me but for my family. You will become weary of hearing my thanks, but I cannot express them enough."

"It is my honour to have alleviated your family's pain in any way. However, Miss Bennet, I must tell you truthfully, my thoughts have been of you alone. You have been constantly on my mind since I left Netherfield last November."

Jane stared up at him, her eyes wide, and stammered, "Oh! I thought, that is, your sister, Miss Bingley...she wrote me a letter and said you were never coming back. She said you were busy, and happy, in London and had no desire to return! She said you preferred the company of Miss Darcy!"

Bingley could hear her voice was wavering and feared she would cry. He stopped walking and turned to face her, taking her hands in his. "Miss Bennet, when I left Netherfield for London last autumn, I intended to return within a few days. Before I could, my family and Darcy quit Netherfield and followed me to London. Caroline told me in no uncertain terms that you did not return my regard. Darcy said he could see no evidence of any particular feeling you might have for me either. My hopes were crushed, but I had always trusted them both, and I believed them. I was so miserable, I did not know what to do.

"By the time Hurst encouraged me to trust my own heart and I came to my senses, the weather had taken a turn. The roads closed, and I could not travel to Hertfordshire. It was when I heard of your father's passing that I had to come, no matter what! Miss Bennet...Jane! Can you ever forgive me?"

She gazed up into his dear, anguished face. "I tried not to think of you, especially with my father so ill, but I could not put you out of my mind. There is nothing to forgive. You have done me no wrong. Although," she looked up at him with a trembling smile, "Perhaps one could wish that you were not such a modest man."

Bingley drew her into his embrace, laughing, almost crying himself. "Jane, I…this is plainly the wrong time and place, as you are in mourning, but I have waited all winter and cannot wait another minute! I must ask you, nay, beg you, to marry me! Please say you will marry me!"

Jane laughed and buried her face in his shoulder.

His smile faded and he gazed intently down at her, raising one hand to stroke her hair. "I made a foolish mistake, and the chances are that I will make more, many more, in my future life. My dear girl, can you be happy in marriage with such a fool as I am?"

She raised her eyes to his. "I know that I cannot be happy without you, my own dear fool. Yes, with all my heart, I will marry you!"

FARTHER ALONG THE PATH, Elizabeth and the Hursts had reached the summit. Mr Hurst breathed deeply and took in the view, the trees showing their pale green haze of budding leaves.

"Miss Elizabeth, what a lovely walk this is! The fresh air and the woods remind me of when I was a boy, rambling through the woods on my family's estate. Even if our design was not to throw Miss Bennet and Bingley together, I would have enjoyed this immensely." He looked at his wife. "Perhaps we should spend some time at Somerleigh Park this summer."

Mrs Hurst took his arm, smiling, and leaned her head on his shoulder.

Elizabeth watched them curiously. "I am glad you have enjoyed it."

Mr Hurst, taking in the scenery before him, noticed another path winding down the other side. He turned to his companions. "I hope you ladies will not mind if I walk on a bit farther?"

"Not at all," said Elizabeth. The two ladies stood next to each other, looking out over the valley. Elizabeth pointed out a few natural features, and her companion duly admired the view. Within a few minutes, there was a pause, and Mrs Hurst turned to her. "Miss Elizabeth, I would not blame you if you were curious about the change in my husband's demeanour since we last met in the autumn."

Elizabeth coloured slightly, but admitted, "I have to confess, I have noticed the difference in both of you, and I have wondered at it." With the barest hint of her old humour in her eyes, she added, "I do not know you well enough to go prying into your affairs, after all."

"Please call me Louisa, as I have a feeling we will be family in the near future."

"Oh, yes, thank you, and you must call me Elizabeth."

With a warm glance in the direction just taken by her husband, Louisa began. "Our marriage was something of a business proposition, and neither of us had any expectations of affection. Yet, each of us began privately to admire the other. After observing Charles's deep regard for your sister, Gilbert decided we needed to begin at the beginning, and enjoy a season of courtship." Louisa's eyes were bright; her mouth curved into a small smile. "We have discovered great happiness with each other, and we both feel extraordinarily fortunate."

"I am happy for you both," Elizabeth said sincerely.

"Of course, it helped that Caroline has been staying with friends, and we had our home to ourselves." Elizabeth could hear the dry humour in Mrs Hurst's voice, and was reminded of her own conviction that Miss Bingley had been responsible for keeping her brother from returning to Netherfield. Dare she ask such a question of that lady's own sister? She hesitated, and the two ladies stood in uncertain silence a few moments longer.

She plunged in while she had the courage. "Please pardon me for asking this question, but I find that I must. It has been bothering me for some time. Your sister wrote to Jane in December, and told her that your brother would not be returning to Netherfield. She implied that he planned to court Miss Darcy."

Louisa stared at Elizabeth. "She did? Oh no! How that must have hurt Jane! The truth is that Caroline told Charles that your sister did not return his affections, and that he was making a fool of himself. It grieves me to say that she does not concern herself with the feelings of others. Caroline wanted Charles to court Miss Darcy because of her own aspirations. Charles is so unassuming that he believed her, as well as his friend Mr Darcy, who only said that Jane was so reserved that he could not tell what her feelings were."

She put her hand on Elizabeth's arm and continued. "My brother spent a long, lonely winter thinking of your sister. It was Gilbert who first told him he should listen to his own heart, and of course I agreed. Later, however, Charles received a letter from Mr Darcy with an apology, urging him to seek out your sister."

Elizabeth was stunned. *Mr Darcy apologised? He encour-*

aged Mr Bingley to court Jane? What could have caused his change of heart? Could I have made a more grievous error?

As if hearing her thoughts, Louisa mused, "I do not think any of us gave the neighbourhood a good impression when we stayed here last autumn. Except Charles, of course. Gilbert and I were each too lonely to be friendly. Caroline was simply too…erm, herself." Her expression grew sombre. "Mr Darcy was…well, from what I understand, something dire had recently happened within his family that had caused him great pain. Now, if you are at all acquainted with Mr Fitzwilliam Darcy, you know that he is a reserved and private man. He did not even speak of it with Charles. We knew only something had occurred that had deeply shaken him and made him even more reticent than usual."

Elizabeth was no longer following the conversation. She closed her eyes as if in pain, her hand rising to cover her mouth. *Fitzwilliam Darcy. FD.* Of course, it was him. A man with fine handkerchiefs and a fine horse. A man who cared for his little sister, who made handkerchief dollies for her, and for the child of a blacksmith. A man who kept his pain to himself. She had believed Wickham over him, and challenged him over it in the middle of a ballroom. Remembered scenes of the autumn unspooled through Elizabeth's mind. *Oh, worse and worse! The ill-mannered things I said to him! Stupid, wretched girl!*

Louisa's voice interrupted her thoughts. "Elizabeth! Are you well?"

She opened her eyes to see her companion staring at her with concern. Flustered, she took a deep breath and answered, "Oh, yes, thank you, I am well. It was kind of Mr Darcy to apologise." She quickly changed the subject. "Will Miss Bingley cause any problems for Jane and your brother?"

"I do not think so," Louisa said. "Charles is the head of the family, after all, and I daresay he has become stronger this year. He will not give her up if she will have him."

Elizabeth liked the new, happy, openhearted Louisa, and relaxed slightly. "I think she will. Jane was heartbroken when she received that letter. She had completely given your brother her heart, and once Jane's heart is given, she does not take it back easily."

The two women heard Mr Hurst coming back up the path and turned to meet him. "Well, ladies, shall we see if we can find our tardy companions? They should have had enough time to plan their wedding by now."

BINGLEY AND JANE CONTINUED WALKING, neither of them aware of nor caring where they were. Her arm was wound around his, and his free hand held hers tightly.

A shadow passed over her face. "Will Miss Bingley be unhappy with our marriage? Or will our marriage damage your friendship with Mr Darcy?"

He smiled at her. "Caroline's opinion does not matter one jot! Darcy's opinion does not matter either, but I neglected to tell you that just as I was leaving for Longbourn, I received a letter from him. He apologised to me and said he felt he had been mistaken about your feelings. He urged me to go to you and see if you still felt the same!"

"Oh, I am so glad! I know his friendship is important to you. Lizzy was utterly convinced that Mr Darcy was behind your family's removal from Netherfield. She made him out to be a cold-hearted villain! I will be glad to tell her that he is not against our marriage."

A few minutes later, Elizabeth and the Hursts came into view. When they saw the couple walking together arm in arm, they exchanged smiles.

Back at Longbourn, the news brought tears of joy to Mrs Bennet. Though she was not her old self, she was able to tell Lydia, Mary, and Kitty, with contentment and reassurance, that they were to move into the dower house at Netherfield. Happiness and love had momentarily taken the place of grief. The sense of relief was palpable.

"Are you going to wait until our mourning is over to set a date?" asked Lydia.

Bingley cleared his throat and exchanged glances with Jane. "We have decided, with the approval of Mrs Bennet and Mr Gardiner, to marry as soon as next week."

"Next week!" exclaimed Elizabeth.

"I know that the propriety of marrying so quickly after your father's funeral is dubious, to say the least, but I believe I can be more useful to my new family if we make our union official," replied Bingley. "I will travel to the bishop's office in London as quickly as possible to obtain the licence while the family moves their belongings to the dower house at Netherfield Park." Mrs Bennet and Jane spoke about the wedding, while Mrs Hurst, the Gardiners, and the sisters began to make plans for the move. For the first time in months, the house rang with laughter and conversation.

CHAPTER 16

Early the next morning, Mrs Philips arrived from Meryton and was informed of Jane and Bingley's happy news. The Netherfield party arrived shortly after, and the planning began in earnest. While Jane, Mr Bingley, and Mrs Bennet sat down to talk about the wedding before his departure for London, Mrs Gardiner gathered up the sisters and they went to sit together in the parlour. Mr and Mrs Hurst, Mrs Philips, and Mr Gardiner joined them.

"The dower house is ready for you," said Louisa. "You can spend this week packing. We shall help you in any way we can."

"There will not be much to pack," said Elizabeth. "Most of the furniture and household items belong to the estate. I had a letter from Mrs Collins," she said, and explained Charlotte's kindness in urging the family to take not only their personal possessions but any cherished mementos.

In planning the move to the dower house, it was tacitly accepted by all her family, even her mother; that Elizabeth would pack up her father's study.

Elizabeth opened the door to her father's refuge for the first time since his funeral, and saw that Davy had already placed several wooden crates on the floor in the centre of the room. She opened the heavy drapes, and the spring sunshine came streaming in, lighting up the dust motes floating in the air. She stood in the middle of the floor and looked about her.

The room had already changed from when it had been her father's domain. Her uncles had sorted the contents of the enormous ancient desk and had removed many of his papers and documents, neatening the perpetual clutter. She wrapped her arms around her waist and sighed. She had spent countless happy hours with him in that room, but she could no longer feel his presence there. He was truly gone. She wished her imaginary friend was there to put his arm around her and help her through this long farewell, but she had been unable to conjure him up. In these past few sorrow-filled days, her dreams—her only escape—had dried up. Just as well; it was better to face reality. She swallowed, took a breath, and set one of the boxes on a footstool.

Sweeping her eyes over the bookshelves, it seemed she had a sweet memory for almost every book and object in the room. Nevertheless, she could not pack up *everything*. Even Charlotte's patience would not extend that far. Elizabeth began by examining each shelf one at a time, removing books, looking at them one by one, and either putting them in the box or returning them gently to the shelves. She smiled at some of the books and leafed through the pages. Over the course of the day, the book-lined shelves began to take on the aspect of a gap-toothed smile.

She packed the chess set, though she knew it had been at

Longbourn since long before her father's time. She folded his favourite old coat and set it in the box. His pen and inkwell, and a little brass telescope also went in, along with his spectacles, which she had retrieved from his bedchamber, followed by a small marble bust of Aristotle, whom he had loved to quote, and one of Cicero. She came across an ancient Bible, written and illuminated by hand in Latin and bound between hide-covered boards. There were several genealogical charts written on vellum stuffed in the covers. *This house will no longer have any Bennets living in it.* She put them into a box. She decided to leave the enormous globe. She had spent many hours dreaming over it as a child, but she was sure even the self-absorbed Mr Collins would notice its absence. She took a box of ancient documents that her father had shown her only a few years before. Some of them went back to the time before old King Henry. They belonged to the family, not to the estate. They went into the growing collection of boxes.

As she finished studying the shelves, she spied her father's fishing rod, along with a smaller one, leaning dusty and forgotten against the wall in the corner. Those would have to come with them as well. Memories of standing next to him on the riverbank, holding her fishing pole, having long conversations, came flooding back to her.

As Elizabeth worked, she pondered her future. She was overjoyed for Jane and relieved for her entire family. Mr Bingley, or Charles, as he insisted they call him, had been the answer to all their prayers when he had appeared at their front door that damp, cold, dark evening only a week before. Not only had he proposed to Jane, but he had given the family a place to live—and settled an allowance on them, no doubt. Elizabeth knew that there had been little money left to her mother and sisters, and that Mr Bing—*Charles*—had spent time closeted with her uncles, discussing settlements and making arrangements. So much had been considered! In the autumn Mary would go to Gracechurch Street for music studies, and other subjects as she chose. Other masters would come to the dower house to make up for the considerable deficiencies in the younger girls' education. Lydia and Kitty would be instructed in music, drawing, French, and most importantly, comportment. Unexpectedly, Lydia's excitement over the coming instruction was as strong as Kitty's.

Elizabeth did not wish to be supported by her new brother, much as she had come to love and respect him. She did not wish to be dependent on *anyone*, even dear Uncle Gardiner. She was determined to be self-reliant. With no formal education, the chances of finding employment she might find enjoyable, or even tolerable, were slim to none; even the position of companion or governess often required some formal education. Not to mention that it was a degradation for a gently born female to work at all.

Her eyes ran over the bookshelves. How she might enjoy being a librarian—an unattainable possibility for a female. She stared into the fire, the bronze paperweight in her hand temporarily forgotten, then collapsed into the old leather chair. How foolish she had been all these years, assuming she would marry and have a husband to love and care for her, and to love in return. A wave of desolation washed over her. Watching Jane and Charles together gave her joy, but oddly, made her chest ache. Still, she was glad that Jane would be loved and cherished forever, as she deserved to be.

The image of Mr Darcy appeared in her mind, but she firmly pushed him away. Another reason to be ashamed. She had been entirely wrong about him, and about Mr Wickham. She remembered how offensive she had been to Mr Darcy at the ball. She had pried into his personal life and plagued him in the defence of a scoundrel.

I hardly know myself. Her faith in her own discernment, in her intelligence, even her self-respect, had been shattered. Elizabeth was grateful with all her heart that Jane's wedding was taking place so quickly, so that she would not encounter Mr Darcy in person. She would be in Cheapside before he was even informed of his friend's marriage, and Elizabeth knew he would never deign to be seen in Gracechurch Street. Not that he would ever consider visiting her to begin with. Not in reality.

She had gladly accepted the invitation from Aunt and Uncle Gardiner to return to London with them right after the wedding. She had been relieved for a chance to escape; her urgent need to be away from Longbourn surprised her. She loved her home dearly, but Longbourn was no longer theirs, and Netherfield's dower house would never be her home; she could not, *would not*, ever live with her mother again. Even though Mrs Bennet was overjoyed by Jane's happy news and relieved by Mr Bingley's efforts to provide her a home, neither grief nor happiness would soften her resentment towards Elizabeth.

How she missed Papa! While surrounded by caring people, Elizabeth was desperately lonely. She had no one to share her humour and love of learning with, to exchange amused glances with when witnessing human absurdity. Jane would be leaving as well, even if it was only as far as Netherfield. Elizabeth would sorely miss their late-night conversations. She would miss Mary, Kitty, and Lydia, too. Life had been difficult and melancholy these past months, but through it all, the sisters had become close, and Elizabeth had seen them all grow stronger.

She would leave them to spend time in London and recover her equilibrium. But where would she go when Mary arrived at the Gardiners' to begin her studies? Another part of

England, or maybe Scotland? She adored Robert Burns, and had dreamt of traveling there. Perhaps a family in the West Indies might need a governess. Or America perhaps, a new land where even a female with no qualifications or formal education might be acceptable as a teacher or librarian. She tried to picture herself in a cabin made of logs, deep in the wilderness, and then snorted at her own folly.

Overcome, she put her face in her hands, a burning tightness in her throat, a weight in her chest making it a struggle to breathe. She pulled her handkerchief from her pocket, hoping she might finally be able to cry it out. That relief did not come, and finally, Elizabeth threw her handkerchief away in frustration.

She was beginning to come to terms with the sadness and loss, and knew that in time she would get used to it. It was the raw pain of her last conversation with her father that she bore alone. She had been so angry with him.

Had he heard the anger in her voice when they last spoke? If he had been hurt by it, she would never know. He had been so dear to her, yet all her life, he had chosen to make light of her when she wished to speak seriously. Elizabeth would give anything to have that last evening back, so she and her father could have shared happy memories instead.

Her sorrow she could share with her family, but her guilt was hers alone, wearing on her night and day. What would her sisters, or worse, *her mother*, think if they knew that she had practically snarled at him only hours before he slipped away?

GIVEN that most of the contents of Longbourn remained with the house, it was the work of only a few days to settle the Bennets into the dower house. The night before the wedding, Jane and Elizabeth stretched out side by side on the big bed in the room that temporarily contained Elizabeth's things. They had been reminiscing about their childhood days, of sharing giggles and deep secrets in their little bedchamber at Longbourn. Jane reached over and stroked her sister's hair.

In the midst of the joy over her marriage, Jane was grieving her father and worried sick about her sister. Now it was Lizzy whose smile did not reach her eyes. "Lizzy, do you remember what Papa said the night before he died? That Charles would return for me?" Jane blushed slightly as she used her betrothed's given name, but she loved saying it.

"Yes, I do."

"What else did you and Papa talk about after I went to bed?" Jane immediately regretted her question. Elizabeth, with an attempt at a smile, tried to deflect the question. "Oh – nothing of consequence. Nothing at all, really." Then, with a slight shake of her head, her eyes bleak, Elizabeth turned her face away from Jane's gaze. "Oh, Lizzy."

A HUSHED SOLEMNITY enveloped them the following morning when Elizabeth preceded Jane into the church. Jane was clinging to Uncle Gardiner's arm, her eyes unswervingly meeting Bingley's. Everyone was in mourning, and every eye was damp. Reverend Blythe spoke the ancient words of the ceremony, and Jane and Charles were married. Elizabeth took in the sorrowful group, huddled together in black. What a different wedding it would have been if it had taken place before the winter!

Elizabeth locked away her childhood the next morning when she boarded the Gardiners' carriage and headed off to London. If only she could leave her sorrow behind as well.

CHAPTER 17

Spring was slow to arrive in Derbyshire. The deep, cold-hardened snows seemed almost impervious to the strengthening sun, even as the equinox drew near.

So it was that when Colonel Fitzwilliam arrived at Pemberley, the roads had been open for almost a fortnight, but there were still snow drifts everywhere. Patches of bare ground were beginning to appear here and there, but the accumulation of snow kept the air chilly.

He rode to the stables, handed off his horse to a groom, and entered the house unannounced through a side door. Mrs Reynolds greeted him as he entered the hall, and led him to Georgiana, who was practising in the music room.

Georgiana leapt up, running to embrace her cousin. He picked her up and whirled her around. "Cousin!" exclaimed Georgiana, "do you know you are the first person I have seen from outside Pemberley since before Christmas? You are like an emissary from another world to me!"

"Has it been awful, my pet?"

"No, though truly it could have been. We were well provisioned, and there are, of course, enough of us here to keep each other company."

Her smile faded slightly. "At least, *almost* all of us passed the winter in good humour." Her eyes again met the older woman's.

Mrs Reynolds nodded slightly in understanding and moved to the door. "I shall bring you some refreshments," she said.

Georgiana watched her leave, and then turned to her cousin, meeting his eyes directly. "We have been concerned about my brother. He has not been himself for such a long time, ever since he returned from London."

"How do you mean, 'not himself'?"

Georgiana considered her words carefully, "It is as if he is not always with us, even when we are having a conversation. He drifts off and is often preoccupied. He is all that is polite and correct, but something is troubling him. He is not sleeping well. Talbot says he has disturbing dreams. At first, I thought he had not forgiven me for last summer." She took a breath, looking at her feet, but then raised her chin to look at her cousin. He smiled gently and put his arm reassuringly around her.

Georgiana went on. "But I recently realised that it does not have anything to do with me. He…he has called me Elizabeth a few times. He does not even realise it when he does."

Fitzwilliam stared at Georgiana. "Really." He paused, his eyes thoughtful, remembering Darcy's troubled aspect when they had last met.

"Yes, and I wondered who Elizabeth could be. I would remember if he had ever been fond of a lady, though he never mentions ladies in his conversations or letters to me. Then I recalled the letters he wrote to me from Hertfordshire, in the autumn. I read them again, and he mentions a young lady named Elizabeth Bennet many times."

"I knew it!" cried Fitzwilliam. "I spoke with Darcy once during those few days he was in London, after he left Hertfordshire and before he came to Pemberley. It was obvious to me that he was upset. I wondered if something might have happened to unsettle him while he was visiting Bingley."

"That thought has crossed my mind as well, but you know how he is. He will not share his troubles with anyone."

"We shall get to the bottom of this, dearest." A twinkle appeared in his eye again. "If necessary, we could tie him to a chair."

Georgiana laughed, happy to have her cousin there to help her with her morose, uncommunicative brother.

MAKING his way to the study an hour later, Fitzwilliam knocked at the door. "Enter," said his cousin's voice.

"There you are, my reclusive cousin. How are you?" He entered the study, a familiar room to him. Familiar, yet different. It had always been Darcy's sanctuary, as fastidiously maintained as his person. A slightly different room met Fitzwilliam's discerning eye.

The enormous desk was cluttered; the stacks of correspondence untidy. There was a glass of brandy, and near it an empty decanter. His eyebrows shot up. Darcy never had more than one brandy, and only in the evening.

His clear unblinking gaze took in Darcy's countenance. He looked drawn and tired. There were harsh lines on either side of his mouth, and deep shadows under his eyes. But it was the bleakness in those eyes that was most disturbing. Fitzwilliam had always teased Darcy about his seriousness, but this change in his cousin's demeanour was worrisome. Something was indeed afoot.

Darcy belatedly manufactured a smile and stood to move towards him, his hand outstretched. Fitzwilliam grasped his hand and held it for a moment. "You have had a hard winter. I can see it in your face." He was intently scrutinising his cousin, his concern palpable, and for a fleeting moment, it looked as if Darcy would unburden himself.

Instead, he looked down at his desk and aimlessly shuffled papers. "How was your journey?"

Fitzwilliam regarded him steadily. His cousin was not going to give up his secrets easily. Perhaps if he went along with the small talk for a while, a deeper conversation would follow.

Darcy moved to resume his seat, but Fitzwilliam took his arm in an amiable manner and sat him down on the sofa, relying on his cousin's impeccable manners to acquiesce. There would be no retreating behind the desk. He seated himself next to the silent man and made bland conversation.

"The roads are clear enough, though devilishly muddy. Our journey to Rosings may take longer than it usually does, so that should be a factor in our planning. Perhaps south of here, where the winter was milder, the roads will be in better condition."

Fitzwilliam went on to fill his cousin in on family news, and all that had gone on in London and other places in England over the winter. "Father has sent my brother to Ireland to assess any weather damage to the family properties there. He was not happy to leave London during the Season, but there was no arguing with the earl."

Finally, met with little more than silence and a raised

eyebrow or nod from Darcy, he paused and stretched out his legs. "I was unsurprised to find you had left town, Cousin. I know how much you love Christmas at Pemberley," he continued. "I saw Bingley on Christmas Day. He was not his usual self. Have you heard from him?"

"I just received a few letters that he sent months ago so no, not recently. We started getting the post regularly again just over a week ago," said Darcy, avoiding his cousin's eyes.

"Were you able to get your household and tenants safely through the winter?"

"Yes. It took much work, but we had had an excellent harvest last autumn; our stores of wood and coal were also sufficient. We moved grain for the livestock closer to the barns and stables after the first snowstorm. After the new year, we also moved all of our outlying tenants to quarters closer to the main buildings."

"Well done! Your father would be proud of you. But what an enormous undertaking! Is that why you look so ill and exhausted?" asked Fitzwilliam, leaning towards Darcy and looking at him steadily.

DARCY BLINKED. It had not occurred to him that he might look as awful as he felt. He realised that there was no dissembling with his cousin. His shoulders sagged.

"Something has been eating at you for months, has it not? I could see it in your face before you even left London. I do not think this has anything to do with Georgiana, does it?"

"No. No, it does not," admitted Darcy. "I do not know that I can explain it to you."

"Try me."

Darcy sat motionless, wondering where to start, when he

himself was unsure when it began. His cousin prompted, "What happened in Hertfordshire to put both you and Bingley in such low spirits, and for such a long time?" Darcy winced, mortified that his trouble was so obvious that his cousin had noticed it after seeing him only twice in three months. He suddenly wanted to let down his guard. For once. To confess the state of his heart. But no, he felt too foolish. Fitzwilliam would surely mock him and never let him forget that he had stupidly fallen apart over a country miss. No, he could not bear that, not over this, it was too personal.

"It is a small matter. I have merely been forced into my own company too much these last months…"

"You are not expecting me to believe that you regret missing London society? What rubbish! Look at this room! Look at that empty decanter! This is not a small matter."

Darcy was at a standstill. Fitzwilliam met his eyes and waited. Finally, he grimaced and began. "I joined Bingley and his family for a stay at Netherfield, an estate he had leased in Hertfordshire, just after Michaelmas."

He stopped dead. Had it only been since October? It seemed as if she had been living in his heart forever.

His cousin cocked his head, eyebrows high. "And?"

Darcy started, then continued. "In addition to investigating the value and potential of the estate, Bingley also wished to become acquainted with the neighbourhood. A few days after we arrived, Bingley insisted we attend a local assembly in Meryton, which is a small market town about two miles from Netherfield."

"Was this where he met the lovely girl with the dreadful family?" Darcy blinked and looked at his cousin. "You told me about her in London. That was the reason you gave for your abrupt departure from Hertfordshire."

"Oh, that," said Darcy. He shifted slightly in his chair and looked away.

Fitzwilliam's suspicions were obvious. "Yes, *that*," he repeated. "You were in league with Miss Bingley on that plot, perhaps?"

Darcy folded his arms and tucked his chin on his chest, too embarrassed to answer; he knew well his cousin's strong aversion to Caroline Bingley.

"And Bingley's heart was broken? I saw him over the winter, and he was still miserable."

Jaw clenched, Darcy nodded. "You need not remind me of my despicable behaviour! I have already tried to make amends with Bingley."

"Well, that is encouraging at least. What could you possibly have done for him from here?"

Darcy sank deeper into the sofa cushions, his elbows on his knees, his hands resting against his temples, remembering the sleepless night a few weeks before when he had rejected the possibility of personal happiness for himself, but embraced it for Bingley.

"Very little until the snows let up. I sent him an express. The road to Lambton had just been cleared, and I wrote to him, apologising. I admitted that I had been wrong to interfere in his life, that I was wrong about Miss Bennet's feelings, and that if his feelings were unchanged, he should go and see her. Then I begged his forgiveness."

"And what prompted your change of heart?" Fitzwilliam asked quietly after a few minutes.

Another silence. Finally, Darcy spoke in such a low voice that his cousin had to lean in to hear him. "I discovered how it feels to yearn for someone you can never have."

"Ah, I see," Fitzwilliam answered softly. After another

pause, he again leaned towards Darcy. "And would this young lady's name be Elizabeth Bennet?"

Darcy's head shot up. "How do you know her name?" he gasped.

"I did not figure that out. Your sister did."

"Georgie?" Darcy was in shock. "How could she *possibly* know?"

Fitzwilliam smiled sympathetically and put his hand reassuringly on Darcy's arm. "My dear cousin, you are not as good at keeping your secrets as you think you are. Your sister has been watching you with great concern ever since you came back from London. She was convinced you were still upset over the events at Ramsgate. That is, until you started absent-mindedly calling her Elizabeth."

"What?"

"You called her Elizabeth. Repeatedly. She remembered the name. Apparently, you made frequent mention of Miss Bennet in your letters from Hertfordshire."

Darcy groaned.

I think you owe her an explanation," continued Fitzwilliam, "which, regardless of what you think, she is mature enough to understand. But first, perhaps you should try it out on me? Let us go back to the assembly." He put his feet up on a footstool, prepared for a long narrative.

Darcy shook his head as if to clear his mind. "It was a dreary evening of country dances in a shabby hall, except for the fact that Bingley fell in love at first sight with Miss Jane Bennet. She is the eldest daughter of five, and the most beautiful woman I have ever beheld."

"That is rather a bold statement!"

"Yes, but she genuinely is that beautiful, and all that is kind and good, with gentle manners," said Darcy.

"And Bingley fell in love with her? And she and her sister

are of the family with a small, entailed estate and relatives in trade?"

"Yes, that is it," said Darcy. He went on. "I was not civil company that evening, but I had promised Bingley faithfully that I would come once he found an estate that interested him. Good manners dictated that I had one dance with Miss Bingley and one with Mrs Hurst, but that was all. Of course, they were the only ladies there of my acquaintance."

"I see. And nobody can ever be introduced in a ballroom," said Fitzwilliam, pulling an innocent face. Darcy tried silencing him with a cold stare, but that just made his cousin laugh. "That does not work on me, and you know it! Now let us continue. You were uncomfortable at the assembly."

"Yes, the evening was interminable and the company dull. Bingley tried to get me to dance with one of Miss Bennet's sisters, but I did not wish to dance at all. Subsequently I discovered that the sister he wanted me to meet was Elizabeth. I now regret that I was quite rude about it to Bingley, and no introduction took place."

"Meryton society is small and insular," he continued. "Over the next days and weeks, we met the same people again and again. Mothers in the country are just as calculating as mothers of the *ton* when it comes to throwing out their lures and pushing forward their daughters. But I began to attend any social occasion willingly, because over the course of all these gatherings, I developed a desire to be in the company of Miss Elizabeth Bennet. At first, I thought I was merely a dispassionate observer..."

Here he broke off, deep in his memories. "She has the most beautiful eyes I have ever seen. She is lovely, not like her sister, but uncommonly lovely. Her face is remarkably expressive. She is artless and unaffected. She never simpers or flirts, or uses disingenuous female arts to attract attention. She sings and plays beautifully, not technically perhaps, but with genuine expression. She is intelligent and witty, and frank, sometimes painfully so, in her conversation. Sometimes a conversation with her resembles more a fencing match! I do not believe she liked me at all. I daresay she thought me rather proud."

"Imagine that," murmured his cousin.

Darcy ignored him, engrossed in his own story. "After we had been there a few weeks, Bingley's sisters invited Miss Bennet to tea. Mrs Bennet, a scheming woman if ever I have met one, made certain that her daughter got caught in a heavy rain while riding horseback between Longbourn and Netherfield. Miss Bennet took a chill and became ill enough to be forced to stay at Netherfield until she was well. The next morning, who should appear at the door but Miss Elizabeth, determined to nurse her sister through her illness." A tiny smile played at the corners of his mouth.

"She had walked three miles through wet paths and fields. Her clothes were damp and her curls had escaped her bonnet. Her eyes were shining and her complexion positively glowed. Miss Bingley was appalled, of course. She was unusually critical, insulting really, of Elizabeth the entire time we were there."

"Of course she was," said Fitzwilliam. "Women like that have an instinct for sensing a rival. Caroline Bingley has had her snares out for you for years. No doubt she knew you were losing your heart to Miss Elizabeth long before you did."

"The two Miss Bennets stayed at Netherfield for five days. I was conscious of Elizabeth's nearness every minute, of being under the same roof as she was day and night. At that point, if she had been of a respectable background, I would have been in some danger. But as a reminder of how dreadful her family is, her mother and younger sisters visited Netherfield ostensibly to check on Miss Bennet. They were loud and uncouth. The girls pestered Bingley into promising the neighbourhood a ball. Of course, Bingley thought it was a capital idea."

"Of course he did."

"I thought I would be relieved when they left, but I missed Elizabeth. I was left to the tiresome society of the Bingleys and the Hursts. The Bennets had a visitor, a distant cousin, and so I did not see much of them, until the day Bingley and I rode into Meryton and found them on the street conversing with George Wickham!"

"What?" Fitzwilliam sat bolt upright, his feet flying off the footstool and hitting the floor. "What was he doing there? Did he follow you?"

"No, it was just a horrible coincidence. Somehow, by fraudulent means, no doubt, he scraped up the money to buy a commission. He was joining the militia there."

"Well, well," said Fitzwilliam, "oddly enough, I may be acquainted with their commanding officer. Colonel Forster, is it not? I knew him years ago when he was in the regulars, before he inherited and sold out. I will make a point to speak with him. Go on."

"Wickham furthered his acquaintance with Elizabeth at a card party. As we know, he is a most captivating liar. He spun a tale of the woe and degradation of his life and fortune, all at my despicable hands. Of course, the dour and stiff Darcy did not compare well with the charming and charismatic Wickham."

Darcy barked a bitter laugh and continued. "A few days later, Bingley's ball took place at Netherfield. Elizabeth looked absolutely radiant. I could not tear my eyes from her. We danced, and she pressed me a bit about my acquaintance with Wickham, but even that impertinence seemed a minor annoyance. I was too busy drinking in the sight of her. I was already lost, though it took me a long time to admit it to myself."

Darcy settled back into his seat, his face turned away. "She had already visited my dreams on a few occasions. After that evening, a night has not gone by that I have not dreamt of her. Still, I did not admit to myself that I had lost my heart. I told myself that it was a mere physical infatuation and that it would fade quickly once I left Hertfordshire. The day after the ball, Bingley left for London on business, intending to return in three days. Miss Bingley immediately began to importune Mr and Mrs Hurst to also leave for town. I now regret it, but I joined Miss Bingley in arguing that Miss Bennet did not love Bingley, and that it would be better for him if we closed Netherfield and returned to London. Curiously, I remember Hurst resisting the removal, but he was soon bullied into agreeing by Miss Bingley. We left for London the next day."

He looked at his cousin. "And that is where I saw you. Less than a fortnight after you called at Darcy House, the thought of staying in town for the Season was so repellent, I left for Pemberley. Within a few days of my arrival, we had the first of our many snowstorms, and I have not left the estate since then."

"But Miss Elizabeth came with you," prompted Fitzwilliam.

Darcy closed his eyes and groaned. "Yes, she is with me, in my thoughts and dreams, day and night. I was too far gone even before we left Hertfordshire. In vain have I struggled! It will not do! My feelings will not be repressed! It is like a madness. I am mortified that I cannot assert control over myself!"

"Many people fall madly in love at least once in their lives. Why should you be any different?"

"Because I am a Darcy. I am expected to exercise control

over my emotions. I owe it to my family and my peers to behave with decorum and dignity. Even if I were to declare my feelings to Elizabeth, even if she returned my love, surely you can see that I could not marry her!" snapped Darcy furiously.

CHAPTER 18

"Because?"

"How could I possibly introduce a woman with such low connexions to our family as my bride, however much I may love her! True, she is a gentleman's daughter, but I am a Darcy of Pemberley. Duty and family honour demand that I enter into an advantageous alliance with a lady of rank and fortune."

"Advantageous alliance? Rank and fortune? Good God, Darcy, you are scaring me. You sound exactly like Lady Catherine! You are speaking of marriage, not diplomacy! You should marry the person you wish to spend the rest of your life with! Who do you think you would offend if you chose Miss Elizabeth as your bride? Certainly not me, nor I think your sister. If I know Georgiana, she would wish you to marry for love. My parents? They consider you an adult who can marry as he chooses. My brother? He never notices anyone but himself. Darcy, the only person in our family who has any concern about whom you may marry is Lady Catherine. She will be outraged if you marry anyone but Anne, even if it were Princess Charlotte! Yes, you are a Darcy of Pemberley, a person who has the fortune and rank to do as he pleases, including marry the woman his heart cries out for."

"I do not know if you understand," began Darcy.

"Oh, I do understand, and much better than you do! *You* will never be forced to marry for money, as I must do to maintain the habits of expense I have been raised with!" retorted Fitzwilliam, vexation showing on his face and in his voice, as he began rising to his feet.

Darcy was embarrassed. The two of them had been as close as brothers all their lives, yet he had never even once thought of what it must be like to be a second son, not to have a fortune of his own. The heir and the spare. Could it be awful to be the spare? How could he have never considered this before? Fitzwilliam was always charming and amusing, seeming not to have a care in the world. Darcy chastised himself for his insensitivity. After a few moments, he said quietly, "Please accept my apology. I have been thoughtless and selfish."

"Indeed," replied his cousin, slowly sitting back down. The room was silent for a few moments before he spoke again. "How well do you know Miss Elizabeth? How much time have you truly spent with her, getting to know her?"

Darcy had been unwilling to confront himself with this question. Irrationally, he felt that he knew Elizabeth intimately. His heart knew everything about her: the silken rustle of her skirts as she moved about Pemberley, how she looked presiding over their dinner table, consulting with Mrs Reynolds, playing duets with Georgiana; how his mother's wedding ring sparkled on her finger, what poetry she liked him to read to her; the pulse point below her ear that he kissed when he wanted to drive her wild with desire, the way her hand fit perfectly within his, how her alabaster skin glowed in the moonlight as she lay in his bed, her wildly curling hair spread across his chest. These mental images, as they always did, made every fibre of his body leap to attention, and he surreptitiously pulled his coat around himself.

"Darcy?"

Darcy groaned, then said slowly, "The truth is I spent only a few days in her company at Netherfield, and even then, she spent most of her time caring for her sister. Several conversations at other gatherings, the one most enchanting dance I have ever danced in my life, and that is the sum total of the time I have spent in the company of Miss Elizabeth Bennet."

"Could it be that you are in love with a dream? With a bewitching creature who exists only in your imagination?"

"I suppose that is possible." Darcy rubbed a hand over his face as he thought more clearly of his acquaintance with Elizabeth. "But during the time I spent in her company, I witnessed her humour and intelligence when challenged by Miss Bingley and her kindness and care of her elder sister. She was all that was admirable."

"So perhaps your instinct, informed by these observations, is correct," said his cousin. "It is not as though you lose your heart every day. We both know that you have no imagination whatsoever—"

Darcy lifted his head and glared, but Fitzwilliam went on as if he had not noticed.

"Maybe your heart is telling you that she is the one." He leaned forward and put his hand on Darcy's arm. "Do you have the courage to find out? I think you need to know. You certainly cannot go on like this."

"Perhaps. Yes, you are right. One way or another, I have to know, even if it comes to nothing."

"How could you meet her again? What excuse can you have for visiting Hertfordshire?"

Darcy set his chin on one hand and considered the idea for several long moments. "Her cousin, who was a guest at Longbourn at the time I was at Netherfield, is Lady Catherine's rector. He is an obsequious, toadying man, and an irksome gossip. When we are at Rosings, I could call on him and see what news he has of his relations."

He looked up, his eyes brighter than they had been for some days. "There is also the possibility that Bingley received my letter and has followed his heart back to Netherfield. If so, I may be able to pay him a visit. If he is courting Miss Bennet, it would only be natural for me to spend time in the company of her family," he mused aloud.

As he spoke, a hint of anticipation began to warm his voice. He was on firmer ground now, used to executing events, not passively reacting to them. He felt a little of his long-lost equilibrium returning, until he remembered Georgiana.

His heart plummeted. "Of course, I cannot even consider visiting her until I speak to Georgiana. Any connexion to the Bennets could damage her future prospects."

Fitzwilliam rolled his eyes. "Georgie has grown up a great deal this year, and she is worried about you. You need to be her brother, not her father or uncle. Do not patronise her. Respect her opinions."

"I do owe it to her," Darcy admitted. He looked at Fitzwilliam. "Georgiana said I called her Elizabeth? Not Miss Elizabeth or Miss Bennet?"

"Elizabeth," his cousin affirmed.

Darcy groaned, wondering what else he might have said in his sister's presence.

"Are you ready to face her? Or do you need some time to collect yourself?"

"Now, I think," responded Darcy. "I gather she is waiting for us?"

"She is waiting for *you.* This is an important conversation for you both, I believe, and I should stay out of your way."

The two men rose from the sofa and walked to the music room, where Georgiana was waiting. Fitzwilliam propelled his cousin through the door and closed it behind him.

As she poured the tea, Georgiana gathered her composure. Her brother had had control of her life ever since she could remember: planning, advising, giving her direction; always with care and kindness. Only once had she made a decision on her own, and it had been a *monstrous* mistake. And her brother, as always, had taken over her life, to repair the damage and protect the family name. He was still sheltering her and refused to discuss the affair out of concern for her feelings. Apparently he thought that if no one spoke of it, her grievous mistakes and actions would be forgotten.

Sweet are the uses of adversity, she reminded herself. She had come a long way since the debacle at Ramsgate, and had used the painful experience to strengthen and grow. She had been greatly concerned for him over the winter, yet a tiny corner of her heart had been relieved to discover that he was human, with feelings and vulnerabilities, not the man on the pedestal; kind and generous, but also remote, self-contained, encumbered with responsibilities and expectations. Perhaps he could learn from his mistakes too.

She handed Darcy his tea just the way he liked it. "I have been worried about you, Brother."

"So I understand," he answered quietly. "I am sorry to have caused you any concern, dearest. I have been, as you surmised, preoccupied with matters of the heart."

She waited a moment for him to continue, but he did not, so she carried on. "Tell me about her."

Keeping his voice carefully level, Darcy gave a brief and rather dry description of Elizabeth. Too dry for Georgiana.

"What colour are her eyes?" she asked innocently, hoping to provoke him into a more heartfelt portrayal.

"They are dark brown," he answered, gazing into the distance, "with gold flecks. Although they flash sparks sometimes."

She chuckled. "At you?"

Darcy smiled ruefully. "At me, I believe. I do not think she liked me, Georgie."

"Sparks are not necessarily bad. In fact, they are probably good. It means she reacts to you. That is far better than indifference."

He set his cup down and looked at her seriously. "She comes from a different kind of society than ours. Her father is a gentleman with a small country estate."

"We are a country family, Brother." she answered lightly, with a slight movement of her head indicating their surroundings.

"So we are. But if I were to marry Miss Bennet, there are people of the *ton* who would look askance at that. Perhaps, as a result, you may not meet the right people when it is your turn to come out."

Georgiana huffed impatiently. "You sound like Lady Catherine! Or worse, Caroline Bingley!"

Darcy grimaced. Twice within an hour, he had been compared to Lady Catherine. And now to Miss Bingley? Did his behaviour resemble either lady? Lady Catherine used her rank as a weapon, a tool to wield power and manipulate others. Miss Bingley desired to raise her rank so she could do the same. Both ran roughshod over anyone in their way. *Surely* he was not like that!

"My dear, it is simply that I do not want my desire for happiness in marriage to affect your future felicity."

His sister's lips thinned in annoyance. "Fitzwilliam, I *do* understand. I have listened to talk of the importance of honour and duty and rank all my life. I have thought long and hard about marriage and the expectations of society and family, and I believe happiness is the most important part of life. How could your happiness affect my felicity, except to make it greater?"

Darcy thought of the Season, the marriage mart, the cold-blooded calculation he had been witness to since he first ventured into society. He looked at his sister, struck by her perceptiveness and intelligence. She was no longer a child, but a young woman who had grown in her understanding of the world.

What could happen if he married Elizabeth? Would he be ousted from his clubs? Would he lose his voucher to Almack's, a place he detested any way? Would the number of invitations and visiting cards he received diminish? In truth, it would be a relief if they did. Would the shades of Pemberley be thus polluted? No, far from it. Pemberley would be made lively, vibrant with music, laughter, spirited conversation and the shouts of children playing on the great lawns. If a man or woman of rank cannot choose their spouse based on affection and love, what good was rank, or property, or influence? What good is it all if one cannot choose to build a life around a happy family?

Nothing truly matters but the felicity to be shared by marrying the woman I love.

"Like you," Darcy said after a moment, "I have examined my life and considered how I wish to live. I have seen married couples of our acquaintance who barely tolerate being in the same room with their spouse, yet their marriages are considered successful. They have children, yet they spend little or no time with them."

"I *do* wish to seek my happiness with Miss Elizabeth Bennet," he continued, as a slow, wondering smile spread across his face. *Is it possible? Can I do this?* Perhaps, he realised, making a happy family at Pemberley *was* his duty. He looked at Georgiana, her wide, warm smile mirroring his own. "*If* I did court her, would I have your blessing, Sister?"

"Only after you tell me everything about her, and how she captured your heart!"

Darcy reflected. *When did she capture my heart?* Again, images flashed before his mind's eye. *At the Lucas's, when she would not dance? The gut-wrenching moment when I saw her speaking to Wickham on the high street? At the ball? When she blushed? Stop it, man, you are sitting with your sister!* Out of the blue, a forgotten picture from that awkward assembly popped into his mind; Elizabeth smirking at him from across the room, her eyes dancing with mischief. What was that about? At that point, they had not even been introduced. *But when were we formally introduced? We must have been introduced,* but he could not remember it. She muddled his brain as much as she muddled his heart.

After a few moments, he mused aloud, "As to when I lost my heart to her, I cannot fix on the hour, or the spot, or the look, or the words, which laid the foundation. I was in the middle before I knew that I had begun. Once I knew that, I tried to ignore it. Then I tried to talk myself out of it. But my heart won out over my head."

"I guess your heart is smarter than your head then."

Darcy stared at her. What had become of his timid, tongue-tied little sister? "When did you get to be so impertinent, young lady?"

Georgiana rolled her eyes at him and waited. Darcy thought about his sister's questions. What was Elizabeth really like? Finally, not knowing exactly what to say, he plunged in.

"I think you would like her. I must confess that I did not spend much time conversing with her, but I did enjoy observing her. I have spent *no* time alone with her, of course." *Except that silent encounter in the library. Good God! I did not sleep a wink that night.* He became conscious of Georgiana, still listening patiently and continued. "There are times I have wondered if I dreamt it all."

He leaned back against the cushions. "I know her to have a mischievous sense of humour. In fact, I have come to believe that she hides her deepest feelings behind her facetiousness. She loves to read poetry, novels, essays—anything at all. She is quite intelligent, but from what I understand rather haphazardly educated. She loves the countryside and the outdoors. You would like this about her: she does not concern herself overmuch with society's expectations. She is her unaffected true self."

Georgiana squealed and clapped her hands. "I cannot wait to meet her! When can you begin?"

Begin? Darcy stared at her for a moment, and then chuckled. His sister looked shocked, and he realised she had likely not heard him laugh since the summer. Then she began to laugh too.

Fitzwilliam, who had had his ear to the door, opened it and put his head around. "May I join the party?"

"Yes, but only if you promise not to be gloomy and cross," said Darcy, his face a mask of innocence. They all burst out laughing, and Georgiana began to slice the cake.

The three spent the rest of the day relaxed in each other's

company, and when they said their goodnights, Darcy thought optimistically that he might sleep deeply. However, Elizabeth Bennet had not loosened her hold on his nocturnal life. He again found himself waking abruptly from a fevered dream of impassioned intimacies. He lay on his back, his palms over his eyes, his fingers entangled in his damp, sweaty hair.

Fitzwilliam is wrong. I have altogether too much imagination.

CHAPTER 19

The succeeding days flew by as Darcy and Fitzwilliam made ready to travel to Rosings. It was a long journey to Kent, and an annual responsibility that the cousins did not enjoy, but undertook as a family obligation. They tolerated their aunt's overbearing haughtiness and pomposity for three weeks every year to look over the estate records, confer with the steward, ride the grounds, and visit the tenants. The duty had fallen on them since Lady Catherine had alienated every other relative she had.

On the day of departure, the coach waited outside the front entrance as Darcy gathered up some papers from his study. Fitzwilliam put his head around the door. "Do you have everything required?"

Darcy glanced up at him. "I do now. The sooner we go, the sooner we get this year's visit over with, and the sooner I can pay a visit to Mr Collins. I cannot believe how much I am anticipating an interview with that fawning imbecile!"

The two gentlemen left the study and proceeded along the hall and down the stairs. A few words of farewell to Mrs Reynolds, and they were out the door. Darcy stopped short at the sight before him.

Georgiana was standing by the coach, dressed for travel, watching her trunks being loaded onto the carriage. She turned to her brother and smiled. "I have decided to accompany you this year, gentlemen. I have been remiss in my own responsibilities towards our family."

"Georgie," began her brother when he was interrupted by their cousin.

"Why, I think that is a capital idea! I am sure Anne will be exceedingly happy to see you!"

"Thank you. I greatly anticipate seeing her. I have not visited Rosings since before I went to school," smiled Georgiana.

"Is that your only reason for accompanying us?" Darcy asked suspiciously.

"Of course not," she replied. "I want to know what you find out about Miss Bennet."

Taking Fitzwilliam's proffered hand, Georgiana climbed into the carriage. Darcy sighed. "Did you know about this?" he asked, turning to face his cousin.

"No, but I think it is a good idea. It would do both Anne and Georgiana good to get to know each other better. They are the only female cousins, after all. And we *all* want to know what you find out about Miss Bennet. I am surprised Mrs Reynolds did not decide to accompany us as well."

AS THEY TRAVELLED TOWARDS KENT, they drove into springtime. The air was warmer, the earth was greener, and the roads in better condition the farther south they went. Their route to Kent took them through Hertfordshire, but nowhere close to Meryton. Even so, Darcy was sorely tempted to diverge from their itinerary to at least drive through the village to see if he could catch a glimpse of her. But Lady Catherine awaited.

They arrived at Rosings early in the evening on the fourth day of travel. After a brief visit to their rooms to refresh themselves, the trio were received by Lady Catherine and Anne in a parlour near the dining room.

Their aunt, a large woman with a heavy-boned countenance and a ringing voice, bellowed her greeting. "Here you are at last! You have kept me waiting. Georgiana, although you did not do me the favour of informing me of your visit, I am pleased to see you. I understand you are alone with servants much of the time at Pemberley. It will do you good to spend time with a young lady of your own station; the better to have the distinction of rank preserved."

Georgiana looked at her cousin and smiled, and Anne smiled back, obviously surprised to see her. She had not seen Anne for several years, and was dismayed by what she saw. Anne had always been small and fine-boned, with a pale complexion and oversized hazel eyes. She was more than ten years older than Georgiana, but the younger girl had grown far taller than her cousin before she was twelve. Anne had never developed a womanly figure, and in many respects looked almost childlike.

Now Anne, still pale and small, was thinner and had shadows under her eyes. She was wrapped in a thick, woolly shawl to fend off some imagined chill. Georgiana felt glad that she had come, but also that she had been neglectful. She should have visited Anne before and corresponded with her. She promised herself to make up for lost time.

Lady Catherine glared imperiously at Darcy till he started and moved to offer her his arm. Grinning, Fitzwilliam took Anne's and Georgiana's arms, and they moved into the dining room. Their aunt asked them about their journey and enquired as to the names of the inns they had stayed at along the way. She, of course, found fault with their choices, listing the names of superior establishments where they could drop her name. She informed them of better routes they should have taken. She held forth on the weather, implying that they had been careless to allow so much snow to fall on Derbyshire over the winter. She interrogated Georgiana about her music and instructed her to practise every day.

When she paused for breath, Fitzwilliam asked his aunt how she liked her new rector, who had come to the parish since their last visit. Her heavy visage grew thunderous. "After all I have done for him, ungrateful wretch, he will be leaving my parish in a few months' time. He has come into an inheritance of a small estate in Hertfordshire."

Darcy looked up from his soup. "An estate?"

"Yes, Mr Collins is heir to an estate entailed away from his cousin's daughters. The cousin, a Mr Bennet, has died. Mr Collins visited them last November to choose a wife from among them, but disregarded my orders and married another lady from the neighbourhood. It was the first sign of the trouble he would cause me, and now I must go to the bother of finding another clergyman for the parish."

Lady Catherine now had the complete attention of her guests.

Darcy, the colour draining from his face, enquired, "Do you know the name of the estate?"

"Oh, it is Longacre or Longview or Longbourn or some such thing. It is insignificant, hardly worth mentioning, except that I will soon lose my parson."

His jaw tightened at the rampant self-absorption of her complaints. "What do you know of the Bennet family, Lady Catherine?"

"They are of small consequence. Five daughters with no dowries, and a mother of inferior birth. With such low connexions and little money, I expect they will go to their relatives until situations can be found for them."

Darcy sat with a rigid posture, breathing slowly and deeply to calm himself, his eyes averted as thoughts of Elizabeth and her family's situation filled his mind. For the rest of the interminable meal, he was silent, pushing food around his plate but not taking a single bite. Fitzwilliam kept the conversation going with occasional help from Georgiana and Anne. Lady Catherine, oblivious to the change in the atmosphere, gave her small audience the benefit of her opinions and advice for the remainder of the repast.

Darcy took notice of nothing, not even Anne's sharp, curious gaze as it darted from one of her cousins' faces to the next for the rest of dinner. At the conclusion of the meal, the travellers begged their hostess's pardon, claiming exhaustion from their journey and retired for the night.

DARCY WENT to his chambers and closed the door behind him, reeling from the news his aunt had so carelessly announced. He paced the floor of the small, gaudy sitting room, his fingers pressed against his temples, trying to digest the information and sort out what to do. His heart ached for Elizabeth; her special bond with her father had been clear to him. When had Mr Bennet died? Elizabeth and her sisters were being forced to leave their home? Her family split up and sent to relatives? Where would she go? *Where is she now*?

There was a quiet rap on the door, and then Georgiana

peered around it. "May I come in?" Not waiting for a reply, she closed the door behind her and ran into the room to embrace her brother. "Lady Catherine said Mr Collins would not take possession of Longbourn for weeks yet! Perhaps the Bennets are still there! There must be *something* we can do for them!"

There was another knock on the door, and Fitzwilliam quickly and quietly slipped in. "Well, this is bad news for the Bennets. What do you think your next move should be?"

Yet another tap, and this time Anne peeked around the door. "What has happened? You have all clearly heard something that has shocked you—especially you, Darcy! What is it?"

Darcy cursed under his breath. He had been staggered by the news of the Bennets' situation, and he did not wish to speak to *anyone*. He wished to think and to plan. In privacy. His immediate instinct was to saddle a fast horse and ride straight through the night to Longbourn. He did not wish to speak about it with Fitzwilliam and Georgiana, much less Anne.

Yet, here she was, and given that Lady Catherine had been filling her head with visions of their marriage since she was a little girl—and that he would be leaving as soon as possible for Hertfordshire—the time had come to speak frankly. Darcy took a deep breath and sank down on an overstuffed rococo settee. "Anne, we must have a conversation that is long overdue."

Anne threw herself down on a chair, groaning. "The only possible topic of conversation that could involve the two of us is that balderdash my mother spouts about our so-called betrothal. We all know that it is a *complete* humbug!"

Three sets of eyes stared at her. Georgiana slowly sat next to her brother and put her arm around him, her eyes on Anne.

"You knew that I never intended, that a marriage between us is out of the question?" stammered Darcy. "I have no wish to injure your feelings, but—"

"I have never paid any attention to that ridiculous idea. We would never suit, of course." Anne's gaze swept over her three cousins. "Now, is anyone going to tell me what you are all so upset about?"

He attempted to placate his cousin. "Anne, I am acquainted with the Bennet family whose home will soon be occupied by Mr Collins. We have spent the last few months snowbound at Pemberley, so I was unaware that Mr Bennet had died. I am shocked and saddened by the news."

"I *see*. The family that has only daughters, and lovely ones at that, according to Mrs Collins," said Anne slowly before turning abruptly to Fitzwilliam. "Which one has Darcy lost his heart to?"

He answered quickly, and as if trying to shield Darcy's raw emotions, joked, "Upon my word, Anne, a lady's imagination is very rapid! To jump from acquaintance to romance in just a moment!" He sat on a footstool next to her chair and patted her hand.

Anne snatched her hand away and poked Fitzwilliam in the arm. "Do not treat me like a child!" She looked at each of them in turn. "I will not bother you for explanations," she said. "But if you were to tell me, I would never breathe a word of it to Mama!"

Darcy looked at Anne with new eyes. *How dull it must be for her here.* She had no one to talk to but her mother and Mrs Jenkinson. She had no one close to her own age, except perhaps Miss Lucas, now Mrs Collins. Darcy remembered that lady to be well-bred and kind, with a sense of humour. Mrs Collins was Elizabeth's closest friend, and she was here, at the parsonage. Here, and far away from the friend who needed her. He would go tomorrow to speak to Mrs Collins and learn more about the situation at Longbourn.

Elizabeth has lost her father and the presence of her dearest friend. How she must be suffering!

Although it went against all his instincts, Darcy understood that he could trust Anne's discretion and recounted an abbreviated version of the previous autumn's events in Hertfordshire, before concluding, "The Bennet sisters are indeed lovely young ladies, and I did come to admire one of them in particular."

Anne's eyes lit up with interest. "What is her name? Are you courting her?"

Darcy chose his words carefully, keeping his voice even. "Her name is Miss Elizabeth Bennet. I am not courting her."

"Whyever not?" cried Anne incredulously. "Did she refuse you?"

Fitzwilliam snorted, and Darcy silenced him with a look. "At the time, I determined that her family was not of sufficient—"

"Darcy! You sound just like my mother!"

Darcy, discomposed, glanced at Fitzwilliam, who was biting down hard on his tongue, trying to keep a straight face. With an effort, Darcy continued, "Since then, I have reconsidered, and I had hoped to pay my addresses to her. Now, with news of her father's death, I need to discover her family's situation. I still wish to pay my addresses to her, Anne, but I know not what they are suffering at the present." His voice trailed off.

Anne's expression changed from incredulity to sympathy. "I am sorry. I do believe you will win her."

Darcy, noting the dark circles under Anne's eyes, nodded at Fitzwilliam.

His cousin peered at Anne and stood. "It is getting late.

For now, let us all try to get some rest, and leave Darcy to consider what he wants to do. Not to mention, we have Rosings's estate business to begin tomorrow. I suggest we all go to bed."

They all filed toward the door, Georgiana embracing her brother before she said goodnight. "You are going to call on Mrs Collins, are you not?"

"Tomorrow morning, as soon as it is an acceptable hour."

"I hope she can put your mind at ease. Will you go and visit Miss Elizabeth and her family?"

Darcy hesitated. "I would like to, although I do not know how welcome I would be. I shall ask Mrs Collins for her thoughts."

"Like Anne, I, too, believe you will win Miss Elizabeth." Georgiana squeezed his hand, and then left, closing the door behind her.

Darcy sat staring at the floor, still agitated. He heard a discreet cough and looked up. It was Talbot with his nightshirt. "Do you wish to retire for the night, sir?" the valet asked impassively.

"Yes, I do. Thank you, Talbot, I will undress myself."

"As you wish, sir" he said, and returned to the bedchamber to lay out his master's night clothes.

CHAPTER 20

Darcy slept fitfully. By sunrise he was dressed. He sat down in the breakfast room, but in his disquietude, barely managed a few bites of toast. He rose and went outside, oblivious to the gentle splendour of the early spring morning.

The sun was warm, and the green haze of new grass freshened the vast lawn. He paced back and forth in the garden, repeatedly taking out his watch and putting it back into his waistcoat pocket, waiting impatiently until such time that he could decently call on the parsonage. He was desperate to hear what the new Mrs Collins knew of Elizabeth's situation.

A short time later, upon consulting his watch for the fiftieth time, Darcy decided that a visit was finally permissible. He strode towards the parsonage, hoping that Mrs Collins would be home and that her grovelling husband would be out. As he approached the house, all was quiet. He did not see anyone in the garden. He walked up to the front door and knocked.

The housekeeper opened the door and ushered him into a small sitting room. Her mistress entered a few minutes later. "Mr Darcy!" said Mrs Collins, with a deep curtsey. "What a pleasant surprise."

SHE WAS, in fact, not surprised. From the moment she became aware that Lady Catherine's nephews always paid her an Easter visit, Charlotte has been expecting to see Mr Darcy.

"Mrs Collins, it is a pleasure to see you. May I take the opportunity to congratulate you on your marriage?"

She inclined her head, and he continued. "I had expected to pay a call on your husband to enquire after our mutual acquaintance in Meryton, and was delighted to discover that you were here."

Charlotte struggled to keep her pleasant smile from turning into a snort. Here was Mr Darcy, too proud to mingle with the neighbourhood when he was at Netherfield, now anxiously enquiring after them. Or at least one of them.

"Thank you, Mr Darcy, you are most kind," she said. "Pray be seated. It is early yet. Have you eaten breakfast? May I offer you some refreshment?" Mr Darcy thanked his hostess and sat down, while Mrs Collins ordered some coffee. Within moments, they were seated beside a low table, and Charlotte poured out coffee and served scones and fruit compote.

They sat for a moment in silence, sipping their coffee, and then Mr Darcy began, "I was unaware that you and your husband were courting while we were visiting Meryton last November."

Mrs Collins chuckled. "At that point in time, sir, we were not courting," she responded. "My husband did, however, visit his cousins at Longbourn with the intention of choosing a wife from among the Bennet sisters, to make peace among the family and to soften the blow of the entail."

Darcy's brows rose at Mrs Collins's frank and matter-of-fact commentary. Ignoring his expression, Charlotte went on, "In fact, my husband first proposed, at the instigation of her mother, to my friend Miss Elizabeth Bennet." Her face was downcast over her coffee cup, but she peeked at Mr Darcy from under her lashes as she spoke.

She was rewarded by the sight of Mr Darcy sitting motionless, his raised cup frozen inches from his lips as an unguarded expression of absolute horror spread across his face.

She bit her lip, suppressing a chuckle. "She refused him, although from what I understand, he did argue with her. It was not surprising to me, however. I have been friends with Eliza since we were girls, and she has always maintained that she will only marry for dearest love."

"After her refusal, Mr Collins and I were able to come to an understanding, and we were married in December. Actually, sir, after our wedding, I invited Eliza to Hunsford for Easter. If fate had not intervened, she would have been here now. As it turns out, we were fortunate that we chose to marry quickly. Shortly after we left Hertfordshire and arrived in Hunsford, the winter storms began and travel became impossible. I received letters only sporadically from my family and friends over the winter."

Charlotte looked up at him and met his eye. "Mr Darcy, has Lady Catherine informed you that Mr Bennet was taken ill over Christmas, and succumbed to his illness in February?"

She watched as Mr Darcy swallowed and avoided her gaze as he spoke in a level voice. "Yes, Mrs Collins. I was shocked and deeply saddened for the family when my aunt told me. Do you know how they are coping? I understand that Longbourn is entailed to your husband. Where will the family go? Do you know what their circumstances are?"

He leaned forward, his voice gaining in intensity before he appeared to remember himself and sat straight again. "I must apologise, Mrs Collins. This is clearly none of my business. It is simply an appalling situation, and I am truly sorry for them." He was silent, looking at the floor, still clutching the cup tightly in his hands.

Charlotte quietly and deliberately set her cup and saucer down on the table and turned in her chair to face him. "Mr Darcy, I think we can be frank with one another," she said in an unruffled, matter-of-fact way. "Unless I am badly mistaken, you and I both share a deep concern for the Bennet family, and for Elizabeth in particular."

At this, Mr Darcy's head came up sharply, his eyes intent. Charlotte calmly met his gaze and went on, "I have corresponded, albeit quite irregularly, with Elizabeth and with my parents and my sister all winter. I believe I can tell you how their situation stands. Mr Bennet, although an intelligent and well-educated man, was never practical, and did not plan ahead or provide well for his wife and daughters. Longbourn estate and its contents are entailed to my husband. What funds they are left with are not enough to provide them with a roof over their heads, nor living expenses."

She dropped her eyes, her countenance becoming troubled, his increasingly agitated.

"When Mr Bennet became ill, Mrs Bennet lacked the, er, let us say the emotional resources to take over his affairs and his nursing care. Jane and Elizabeth took on most of their father's care, and Elizabeth has also been handling much of the estate business. Their younger sisters, I am relieved to say, proved far more helpful than anyone expected. Their uncles have also offered as much assistance as they can, although the fierce weather kept them from visiting for much of the winter. In her letters, Elizabeth never complained, but my father and mother have described the extreme difficulty and trauma she has experienced over the past few months."

Mrs Collins paused, her troubled eyes staring out the window. She took a deep breath and continued. "Ever since we were young, Elizabeth was always the indomitable one, seemingly formed for happiness, and it has been painful for me to know that she has been so deeply distressed. Out of a desire to comfort her and assist her family, I have contrived to influence your aunt to retain my husband here as long as possible. I dare say she will find it difficult to find another parson who will offer such abject loyalty and submission to her wishes," she said with a rueful smile. "I have written to Elizabeth and informed her that we will not take possession of Longbourn until June. She and her sisters Jane and Mary plan to seek positions as governesses or ladies' companions to augment the family income."

At this, Mr Darcy set down his cup, and rose to pace back and forth in the small room, clasping and unclasping his hands. Charlotte watched him for a few moments, reminded of a tiger she had once seen in a cage at a traveling exhibition. She heard Mr Darcy mutter to himself, "I must go to her."

Mrs Collins looked at him with great compassion, grateful that she did not share the same passionate, romantic nature of her closest friend, and of this anguished gentleman before her.

"Mr Darcy, what are your intentions towards Elizabeth?"

Darcy looked up, surprised, and saw Mrs Collins's expression, though not unkind, was serious and direct.

His first instinct was to put this lowly parson's wife in her place and refuse to even answer the question. Then, meeting her gaze, he understood that Mrs Collins, Elizabeth's dearest friend, wished to be his ally. So to his great chagrin, he found himself again, for the fourth time within a fortnight, in the position of divulging his feelings—sparingly this time—to Mrs Collins. He said only that he had belatedly realised his attraction to Miss Elizabeth, that she had been much on his mind, and that he wished to renew the acquaintance and pay his addresses. His countenance reflected his suffering as he admitted that they had been barely acquainted, and that Elizabeth would most likely not share his feelings, perhaps even regard them as unwelcome.

"Mr Darcy, it is my belief that Elizabeth was not unaffected by your presence at Netherfield last autumn. The elder Miss Bennets, having been unable to rely on their parents for counsel, are both in the habit of keeping their deepest feelings disguised. I think that might explain some of her impertinence to you. She can be rather flippant, even impudent, as I think you know. I must tell you, however, that not having seen her in person since before Christmas, I cannot say how much this dark time may have altered her. I urge you to see her as soon as possible. I believe she needs someone who will cherish and care for her."

"There is nothing I would rather do," he said feelingly.

Mrs Collins looked down at her hands, and then raised her eyes to his. "I know you have much estate business to work through for Lady Catherine before you can go on to Hertfordshire, so I shall not be offended if you wish to take your leave. I am glad to have had this conversation." She rose and offered her hand.

Darcy was gratified that Mrs Collins understood his need to make haste and bowed over her hand. "Mrs Collins, I marvel at your frankness, and I am most humbly grateful for it. Miss Elizabeth is fortunate to have you as a friend."

DARCY WALKED QUICKLY BACK to Rosings, his heart pumping and mind racing, Mrs Collins's words swirling and dancing in his head. *She was not unaffected by your presence.* Could she welcome his call, his attentions? Could she love him?

As he neared the manor house, he was seized from his absorption by the sound of his aunt's stentorian voice. "There you are, Darcy! Where have you been? Fitzwilliam and Houston are waiting for you!" Lady Catherine was standing outside the front door, glaring at him as if she had been going to hunt him down herself.

Darcy struggled to tear his mind away from Elizabeth. He wished he had the sort of connexion to her that would allow him to directly assist her family. If only he had not been so harshly judgmental, so insufferably conscious of his rank, and had tried more to be amiable, they could have been friends. Even so, he could not just gallop off and leave everything for Fitzwilliam to do—but he could hasten the process and shorten his stay at Rosings. He bowed slightly to his aunt and went to the study to find his cousin and the steward.

SEVERAL HOURS LATER, after ploughing through stacks of crop reports and accounts, the three men almost staggered from the study. "Well, gentlemen, I believe we have done at least two days' work this afternoon!" said Mr Houston. Darcy nodded. "We will meet by the stables in the morning, and ride through the farm."

"Yes, sir," answered the steward, wondering what on earth all the haste was about. "I can let myself out, gentlemen," he said, and almost ran for the door.

Fitzwilliam watched him go and turned to look at his cousin. "What was all that about? You were driving us as if the devil himself was at our backs!"

"I wish to work through the estate business as quickly as possible, so I may proceed apace to Hertfordshire. I do not wish to take three weeks to do this work as we usually do."

"Is this your decision based on your visit to Mrs Collins this morning?"

"My decision is based on Elizabeth," answered Darcy gravely. "What I learned from Lady Catherine nearly prompted me to leave for Longbourn last night, but I cannot leave you to do all the estate work alone."

"Thank you for that, at least!" His cousin looked at him curiously. "What did Mrs Collins tell you?"

Before Darcy could reply, their aunt's butler appeared. "Lady Catherine is waiting for you in the saloon, gentlemen." Darcy looked at his watch and muttered an oath. "Thank you, Ralston. I had not realised it was so late. We will change quickly and join her there."

A quarter of an hour later, they joined the ladies. Lady Catherine was furious. "I expect you to be on time for dinner, Darcy. I am most seriously displeased. Do not be late again," she commanded.

Darcy looked down at his aunt, coolly matching her hauteur with his own. "Lady Catherine, Fitzwilliam and I spent the entire day working on Rosings estate business. A word of gratitude would be in order." Fitzwilliam's eyebrows shot up. Anne and Georgiana, sitting side by side on the settee, exchanged incredulous glances. Darcy usually let his aunt's rudeness go unremarked. Anne turned to meet her cousin's eye and offered him a silent salute. Lady Catherine did not notice her daughter. She was too furious.

At that moment, Ralston entered. "Dinner is served, my lady." Stiffly, Darcy offered his arm to his aunt, and she took it, still glowering. Dinner conversation was sparse and frosty. After dinner, the two men once again excused themselves, announcing that they intended to get an early start in the morning.

No sooner had Darcy entered his sitting room and closed the door behind him, he heard a light tap. *Am I not to have any privacy?* He stepped quickly to the door and opened it. All three of his relatives were there; Anne bent over, apparently having been trying to peer through the keyhole. He swore under his breath, but stepped aside for them to enter. Anne, Georgiana, and Fitzwilliam quickly stepped through, and Darcy quietly closed the door again behind them.

He turned to find them all settled into the same places they had been in the night before, looking at him expectantly. They were obviously not going to allow him to work through his dilemma alone.

"Well?" Anne finally said. "What did you learn from Mrs Collins?"

Darcy sat down on the settee, his elbows resting on his knees, his hands steepled in front of his face, and related his conversation with the rector's wife regarding the Bennets' circumstances. He held back the awful revelation that the toady parson had first proposed to Elizabeth; the worthy Mrs Collins deserved to retain her pride.

"Mrs Collins has also informed me that Miss Elizabeth intends to seek employment, although her uncle has asked her to delay that. I hope I can see her before she takes any steps in that direction."

"Employment!" cried Georgiana. "Do you mean as a companion or governess?"

"I believe that is her intent," her brother answered sombrely.

Fitzwilliam rose and knelt next to Darcy, putting a hand on his cousin's shoulder. "We will get you to her as soon as humanly possible. We will put in a long day's work with Mr

Houston tomorrow, and every day until it is done. I will cheerfully let you drive me like a dog!" he quipped, squeezing Darcy's shoulder.

One side of Darcy's frown turned up. "I will hold you to that."

Anne piped up, "Is there anything that Georgie and I can do to help you to complete your task?"

Georgiana brightened. "What a good notion, cousin! Perhaps we can check figures in your ledgers or summarise the reports."

The cousins agreed to meet in the study in the afternoon, after Fitzwilliam and Darcy had ridden the estate with Mr Houston. The four of them worked companionably together over the next few days. Much as Darcy wished to be in Meryton, providing help and solace to Elizabeth, he was grateful to lose himself in the estate work. Mr Houston was, on the whole, gratified at their interest in the estate, though the young people were exhausting him.

CHAPTER 21

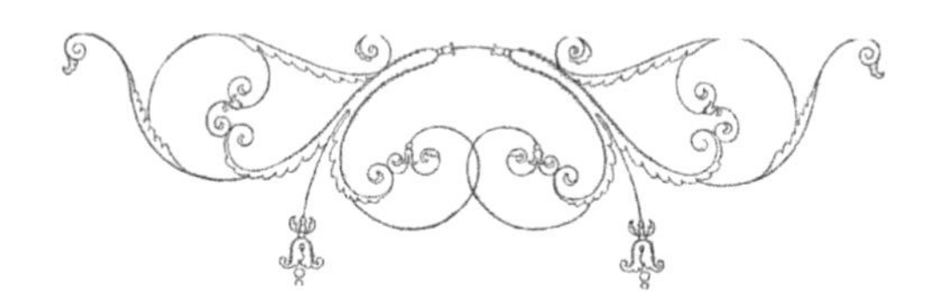

Lady Catherine was incensed. She tired of having only Anne, Mrs Jenkinson, the Collinses, and a few assorted neighbours to bully about, and looked forward to using her nephews' annual visits to hold court. Accustomed to being the centre of attention everywhere she went, she deemed it her right. Yet she had scarcely seen them since their arrival!

She had not yet taken Darcy and Fitzwilliam to task for neglecting her, but another afternoon of being forced to endure the sole company of Mrs Jenkinson pushed her over the edge. Lady Catherine marched down the corridor, bellowing her nephews' names. "Darcy! Fitzwilliam! I demand to know what you are doing!" She threw open the door to the study.

Her nephews stared at her, startled. Darcy sat at the enormous desk that had belonged to his uncle; Fitzwilliam stood next to him, looking over a map of drainage ditches that had been dug in the fields.

Lady Catherine's eyes took in the room. Near the desk, there was a large oaken library table covered with an enormous paisley shawl and topped with a clutter of ledgers and papers. The two men followed her gaze to where Anne and Georgiana had been sitting seconds before. The two men exchanged questioning glances, and Fitzwilliam gave a slight shrug of his shoulders.

"I am sorry, Lady Catherine, but there is more than the usual amount of business to attend to this year," said Darcy in a defensive tone. "Fitzwilliam and I have much to do."

"Well, I suppose if you must. You have my permission then. I will expect you to attend me after dinner this evening, however. Surely by *now* you are rested from your journey."

"Now, where have Anne and Georgiana gotten to?" their aunt continued.

Fitzwilliam quietly put one hand behind his back and crossed his fingers. "I do not know. Perhaps Anne has taken Georgiana out in her phaeton."

"I am sure they will be back shortly, wherever they are. I shall have them keep me company then." Lady Catherine swept out of the room, slamming the door behind her.

For several minutes, there was silence. Then a small hand grasped the edge of the great library table, and Anne climbed out from underneath it. Another hand appeared, then Georgiana's beaming face, as she, too, rose to her feet. "Upon my word, Anne, how on earth did you learn to dive under the table so fast?" she giggled, shaking out her skirts and smoothing her hair. "I almost hit my head on the edge when you pulled me in after you!"

"Oh, I hide from Mama all the time, though not so often as when I was little. Papa used to hide with me too!"

Darcy stared at Anne. He had no idea how to react, whether to laugh at or console his cousin. He was brought back to attention when Fitzwilliam said dryly, "You heard Lady Catherine, ladies. We cannot avoid her much longer."

"You are right. Georgie, do you agree that we should attend my mother for the rest of the afternoon?" asked Anne.

"Yes, I do. And tomorrow morning, let us go for a drive in your phaeton!"

"Done and done!" agreed Anne. "We will see you gentlemen at dinner," she added as the two girls left the room arm in arm, looking for Lady Catherine.

Darcy smiled after them, but then his humour faded. He turned to Fitzwilliam, who also was looking at the door after them, a thoughtful expression on his face. "What a lonely life Anne has led," Darcy said. "I chastise myself for never having considered it before."

"And I as well," said his cousin ruefully. "But we know now, and none of us will ever neglect her again. Now, I shall see what the girls have accomplished over the morning, and then perhaps we should conclude our business a bit earlier today. We do not want Lady Catherine to be suspicious of your plans for an early departure."

Fitzwilliam stepped over to the table and turned the pages of the ledger where Anne had been entering figures and checking sums. He marked the page with the ribbon affixed to the binding, and then picked up the report Georgiana had been working on. "The ladies are doing first-rate work. Maybe they should be in charge next year."

Darcy looked up at him sceptically and began to speak, but then stopped.

His sister had had an excellent education and had been trained to run a large household. How different was that from running an estate? Anne was as smart as a whip, he now knew. And Elizabeth had been running Longbourn estate for months, according to Mrs Collins. *Of course she had, and likely better than her father. Her quick intelligence, principled integrity, and active habits would do much good for the tenants of Longbourn, or indeed anywhere she went.*

Darcy looked at his cousin. "I astonish myself. I am in complete agreement with you."

THAT EVENING, Darcy again heard the now-familiar tap on his chamber door. He opened it and his cousins and sister slipped in, sitting in their usual places. "How much more time do you think you need to complete your work, Brother?" asked Georgiana.

Darcy looked at Fitzwilliam. "I should hope to finish tomorrow and travel on Monday."

When Fitzwilliam nodded his agreement, Darcy smiled warmly at his sister and cousin. "Anne, Georgiana, your assistance has been brilliant. I can never thank you enough."

"Are you *all* going to Hertfordshire?" asked Anne wistfully. There was a silence. It was clear that Anne was revelling in the company of her cousins.

"I will remain here with you, Anne, with Lady Catherine's permission, of course," said Georgiana with a wry smile, putting her arm around her cousin's narrow shoulders. "I do not think my brother needs my assistance in wooing Miss Bennet."

Darcy cleared his throat and turned to Fitzwilliam. "Would you care to accompany me to Hertfordshire?"

It seemed that his cousin understood his unspoken plea for moral support, for he immediately agreed.

THE NEXT DAY WAS SATURDAY, and Lady Catherine was occupied, having determined to visit the dean of the diocese to personally instruct him as to her expectations of any candidates for the Hunsford living.

The two men toiled away through the morning while Anne and Georgiana went for a drive. After a light luncheon, the ladies joined them in the study to see what tasks were waiting for them.

"Anne," said Fitzwilliam, "since Darcy wishes us to leave for Hertfordshire early on Monday, perhaps you should meet with Mr Houston and discuss the plans he is considering for Rosings this year."

"You think *I* should—?" gasped Anne.

"Why not?" smiled her cousin. "You now have an education of sorts of how Rosings works. You know more about it than your mother, I would venture to guess."

"He is right," agreed Darcy. "And do not forget, Anne, Rosings belongs to you."

"It belongs to *me*?"

"Of course, your father left it solely to you." Darcy looked at her intently. "Has no one ever informed you?"

"No. No one ever told me. I assumed Papa had left it to Mama."

Darcy opened a drawer of Sir Lewis's desk and took out a small key. He used it to open a small drawer in a cabinet behind the desk and took out a leather folder. Opening it, he removed a document and placed it in Anne's hands. "That is your father's will. You should read it. You should also consider keeping it in a safer place."

Anne's eyes swept over the pages in her hands before she looked up, wide-eyed, at her three cousins. "This changes everything."

The inmates of Rosings attended church the next morning. Mr Collins was as Darcy remembered him, all scraping and bowing and babbling flattery. He was not a sensible man, and the deficiency of nature had been but little assisted by education or society. He preached a long, rambling sermon, his eyes constantly moving to his patroness to be sure his monologue met her approval.

After the service, Mr Collins perfunctorily greeted members of his congregation as he brushed past them, obviously impatient to hobnob with Lady Catherine and her noble guests. Darcy watched as Mrs Collins spoke graciously to all their parishioners, calling them each by name, remembering particulars of their lives. They gathered around her, making clear their preference for the wife over her husband.

While Collins listened submissively to his patroness's evisceration of the sermon, Darcy introduced his cousin and his sister to Mrs Collins, albeit briefly, conscious of the demands on that lady's attention from her parishioners.

The Collinses, as was customary, had been invited to Rosings for dinner that evening. Darcy, as always, was seated at Lady Catherine's right, captive to her continuing interrogation of her rector. Anne, Georgiana and Fitzwilliam enjoyed talking with his wife, appreciating her wry humour and good sense.

The conversation turned to the Collins's upcoming elevation in status to master and mistress of Longbourn. Anne asked Mr Collins if he would be able to assuage the difficulties now facing the Bennet family.

Mr Collins paused for a moment and considered. "Conscious as I always am of familial obligation, I shall endeavour to assist in some small ways. Yet I cannot help but feel that their situation is at least partly of their own making. My late cousin's second daughter, when presented with the opportunity to assure her family's future by joining me in the married state, chose not to do so, with her father's approbation. In spite of her manifold attractions, it is now more than probable that neither she nor her sisters will ever again receive offers of marriage. Their portions are unhappily so small, and their connexions so low, it is to be wondered who, as your ladyship has so condescendingly said, would connect themselves with such a family? Indeed, as a man of God, it is apparent to me that our Lord himself has chosen to correct their pridefulness by taking their father Mr Bennet to His bosom, so that they may learn the value of humility."

His words echoed in the shocked silence. Georgiana, Fitzwilliam, and Darcy stared at him, stunned that anyone, even a man of such mean understanding as Mr Collins, could utter such offensive and mean-spirited words. Anne's eyes flared, her expression furious, and she had opened her mouth to condemn his remarks when her mother interrupted.

"Perhaps I can offer my guidance, Mr Collins. I will write to several of my acquaintances whom I know to have children being educated at home and might have need of a governess. It is wonderful how many families I have been the means of supplying in that way," Lady Catherine preened. "I am always glad to get a young person well placed. Indeed, I found situations for two of Mrs Jenkinson's nieces last year."

Lady Catherine and Mr Collins moved on to other subjects, but none of the other diners could find their voices, much less converse, so shocked were they by the rector's callous dismissal of his cousin's family.

Mrs Collins was motionless, staring at her plate, her face flaming scarlet. Georgiana, nonplussed by the rector's heartlessness, recovered enough to reach over, and patted the lady's hand. Darcy, however, was fighting for control. His face was pale, especially about his mouth, and his teeth were clenched.

He gripped his knife and fork so tightly his knuckles were white. His cousins, alert to his insensibility, began conversing quietly and drew his notice; he forced himself to carry on an unexceptionable conversation, managing to make it through the rest of the interminable meal.

After dinner, the assembled company sat in the drawing room. Georgie sang and played while Mrs Collins turned the pages. As the clock chimed and the party began breaking up, Darcy announced to his aunt that he and Fitzwilliam had been called away to town on business, but that his sister would stay to keep Anne company. Fitzwilliam would return with the carriage in a few days to collect Georgiana.

Lady Catherine scowled, red-faced, at her nephew. "This is not to be borne! What business is it? Who sent for you? I saw no letter arrive for you, Darcy!"

"I received the message yesterday while you were consulting with the dean, Aunt," Darcy lied smoothly, his eyes avoiding Fitzwilliam's smirking face. "And the business is confidential."

Lady Catherine stormed and ranted and threatened, but he would not be moved. "Rosings' estate business has been concluded for this year," he said implacably. "There are other pressing matters that require my attention. Fitzwilliam and I will leave first thing tomorrow."

Charlotte was relieved when the clock chimed; her mortification had been thorough that evening. But as she prepared to take her leave, Mr Darcy moved to say his farewells to her, making it clear that he in no way blamed her for her husband's outrageous utterances. "Mrs Collins, I am exceedingly glad to have seen you before I take my leave. I must thank you again for your kindness to me."

Although still struggling with her embarrassment, Charlotte smiled tentatively. "And yours to me, Mr Darcy. Will you and the colonel be going to Longbourn?" she asked softly. "If so, I wonder if I could beg you the great favour of taking a letter I have written to Elizabeth." She fished in her reticule and brought out a sheet of paper sealed with a wafer. She held it out to him, smiling up at him and meeting his eyes fully.

Darcy immediately understood that she was giving him an excuse to call on Elizabeth, and returned her smile. "Thank you, Mrs Collins. I shall be only too happy to deliver it to her." He took the letter and tucked it in his inside coat pocket.

Mrs Collins stepped away from him, her brows furrowed. "Thank you, sir. I have had no word from her since her father's death, and I am a trifle concerned." With an effort, she banished the troubled expression from her face with a slightly too bright smile. "Goodbye, Mr Darcy."

"Goodbye, Mrs Collins," he said, bowing over her hand.

After the Collinses took their leave and Lady Catherine had gone to her rooms, Darcy turned to Anne. "Fitzwilliam and I shall first go to Meryton to discover how things stand with the Bennets. When he returns here to fetch Georgiana, I would like you to come and stay with us in London for as long as you would like."

"My mother would also enjoy your company. She has wanted to pry you from your mother's clutches for quite some time," said Fitzwilliam.

Anne's eyes sparkled with excitement. "I would love to come to London. I have not been there since I went with Papa more than fifteen years ago!"

Georgiana smiled. "We shall find a way, cousin!"

CHAPTER 22

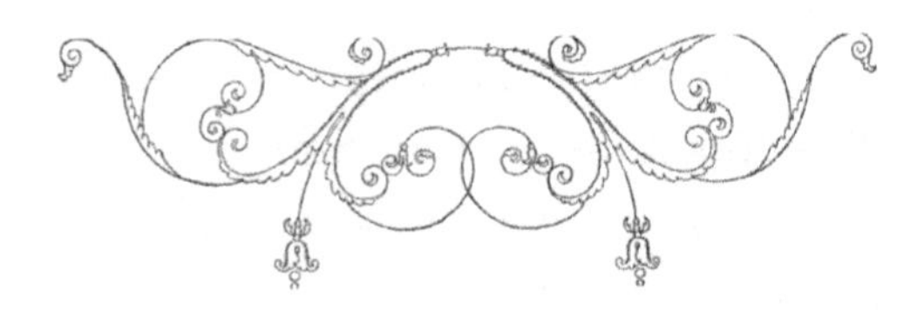

As the carriage pulled away from Rosings early the next morning, Fitzwilliam studied his cousin solicitously. "How are you?" he asked gently.

Darcy shook his head and gave a short laugh that sounded more like a groan. "Full of trepidation. I only know I need to see her," he answered. "But I am unsure of how difficult it will be. Mrs Collins says that Miss Elizabeth will only marry for love. She does not love me, does not even know me well. My feelings for her will come as a surprise, even a shock; I was so careful to conceal them from her. With her family in such distress, all she may feel for me might be resentment for my interference or gratitude, or both—certainly an unsound foundation for marriage," he continued, somewhat dispiritedly. "I need to find her, determine whatever means by which I can alleviate her suffering, and then somehow make her fall in love with me."

"Mrs Collins did not discourage you from seeing her," said Fitzwilliam encouragingly.

"No, she urged me to go to her. She even said that she thought Elizabeth was not unaffected by our acquaintance last year."

"That is good news, then. There is hope for you yet."

Darcy smiled slightly. There *was* hope. He was still concerned over what he would find at Longbourn. He had spent long nights in his rooms at Rosings, once he was alone, ruminating over the Bennets' situation. With the Collinses' willingness to postpone taking possession of Longbourn until summer, the Bennets had had time to absorb the loss of their patriarch and to think of the future. A dire one indeed, if Elizabeth was thinking of a life in service! Any family, any gentleman, would value her intelligence and kindness, but she deserved so much more. He was so tired of thinking. He needed to see her, to take action to help her.

Today. I shall be in Hertfordshire this evening.

Darcy and his cousin sat quietly for long intervals, occasionally chatting about Anne or Georgiana, until Darcy remembered another thing that had been troubling him.

"Am I really so similar to Lady Catherine?"

His cousin snorted.

"No," he said consolingly upon seeing the apprehension on Darcy's face. "Not exactly. You have always been decidedly *conscious* of rank, as our aunt is. You have a tendency to judge others depending upon whether you consider them above or below you in society. But where Lady Catherine abuses the privileges of her rank, you have always seen *yours* as a great responsibility."

Fitzwilliam paused briefly, choosing his words with care. "However, I was concerned for you when you were willing to give up the only woman you have ever loved because of her connexions."

Darcy stared out the window, frowning ferociously, but did not answer.

"You know, within the family, you were considered a sensitive, emotional child. Much unlike me, of course," Fitzwilliam said lightly.

Darcy turned to stare at him, puzzled at the change in subject.

"My mother," he went on, "always felt that your parents' emphasis on your status was, in part, an attempt to curb your naturally passionate nature. Mama loved your parents, they were all that is good, but she always worried that in impressing upon you the importance of duty and self-control befitting your station, they were causing you to suppress your natural feelings too much. I find myself in agreement with her."

Darcy nodded slowly. Fitzwilliam smiled at him, leaning over and grasping his arm. "That is another great difference between you and Lady Catherine. You have the ability to love."

THAT AFTERNOON, Darcy's carriage drew up to Netherfield, and to his relief, the house was occupied. He was feeling no little embarrassment about the impropriety of arriving without notice, adding to his worry over what kind of reception he would receive. It had been several months since he had seen Bingley, but he hoped his friend had received the express he had sent to him in February.

The butler ushered both men into a small parlour and went looking for his master. Within a few minutes, Bingley stepped into the room, a wide smile on his face. His smile faded slightly when he saw the effects of the winter on his friend's countenance.

"Darcy, how glad I am to see you! You must not trouble yourself about visiting us without notice! You will always be welcome. Have you come from London?"

Darcy nodded, relieved at their reception. Despite the black armband Bingley wore over his coat sleeve, his friend's mood was far cheerier than when last he had seen him. Before he could reply, Fitzwilliam spoke up.

"We have come from Kent, where we were making our annual visit to Lady Catherine. Her parson is married to the former Miss Charlotte Lucas. She informed us of Mr Bennet's death, and we came as soon as we could to offer our condolences and assistance to the family. Is there anything we can do?"

Bingley's countenance sobered, and he invited the gentlemen to sit with him in his study. After they had settled themselves into armchairs by the fire, he began to describe the events of the previous month. He recounted how Hurst had learned of Mr Bennet's death at a business meeting. He described the mourning family and their dire circumstances, and how they had passed the winter. Finally, Darcy spoke.

"That is similar to what Mrs Collins told me. She said that the family has had an extremely traumatic time; that they must vacate Longbourn and are distressed financially. I wish to do whatever I can for them."

Bingley looked at his friend. "Darcy, I was on my way to Longbourn when I received your letter. I had already made up my mind to see if Miss Bennet would receive me, but I must tell you that your opinions on that subject meant a great deal to me. After the funeral, with the approval of her uncle Gardiner, I made her an offer of marriage, and I am most fortunate that she accepted it. Her feelings towards me had not changed, and she forgave me for leaving Netherfield so abruptly last November."

At this, Darcy shifted in his chair uncomfortably, but it was obvious that his friend had forgiven him, and had found his happiness. A slight smile appeared on his face. "That is wonderful—"

"Oho, Bingley, that is good news in the midst of all this sadness!" cried Fitzwilliam. "When is the wedding?"

Bingley beamed. "We were married almost a month ago! I cannot express to you how delighted I am to be married to my angel, and to take care of her and her family in their hour of need! It is all I could ever have wished for!"

"You are already married?" gasped Darcy in astonishment.

"Yes," said Bingley, his voice once more growing serious, "While the propriety of such a quick wedding is clearly debatable, once Jane and I discussed the situation, the needs of the family, and our longstanding attachment, it seemed the most natural thing in the world."

"What of *your* family?" asked Darcy. "Did you consult them?"

"Louisa and Hurst had been encouraging me all winter to visit Jane as soon as the weather would permit. They have become friends with Mrs Bennet's brother and sister-in-law, and wished to be of service to the family, and stayed here for several days, assisting the Bennets."

If Bingley noticed the sceptical expression on Darcy's face, he was too good to mention it as he continued. "Caroline, well, no doubt she will disapprove, but she has been staying with Baroness Riverton for months now, and given that she has not responded to any of Louisa's letters, we are not at all concerned with her opinions!"

Darcy felt as if the planet had shifted under his feet. While he had been confined at Pemberley, stewing in his own juices, apparently everyone else had been busy.

"Where is Mrs Bingley now?" he asked.

"At this moment, she is with her family at the dower house. We moved the family over there from Longbourn the week after the funeral. She will return shortly."

"Is the entire Bennet family living there?"

"Mrs Bennet and her three youngest daughters are there. Elizabeth is staying in London with her aunt and uncle for at least a few months."

Elizabeth is in London?

Darcy's face fell, and he made no attempt to disguise his deep disappointment. "She is not here?" he asked. He rose abruptly and walked to the window, his back to the two other gentlemen.

Bingley shook his head gravely. "She had the worst of it. She took a great deal of responsibility on her shoulders during her father's illness, and she was the closest of the daughters to him. She misses him terribly, and Mrs Bennet was cruel to her, blaming her for much of their situation. Elizabeth is deeply bereaved, well, truthfully, to the point where it is almost hard to recognise her. Her aunt and uncle decided that it would be best for her to be away from Meryton, and her mother, for a while."

Bingley's speculative gaze moved back over to his friend, still staring out the window. "Let us get you both settled into your rooms. There will be more time for talk after you have had a rest and dinner."

Though Darcy desperately wished to know more of the events of the past few weeks at Netherfield, he agreed with Bingley that a rest was needed. He required privacy to think about what he had already learned.

Once he was in his chambers, however, he found that he

could not relax. He took off his boots and coat, lay down on the bed, got up, paced, looked out the window, sat down, tried to read, and got up and paced some more. Finally, unable to concentrate on any task, he decided to go for a walk. There were still a few hours before dinner, and the day was clear.

He set out, every step reminding him of his time there the previous autumn. He wished more than anything that Elizabeth was there to walk alongside him. He smiled at the memory of her, standing at the door of Netherfield in her muddy petticoats, her eyes bright with determination and some defiance. He walked without intention, letting his feet take their own direction, but after a time realised that he was nearing Longbourn. Within minutes, the house came into view. There was no sign of activity, but the front door stood wide open. Darcy walked up to the house and looking around, saw no one. Casting a guilty glance about him to see if he was being observed, he stepped through the door.

THERE WAS INDEED someone at Longbourn, in the person of the housekeeper, Mrs Hill. She had come to air out the house, and to say goodbye to it, her home of over five and twenty years. She loved the house and the Bennet family, even her ofttimes difficult mistress. Most of the servants would stay at Longbourn and work for the Collinses, but Mrs Hill had decided to go with the Bennets to the dower house at Netherfield, and then wherever they would go after that. She liked Mrs Collins and had known her ever since she was little Charlotte Lucas, but she was also well acquainted with her insufferable husband, and refused to be in his employ.

She was in the kitchen garden when she glimpsed a tall figure striding towards the house, and came around the corner of the building just in time to see him step inside. She realised that the person was known to her. *That haughty man who was Mr Bingley's friend, what was his name? Mr Darcy! What is he doing here?* Such a respectable gentleman certainly was not up to any nonsense, but why would he go inside the house? Surely he knew the Bennets were gone?

She recalled an evening the Netherfield party had dined at Longbourn. The footmen had laughed whenever they came back into the kitchen after serving each course. Davy had hooted, "He could be eating straw for all the notice he is paying to the food!" That had rankled Cook, for it had been one of her best efforts. Mr Darcy had spent the entire evening staring at Miss Elizabeth. Hill had wondered if there would be not one, but two, announcements, but then the entire party had left Netherfield without so much as a by-your-leave, and were not heard from again until the evening a few weeks before, when Mr Bingley had pulled up to the front door covered in mud.

She decided to investigate. She knew every creaky board and squeaky hinge in the house, and so, slipping off her shoes, followed him in complete silence.

DARCY WALKED WITH SLOW, measured steps through the house, pausing in every room, remembering the few occasions he had been there before. He could see that the Bennets had removed some things, but most of the contents of the rooms were as he remembered them. The bonnets and shawls strewn about, the sheet music, and the sewing baskets were missing, and the house had a cold, impersonal look to it. It no longer seemed like a home. He stepped into the library and stood looking at the battered desk and the deep leather chair where Mr Bennet had spent the better part of his days. He noticed gaps in the shelves, and understood that Elizabeth had acted on Mrs Collins's advice and taken some books with her.

Moving to the bottom of the stairs, he suddenly had the sense that he was not alone. He stood absolutely still and listened, but heard nothing but the sound of swallows chirping under the eaves. After intently looking about him again, he began to climb.

When he came to the room that Jane and Elizabeth had shared since they were little girls, he knew it was theirs from the faint scent of their mingled perfumes. Mrs Bingley favoured lilac scent and Elizabeth always smelled like roses and spring air. He breathed deeply and sat down on one of the little beds.

Mrs Hill had followed him up the stairs in stealthy silence, and quickly slipped into the big linen closet, leaving the door slightly ajar. She stood in the dark of the closet, watching, her eyes wide. Mr Darcy sat on Miss Elizabeth's bed. He picked up her pillow and inhaled deeply. Then he buried his face in it, hugging it to his chest. He stood up with the pillow in his arms, deep in thought. After a few moments, he set the pillow gently down, squared his shoulders, and walked out of the room, down the stairs, and out of the house.

Hill quickly ran to the front bedroom and looked out of the window. Mr Darcy was walking slowly back down the lane in the direction of Netherfield. She shook her head in wonder. *Pride goeth before a fall. That poor man.*

She ran back to the little bedroom, snatched up Elizabeth's pillow, and then ran to the stables to retrieve the little brown cob she had ridden to the house earlier in the day. She had an errand to run, and trotted her horse off to Netherfield, taking the bridle path.

Fitzwilliam, too, had been unable to rest for more than half an hour. He left his chamber and sought out his host. He found Bingley still in his study, and knocked on the open door. "Ah," smiled Bingley, standing and gesturing him into the room. "Do come in. Where is Darcy?"

"I do not know, but I hope he is asleep in his room. He is a deeply unhappy man these days, and has not slept well in weeks, if not months."

"I noticed the change in his appearance the minute I laid eyes on him. He looks positively ill!" said Bingley with concern. "Is everything well at Pemberley? How is Miss Darcy?"

"Georgiana is well, and all is well at Pemberley, although they had a harrowing winter," replied Fitzwilliam. "No, Bingley, Darcy has one problem, and it is affecting him deeply. I do not know how much my cousin would wish for me to share on his behalf, but I know he thinks of you as one of his closest friends, and it does concern you as well. Do you recall how last December he told you that the reason he and your sisters removed from Netherfield was that they doubted the wisdom of your attachment to Miss Bennet?"

"How could I forget?" shuddered Bingley. "It was one of the worst days of my life."

"My cousin had convinced himself that the reason he wished to leave Hertfordshire was to prevent you from making a dreadful mistake. It was not until after many weeks of misery and forced introspection that he understood he was actually running away from his own growing attachment to Miss Elizabeth Bennet."

Bingley's face lit up. "I knew it!"

"Darcy is not a man accustomed to self-doubt. He has

always congratulated himself on his exemplary, well-ordered life," continued Fitzwilliam. "Miss Elizabeth Bennet has managed to shake my cousin's life to its foundations without even being in his presence. I hope I have the honour of meeting the lady soon."

Thinking back to that day, Bingley spoke thoughtfully. "To be truthful, if Caroline's had been the only opinion I had heard on the subject of love, I would have been sceptical, to say the least. I believed at the time that Darcy never made mistakes. I was completely taken in by his judgment, and was utterly anguished. I have always trusted his opinion. I still do, but I am also pleased to find that my dear friend is a mere mortal. You know, Colonel, Darcy sent me an express, and I received it just as I was leaving for Longbourn. He told me of his changed opinion and encouraged me to go to Jane. The tone of the letter was so...*desolate*, it made me wonder what had happened to him. Even his handwriting was uneven. At the point of reading his words, a picture of your cousin dancing with Miss Elizabeth at our ball popped into my mind. Jane and I have been speculating about it."

"Darcy is now intent upon pursuing Miss Bennet, if she will see him," said Fitzwilliam.

"He was obviously deeply disappointed to find that she is not here," agreed Bingley.

DARCY RETURNED to Netherfield as the glow of twilight was fading. His walk had calmed him somewhat, and he felt ready to be in company again. When he let himself in the side door, he was met by a footman who informed him that his cousin and Mr and Mrs Bingley were in the sitting room.

Jane Bingley was a goddess in black bombazine. The effects of her bereavement remained on her countenance, but

Darcy could also see the solace and joy she took in her husband's presence. She greeted Mr Darcy cordially; he walked to her and bowed over her hand.

"Mrs Bingley, I wish to express to you my profound sympathies on the loss of your father. "

"Thank you, Mr Darcy," she said, "On behalf of my family, I appreciate your taking the trouble to visit us."

"I only wish I had known sooner," Darcy replied with more feeling than he had intended. "I came as soon as I learned of his death. I am especially grieved to have missed your wedding."

"I am sorry too. But you are here now, and Charles and I are grateful, and most happy to see you."

Darcy hardly knew what to say, so humbled was he. Here was a marriage that he had done his best to prevent, and they still welcomed him with open arms.

Dinner was served shortly after Darcy's return to the house. Bingley kept the conversation light, catching up with news of his guests and their families. After dinner, they removed back to the sitting room, rather than to the more formal drawing room.

The four of them sat together, talking companionably for a while longer. At length, Mrs Bingley rose and said goodnight to her guests, and left the room. Her husband took his leave a few minutes later. The two remaining gentlemen sat silently in front of the fire for a few moments, but the strong emotions of the day had had an exhausting effect on Darcy as well, and he said goodnight to his cousin.

HE TOOK a candle and was making his way to his chamber, but stepped back when he saw his hosts in an embrace at the bottom of the stairs. Mrs Bingley was leaning on her husband,

and Darcy could see that her cheeks were wet. She had been so gracious that one could almost forget that she was still in a state of deep bereavement. Bingley murmured comforting words to his wife, and then kissing her, swept her up in his arms and carried her up the stairs.

Darcy stood still, looking after them, his hand unconsciously rising to rest on his heart. He had an unfamiliar, empty, hollow feeling. He did not recognise it at first, but then understood that it was envy.

He did not like feeling this way. He had never been envious of anyone in his life. He was not supposed to envy Bingley; *Bingley* was supposed to envy him. Yet Darcy now saw a lot to envy in his old friend.

Bingley was an uncomplicated man who was not afraid of his feelings. He was kind, amiable, and generous. He had literally come riding to the rescue of the Bennet family, providing them with a home, and no doubt, much needed income. He had done it all for love, and received love in return.

He had also quite taken the wind out of Darcy's sails.

Darcy could now add envy to his collection of new and unhappy sensations: doubt, anxiety, jealousy, worry, loneliness, humility. *How does one even begin to live like this?*

He walked the familiar corridors to his chambers, recalling that when he had previously stayed at Netherfield, he had spent several nights uncomfortably aware of Elizabeth sleeping only a few doors away. As he opened the door to his chamber, the faint scent of roses greeted him. He stood motionless for a moment, then set his candle on the bedside table and discovered its source. There on his bed lay the pillow that had been on Elizabeth's bed at Longbourn. He stared at it in utter disbelief.

Talbot appeared with his nightshirt, and helped him undress; the valet's carefully impassive face never once looked in the direction of the bed before he left the room without saying a word. Darcy climbed into bed, his hand reaching for the pillow, wondering if he had a guardian angel. He wrapped his arms around it, sighing with relief and pleasure. He fell into a deep sleep and slept well through the night.

CHAPTER 23

When Darcy entered the breakfast room the next morning, he found the Bingleys sitting side by side at the table with their heads together, planning the day. When they both looked up and smiled at him simultaneously, he was struck by what a handsome couple they made. *They were made for each other, you idiot.*

After filling his plate, he sat down across from them. "Now, Mr and Mrs Bingley, how may I be of service to you today?" he asked. "Of course, I would like to pay my respects to your family, Mrs Bingley."

"It might be appropriate to begin by visiting Mr Bennet in the churchyard," replied Bingley. "After our visit there, we can call on Mrs Bennet and the girls at the dower house."

"My mother would be honoured if you and Colonel Fitzwilliam would consent to have luncheon with the family," said Mrs Bingley.

"I would be delighted to renew my acquaintance with your

family," Darcy said, "and I am sure my cousin would be pleased to meet them."

Within a few minutes, Fitzwilliam had joined them. He filled his plate and sat down with a greeting to his hosts. Darcy and Bingley briefed him on the plans for the morning, and he readily agreed.

Less than an hour later, the three gentlemen were riding into the old churchyard at Longbourn, black armbands decorating their coat sleeves.

Darcy studied the ancient structure. "This church must be many centuries old," he marvelled.

"The church is Anglo-Saxon and the tower is Norman. The Longbourn estate and village themselves are almost as old," said Bingley. "There have been Bennets on this land for over four hundred years. Mr Gardiner showed Hurst and me some ancient family records kept at Longbourn. They list Bennets who were knights and went on the Crusades. The family can be traced back to the Conquest and beyond."

Darcy turned and stared at his friend. "Mr Gardiner? Do you mean the gentleman at the theatre? He was here?"

"Oh—you did not know! Mr Gardiner is the brother of Mrs Bennet. He and his wife were here for more than a week after Mr Bennet's death. Through their business partnership, the Gardiners have become particular friends with Louisa and Hurst. It is through Hurst that I discovered that Jane's father had died, and that is when I returned to Longbourn. Hurst did not realise that Gardiner was Jane's uncle until they informed him that they were going to Hertfordshire to care for their relatives. That was when he discovered the connexion."

"Mr Gardiner is the uncle in trade? The uncle in Cheapside? The Hursts are friends with them?" Darcy repeated helplessly. Had *all* his assumptions been incorrect?

"Yes, they are a delightful couple," enthused Bingley.

"Louisa and Hurst have been most fortunate with their investment in Mr Gardiner's company. It has been extremely lucrative, and they have made two dear friends as well. They spend time together quite often. The Gardiners are acquainted with many fashionable people in town."

Darcy, although mired in his own thoughts, saw Fitzwilliam's interest was captured. "Really! Are you invested with Mr Gardiner's company as well?"

"Yes, recently, and I am already glad I did."

Fitzwilliam smiled. "I should like to know more about this, later of course, at your convenience."

Darcy was still struggling to piece together the events of the last few weeks at Longbourn, and feeling more behindhand by the minute, as they left the church and walked on the new spring grass to the crypt. They entered, and Darcy looked about him, impressed by the Bennet family genealogy. He was silent and thoughtful on the ride back to Netherfield, rebuking himself for the erroneous conclusions he had drawn about the family.

Once on the Netherfield estate, they returned to the manor only long enough to leave their horses at the stables. Their host led them down a tree-lined lane to a pretty house with a cottage-like appearance, built from the same pale golden limestone as the main house. As they neared the front entrance, Mrs Bingley and Miss Catherine emerged to greet them. Bingley's eyes glowed as he took his wife's hands and kissed them, while her sister grinned and rolled her eyes. Bingley laughed at his new sister and introduced her to the colonel.

Miss Catherine curtseyed gracefully and held out her hand to Fitzwilliam and then to Darcy. "It is a pleasure to see you again, Mr Darcy," she said. "You honour us with your visit. Pray let me take you in to see our mother."

Darcy had by now passed astonishment and was well on

his way to stupefaction. He had described the raucous, out-of-control behaviour of the two youngest Bennet sisters to his cousin and now here was Miss Catherine, a model of decorum.

The three gentlemen entered the house and were conducted to a pleasant sitting room where Mrs Bennet, Miss Mary, and Miss Lydia were sitting quietly together. Mrs Bennet and Miss Lydia were sewing, and Miss Mary was writing a letter.

All three daughters seemed older and more mature, more like young ladies instead of girls. Their trauma had had its effect, but there was something more. Darcy took in the scene of domestic refinement—a mother and three pretty girls in full mourning—and compared it with his memories of only a few months before: a chaotic household full of raucous conversation about balls, officers, and finding rich husbands.

DARCY COULD PERCEIVE THE ALTERATIONS, but not the underlying experiences that had promoted them. He could not know that Catherine's self-confidence grew as her manners became more assured, or that Mary, having become closer to her sisters, no longer felt the pressure to distinguish herself with affected manners and conspicuous accomplishments. As a result, her conversation and musical abilities had improved, and her plain face looked relaxed and almost attractive.

He could see that Miss Lydia was still struggling to curb her unruly tongue, but did not know her eagerness to exhibit her much-improved self to 'certain' people in Meryton. Mr Hurst had told her his motto was 'Living well is the best revenge', and Lydia had taken it as her own.

Though still fragile, Mrs Bennet had found a tenuous calm since Jane and Bingley had married and brought a modicum of security to her life. She rose to greet her son-in-law warmly, but Darcy was received with cool civility.

To Mrs Bennet, Mr Darcy was still the man who had insulted her daughter at the assembly, never mind that she herself had treated that same daughter with bitterness and cruelty for months. Bingley introduced Colonel Fitzwilliam, and Mrs Bennet invited the gentlemen to sit down for refreshments. Darcy expressed his condolences to Mrs Bennet, and she communicated her gratitude. "Hill and Jenks will have luncheon ready shortly, gentlemen," she said.

"Did your housekeeper and cook remain with you, Mrs Bennet? That is indeed fortunate for you. I remember the fine table you set when I dined at Longbourn," said Darcy.

Mrs Bennet's expression softened, and as she left the room to confer with Hill, it appeared she could find it in her heart to forgive Mr Darcy.

Bingley recalled that he wanted Darcy to advise him about a faulty culvert near the house, and he and Mrs Bingley walked him back to the road to have a look. Fitzwilliam waved them off, claiming he was a soldier, not a steward. He would much rather take the opportunity to sit with three pretty girls. "How do you like the dower house, ladies?" he asked kindly.

After a few minutes of discourse, it was clear that underneath their grief, the Bennet sisters remained a group of unusually high-spirited young women. The conversation flowed almost immediately. Before Darcy and the Bingleys returned, Fitzwilliam heard humorous accounts of his cousin's obvious disapproval of Meryton, as well as his ill-timed remark about Elizabeth's appearance at the assembly where they had all become acquainted.

Laughing, he said, "It has been an age since I have enjoyed a conversation so much! How on earth did your father deal with you lively young ladies?" The room went silent, the three girls looking at each other for a long, poignant moment.

"Most of the time, he did not," Miss Mary finally said quietly, "until his illness, when we all became closer to him."

After a brief pause, Fitzwilliam leaned forward towards them. "That makes me very sorry for him," he said feelingly. The conversation began again and recovered its animated flow until the trio returned from their drainage inspection; Darcy warily eyed the expressions of amusement shared by his cousin and the three younger Bennet sisters when he entered the room

AFTER A DELICIOUS AND COMFORTABLE MEAL, the gentlemen made their farewells. Feeling relaxed and particularly well-fed, they strolled leisurely back to Netherfield in thoughtful silence. After some minutes Fitzwilliam spoke. "What lovely young ladies! From how you have described their past behaviour, it appears that their father's illness must have forced them to grow up quickly."

"Yes, there has been quite a substantial change in the daughters, and even with their mother!" agreed Darcy wonderingly.

"It is my opinion that the younger girls will do well. I do not know that I would have said that last November," agreed Bingley.

The gentlemen arrived back at the manor house. Mrs Bingley, lingering with her family as her mother had desired a further conversation, joined them shortly after.

AS THEY SETTLED themselves in the sitting room, the butler announced Colonel Forster. "What a pleasant surprise," said

Bingley, as the gentlemen rose. "To what do we owe the honour of your visit?"

"Bingley, it is always good to see you. But I confess today that I have come to see Colonel Fitzwilliam and Mr Darcy," said Colonel Forster with an apologetic smile.

"I had been intending to speak with you as well, Forster, so this is a happy coincidence," said Fitzwilliam. He saluted, then shook Forster's hand. "How did you know that we were here?"

"I heard of your presence from one of the shopkeepers, who had it from a farmer who saw you riding this morning. This is a small community, and visitors are always noticed around here."

"Now that you are here, what can we do for you?"

"We had been dealing with a junior officer over the winter who had become something of a problem," he began. "Initially, he seemed quite the gentleman, and his charming manner won over his fellow officers and the townspeople. It started gradually with the usual; gambling, intoxication, dereliction of duty, but as the winter progressed, his behaviour became criminal. He was in debt to the local merchants, swindled some young enlisted men, and even tried to abduct the innkeeper's daughter. He was put in the brig until a court martial could be held. One of my junior officers recently informed me that he has claimed some relationship to you, Fitzwilliam, and to you as well, Mr Darcy."

The cousins exchanged glances, and Darcy's face paled, his mouth forming a grim, angry line.

Fitzwilliam said, "His name would not happen to be George Wickham, would it? Are we expected to bail him out of some trouble, Forster?"

"No, no, nothing like that. In fact, it is too late to do

anything for Wickham except wish him bon voyage. As of a week ago, he is on his way to Botany Bay."

"What?" both gentlemen exclaimed.

Fitzwilliam shook his head slowly. "So Wickham's maliciousness finally caught up with him. Unbelievable."

"Believe it. The court martial stripped him of his commission and sentenced him to transportation," said Colonel Forster. "He will not be troubling anyone in Meryton, or England, again."

"What a relief!" cried Fitzwilliam. "He has been a problem for Darcy for years. What say you, Cousin?"

Darcy's expression of astonishment faded to sadness. After a moment, he spoke. "It would have grieved my father deeply to think that something like this could happen. I also feel regret for my childhood playfellow. He grew from a happy, boisterous boy to a dissolute, conniving man. The person he became wanted only to use others for his own benefit." His eyes focused on something miles away, but then he smiled slightly. "Yes, it is a great relief!"

"When I became aware of the connexion, I thought you might wish to be informed," said Colonel Forster, who then refused the offer of refreshments, excusing himself to go back to his headquarters. "The regiment has orders to remove to Brighton for the summer months. We have already been delayed by the court martial and I do not want the preparations to fall farther behind. Perhaps you could join the officers for dinner this evening, Colonel." He bowed to the company and saluted Fitzwilliam. "Do not go to any trouble, Bingley, I know my way out," he said with a smile as he left the room.

After he departed, Mrs Bingley spoke. "We were unaware of the court martial! After Papa became ill, we were almost completely housebound, but we did hear that Mr Wickham was wearing out his welcome in Meryton rather quickly. Lizzy said she had tired of him before Christmas!"

At that, Darcy felt some of the tension he had been carrying around for months evaporate.

FITZWILLIAM TURNED TO HIS COUSIN. "I know you wish to travel on to London as soon as possible, but it is too late to leave today, so I will take Forster up on his invitation. The night will be clear and a moonlight ride from the encampment would suit me very well."

"Of course. It sounds like an enjoyable evening," Darcy answered. He *was* becoming increasingly anxious to get to London. He was relieved to have been welcomed by the Bingleys and the Bennets, but he had come to see Elizabeth. Her absence had been a profound disappointment, and the descriptions of her ordeal had greatly upset him. He would have to wait one more day to see her.

"I regret that your visit must be so short, Mr Darcy," exclaimed Mrs Bingley.

Her husband joined in, adding, "Of course it is too late to be starting for London today. Pray stay with us at least until tomorrow!"

"Yes, and you may be able to see Mr and Mrs Hurst," said Mrs Bingley. "They were so kind to us after my father's death! Louisa sat with my mother and assisted my aunt with our mourning clothes. She even helped arrange the shoulder feast. Gilbert supervised the work on the dower house and helped my family move. Once we were settled in, they took some time to travel since the weather has been so pleasant. They said they had long wished for a second wedding trip, and we expect their return any time now."

Fitzwilliam's eyebrows rose in disbelief. "I must own that

I am surprised that Hurst would go to such great lengths to help anybody, much less someone not of his own family."

Bingley chuckled. "Hurst is a changed man. With Caroline staying with friends over the past few months, he and Louisa have become much happier together. One would think they were in the first flush of love themselves. They are, of course, on intimate terms with the Gardiners, and now with our marriage, they think of the Bennets as family."

"After the funeral, when we all sat together and discussed the future of the family as a whole and individually," he continued, "Louisa offered some guidance in the manner of selecting masters, and what the girls will be expected to learn. My mother-in-law," he added, looking apologetically at his wife and reaching for her hand, "is unable to take responsibility for the girls' education herself. Both Kitty and Lydia have matured a great deal over the last few months, but we felt that they should have the opportunity to broaden their education and acquire a bit of polish, shall we say."

"And Miss Mary?" asked Darcy. "I am sure she would have wished to study under a music master."

Mrs Bingley smiled. "Since Mary is nineteen, my aunt and uncle thought she might find a stay in town more beneficial. They have asked her to stay with them in London come autumn, and she will be able to study with a music master and other tutors. She is happily looking forward to it."

Darcy took a breath, eager—nay, desperate—to ask about Elizabeth, but the words did not come. What of Elizabeth? What were her plans? Mrs Collins had said she was planning to seek employment, but surely with Bingley as her brother, she would not need to. As a member of Bingley's household, she could live as a lady.

No sooner had that thought appeared, than he realised that Elizabeth could never be content as Bingley's dependent. He could picture her chin rising mulishly at the very idea. Not trusting his voice to remain level, he kept silent.

AS FITZWILLIAM WAS DINING with the officers, there were only three for dinner at Netherfield. Darcy spoke little as the Bingleys carried the conversation. After dinner, they settled back into the sitting room. Finally, Bingley said, "You are quiet this evening, Darcy."

"Yes," he answered slowly. "Actually, there is something I would like to speak to both of you about," he said, raising his head to look directly at the couple.

Their fleeting exchange of glances put Darcy on his guard. *What are they thinking?*

Mrs Bingley's smile was kind. "Of course. How may we help you?"

"How is your sister, Miss Elizabeth? Do you think she would welcome any visitors? I should like to renew our acquaintance and extend my condolences to her personally."

Mrs Bingley's eyes met his gravely, her brow slightly puckered. "Lizzy needs time to recover, to let others care for her for a change. She shouldered the heaviest share of responsibilities during my father's illness and seems unable to shed them. She still insists on finding employment, but my aunt and uncle have persuaded her to put that off at least until the summer. My sister values self-reliance, and does not wish to be dependent on anyone." She paused for a moment. "It would be helpful for Lizzy to have some visitors. According to my aunt, she never leaves the house, and rarely leaves her room."

"She does not go outdoors? She does not go walking? That is completely unlike her!"

"Yes, it is, but she is not at all herself, Mr Darcy. Perhaps if you visited her, she might consent to go walking with you."

"Yes, and I do not think Elizabeth has seen the British Museum yet, has she, my dear?" suggested Bingley. "That might be a pleasant distraction for her, and a suitable pastime for a lady in mourning. You are right about her walks though." He began to relate the memory of how he had found Elizabeth shivering outside the day before the funeral but his voice faded as Darcy grew visibly distressed.

"I greatly anticipate seeing her again," Darcy said, with more feeling than he had intended. "That is, I have been concerned about her. Since your father's death, of course. And through the winter. That is to say, the winter was difficult for everyone, but..."

He looked up to see Mrs Bingley looking at him with compassion, and Bingley grinning with amusement. *Oh, blast, might as well come out with it.* "I wish to see Miss Elizabeth again, to spend time with her and pay her the attentions she deserves. Your sister is precious to me, and I wish to help her regain her spirit. Her joy. If she is willing...if she thinks I am suitable to the task, I wish to court her. Marry her." Darcy trailed off quietly, suddenly overly conscious of exposing himself. "You must think me a great fool."

Bingley moved near and clapped Darcy on the shoulder. "To be a fool is one thing, to be a fool for love is something else altogether. Believe me, I know the feeling well. You should not be embarrassed or afraid of your feelings," Bingley said, as if he could read Darcy's mind. "I have been a fool, and now I am a fool for love," he continued, stepping over to his wife. He took her hand and kissed it tenderly. "It is a much higher calling."

Mrs Bingley gazed at him, her countenance calm as always, but her heart was in her eyes. "My own dear fool."

Darcy did not have the slightest idea how to react to this. He was saved by the butler opening the door and announcing

Mr and Mrs Hurst. He had not seen the couple since that evening at the theatre in December when Caroline had made him the laughingstock of the *ton*. He rose to greet them, trying not to stare. Here were two people he had been acquainted with for years, entirely transformed. Hurst had an easy, relaxed smile on his face as he spoke genially with the Bingleys. Mrs Hurst was also smiling and warm, vivacious and laughing. They greeted him cordially and he reciprocated, a bemused expression on his face

"Darcy! Good to see you, old man! What a terrible winter you must have had! On your way to London, are you?"

Mrs Hurst smiled up at him. "How nice to see you again! We wondered how you survived the winter up in the wilds of Derbyshire. How is Miss Darcy?"

Darcy found himself smiling back before conversation was launched about the long winter, their families, and travels. Apparently having Miss Bingley absent from their home had contributed greatly to their marital felicity. In fact, he realised, everyone he had encountered here was in good spirits and creating their own happiness. He hoped he would soon be doing the same with Elizabeth; if he could help her recover, if she would have him, if they could find their way together.

CHAPTER 24

The morning of Darcy's return to London, he rose before the sun and, not waiting for Talbot, dressed quickly. He had an important errand to attend to, but had not shared it even with Fitzwilliam. *Gad, if he knew, he would never let me forget it!* Finding a stable boy up and about, he had him saddle a horse, and then cantered down the road towards the old church. Upon arriving there, he dismounted and began walking towards the crypt, but then stopped abruptly when he realised that he was in the wrong place.

He again mounted his horse and turned in the direction of Longbourn. The sun had now cleared the horizon, sunbeams beginning to move through the trees. He knew that the house would likely be locked this time but had to try nevertheless. He pulled up at the front door, dismounted and tied the reins around a post. Raising his hand to the knocker, he felt the door move. It was unlocked.

He again stepped into the empty house, but did not wander. He went directly to the library. Entering the half-lit room, he took a seat opposite the old leather chair. Self-consciously, but with a deep desire to do things properly, he spoke aloud into the empty room. "Mr Bennet, I wish to marry your daughter Elizabeth, if she will have me, and I am most humbly asking your blessing." The room echoed slightly with his voice and then all was silent.

Darcy felt like an idiot. What on earth had he been expecting? Embarrassed, he rose from the chair to leave. As he did, dappled light from the rising sun shone through the window and moved over the bookshelves. Something white at the back of an empty shelf caught the corner of his eye, and he went to pick it up. It was a crumpled handkerchief. He gently smoothed it out, seeing the embroidered initials E.B. It was Elizabeth's! Darcy carefully tucked it into his inner coat pocket. His feelings of foolishness gone, he spoke again. "Thank you, Mr Bennet! I swear to you I will make her happy!" He left the house and rode back to Netherfield.

AFTER HANDING his horse off to the same stable boy, he made his way to the breakfast room, hoping to catch Bingley alone. It was not his host in the room, however, but Mrs Bingley. He stood on the threshold, wavering, but then she saw him and greeted him. He had no choice but to come in. He mechanically put some food on his plate, even though he had no appetite, and sat down with his hostess.

"You have excellent weather for your journey today, Mr Darcy. I am sure the roads are much improved as well."

After several minutes she continued, "I wonder if I might ask a great favour, sir. I have written a letter to my sister Elizabeth. Might I possibly send it to London with you?" Like

Mrs Collins, she was giving him a pretext to call on Elizabeth.

"Of course, I would be happy to deliver it myself," he answered. "Mrs Collins also entrusted me with a letter to your sister." He paused, and then decided he might as well dive in. "Mrs Bingley, do you believe your sister will be willing to see me?"

"My sister is suffering a deep melancholy. I believe it to be something more than grief that afflicts her, but I have not been able to understand the depths of her sorrow, and she does not share them with any of us. I do believe that if there is anyone who can help her, it is you."

Darcy was beyond surprise. A mixture of hope and fear rose in his chest. "You believe *I* can help her? I would like nothing more, but Mrs Bingley, I had the distinct impression last November that Miss Elizabeth found me, er...disagreeable." He regarded her uncertainly.

"I believe that you and Lizzy got off on the wrong foot during your stay here last November. I have reason to believe that her opinion of you has improved."

She was quiet for a moment, considering her words. "Mr Darcy, I am going to share something with you that I have not even told Charles." She hesitated. "I have deliberated much on the wisdom, not to mention the propriety, of sharing this with you. It is something especially private, but it does concern you, in a way. I have decided to tell you because I believe it may reassure you as you seek to become reacquainted with my sister. I also find that I have complete trust in you."

Darcy was riveted, staring at his hostess.

She returned his gaze and said gently, "Mr Darcy, Lizzy dreams about you."

For a moment he could scarcely breathe. Finally, he rasped, "She...dreams about *me*? How can you know this?"

Mrs Bingley leaned slightly forward, her voice low and confidential. "She talks to you in her sleep. It began over the winter. Lizzy was under such strain and truly had no one she could go to for comfort. It is my belief that somehow she understood that you would be such a person, had you been there, and that she could go to you with her troubles. I believe it was a source of some comfort to her."

She smiled a little slyly at him. "She always sounded happy to see you, at least. But I must also caution you that Lizzy does not know that I overheard some of her dream conversations with you. I do not know how she would feel if she knew. For all her levity, she is a deeply private person, sir, a trait which I believe you share. I have always seen a great similarity in the turn of your minds."

"Yes," he said thoughtfully, "We neither of us perform to strangers." He looked earnestly at her. "I will keep your confidence, of course. I do not know that I will ever be able to express my gratitude to you for trusting me with it."

Mrs Bingley met his eyes with an intensity and earnestness he had never seen on her before. "It is I who must express gratitude to you. Mr Darcy, if you can help Lizzy come out of her melancholia, my family and I will be forever in your debt."

BY MIDMORNING the Bingleys and the Hursts had left for the dower house. Darcy and Fitzwilliam followed in their carriage to take their leave of the ladies on their way to London.

The two cousins sat in meditative silence in the carriage, each reflecting upon the events of the last few days. They expected to reach London by the middle of the afternoon. Darcy had made up his mind to stop at Darcy House only long enough to freshen up. Though an unannounced visit to

Gracechurch Street so late in the day might be considered ill-mannered, he simply could not wait any longer. The last time he had made the same journey, he had been running away from Elizabeth. Now he was running after her, and the carriage could not move fast enough.

He patted his coat pocket, feeling the letters he had promised to deliver; two to Elizabeth from Mrs Bingley and Mrs Collins and one for Mrs Gardiner from Mrs Hurst. He felt like a courier. The three ladies wished to send communications where they were needed, but it was patently obvious that each of them wanted to give him a pretext to call on Elizabeth.

He thought back to their stay at Netherfield the previous autumn. Had he really been that transparent? Had half the guests at the ball observed that he was falling head over ears for Elizabeth? It was all extremely mortifying, yet he felt warmed and humbled that Elizabeth's family and friends wished him to succeed.

His mind returned to the disturbing tale Bingley had related, of Elizabeth shivering in the cold. He frowned at the mental image of Bingley lifting her in his arms and putting her on his horse. He himself had only ever touched her hand, and through two layers of gloves!

"Why the frown, Darcy?"

He looked up, startled, to see his cousin watching him. He related the story to him.

"But is it not fortunate that Bingley happened along?" Fitzwilliam asked, his eyebrows raised. "She could have made herself ill! Not to mention, she was wrapped in Bingley's greatcoat!"

"Yes, yes, I know that. My reason fails me when it comes to Elizabeth."

"Your entire acquaintance with Miss Bennet seems to have thrown you off balance, causing you to say and do things you ordinarily would not. Even the first time you laid eyes on her, judging from the story her sisters tell," said Fitzwilliam. "I heard an excessively diverting account of your behaviour at the Meryton assembly, where you found Miss Bennet 'tolerable, but not handsome enough' to tempt you."

Darcy gaped at his cousin in horror. "She heard me say that?"

"That she did," said Fitzwilliam, "and apparently found it highly amusing. She must be quite an exceptional girl."

Darcy put his head in his hands. *Good God!* Elizabeth must indeed have been under a terrible strain if she had dreamt of him with any kind of regard at all.

"Darcy." His cousin's voice held a note of command. Darcy looked up. "Show her your true self. The person you are with us, your family. Show her the loving brother, the caring friend, the sensitive man. That is who you really are." He flashed a grin, a return to his teasing aspect. "Why else do you think we put up with you?"

HAVING ALREADY SPENT much of the day in a carriage, Darcy elected to ride to Gracechurch Street. He had quickly bathed, shaved, and changed his clothes, and now the crisp cadence of his horse's hooves helped him centre his mind on his mission. He again checked his coat pocket for the letters he was delivering, a corner of his mouth turning up slightly. *A courier, indeed.*

Following the direction given him by Hurst, he found himself in front of a handsome town house, uncomfortably aware that only a few weeks ago, he would have not even considered coming into this part of town. He tied up his horse, and upon reaching the door, closed his eyes and took a deep breath. "Smile and be amiable, Darcy," he said to himself, and reached for the knocker.

The butler answered and bade him enter. He invited him to wait in a small side room and went to find his master. Darcy shifted from foot to foot, and then paced nervously, unable even to sit down.

Within a few minutes, Mr Gardiner hurried into the room. "Mr Darcy! This is a happy surprise! Welcome to our home!" Darcy bowed and shook Mr Gardiner's outstretched hand.

"It is a pleasure to see you again, Mr Gardiner. I apologise for any inconvenience caused by my unanticipated visit. I have just come from Netherfield today. I have some letters to deliver to Miss Bennet, as well as one for your wife from Mrs Hurst."

"Ah," said Mr Gardiner sadly, "so you have been caught up on all the family news."

"I have, sir, and may I offer my deepest condolences."

Mr Gardiner bowed. "Thank you, sir. And your visit is not inconvenient in any way. We are honoured. Come into the parlour and take some refreshment."

Darcy followed Mr Gardiner through the gracious and elegant home, a modern town house built on a smaller scale than those in Mayfair. The décor was a deft combination of sophistication and comfort. Mrs Gardiner had excellent taste indeed. The two men entered the parlour where she was sitting. Mrs Gardiner, though in black, was dressed in the same understated elegance he had noticed when they had been introduced.

She rose to meet their guest. "Mr Darcy, how delightful to see you again! Welcome to our home!"

"Mrs Gardiner, the pleasure is mine. I am deeply sorry to be calling upon you in your mourning, but I have a letter for you from Mrs Hurst, and some letters for Miss Bennet as well."

Darcy felt his hostess studying him. He knew she was an intelligent lady from their conversation at the theatre. His expression was polite, as was hers, but he thought it likely she saw right through him.

"Elizabeth is upstairs. I shall let her know that she has a visitor." Mrs Gardiner rang for tea, and then sent a maid to fetch her niece.

A short time later Elizabeth walked into the parlour. When Darcy turned to greet her, she stopped in her tracks, her eyes widening in surprise. He stepped over to her and bowed over her hand, hoping she could not hear his heart hammering in his chest.

He was unnerved and shaken at her appearance. Bingley had not exaggerated the effects of her grief. He arranged his face into a smile, hoping that she had not seen his dismay. As he straightened, their eyes met for several seconds.

Gathering himself, he was the first to speak. "Miss Bennet," he said gently, "I have just come from Netherfield. I have a letter for you from Mrs Bingley, and one from Mrs Collins as well. Most of all, I came to express my deepest sympathy to you. I was distressed and saddened to hear of your father's death. Is there anything at all that I may do for you?"

CHAPTER 25

Elizabeth fought to hide her emotions. She had known she might encounter Mr Darcy occasionally since he was Charles's dear friend, but she had never expected him to seek her out. Indeed, once she had understood how wrong she had been about him, and by extension how rudely she had behaved towards him, she had expected him to actively avoid her. Yet here he was, looking at her with concern and offering what appeared to be heartfelt condolences.

She looked up at him and saw sympathy on his face, and perhaps some uneasiness. *Of course, he is out of his element here in Cheapside.*

Clearly he had changed since their last encounter. He was thinner, and his face, while not precisely gaunt, had lines and hollows that she had never noticed before. They made him look a little sad. Certainly there were no traces of the haughty and severe countenance she had come to know the previous year. What could have happened? Had he been ill? Whatever it was, he was not the same. But neither was she. Nothing was the same.

"Thank you most kindly, Mr Darcy." Elizabeth made her way to a sofa and sat down. "It is a pleasure to see you again."

Mr Gardiner gestured Mr Darcy to take the seat next to Elizabeth, and he complied with alacrity. She was relieved that he did not look at her, and she, too, kept her gaze on her uncle.

"How did you cope with our severe winter, Mr Darcy?" he asked. "You live in the north, I understand? It was much worse there, I believe."

"My estate is in Derbyshire, and yes, it was the worst winter in living memory. The cold was extreme, and we were utterly buried in snow. It felt as if I continually had a shovel in my hand for more than two months. Everyone, including the servants, my tenants—even my younger sister—worked to make sure every family was kept warm and well fed."

Mr Gardiner nodded. "An impressive effort, sir."

Elizabeth listened silently, her eyes averted from Mr Darcy, wondering at the picture he presented of himself and Miss Darcy working in concert with everyone at Pemberley to ensure their well-being, and marvelling at the idea of Mr Darcy shovelling snow.

"I am familiar with Pemberley, Mr Darcy," said her aunt. "I spent part of my childhood in Lambton."

Just then refreshments were brought in, and over tea and biscuits, Aunt Gardiner and Mr Darcy spoke of the neighbourhood near Lambton, discovering several mutual acquaintances.

To his relief, Darcy felt himself relaxing in the company of the Gardiners, his usual reticence subsiding slightly. While he was enjoying the conversation, he could not keep his eyes from Elizabeth. She was subdued and seemingly distracted, offering little in conversation unless she was addressed directly. He had noticed as she crossed the room how stiffly she moved, so unlike the light and graceful step that had danced through his dreams. She was thinner and pale. There were dark circles under her eyes, which were mostly downcast.

But it was what was missing within those eyes that was most distressing. Darcy had spent the winter envisioning Elizabeth's eyes: bright, sparkling, expressive, laughing, filled with spirit and intelligence. They were still a beautiful deep brown, but flat and dull. The light, the spark, was gone. His worried gaze returned to her again and again.

Darcy reached into his pocket and drew out the letters, handing one to Mrs Gardiner and two to Elizabeth. She eyed the letter from Hunsford with curiosity. "Where did you meet Mrs Collins, sir? Was she visiting in Meryton?"

Pleased that she had addressed him directly, he gave her a small smile. "My cousin, Colonel Fitzwilliam, and I make an annual Easter visit to Hunsford to visit our aunt, Lady Catherine de Bourgh, and attend to estate business for her. I was pleasantly surprised to find Mrs Collins there. I had not known that she and Mr Collins were married. She provided me with intelligence on Hertfordshire, including the sad news of your family," he said in a kindly voice. "We concluded our business at Rosings as quickly as we could and travelled to Meryton to offer our condolences and assistance. Mr and Mrs Bingley made us welcome at Netherfield. I was pleased to discover that they were married, but deeply regret missing their wedding."

Elizabeth averted her eyes to hide her confusion. Mr Darcy had travelled to Meryton out of concern for her family? She could make no sense of the idea, then realised guiltily that he was still speaking.

"Miss Bennet, how have you been spending your time in London?"

"Oh, I have been...helping my aunt with my young cousins," replied Elizabeth vaguely, looking down at her hands.

"Unfortunately, my niece has been somewhat confined to the house," said Mrs Gardiner, who was carefully attending to their dialogue. "I am sure she misses walking out as she used to do."

"Miss Bennet, could I persuade you to accompany me on a walk? I saw a pretty little park just a short distance from here today. The weather has been so fine, it would be a pity not to see the spring flowers there."

As Elizabeth began to offer a polite demurral, her aunt spoke up. "What a lovely idea, Mr Darcy! I think some fresh air would be rather beneficial, do you not agree, Lizzy?"

Elizabeth was on the spot. She did not want to go walking with Mr Darcy. She knew he was just offering out of politeness. But to refuse out of hand would be rude, just another in the succession of discourtesies she had dealt him. She realised she had to accept, and oddly, just for an instant, felt a sense of relief.

"Yes, Mr Darcy, I should like to accompany you," said Elizabeth, pinning a semblance of a smile onto her face.

"Would tomorrow afternoon be acceptable, Miss Bennet?"

Why not? Then Mr Darcy will have done the polite thing and he can be done with me.

"Yes, sir, I shall look forward to it."

LATER THAT EVENING, after dinner, the Gardiners sat together discussing the events of the day. "Louisa writes that they will soon be returning to town. She suggested the names of a few masters and spoke with the girls about it." She handed the letter to her husband and smiled up at him. "Jane slipped a note in with Louisa's letter. She tells us that Mr Darcy wishes to help Lizzy recover from her melancholia."

Gardiner, with raised eyebrows, took the letter from his wife and skimmed it briefly. "Well, perhaps he will succeed where we have failed. We have scarcely been able to interest her in leaving her room, and he has already persuaded her to go out walking. But I was under the impression that they disliked one another."

"Jane and Charles believe otherwise, my dear. They are convinced that Lizzy and Mr Darcy were rather attracted to each other last November, but that they got off to a bad start. I also had a sense that he admired her from Lizzy's letters last autumn." She paused briefly and continued. "Do you remember meeting Mr Darcy at the theatre last year? Does not he look rather ill in comparison?"

He reflected for a moment. "I did think he looked thinner, and tired perhaps. They did have a terrible winter in the north, you know," he said, stifling a yawn. "Let us see what tomorrow brings. Then we will be able to further our acquaintance with Mr Darcy."

CHAPTER 26

That gentleman was sitting in his study at Darcy House, describing his visit to Gracechurch Street to his cousin. "She seems to be utterly vanquished," Darcy said anxiously. "I have always known Elizabeth to have an inner fire, a spark. I could always see it in her eyes. But now it seems to have been completely extinguished." He shook his head. "I was not there when she most needed solace —I had no proper role in her life then. But I will bring her back. I have no idea how to go about it, but I will figure it out along the way."

He needed solitude to think, and needed his cousin to conclude his visit. Determined to spend his evening—if not the rest of his days—discerning how to improve the spirits of the woman he loved, Darcy changed the subject and asked after the health of his aunt and uncle.

"My parents are well. However," he said, his voice taking on an edge, "I told them that no one had ever informed Anne that she had inherited Rosings. That is concerning to my father. There is no love lost between him and Lady Catherine, as you know. He does not trust her. If Anne dies before Lady Catherine, and there is no will, Rosings will go to our aunt."

Fitzwilliam sipped his brandy. "We also discussed the state of Anne's health. My mother has been trying to get Lady Catherine to permit Anne to come to London to see her physician for years." He paused. "I will be driving to Rosings again in a few days to fetch Georgiana. My father has decided to accompany me, and to bring Anne back with us as well, for a visit."

Darcy's countenance eased, and he smiled. "Anne would love that. I wish you every success with your mission."

THE BREEZE WAS STILL COOL, but the sun was shining brightly the following afternoon when Darcy arrived at Gracechurch Street. He paused momentarily on the doorstep, took a few deep breaths, adjusted his neckcloth, squared his shoulders, and raised the knocker. He was again admitted by a footman. Mrs Gardiner came downstairs to the entrance hall and greeted him warmly, informing him that Elizabeth would be down directly.

Seconds later, she appeared at the top of the stairs, completely in black, tying the ribbons of her bonnet under her chin. Darcy's heart skipped a beat as he watched her descend, although she kept her eyes downcast and did not meet his gaze. As she reached the bottom step, he stepped forward.

"Miss Bennet," he said softly, bowing slightly, and she finally raised her eyes to meet his.

"Mr Darcy," she answered, with a curtsey.

"The park is only about half a mile away. Shall we walk from here?" he asked gently.

"Yes, that would be agreeable."

They left the house through the front door, and for a few moments, she appeared dazed, blinking in the bright sunshine. He offered her his arm, which after a brief hesitation, she took. They walked in silence for a while, each of them seemingly at a loss for words.

With a deep breath to steady himself, Darcy rose to the occasion by telling her of his chance introduction to the Gardiners at the theatre in December. "Do your aunt and uncle often attend the theatre? They certainly are knowledgeable about playwrights."

"Yes, I believe they do, sir. I believe you could say that they are both of a literary bent; they enjoy plays, poetry, and read widely."

"Indeed? I look forward to getting to know them better."

Mr Darcy watched her eyes widen slightly as she took in the spring beauty before her and felt some relief. It had been right to take her outdoors. Then, just as quickly, the sadness returned to her face.

He swallowed. Time to take a chance. *None but the brave deserve the fair*. He took a deep breath. "Do you miss Longbourn? I would miss my home if I were in your place," he asked gently.

"Yes, I do," she said quietly, "All the more because it is no longer ours."

"If it does not pain you to speak of it, I should like to learn more about your old home." He knew she might not wish to speak of it to him, and had to remind himself that they were not as intimately acquainted as they were in his imaginary life.

ELIZABETH WAS in danger of slipping into her dream persona as well. He was speaking to her so kindly, she could not keep herself from looking up at him again. His head was bent toward hers, listening earnestly. He seemed to be the Mr Darcy of her dreams, not the frowning, disdainful man she had known months ago.

As they continued their steps along the path, Elizabeth looked around her in wonder. She had been indoors for weeks and had nearly forgotten that it was springtime. Green grass and bright flowers carpeted the ground, and the trees were completely leafed out. Memories of the orchard in bloom at Longbourn seized her, and her heart twisted.

Even as she sternly told herself not to be too familiar with the tall, dark gentleman beside her, her voice disobeyed, and she found herself falteringly describing the orchard in bloom. He quietly and solicitously drew her out, as Elizabeth described her favourite places on and surrounding the Longbourn estate.

As they strolled by a hedge, they frightened a flock of sparrows into flight, which in turn startled them out of their discussion. Elizabeth looked at her watch and exclaimed at the time.

"Much as I would like to keep walking, we had better return to your uncle's house, or we will be late for tea," said Mr Darcy. He was being solicitous of her and mindful of propriety, but in truth, Elizabeth felt refreshed by the exercise and could have walked much farther. However, she nodded her agreement, and they turned back to Gracechurch Street and entered the house, where a footman led them to the drawing room.

Mrs Gardiner was waiting for them, having laid out tea with a generous assortment of sandwiches, biscuits, and cakes. Mr Gardiner was in attendance, home early from his offices. Elizabeth realised that she was hungry.

As they sat down, two maids entered the room with the

four Gardiner children; aged ten to two. Margaret and Rebecca were ten and seven respectively, John was four, and little Henry was two. The girls made their curtseys, trying not to stare at the sweets on the table. John was also bashful, and after his bow, walked quickly over to his father and hid his face against his legs. Little Henry pulled away from the maid and made an unsteady beeline for the cakes until Elizabeth stepped forward and picked him up.

She sat down again in her place next to Mr Darcy. Henry began to protest until Darcy pulled a fob from his waistcoat pocket and sombrely held it out to the squirming child. Henry went still, his eyes moving back and forth between the fob and the silent stranger. He tentatively reached out for it and took it in his chubby hand, then happily played with it, the cakes temporarily forgotten.

"I see you know how to communicate with savages, Mr Darcy," quipped Mr Gardiner.

Darcy smiled. "Perhaps we are all small children at heart, Mr Gardiner. If it were not for the rules of civility, we would all be fighting over the cakes."

Mr and Mrs Gardiner laughed, and the girls regarded Mr Darcy with renewed interest. Elizabeth, with the now content Henry on her lap, stared at him in disbelief. Mr Darcy had made a joke! She averted her eyes just in time, as Darcy turned his head to regard her again, a small smile enhancing his handsome face.

Tea and refreshments were served, with the children on their best behaviour. After finishing his biscuit, little John, who had been solemnly staring at Mr Darcy, squirmed off his father's lap and went quietly over to him, reaching out and touching the tassel on one of his boots with a curious little finger. He smiled down at the boy and detached it, holding it out to him, and he warily took it.

Then, as if their guest had passed inspection, he climbed up into his lap. The expression on Darcy's face went from pure panic to embarrassment, and then to sheepish delight, as Henry quickly crawled from Elizabeth's lap to join his brother.

Mrs Gardiner exclaimed, "John! Henry! You must get down! Mr Darcy is our guest!" as she rose to take the children.

"I do not mind, Mrs Gardiner! I rarely have the pleasure of visiting with children," replied Mr Darcy. "And no doubt they will become bored with me quickly. Now if my cousin were here, he could keep them entertained for hours."

As the little boys settled into his lap, playing with the fob and tassel, Mr Darcy again turned to Elizabeth. "Miss Bennet, have you ever visited Hyde Park? The gardens there are particularly lovely this time of year. Can I interest you in walking there tomorrow?"

Elizabeth blinked, rather dumbfounded. Even though Mr Darcy had seemed to be enjoying himself all afternoon, she had been certain he was merely discharging a social obligation. Now here he sat with her little cousins on his lap, asking to see her again. She heard her uncle's voice. "Lizzy, you must see the spring flowers at Hyde Park!" She looked up to see that everyone, even the children, were looking at her expectantly.

"You can feed the ducks, Cousin Lizzy!" cried Margaret.

"Why, yes...yes, thank you Mr Darcy, that would be most enjoyable," she managed to answer.

"Mama, may we go to Hyde Park with Mr Darcy?"

Mrs Gardiner opened her mouth to refuse her eldest daughter, but Mr Darcy looked at Elizabeth. "Miss Bennet, shall we have these rascals accompany us?"

Elizabeth was now beyond bafflement. Who on earth was this gentleman who looked exactly like Mr Darcy?

"I believe that we may be able to handle three out of four,

sir," she said, looking doubtfully at Henry, who was dozing off on Darcy's lap.

Mr Gardiner agreed. "He still needs a lengthy nap in the afternoon, so Henry will not be joining you." He turned to his guest. "Are you sure you wish to take the children along, sir? You yourself said you are not often in the company of youngsters."

Mr Darcy, though he had perhaps surprised himself with the impulsive invitation to the children, confirmed it. "Your children seem especially well-behaved, Mr Gardiner. I have the impression that Miss Bennet deals well with her cousins, and with children in general. In addition, I have every intention of calling out the cavalry for assistance on this excursion."

Within an hour, all of the tea was gone and most of the cakes. Mr Darcy rose to take his leave, shaking hands warmly with Mr and Mrs Gardiner. Elizabeth stood in confusion, wondering what exactly had happened as she watched the gentleman mount his horse and ride away.

LATE THAT EVENING, the Gardiners again reviewed the day. "Can this truly be the haughty 'Mr P' of Lizzy's letter?" asked Mrs Gardiner. "His behaviour goes far beyond civil to us, and he is showing himself to be exceptionally attentive and solicitous of Lizzy!"

"Perhaps he may be a little whimsical in his civilities. Your great men often are," her husband yawned. "Maybe he will cry off on tomorrow's excursion to Hyde Park. Although Bingley, our 'Mr A', holds him in great trust and esteem. We shall just have to wait and see."

For the first morning since their arrival at Abbotsford Park, Baron Riverton stayed in his rooms. The ancient family seat had always been his heart's home, and a surge of euphoric energy had buoyed him for weeks after his arrival. He had spent hours walking around the park and had even briefly ridden horseback one afternoon. But now he woke up exhausted, as if he had not slept at all.

He sighed. Sophy would scold him for having overreached his limits. He rose and his valet helped him dress, but then he rested on a chaise longue in his sitting room, too tired to go downstairs just yet. He slipped into a doze.

Shortly after, Sophronia entered his rooms to check on him. She sat down on the footstool next to the chaise longue and studied his face. He was paler than she would have liked.

"Rupert," she said quietly. His eyes opened.

"Oh, good morning, Sophy," he said, smiling, he hoped, in a casual way. "I was just on my way down, but I have decided to read for a while. I will take my breakfast up here. What are your plans today?"

She eyed him. "I have no firm plans yet. I take it you will not be traipsing all over the park today?"

He barked a laugh, which ended in a fit of coughing. "No, my dear, but I will come down later and spend time with our guests." He smiled and patted her hand. "They are true friends, to keep company with you while I continue my decline. Even Miss Bingley is entertaining, not that that is her intention. Do you know when she bent to fawn over me yesterday, I could see straight to her navel." He threw her a wicked look.

Ignoring his attempt at humour, Sophronia cried tearfully, "I do not know how you can be so calm about it..."

The old man sat up and leaned towards her, taking her hand. "You are the child of my heart, Sophy. When your aunt brought you to live with her, it was as if she and I were raising a child of our own together. I hate to leave you. But I am ready to go. Oftentimes I think I have lived too long already. Most of my generation is long gone. And I long to see my Gussie again." He lay back against the cushions but kept her hand in his.

"You will not be alone my dear! Your friends are like family to you, closer than many families by blood. Broughton adores you. I wish Gussie had not been quite so cynical with you about marriage, Sophy. There is still real love in the world. You are loved, my child, and you will always have your aunt's love with you. And mine. We are part of you." He closed his eyes briefly, then opened them and smiled at her. "Now, my child, why do not you take your young man for a ride out to the folly? After playing suitor to Miss Bingley, he deserves some peace."

DARCY'S largest barouche rolled up to the Gardiner town house shortly after noon the next day. Instead of one, two gentlemen alighted and walked to the door. They were ushered in to find Elizabeth and her aunt buttoning coats, fastening hats and reminding the children of their manners. Elizabeth looked curiously at the smiling man with Mr Darcy, while John's eyes lit up at the sight of his regimentals.

"Mrs Gardiner, Miss Bennet, may I present my cousin, Colonel Richard Fitzwilliam."

"At your service, ladies," Fitzwilliam said, with a slight bow. "And gentleman," he added, grinning at John.

The three children quickly climbed into the carriage, and Darcy handed Elizabeth in, their eyes meeting briefly as she took his hand. It was a short ride to the immense park, and the children were wiggling with excitement, even John, who was struggling to maintain composure in front of the two impressive gentlemen. After everyone disembarked from the carriage, Mr Darcy reached under the seat and pulled out three bags of breadcrumbs for the children to feed the ducks. "Well done, Darcy!" exclaimed Fitzwilliam as the children shouted their thanks.

The group made their way towards the Serpentine, passing flower beds and trees in early bloom. The air was scented with blossoms. Elizabeth was watching the children, Darcy was watching Elizabeth, and Fitzwilliam was watching Elizabeth and Darcy.

THE CHILDREN THREW the breadcrumbs out onto the water with varying degrees of success, John having difficulty throwing them more than a few inches beyond his shoes. Nonetheless, the ducks swam in close to the banks, delighting their audience.

Colonel Fitzwilliam spied a flat stone and tossed it over the surface of the water, where it skipped three times and then sank. The children immediately forgot about the ducks and started searching out flat stones, importuning the colonel to demonstrate for them again. Laughing, he told them, "If you want to learn, you must ask Mr Darcy! My best is only five skips, his is seven!"

Darcy's face froze for an instant, his natural reserve temporarily overwhelming any response. Elizabeth saw expressions of embarrassment, uncertainty, then aloofness, rapidly flit across his face before he donned his reserved mask once more. *So it is true, he does not like attention.*

Strangely, she felt moved to reassure him. "Mr Darcy, if you will try it, so will I," she said encouragingly, admitting that she had often practised skipping stones as a child. He smiled. "So be it, Miss Bennet." They all searched for flat stones, and soon each had a handful. Mr Darcy and Colonel Fitzwilliam bent over the children, showing them how to flick their wrists to get just the right angle. In the pleasant spring sunshine, as Elizabeth competed with the gentlemen and watched her little cousins shout with delight, she felt a gradual relaxation of her body; a fleeting sense of ease. She achieved a respectable four skips with one throw. The gentlemen congratulated her but Margaret was quick to point out some flaws in her style.

"Cousin Lizzy, why can you not throw the stones as far as Mr Darcy?"

She answered with pretended indignation. "Mr Darcy and Colonel Fitzwilliam have an advantage, in that they are tall and have very long arms. It is quite unfair. Though I would look very silly with long arms, would I not?"

The sun was lowering in the sky, and it was time to leave. The party again boarded the carriage and were on their way back to Gracechurch Street. John fell asleep in Elizabeth's lap, but the girls chatted happily with the colonel, with a few remarks from Mr Darcy.

Elizabeth was abstracted, half listening to the conversation, her mind wondering at the side of Mr Darcy that she had never seen before. Of course, he had once been a child, but she was having difficulty imagining him as a little boy. An image of a small boy, dressed sombrely as a gentleman, skipping stones with a fierce, gloomy expression popped into her mind, and a corner of her mouth turned up slightly. She looked up at him only to find his eyes were fixed on her. Her breath caught slightly, and she looked away. A few minutes later, they had reached their destination, and all disembarked from the carriage and into the house.

THEY WERE MET by Mrs Gardiner, who took the sleepy John from Fitzwilliam's arms. The girls thanked the gentlemen with curtseys and ran upstairs. As the gentlemen made to leave, Mrs Gardiner mentioned that she had received a message from Mrs Hurst that afternoon. "Mr and Mrs Hurst have returned from Hertfordshire today. They have invited my husband and me, as well as Elizabeth, to join them for an informal dinner tomorrow evening. I believe you gentlemen will each find an invitation when you return home."

Darcy was relieved. He had been trying to think of an excuse to call on Elizabeth the next day. Now he could see her at dinner with a small group of friends. Darcy and Fitzwilliam made their goodbyes to Mrs Gardiner, and then he turned to Elizabeth. "Thank you for a delightful afternoon, Miss Bennet. I should have known that you would be a talented stone skipper. Will we be seeing you at Mrs Hurst's dinner tomorrow?"

Elizabeth looked at her aunt. "I believe we will be there. Thank you, Mr Darcy, Colonel Fitzwilliam," she said, dipping a curtsey. "The children enjoyed themselves immensely."

There was a thoughtful silence in the barouche as it pulled away from the kerb. When Darcy looked away from the window, he found his cousin's gaze was settled on him.

"She is a lovely girl. I understand why you are drawn to her. But," Fitzwilliam said, more seriously, "she is not recovering as well as her sisters, I do not believe. Her sorrow is plain, though I did glimpse some ease of her pain. She did smile a little."

Darcy sighed. "It was a ghost of a smile. Elizabeth's typical smiles brighten the entire room. I shall do whatever it takes to see her smile that way again. Even if her smiles are not for me."

CHAPTER 27

The Hursts had invited the Gardiners to arrive earlier than their two gentlemen guests. Elizabeth listened to Louisa and her aunt describe their work in redecorating the drawing room, and she sincerely admired it. The two ladies walked her through the house while Mr Hurst and Mr Gardiner settled themselves comfortably in the study. It was clear that the house had seen better days, but Elizabeth enjoyed Louisa's happy enthusiasm about her future plans. She was genuinely pleased for the Hursts. The house was a metaphor for their lives together as well. Their marriage had originated in the failures and ambitions of others, but now they were creating a home and a life for themselves.

A thought intruded that she herself was now homeless—unwelcomed by her mother and dependent on her aunt or Jane for a bed. A wave of sadness assaulted her. She pushed the thought away and concentrated on listening to the discussion.

At that moment, Darcy and Fitzwilliam were approaching the front door, Darcy with considerable trepidation. He had not set foot at the Hursts' since the ghastly evening he and Caroline had deliberately broken Bingley's heart. He shuddered and stopped briefly to compose himself.

He need not have worried. Stepping into the drawing room, he was delighted to see the entire room was sparkling and new. The atmosphere was comfortable, and the company so convivial, that that wretched autumn afternoon was soon forgotten. The conversation over dinner, and later back in the drawing room, flowed, although Elizabeth continued to be uncharacteristically silent. Darcy was by nature not a talkative man, but he enjoyed the intelligence, humour, and ease of the discussion. He directed a few quiet remarks to Elizabeth, but mostly contented himself with watching her.

As he and his cousin made their goodbyes that evening, Darcy quietly asked Mr Gardiner's permission to call upon his niece regularly with the aim of lifting her spirits, and it was quickly given.

Mr Gardiner continued cautiously, "Ordinarily I would send a maid with Elizabeth at all times, Mr Darcy. Since there is already an acquaintance between you and our niece, and because of your reputation for propriety and rectitude, I think we may forego that. My wife and I are hoping that she will find it easier to share her grief with you privately." Darcy nodded sombrely, aware of the irony that the stiff and cheerless reputation which had so repelled Elizabeth early in their acquaintance was serving him well now.

Between themselves, Mr and Mrs Gardiner debated whether what they were witnessing were condolences or courtship, but decided to allow events to unfold as they would.

"And so, Maddie, I impulsively gave my permission to Mr Darcy to call on Lizzy, and to escort her when walking or making visits without a maid present. Do you think I have done wrong?" Edward looked slightly worried.

His wife returned his gaze thoughtfully. After a moment, she answered, "No, in this case, I do not believe you have. I expect that they will always be out in public, walking or making visits. We also know him to be a sober, respectable man. He has already shown great gentleness and care with her. I believe that he truly understands her emotional state." She smiled at her husband. "He cares for her enough to put off his own suit, if indeed that is what it is, until she is more herself. He is putting her needs ahead of his own wishes, which indicates a fine character. And somehow Lizzy already trusts him, even if she does not quite understand that herself."

THE FOLLOWING DAY, Darcy saw his cousin and uncle off for their journey to Rosings and began to call on Elizabeth almost daily. If Elizabeth was confused by his continuing presence, she came to appreciate the distraction from the despondency in which she was mired. He took her walking most often, but there was a trip to the lending library and visits to galleries. Often Mrs Gardiner would invite him to stay for tea. The watchful eyes of her aunt and uncle noted a lessening of the tension in her manner, and a growing inclination to initiate conversation.

It was with rising hope that Darcy, too, observed these subtle changes. He took Elizabeth to the British Museum, hoping it would awaken her natural curiosity and kindle a spark within her. They strolled slowly through the galleries, immersing themselves in the wealth of antiquities on display. They walked towards the Rosetta Stone and studied it.

Elizabeth gazed at it in rapt fascination. After several minutes, she exclaimed, "Oh, I wish my father could—" and then stopped, her face crumpling. Darcy's arm reflexively went up to encircle her shoulders, but he caught himself just in time. Instead, he put her hand on his arm and covered it with his, steering her to a bench in a quiet corner. Elizabeth sat down and he took a seat next to her.

"Miss Bennet, would you rather I take you home?" She looked up, seemingly startled by the genuine concern on his face.

"No…no, I will be all right. It just struck me how much my father would have enjoyed this. All of a sudden, I missed him dreadfully." She shook her head, her eyes downcast. "I am sorry."

"You must not apologise for your feelings. I understand completely."

Darcy drew in a steadying breath, but the words tumbled out in an unexpected rush. "I know what it is to sit at a beloved parent's bedside, unable to do anything but watch them die. I know the heartache and helplessness and anxiety. Missing someone you love never ends, even though it becomes easier to bear. Even now, there are times when it all comes back to me, and it is as if the grief is still fresh—"

Suddenly realising that he was gripping her hand too tightly; he loosened his hold but did not let go. Feeling awkward and self-conscious, he turned his face away from her and trailed off lamely, "I just wanted you to know that I understand."

ELIZABETH COULD NOT TAKE her eyes from his face. She felt as if she was seeing him for the first time. Here was a man who had, at an impossibly young age, been left not only with sole responsibility for a great estate with all its dependents, but the raising of an orphaned child, all while in the depths of bereavement himself. He had sacrificed what should have been carefree years to do his duty, and had succeeded admirably. What a remarkable man he was. Her regard for him, already having risen, now soared, and her heart swelled with sympathy and understanding.

Her hand was still on his arm, with his other hand covering hers. She laid her other hand atop his and tentatively squeezed, and he raised his head to look at her. "Thank you, Mr Darcy," she said quietly, her eyes meeting his. "Thank you for sharing your feelings with me. Your sympathy means a great deal, and I deeply appreciate your friendship." Lost in his gaze for a few seconds, her eyes suddenly widened and she looked away, carefully removing her hand.

She managed a tentative smile before joining him to walk through another gallery, and then returned to Gracechurch Street. Before Mr Darcy took his leave of her, he mentioned a return to the lending library, and she consented.

AS THE CARRIAGE took him back to Darcy House, he replayed her words in his mind. She considered him a friend, and appreciated his friendship. *We are friends.* He had never expressed his own sorrow to anyone else before, not even Fitzwilliam. He and Elizabeth were certainly on better terms than ever before, yet it was not enough. In his dreams she was his wife, his lover, the mother of his children. Would she ever be able to think of him as a suitor?

Or was it perhaps through friendship that he could win her trust and respect—even her love? To be ardent lovers and the dearest of friends, to be her closest confidant and she his, to be their truest selves with each other; that would be true intimacy.

He leaned his head back against the squabs and closed his eyes. The mere thought took his breath away.

Georgiana and Fitzwilliam were just returned from Rosings and waiting to greet him when he walked through the door. His sister threw herself into his arms. "Oh, Brother, I have missed you! You have been constantly in my thoughts. Fitzwilliam told us all the news from Netherfield. How is Miss Bennet faring?"

Darcy embraced his sister tightly. He had missed her, too. "She still suffers and grieves, but I believe she is coming back to herself. It will take time, much more time, as we ourselves understand, Sister, but I see evidence of her spirits returning," said Darcy. "So far, she has agreed to spend time with me almost every day, though she does study me rather curiously at times, when she thinks I do not notice."

"When will I be able to meet her? I was envious when I heard about your adventure in Hyde Park," she grinned.

Fitzwilliam laughed. "No one was more surprised than I when I found that we were taking three young children to the park, and that it was your brother's idea! I do think it did us all some good. I have not seen you skip stones since we were boys. And Miss Bennet has quite an arm herself."

"Perhaps I can prevail upon her to teach me," said Georgiana. "I thought to invite her to tea first, however."

"Tomorrow, perhaps?" asked Darcy. "I had asked her to accompany me to Hookham's but I so much want you to meet her."

"Perfect!" Though mindful that Miss Bennet was still bereaved, Georgiana could not contain her excitement and clasped her hands together. "I cannot wait!" She hurried away to speak with the housekeeper and Mrs Annesley.

Darcy turned to his cousin. "Where is Anne? Did Lady Catherine prevent her from coming with you?"

"Lady Catherine has become so consumed with finding an amenable rector to bend to her will, that she has temporarily lost interest in her daughter. Anne was delighted to come to town with us, but traveling has completely exhausted her. She is resting at Matlock House. My mother is busily making arrangements with her physician to attend Anne, and Georgiana wants to bring her dressmaker to see her."

He grinned at his cousin. "Picture this, Darcy. While we were in Hertfordshire, our little Annie, with Georgiana's help, mind you, hied herself off to see a Mr Kendrick, who is Lady Catherine's solicitor. Mr Kendrick was quite disturbed to discover that Anne was never informed of her status as mistress of Rosings Park. He immediately set aside his work and went through Sir Lewis's will with her, item by item, and they discussed at length not only the estate, but her obligations to her tenants and the residents of the village, including the Hunsford living. They made a temporary will at that time. Anne signed the final version of the will just yesterday, and my father and Mr Houston provided witness for her. Anne is determined not only to care for Rosings Park, but to mend the frayed relations between the de Bourghs and the local citizenry. I daresay she will succeed admirably."

THE NEXT DAY, when Mr Darcy was again welcomed to the Gardiner home, Elizabeth was surprised when he asked if she would object to a change in plans. "Miss Bennet, my sister, Georgiana, has arrived in town, and most particularly wishes to be known to you. Will you allow me, or do I ask too much, to introduce her to your acquaintance?"

Elizabeth stared at him. Miss Darcy wished to make her acquaintance? She realised that Mr Darcy was still waiting for her reply. "Thank you, sir," she said, blinking, "It would be my great pleasure."

He handed her into his carriage, and they made the journey across town. As she alighted, she raised her eyes to the formidable grandeur of Darcy House and drew in her breath. Glancing nervously down at her simple black walking gown, she hesitated, looking up at the house again. *Where is your courage, Lizzy?* Nothing could be done about it now. At least it was well-made and of the excellent fabric Louisa had brought them. Her chin rose and she took a deep breath.

"Are you well, Miss Bennet?" She jumped slightly at Mr Darcy's deep voice at her ear.

She met his eye, one brow arched. "I am, sir. I was just speculating as to the size and number of sinister retainers who will greet us at the door."

He looked puzzled for a moment, then caught on. "I will expect no less than three or four. I hire my servants based solely upon their menacing qualities."

"And their proficiency at lurking in the shadows? Or appearing out of nowhere?" she countered.

He managed to look affronted, even as his eyes crinkled. "Only the best, madam. Prepare to be intimidated."

She took his proffered arm, and they went into the house, where they were met solely by a kindly, silver-haired butler. Elizabeth managed to smile rather than laugh when a young lady, presumably Miss Darcy, walked quickly into the entry hall to greet them.

Elizabeth curtseyed before the younger girl took Elizabeth's arm from her brother and led her to the music room. "Miss Bennet! I am so happy to make your acquaintance at last! Pray be seated and make yourself comfortable."

Elizabeth in turn studied her young hostess. Miss Darcy's expression was kind and intelligent, with a lovely smile; her straight back and perfectly aligned head lending her a stateliness beyond her years. She moved gracefully and naturally. The two young ladies sat side by side on the settee, and Darcy seated himself on a chair on the other side of the low table.

Miss Darcy's rigorous training as a hostess came to the fore. She rang for tea and re-seated herself, laying a gentle hand on Elizabeth's arm. "Miss Bennet, please accept my sincere sympathy on your father's death. I am deeply sorry for what you and your family have been through."

Elizabeth's throat tightened and tears stung her eyes, but she understood immediately that Miss Darcy's condolences were sincere. How was it that the simplest condolences affected her the most deeply? "Thank you," she answered quietly. "You are most kind."

Miss Darcy smiled gently and gave Elizabeth's hand a little pat as the tea tray was brought in. She poured Elizabeth a cup and handed it to her. "I am sorry to have missed the outing with your little cousins in Hyde Park. My brother and I are a small family and have no young children on either side of our relations. I hope I have the opportunity to meet your young cousins someday."

Elizabeth smiled slightly, not as surprised as she would have been several days before. If Mr Darcy had no qualms about spending time with a businessman's children, likely neither would his sister. "I daresay they would enjoy meeting you."

Elizabeth admired the music room, which her hostess acknowledged was her favourite room in the house. "My brother tells me that he has on several occasions greatly enjoyed your singing and playing. Does your aunt have an instrument for you to use?"

Elizabeth looked at Darcy, her expression quizzical.

Really? He coloured slightly but smiled a little sheepishly back at her.

"Yes, Miss Darcy, she does. I must confess that I have not made good use of it," she admitted.

"I hope I have a chance to hear you someday. I adore playing duets, but rarely have the chance. Perhaps we can work on some music together."

"I should like that," answered Elizabeth, her mind whirling at the amiability of her hostess, as well as that young lady's seeming assumption that they would be spending time together in the future.

AFTER THE TEA had been finished, Darcy excused himself, wishing to give the ladies private time together. He went to his study, intending to see to some correspondence, but was helpless to do anything but pace back and forth, with occasional long pauses to stare out the window. Finally, after an hour had passed, he found them still in the music room, seated together at the pianoforte with their heads together, looking over sheet music. His heart beat faster at the sight of the two most important people in his life sitting side-by-side. Clasping his hands together tightly, he was unable to think of a thing to say that would not betray his feelings, and so managed only an apologetic interruption.

"Ladies, I regret that it is time to take Miss Bennet back to her uncle's home," he said, his smile warm and unaffected, his eyes crinkling in pleasure at the sight before him.

Elizabeth turned and stared at him, as if she were confused by his presence. "Oh! Yes, of course. Miss Darcy, thank you for your kind hospitality. I have enjoyed meeting you exceedingly. I hope we will be able to further our acquaintance," she said a little breathlessly.

"I also wish it, Miss Bennet! In fact, I am counting on it!" Georgiana said with a wide smile that resembled her brother's.

The ride back to Gracechurch Street was quiet. Darcy spoke occasionally in quiet tones, and Elizabeth answered him, but she seemed somewhat discomposed. He looked out the window but could feel her eyes on him. Darcy was trying not to let his hopes get too high. Still, for the first time, Elizabeth seemed to have awakened to him, to be as aware of him as he was of her.

IN FACT, Elizabeth had become acutely and physically aware of Darcy. When he had come upon them in the music room, she had been mesmerised by his appearance, her wide eyes riveted to his face. She had always recognised that he was a handsome man, even in their earliest acquaintance. But when he was smiling, his eyes aglow, he was breath-taking. Their eyes had met and briefly held, and then Elizabeth hastily rose from the bench, a blush rising over her cheeks.

Now, sitting across from him in the carriage, she remained a bit dazed, but suddenly remembered her manners. "Mr Darcy, thank you for inviting me to make your sister's acquaintance. I cannot remember when I have enjoyed anything more."

"I am delighted, Miss Bennet. I have long thought that you and Georgiana might take pleasure in one another's company."

The carriage halted at the Gardiner town house. Darcy handed Elizabeth down, but did not relinquish her hand as they walked to the door, tucking it again in his arm. He looked down at her. "Will I see you tomorrow, Miss Bennet? Shall we make our visit to Hookham's after all?"

She was looking back up at him, her eyes arrested,

searching his face. "Yes, sir, I would enjoy that." Still holding her gaze, he bowed over her hand and waited on the step as she went inside.

Elizabeth stood inside the closed door, trying to soothe her strange disquiet by breathing deeply. What was Mr Darcy up to? She felt a tingly shiver run up her spine and shook it off. Yet later, as she sat at her aunt's pianoforte and played for the first time since Christmas, she carried with her a quiet elation, a soft, undefinable joy that she had not experienced for many months.

CHAPTER 28

It was with consternation the next morning that Elizabeth regarded herself in the mirror. *When did I become so pale and drawn? How lifeless my hair looks! How dull my eyes!* She called her aunt's maid to style her hair and touched some scent behind her ears. She looked through her gowns: black, black, and more black. *I miss wearing colours*, she thought wistfully, but then rebuked herself guiltily for not being more respectful of her father's memory. It was under three months since he had died. She could endure black crape and dyed gowns a little longer.

Still, she would prefer to be more in looks when meeting her tall, handsome friend.

However, when his carriage arrived in Gracechurch Street, it contained two extra passengers. Miss Darcy had accompanied her brother, as had his cousin, Miss de Bourgh.

Anne de Bourgh! Mr Darcy's intended bride! Elizabeth felt

the bottom drop out of her stomach, but smiled with an effort as the introductions were made.

After Mr Darcy had settled Elizabeth in her seat beside his cousin, Miss Darcy looked at her apologetically. "I do most sincerely beg your pardon, Miss Bennet. Anne and I have been ever so rude and invited ourselves along on your visit to the lending library. I hope you do not mind terribly."

Elizabeth demurred, smiled, and replied that she welcomed their company. She examined her newest acquaintance and recalled what she had been told of her. Miss de Bourgh truly did not look well, although her eyes were bright, curious, and friendly. Mr Darcy would appreciate such traits.

The lady interrupted her thoughts. "This is my first outing since I have arrived in London two days ago, Miss Bennet. The journey from Kent quite knocked me flat. I have never been to a lending library, and I am looking forward to it!"

Never been to a lending library? Elizabeth surreptitiously studied Miss de Bourgh. She was tiny and fine-boned, pale and wan, except for her expressive eyes. Her conversation was lively, even ebullient. Elizabeth regretfully found herself warming to the diminutive lady. They chatted about Rosings and Hunsford, and their mutual friend Mrs Collins. Elizabeth watched for any sign of particular regard between Mr Darcy and Miss de Bourgh, but they seemed to converse more in the way of a brother and sister.

ONCE AT THE LENDING LIBRARY, they enjoyed an hour browsing the shelves, together and separately, randomly meeting in twos or threes and consulting over what they had each read. Mr Darcy stayed close to Elizabeth, sometimes walking and talking with her about their favourites, other times simply remaining within earshot of her. Though she enjoyed his amiable, well-read company, Elizabeth wondered at Mr Darcy's attentions to her. Should he not be attending to his betrothed? He hardly looked at Miss de Bourgh, though she and Miss Darcy appeared to be having a fine time together, arm in arm, giggling and whispering. *Perhaps because they will soon be sisters.*

She spied a copy of a history that her father had added to his collection just before Christmas and examined it. He likely had never had the chance to read it. She pushed away the now-familiar sense of loss such memories engendered, and centred her thoughts, as Mr Darcy had described, on the present.

That gentleman, as if he had been summoned by her thoughts, appeared at her side. "Improving your mind with extensive reading, Miss Bennet?"

She smiled at his teasing reference to that long ago conversation. "I will not admit to that, sir. A lady, should she have the misfortune of knowing anything, should conceal it as well as she can. I shall cover a screen or net a purse, and enjoy a mere novel." She did, however, add the history to her small stack of books.

When all had made their selections, they stepped back out into the sunshine.

"Miss Bennet, can I persuade you to join us for tea at my aunt's home?" asked Miss Darcy. "Anne is staying with Lady Matlock while she is visiting London. I think it would be best to take her there first so she can rest."

Elizabeth looked at Miss de Bourgh. Her face was ashen and her lips had a bluish tinge. It did seem to be an effort for her to stay on her feet. "Of course, Miss Darcy, I would be honoured. But what will your aunt think of an uninvited guest accompanying you to her home?"

"Lady Matlock has already included you in her invitation

since my brother told her of your planned visit to Hookham's. I am glad you will have a chance to meet her."

The carriage pulled up to a splendid town house, even more impressive than Darcy House, and they disembarked. Miss Darcy handed her cousin's books to a footman and said, "We will show ourselves up to the saloon, Gordon."

SHE LED THEM TO AN AIRY, sunlit sitting room with the most elegant furnishings Elizabeth had ever seen. Even though it was only April, there were vases of flowers everywhere. Beautiful paintings hung on the pale damask-covered walls and exquisite, intricately woven rugs covered the polished floors.

A handsome silver-haired woman came forward to greet them. Lady Matlock was stylish and graceful, yet her kind expression and the tiny laugh lines by her eyes made her look motherly. She welcomed them and held out her hand to Elizabeth. "Miss Bennet, I am so happy to make your acquaintance. My son tells me you can skip a stone with the best of them!" She turned to her niece, touching her cheek and peering into her eyes. "Anne, oh my dear, you look dead on your feet!"

"I will be better once I have had some tea, Aunt," said Miss de Bourgh as she sank into a chair. They settled themselves, and a few minutes later the tea tray was brought in. They chatted briefly about the books they had chosen at the library, followed by a silence as they all sipped their tea.

"Miss Bennet, Georgiana tells me you are staying with your aunt and uncle?" Lady Matlock asked.

"Yes, my lady, their name is Gardiner. They live on Gracechurch Street," replied Elizabeth, waiting for the countess's reaction to having a denizen of Cheapside in her elegant saloon.

Lady Matlock's eyes lit up. "Oh, Miss Bennet, is your aunt

Mrs Edward Gardiner? We served on a hospital charity committee together! Pray send her my regards!"

"Thank you, your ladyship, I shall be happy to convey them," said Elizabeth, taken aback. She let out her breath and allowed herself to relax into the congeniality of the company.

GEORGIANA CAUGHT her brother's eye and looked down her nose at him. Darcy bore her teasing well. Having become acquainted with Elizabeth's aunt and uncle, such information no longer surprised him, but the memory of his own arrogance caused him considerable chagrin.

At that moment, Fitzwilliam entered the room, calling out his greetings to the assembled group. "Good day, cousins!" he said grinning, "and Miss Bennet! Did you each content yourselves with one or two books today, or did you completely clear the shelves at Hookham's, since there is nary a book to be found either here or at Darcy House?" He walked over to his mother and kissed her cheek.

Lady Matlock chuckled. "Pray pardon our informality, Miss Bennet! When it is only family in attendance, we are much at our ease! My son is not the reader that Darcy and Georgiana are, and I daresay he thinks that two rather grand libraries in the family are more than enough."

Elizabeth pursed her lips as she had used to do when she was teasing, and a dimple appeared. "Please do not apologise, your ladyship! Mr Darcy can attest that my family is also rather, er, informal."

She turned to Darcy, one corner of her mouth turned up and a mischievous sparkle in her eye. His heart leapt. She was teasing him! He laughed and returned her smile. "Yes, Aunt, I can verify that Miss Bennet's family is delightfully unaffected."

"You have four sisters, is that correct?" asked Georgiana. "I always wished for sisters, even one sister, but you have them in abundance!"

"Yes, I do. One might almost say an oversupply, do you not agree, Mr Darcy?"

He appeared to consider that gravely. "A plethora perhaps."

"Certainly a surplus."

"A profusion."

"A surfeit, most definitely." Although his attention remained on Elizabeth, Darcy could feel the speculative gaze of his aunt, her eyes moving back and forth between them. She would most certainly be interrogating Fitzwilliam later, but Darcy was too content to mind, recognising that his cousins and Georgiana were nearly as delighted as he, for they had at last caught a glimpse of Elizabeth as she really was.

Their brief badinage having ended, general conversation flowed easily. As they prepared to take their leave, the three young ladies chatted while Darcy and Fitzwilliam spoke to the countess. Darcy attended poorly to the conversation, as he was more focused on the ladies' spirited discussion.

"You can see why I am so pleased to visit my relatives in town, Miss Bennet," said Anne. "We are far more formal at Rosings. When we are gathered there, my mother rather prefers to hold court, does she not, Georgiana?"

"Oh, you have put me on the spot in front of Miss Bennet," laughed Georgiana. "Yes, I am afraid that is true."

"And then she makes my cousin Darcy sit next to me all the time so she can pretend we are courting. The poor man! It is a wonder he ever visits at all."

Elizabeth spoke to Anne in a cautious tone. "Mr Collins informed my family that you and Mr Darcy were betrothed when he visited us last December."

"Oh, that ridiculous man! Pardon me, Miss Bennet, but he parrots whatever my mother says. We are most definitely not engaged, and never care to be."

A peculiar sense of lightness washed over Elizabeth. She had to consciously refocus her attention on Miss de Bourgh, who was still talking. As Fitzwilliam and Darcy came to join them, Anne continued. "Miss Bennet, I cannot believe that you and Mr Collins are cousins. There is nothing about you that is similar in any way."

"We are *distant* cousins." Elizabeth's mouth turned up at one corner, and again the dimple appeared. "Very, very, very distant." Georgiana's hand came up to cover her mouth and Darcy looked down to hide his smile, but Anne and Fitzwilliam laughed heartily.

They made their farewells, and went on to Gracechurch Street, where Georgiana was introduced to the children, albeit briefly. As it was late in the day, they regretfully took their leave, but not before Darcy had invited Elizabeth to walk in Hyde Park yet again the next day.

AS THEY RODE HOME, Darcy was exultant. "Did you see, Georgie? Did you *see* how she sparkles?"

Georgiana smiled at her brother. "Yes, I did. We all did. Even our aunt. I am certain that even as we speak, Fitzwilliam is undergoing a thorough interrogation about her. You truly are helping her recover." She smiled into her brother's eyes. "Love can heal all wounds."

Darcy blushed faintly. "I am counting on that. But I also credit your kindness, Fitzwilliam's affability, and Anne's tendency to blurt out just about anything that pops into her mind as being extremely helpful."

"MOTHER, I can tell you that I have never seen a man more head over ears, nor less equipped to deal with it than Darcy!" said Fitzwilliam to Lady Matlock. They were still sitting together in the saloon, the tea tray having been cleared away.

"It is certainly written all over his face," his mother agreed. "Miss Bennet seems to be a delightful young lady. One would not need the mourning clothes to see that she is bereaved, however. Poor girl! Such lovely eyes, especially when she smiles! And you say she has not a penny to her name? Remove your boots from the sofa, Richard."

Fitzwilliam chuckled, swinging his feet to the floor. "Well, perhaps more than a penny, but not much." He looked at his mother. "Do you know that Darcy was trying to suppress his feelings for her? He spent the winter in utter misery because of it. He felt that her lack of fortune, and her relatives in trade, made her much too far beneath his touch. There he was, madly in love, yet he had decided not only that he could not court her to preserve family honour, but that he would never marry at all!"

Lady Matlock tutted and shook her head. "That is how he was raised, poor boy. His parents were such sticklers! It has made his life that much more difficult. I hope he can learn to relax a bit. Not that we would wish him to marry a washerwoman, of course. Miss Bennet's father *was* a gentleman, you say?"

"I believe even my aunt and uncle Darcy would have been satisfied with the Bennet family history, which is quite distinguished even though the estate itself is small." Fitzwilliam shrugged. "Although perhaps not, since, of course, her mother's relations are in business."

"No doubt Lady Anne would not have accepted Miss Bennet." Lady Matlock sighed and then smiled. "But she is not here to prevent her son from pursuing his heart's desire, and I think it is high time for Darcy to find his own happiness. My acquaintance with Mrs Gardiner gives me reason not to concern myself overmuch about what the *ton* may say," said Lady Matlock. "They are respectable and cultivated people."

AT GRACECHURCH STREET, Elizabeth was at loose ends. After telling her aunt and uncle about the afternoon and relaying Lady Matlock's regards, she had played the pianoforte and then excused herself for the evening. Now in her room, grateful for the solitude, she was feeling curiously light-hearted, but mostly confused. Why was Mr Darcy paying her so much attention? He was the last man in the world she would have expected to do so. He was the last man whose company she would have expected to enjoy so much. She had come to greatly anticipate their outings together. His attentions were almost as if he was courting her? *Surely not!* Her rising heart sank once more. *Foolish girl!* Despite the kindness shown by his family, any alliance between them would be a degradation for him; family obstacles would oppose such an inclination on his part. That had been true even before her papa had taken ill. Now she was just a penniless, homeless country girl.

She remembered his words in the museum. He was merely showing her great kindness and condescension. He had experienced devastating loss in his life and understood her pain. *We are friends*, she thought wistfully. Still, Elizabeth was glad that Mr Darcy had turned out to be the warm, kind-hearted, gentle man he had been in her dreams.

But he would never consider her to be more than a friend, she was certain, her spirits slipping and her throat tightening. Even though he was not betrothed to Miss de Bourgh, someday he would marry a wealthy or titled lady and then they would not be able to maintain their friendship. She would enjoy it while she could. Perhaps she could build a continuing friendship with Miss Darcy. She fell into a restless sleep, swirling with visions of Mr Darcy smiling at her in the music room and laughing with her over tea.

CHAPTER 29

Elizabeth awoke the following morning, tired and unrefreshed by her fitful sleep. The dark numbness of the last several weeks had lifted, to be replaced by a slight despondency and a jangling unease. She had a sense of rawness, as if she was just barely holding herself together, yet could not pin down specific emotions. She spent the morning with her aunt, and after helping with the children's meal, went up to her room to change out of her morning frock into walking clothes for her planned outing to Hyde Park with Mr Darcy.

His carriage arrived punctually as usual, and her heart warmed. Mr Darcy's careful dependability endeared him to her, where she once would have considered it evidence of inflexibility. He was ushered in for a brief, friendly greeting to her aunt, after which he took Elizabeth's arm and led her out to his carriage for the trip to Hyde Park.

They walked in a different direction, away from the

Serpentine, along paths that wound through a stand of ancient, towering oaks and elms. The sky was blue with small puffy clouds and a gentle breeze. It should have been calming to her, but it was not. The two conversed more comfortably than they had a few weeks earlier, but Elizabeth's discomposure kept her relatively quiet. Mr Darcy also seemed to be silently reflective.

After almost an hour, he asked Elizabeth if she would like to walk the short distance to Darcy House for some refreshment. She agreed, and they turned their steps towards his home. Georgiana sat with them and enjoyed a glass of cool lemonade, and then left for Lady Matlock's house.

"My dressmaker is meeting me there today. Lady Catherine has always chosen Anne's clothes, and she is choosing for herself for the first time! My aunt and I wish to give her some new gowns." At this she smiled softly. "I enjoy Anne's pleasure in this more than I have ever enjoyed shopping for myself."

"And I know how much you adore new gowns," her brother teased gently. She smiled and took her leave.

WITH GEORGIANA GONE, they were without a chaperon, so it was time for Darcy to escort Elizabeth home. He had been quietly studying her throughout their walk and had noticed her distraction. He hit upon an idea that he hoped would lighten her mood.

"Has my sister given you a tour of the house?"

"Only the music room and the drawing room," she answered, "so not a complete tour."

"Before I return you to your aunt, would you allow me to show you *my* favourite room?"

He led her back through the entrance hall and down a short

corridor that ended in a set of double doors, which he threw open and followed her through. She gasped at the sunlit room before her, a high-ceilinged room whose ranks of bookshelves were broken up at intervals with tall windows that went from floor to ceiling. A large fireplace graced the end of the room, and comfortable chairs were placed in small groupings. There was even a large globe on a table near a window, much like the one at Longbourn.

"Oh! Oh, my! What a magnificent library!" she breathed, turning in a slow circle to take in the entire room.

Darcy was smiling, thrilled with Elizabeth's reaction. He was right to have shown it to her, to have given her the pleasure. He had imagined them together in this room many times. "I understand you spent many happy hours in your father's library," he said as he stood behind her. As the words left his mouth, there was a silence, and he felt the air change.

"Oh, how Papa would…And you even have a globe. I remember…" Elizabeth faltered. Memories of time spent with her father unspooled like lightning through her mind, shocking her to the core with their intensity. She took a shuddering breath. Suddenly, her body slumped and her shoulders began to shake.

"Miss Bennet," he said with some alarm, and stepped around to look at her.

The colour had drained from Elizabeth's face, and her eyes stared unseeing at the wall. Tears filled her eyes. "Miss Bennet!" he said, bending over her, and putting his hands on her arms just below her shoulders. "Please, have I upset you?" She did not answer, but her hands came up to cover her face, as weeping silently, she began to sink to the floor.

With a muttered oath, Darcy caught her up in his arms and carried her to a large sofa directly in front of the hearth. He knew he should set her down but, afraid to let go of her, he sat down and held her as she wept against his chest. "Forgive me, I did not mean to cause you pain!" His arms encircled her and he held her tightly. "Elizabeth, please talk to me," he said into her ear.

And so, her head on his chest, she did, the words spilling out of her. She told him about watching her father fade away, enduring her mother's cruelty, trying to manage the estate under dangerous conditions, and the mixture of despair, anxiety, and fury she had carried locked in her heart all through the harrowing winter.

"The last evening—his final night on this earth—even then, he did not share stories or speak to me of tender memories, or even offer any wisdom that could help my mother, sisters, and me. He had done little to guide us or plan for our futures. He left those tasks to my uncles. Even when death was imminent, he chose teasing over serious conversation."

Darcy was disgusted, but not surprised. Mr Bennet had not appeared serious about anything but his own pleasures and convenience. His own father had imparted all he could, in word and on paper, to advise him—his son and heir—to be a principled man and a successful master of Pemberley. He held Elizabeth closer as she shuddered, tearfully revealing the guilt she still felt over expressing her anger at her dying father.

Darcy listened, murmuring soothingly, aghast at what she had endured. Gradually her words subsided. The storm had passed, and his shirt and neckcloth were damp with her tears. The release of her pent-up emotions had exhausted her; he felt her body relax against him, and her breathing become even. She had fallen asleep in his arms.

He stroked her hair, wondering if Mr Bennet had ever understood how much he had failed his family, or how rare and courageous and strong his daughter was.

Elizabeth dozed, feeling safe and content for the first time in months. It was just another dream, but it was so comforting. She sighed and snuggled against Mr Darcy's chest, and felt his arms tighten around her. She felt his cheek against her hair and his kiss on her forehead. He had never kissed her before. This was a good dream. His arms were strong and warm, and he smelled of sandalwood and leather, and a little bit of horses and...

She had never noticed smells in her dreams before.

Except it was not a dream. Her eyes flew open. "Oh, no! No, no, no!" She looked up into Mr Darcy's eyes, only inches from her own. She pushed herself away from his chest, trying to get to her feet, but clumsily sliding off his lap to the floor. She struggled to her feet. "Oh…Oh, Mr Darcy! I am sorry! Do please forgive me! What must you think of me? Oh! I must go!"

Darcy stood and caught her gently, his hands on her shoulders, forcing her to face him. She could not look at him, and covered her face with her hands. She was humiliated, disgraced; realising not only the impropriety of what had just passed with Mr Darcy, but how she had completely lost her composure. Tears sprang to her eyes again.

"Miss Bennet," he said quietly, his deep, gentle voice cutting through her panic. He took her hands, and she tentatively raised her eyes to his. "Miss Bennet," he said again, his tone a caress. "Remember I said you must never apologise for your feelings?" She nodded, looking into his serious dark eyes. "I meant it," he said. "We are friends, are we not? I am honoured and deeply touched that you shared your feelings with me." He pulled his handkerchief from his pocket and set about drying her tears. Smiling down at her, he slid his hands down her arms to take hers. "I think you were exceptionally brave. Your father must have been quite proud of you."

She stared at him, confused, and then noticed his dishevelled shirt and neckcloth. "I…I have ruined your shirt," she stammered, blushing furiously.

"It will dry," he said calmly. "You are exhausted. Let me take you home."

She nodded numbly, too shamed and distraught to meet his eye.

They rode in silence, until Mr Darcy leaned across the carriage to her and touched her arm. "Miss Bennet, can you recall what your father's last words to you were?"

Elizabeth, pulled out of a brown study, had to think for several long minutes. "They were...take joy," she said at last.

"Take joy?" repeated Mr Darcy.

"Yes," said Elizabeth, her eyes fixed on a point far away. "My father said he wished me not to grieve, to be happy and to take joy...to *find* joy in my life. He said he loved me." She looked up at him again, into his serious dark eyes. "I had forgotten. I had forgotten he said that."

"Those are not the words of a man who was hurt or upset by your feelings. I daresay he understood your distress better than you thought. He wanted you to be happy."

At that moment, the carriage came to a stop. Mr Darcy carefully handed her down, walked her to the door, bowed over her hand, and then stepped back. She opened the door, but as she made to step inside, she suddenly turned and moved quickly back towards him, embracing him tightly. "Thank you," she said in a small voice, her face buried against his chest, clasping him fiercely, and then just as quickly, she turned and ran through the door, closing it behind her.

Once inside, Elizabeth slumped against the door, breathless, her mind whirling. *What have I done?* She covered her face with her hands. Overwhelmed by emotions and sensations she was unable to even recognise, much less untangle, she bolted up the stairs in full retreat.

DARCY SAGGED against the cushioned squabs in his carriage. Elizabeth had embraced him. She had wrapped her arms around him and hugged him tightly, but it had all happened too fast for him to react. He had just stood there like a great stupid ox!

He reeled under a staggering rush of emotions: awe, euphoria, exultation, humility, and love. She had opened her heart to him and entrusted him with feelings that she had been unable to share with her own family. He could still feel her on his lap, in his arms; how she had nestled against his chest. He could still smell her scent of roses and feel the glorious silkiness of her hair.

Damnation! He sat up straight, vexed with himself. He had not thought to ask when he could next call on her. The amount of time he had spent with Elizabeth, in public and in private, would indicate to society that he was courting her. In his heart, he was; would it be too soon to ask her if their friendship could lead to more? He tried to lay out a strategy, but his mind was still whirling too much for any clear thinking.

He could not go a day without seeing her, but would she need time to recover from the wrenching emotions of the day?

And truly, what were her feelings towards him? Did she think of him as a friend? Of course they were friends. They had spent the last few weeks and more together, almost every day. They had conversed at length on many subjects, although at first, he had been the one doing most of the talking. He had seen her slowly relax and come back to herself. He had seen the sparkle in her eyes rekindle. And she had opened her heart to him. A dreamy smile flitted over his face.

Perhaps not her *whole* heart. But she *had* embraced him. Very tightly.

Darcy remembered Fitzwilliam's words. Had he shown Elizabeth his true self? Yes, he thought so. The only truth he had not shared with her was how much he loved her. How much he wished to protect and care for her. How much he *desired* her. He closed his eyes. That would never do. At least not yet.

ELIZABETH SAT IN HER ROOM, breathing deeply, struggling to pull herself together before she spoke with her aunt and uncle, to tell them that she had arrived home safely.

She did not *feel* safe. She felt raw and exposed. She had revealed her darkest self to none other than *Mr Darcy*! What on *earth* had come over her?

She could still feel his arms tighten around her, his cheek resting on her head. He had *kissed* her. On the forehead, yes, but it was still a kiss. He had called her by her given name and whispered it in her ear. She shivered. She felt raw and exposed, but also somehow thrilled. Shocked at her own behaviour and, oddly, light-hearted. And afraid. Her fingers itched to touch him again. Elizabeth shivered again, and a hot, tingly sensation swept through her body, pooling in her lower belly like warm honey. She closed her eyes, giving in to the wonder and agitation and pleasure of it. Was this desire?

She was not afraid of Mr Darcy. The time they had spent together over the last few weeks had taught her that she could trust him implicitly, and that he was a dear, gentle, caring man. A loving man. She had become as attached to the corporeal man as she had been to his dream persona. Maybe more. *I am afraid of my own feelings, because I am in love with Mr Darcy.* A man she could never have. *Stupid, pathetic girl.*

Elizabeth then remembered that she had also been given a gift that day, from her father. How could she have forgotten his last words to her? Maybe because she had been in such despair, and so upset with him. Her father had given her a gift, but she had lost it, and Mr Darcy had helped her find it again. 'Take joy', she remembered him saying. *I will, Papa.*

There was a tap on her door and Mrs Gardiner peeked into the room. "Is everything well, Lizzy?" she asked, with such an overt mixture of concern and blatant curiosity on her face that Elizabeth laughed shakily as she replied, "Yes, all is well."

"Oh, Lizzy," gasped her aunt, with tears in her eyes, "You laughed!" They spent the next hour deep in conversation, and then the two ladies turned their attentions to putting the children to bed.

The atmosphere at dinner was lighter than it had been for weeks. "Will you see Mr Darcy tomorrow?" asked her uncle.

Elizabeth was brought up short. "I do not know," she said. "I think we both forgot to mention it."

Mr Gardiner chuckled. "I will wager that there will be a note or an invitation delivered first thing in the morning!"

His wife smiled. "Edward, what would you think of hosting a small gathering ourselves. We certainly cannot formally entertain while we are still in our mourning, but perhaps a small dinner and some music? We could invite Mr and Miss Darcy, Colonel Fitzwilliam, Miss de Bourgh, and the Hursts."

Her suggestion was gladly met, and the evening ended with Elizabeth playing the pianoforte and singing. Her aunt and uncle sat together on the sofa and exchanged relieved smiles. "I will write to Jane tomorrow," she whispered to her husband, taking his hand. He squeezed hers. "I daresay everyone at Netherfield will be relieved to hear that Lizzy is almost her old self again."

Mrs Gardiner had not yet found the time to write her invitations the next morning before two invitations were delivered by messenger: one from Miss Darcy, inviting Elizabeth to practise duets together that afternoon, and the other from Lady Matlock, inviting them all to Matlock House for dinner in three days' time. Acceptances were sent immediately.

A HAPPY, glowing Louisa Hurst called at Gracechurch Street that morning as well. She had embarked upon another project, and it had been several days since she and Mrs Gardiner had had time for leisurely conversation. They had much catching up to do.

"I am glad you were at home this morning," Mrs Hurst said. "The painters are working in the great hall today, and there are buckets and ladders and sheets everywhere. The chandelier has been removed for repair, and workmen are replacing the broken tiles on the floor. I had the distinct impression that I was in the way!"

"Are you purchasing any new furnishings?"

"No, but I am having some tables refinished and that fine old Persian carpet is being cleaned and repaired. I am still doing my utmost to be economical!" Mrs Hurst rolled her eyes.

"Do you plan to renovate every room in your house?" asked Elizabeth, who was enjoying a short visit until it was time to leave for Darcy House.

"Perhaps over time. We shall do the public rooms first. Mr Hurst and I have agreed on that. The entrance hall now; I suppose the music room and the dining room next year, and perhaps one of the guest chambers. We shall put off our private chambers for now, although there is one smaller room I wish to redecorate."

Just then a footman entered with the news that the Gardiner carriage was waiting, and Elizabeth took her leave.

After her niece had made her goodbyes and quitted the room, Mrs Gardiner leaned forward and took her friend's hand, looking fully into her eyes. "Louisa," she said gently, "would that smaller room happen to be the nursery?"

"Yes! I mean, I hope so!" Mrs Hurst's eyes filled with happy tears. "That is what I wish to speak with you about most of all! There is so much I do not know!"

CHAPTER 30

As the butler led Elizabeth through Darcy House, her eyes roved each corridor, trying to catch a glimpse of a tall, masculine form. Instead, she found Miss Darcy and Miss de Bourgh awaiting her in the music room. Elizabeth was delighted to see them both, and the three ladies chatted over tea until Miss Darcy rose and carried over a stack of sheet music.

"Do you play an instrument, Miss de Bourgh?"

The diminutive lady huffed "No, my mother deemed it too taxing for my health. Georgiana is giving me lessons while I am in town, however, and I am enjoying it."

Elizabeth gazed sympathetically at Miss de Bourgh. *I might even prefer my own mother to hers.*

She and Miss Darcy sifted through the music, finally agreeing upon three duets. "Your proficiency is far greater than mine, so let us keep that in mind," said Elizabeth when they were considering which parts to play. "It is my own fault because I will not take the trouble of practising," she continued, ruefully laughing. Focused on the music in her hands, she did not notice the two cousins exchanging secret smiles at the sound of her laughter.

After sight reading and briefly practising the three pieces, the pair made their choice. They had played through it a few more times when Mr Darcy walked into the music room. Sensing his presence even before she raised her eyes, Elizabeth immediately played a series of wrong chords.

"Oh, dear," she groaned, blushing and flustered.

"Do not even think of it, Miss Bennet," said Georgiana. "We have practised long enough for today, I believe."

"I am happy to hear that," smiled Darcy, his eyes intent on Elizabeth. "Miss Bennet, may I borrow you for a moment? I would like your opinion on something in the library."

"Oh! Yes, of course. Miss Darcy, Miss de Bourgh, would you excuse me please?" Elizabeth rose quickly to her feet, clearly rattled, scattering sheets of music to the floor and catching her foot on a corner of the carpet.

"Of course! Pray, take all the time you need," said Miss Darcy, stifling a grin as the pair left the room.

Neither of the blushing couple heard the ladies' laughter as they walked down the corridor to the library. Elizabeth's eyes again took in the beautiful room, but then she flushed deeply, remembering her visit the previous day. She cleared her throat uncomfortably and turned to him. He was standing inches away, looking at her, his eyes intent.

She swallowed and forced herself to meet his eyes. "Mr Darcy," she began, her voice unnaturally high and quavering, "Pray pardon my rudeness in speaking first, but I must say my piece. I can never thank you enough for lending me your ear yesterday."

Not to mention your lap, your arms, and your lips. Such

thoughts turned her cheeks an even deeper shade of pink. "I wish...I have *long* wished to apologise to you, sir, for my impertinence to you when we first began our acquaintance last autumn in Meryton. Ever since then, I have looked back at my abhorrent behaviour and been most heartily ashamed of it. Even before my father's illness, I began to understand that I had been completely mistaken about you. I had so sorely misjudged you. I, who had prided myself on my discernment..." Her voice trailed off unevenly.

She took a shaky breath and looked down at her tightly clasped hands. "And then you rewarded my dreadful behaviour by treating me with the kindest attention I have ever known, listening to me, and understanding my feelings and—" She searched for the words. "And bringing me back to life again. I consider you the finest man of my acquaintance." She raised her eyes to his again. They were luminous with tears. "You saved me, Mr Darcy."

DARCY HAD HAD A WAKEFUL NIGHT. He had lain in the dark, searching his mind for just the right words to make clear his intentions. Now, he looked down into her shining eyes, unable to move or speak. All those fine words had evaporated from his mind. He opened his mouth to speak, but nothing came out.

Then he took her hands in his and held them against his chest. "Miss Bennet, I would…I wish to…" Finally, his head swimming, he blurted, "Miss Bennet, you must allow me to tell you how ardently I admire and love you."

Perdition, had he actually said that? Was it even possible to be more awkward? He did not want to frighten her away. He swallowed, steeled himself, and in a calmer voice said,

"Miss Bennet, I would be the happiest of men if you would allow me to pay my addresses to you."

Elizabeth stared up at him, her lips slightly parted, her dark eyes shining but unreadable. "Oh, yes. Yes, please," she breathed, leaning into him.

He released her hands and gathered her into his arms. "Elizabeth," he breathed, laying his cheek on her hair, "my heart." He closed his eyes, savouring the scent of her hair, its silken touch on his skin, his awareness of their hearts beating so close together. He raised his head and looked down at her, taking her chin between his thumb and forefinger and raising her face to look at him. "My love," he whispered, and gently brushed his lips against hers.

ELIZABETH WAS STRUGGLING to cope with an onslaught of sensation. How could a mere embrace cause such a rush of feelings? Her knees weakened. He was warm, and soft and hard at the same time. His arms felt so strong. When his lips touched hers, she lost all consciousness of anything else. Her eyes closed and her bones melted. She clutched his lapels, attempting to stay on her feet.

He again swept her up into his arms and carried her to the same spot where they had sat the day before. He kissed her again, the kiss now deep and lingering. Her arms wrapped around his neck; her fingers twined in his hair. She leaned into him and sighed. He kissed her again and then lifted his head and slightly loosened his hold on her.

"Elizabeth," he said, "I have loved you almost since the day we met. But before you agree, my dearest, I must make a confession of my own. My honour depends upon it. Please hear me out, and then you can decide if you still wish to accept my suit."

Elizabeth looked at him in confusion as he lifted one arm away from her and ran a hand over his face. She had seen Mr Darcy look disdainful, irritated, condescending, haughty, as well as kind, warm, happy, and even fleetingly unsure of himself. She had never seen him look anxious, as he did now.

"What is it?" asked Elizabeth, searching his face with concern.

"Elizabeth," he began, and then paused as if searching for words. He closed his eyes for a moment, dragging in a deep breath, then opened them and looked at her. "Elizabeth," he began again. "It is I who must apologise to you. Your impressions of my character and actions last autumn were not mistaken. I *was* the arrogant, conceited man you believed me to be."

He shook his head, as if trying to rid his mind of the idea. "I came to Netherfield at Bingley's request. The few months previous had been extremely difficult."

As his gaze returned to her face, Elizabeth recalled Mrs Hurst's words on Oakham Mount: 'something had recently happened within Mr Darcy's family that had caused him great pain.' Realising he was going to share his pain with her, her heart swelled for him. Darcy continued. "A few months before we met, my sister nearly eloped with a man who wanted her only for her fortune, and to wreak revenge on me, who he blames for all his misfortunes. I refer to George Wickham."

Elizabeth looked up at him and saw that he was becoming distressed. She reached up and lightly touched his cheek. His eyes closed briefly and he turned into her hand, softly kissing her palm and tightening his hold on her before continuing.

"Georgie was much more innocent then, more of a child, not even a year ago. Wickham made her believe that he was in love with her and wanted to marry her. If I had not impulsively decided to visit her the day before they were to have eloped, he would have succeeded. I have never been so angry in my life. Wickham, having been forewarned of my presence, left her without a word. Georgie was deeply hurt, especially when she learned her companion had been in league with Wickham. I sacked the woman, took my sister home, found her a new companion, and settled in back at Pemberley."

"Several weeks later Bingley asked me to join him at Netherfield. I had promised I would come and help him assess any estate he became interested in purchasing. Instead of the brief visit I was hoping for, Bingley insisted that we become acquainted with the neighbourhood." He looked at Elizabeth apologetically. "I have always found the curious stares of strangers to be excruciating. I know that I made a bad impression. I deserved your ill opinion. I was disagreeable and disdainful to a ridiculous degree. I know that my company was only tolerated because I was Bingley's friend. I was too ill-tempered to care. Until, shortly after I arrived, I began to be entranced by a lively, bewitching young lady, the like of whom I had never met before."

He gently took her chin in his hand and kissed her. "Elizabeth, the morning you marched into Netherfield with your muddy skirts and your glowing face, I was lost, although I could not admit it, even to myself, for quite some time. My feelings for you only deepened, but at the time, I believed that I was impervious to you, and that I was above your company."

Elizabeth made no move to pull away from him, so he continued. "The night of the ball, when we danced, I understood that my feelings for you were getting the better of me.

"The following day, after Bingley left for London, Miss Bingley began urging Mr and Mrs Hurst and me to leave Netherfield, insisting that it was of vital importance to remove her brother from your sister's company before he could declare his feelings to her. I am deeply ashamed to admit that I agreed with her, and we quit Netherfield the next morning. I had convinced myself that it was concern for Bingley that drove me to leave, but I did not admit to myself the real reason I fled. I *fled*, Elizabeth. That is the only way to describe my cowardly, despicable actions. And I willingly assisted in breaking the hearts of two of the kindest, most loving people in the world."

Elizabeth could hear her father's voice as if he was sitting next to her. *I almost pity the man. When actually confronted with a woman worthy of him, he turned tail and ran.* Papa, that inveterate observer of human folly, had been right all along.

Mr Darcy continued. "Of course, the truth will out, even with a man as blindly conceited as I was. I could not stop thinking of you all winter, Elizabeth. I could not sleep. I could barely eat. It was Fitzwilliam and Georgiana who finally made me see what a fool I was. Georgiana, whom I had always treated like a child, had not wallowed in self-pity after her experience in Ramsgate, but had grown and matured as a result of it, to the point where she has become much wiser than I." He sighed. "That tale is another example of my propensity for misapprehension that I will describe to you another time. But it was by you, my dearest, that I was properly humbled." He hugged her tightly to his chest. "*You* saved *me*, Elizabeth."

Elizabeth looked up at him. He was looking anxiously at her. "Now, my love, tell me what you think of me. I love you with my whole heart, and I would marry you today if I could."

She was silent for a several long moments, thinking of how her feelings towards Mr Darcy had changed over the course of the winter and spring. She remembered being fiercely angry with him, but could not feel that way towards him now, even with his confession of being partially behind Bingley's removal from Netherfield. She was only sorry that he still tortured himself with guilt, as she had done. He had told her the truth about his feelings and actions, even though it was unlikely that she ever would have found out if he had not. She was glad to have discovered his real self, and happy he had discovered it as well.

She felt his body grow tense, and realised that he was waiting for her response. She wrapped her arms around his neck again and leaned upward to kiss his chin. She felt him relax and his eyes met hers again.

She smiled ruefully up at him. "I must admit, sir, that I was furious with you after your party left Netherfield in November. My opinion of you began to change within a few weeks, however, thanks in part to none other than Mr Wickham, whom I finally recognised as a narcissist and a scoundrel. It pained me no end to realise that you had the right of me, Mr Darcy!"

She felt his chuckle rumble in his chest and rested her head on his shoulder. "And then, when my father was so ill and I was trapped indoors and had no one to confide my deepest fears to, you began to visit me in my dreams." She buried her face against his chest. "Oh, how mortifying this is to admit! We had many long conversations, oftentimes sitting as we are now, sir. I fear you must think me ridiculous, but I found my dreams of you to be extremely reassuring," she said into his coat.

DARCY CLOSED his eyes and laid his cheek on her hair. Moments ago, he had steeled himself for disappointment, and now, not only were they suffused in mutual happiness, she had admitted her dreams of him.

Would he ever tell her of his dreams, full as they were of raw passion and fervent intimacy, where night after night he had loved and worshipped every inch of her? Perhaps after they were married. For ten years.

Elizabeth raised her head, her cheeks pink. She gently laid her hand on his chest. "Let us not quarrel for the greater share of the blame. I have not changed my mind about your suit, Mr Darcy. I have come to love you dearly. You have only reinforced my belief that you are the best of men."

Darcy felt as if his heart might burst from his chest. He tipped his head down towards hers. "How long must our engagement be?" he murmured in her ear. She laughed, then pursed her lips and raised an eyebrow at him. He flushed and then laughed sheepishly. "That is, will you do me the great honour, madam, of accepting my hand in marriage?"

She held his gaze, her eyes softening. "Yes, Mr Darcy, I will marry you. There is nothing that would give me greater joy." She reached up to cup his cheek and guided his lips down to hers once more.

Darcy wrapped himself around her, holding her as tightly as he could. He knew that as long as he lived, he would never be happier than he was at that moment. He deepened the kiss, one hand moving from her back to grasp the curve of her waist. A voice in his head was shouting *Stop!* but then he felt her hands on his neck, in his hair. *Elizabeth.* She was holding him as tightly as he held her.

His hand was moving up from her waist when Darcy began to drag the fragile threads of his self-control together. She was naturally passionate, as he had hoped she would be, but she was still an innocent. He loved her too much to maul her on a sofa. He began to gently pull away from her, watching her face as she opened her eyes, bereft of his touch at first, and then averting her face from his as she came back to herself, seemingly shocked and overwhelmed at her own passion.

"Do not be ashamed, my darling. Our passions are natural and just. I-I apologise for my lack of control," he whispered in her ear.

"Yes…yes, of course," Elizabeth said, her voice shaking as he pulled them both again to a sitting position. She took a deep, shuddering breath. "Miss Darcy and Miss de Bourgh will be wondering where we are."

They rose to their feet unsteadily, clutching each other, embarrassed, self-consciously laughing at their own shakiness, when she looked up at his hair. His naturally unruly curls were practically standing on end. "Oh! Mr Darcy! Your hair!" She reached up and attempted to smooth it with her fingers, as he gently tucked a loose chestnut curl behind her ear.

She tilted her head back to look into his eyes, one corner of her mouth turned up. "Am I to call you Mr Darcy, even when we are married?"

He stared down at her for a moment, and then threw his head back and laughed. "You may call me anything you wish! Especially since I have been making free with your name without even begging your permission. I have been calling you Elizabeth in my mind for months. But I would very much like to hear my name on your lips."

They hurriedly smoothed the creases in their clothes, and Elizabeth reached up to adjust his cravat. Her hands resting on his chest, she met his eyes. "Fitzwilliam. Just one more," she whispered, and he bent his head to hers for a slow, gentle kiss. As their lips parted, he looked longingly at the sofa and then smiled at her. "I do like holding you on my lap, Elizabeth. When we are married, we should have all our conversations that way."

She laughed, joining in the game, clearly delighted that he was teasing her. "Perhaps not *all* our conversations, sir! We would look decidedly silly walking through Hyde Park with you carrying me in your arms."

"You are correct, as usual, Elizabeth. I shall just have to throw you over my shoulder when we go walking in the park."

She stared at him incredulously. He was looking particularly pleased with himself. "Is this really *my* Mr Darcy? I am all amazement that you can tease and laugh so much!"

He smiled down at her. "I am completely *your* Mr Darcy. That is what you have done for me, my dearest."

He sighed and pulled her into his arms once more. "Now we will leave this room and tell our families that we are betrothed. We will always have a chaperon with us now until the wedding, my love. We will likely not have a moment to ourselves. We, and especially you, will be fussed over and never left alone while everyone is making plans for our wedding. So, what say you, Elizabeth? Have you always dreamed of a large, formal wedding? If that is your wish, you shall have it, but we will have to wait until your mourning is over."

She was quiet for several long moments. "I have never wished for a large wedding. My mother is the one who always dreamed of elaborate weddings for her daughters. I would prefer us to be married as soon as possible, with a minimum of fuss. What do you prefer?"

"I also wish to marry as quickly as possible. A common licence then, and a small wedding as soon as your family can arrive from Hertfordshire? Within the next week or so?"

"That would be perfect," she agreed. He lowered his head to hers for another kiss, and then opened the door to return to the music room.

Elizabeth cast a wistful look over her shoulder. "What a wonderful library you have. Perhaps one day I might even come in here to choose a book."

THE TRUANTS RETURNED to the music room to find Anne and Georgiana had been joined by Fitzwilliam. Their announcement was met with unbounded joy, but no surprise. Toasts were drunk with lemonade, and the three young ladies embraced and laughed.

Fitzwilliam threw his arm around Darcy's shoulders. "You are a lucky man. Miss Bennet is just who you need in your life. I knew it as soon as you first described her to me."

Darcy sighed. "I might never have come to my senses if it had not been for you, Cousin. My hope is that you will soon find a woman who gives you as much happiness as I feel today."

Grimacing, Fitzwilliam replied, "That will not be easy. Especially since I anticipate following the drum for the foreseeable future."

"You never know. I certainly did not expect to find my bride in a backwater village in Hertfordshire. It will probably happen when and where you least expect it."

Fitzwilliam studied his cousin's face, infused with a joy that he could not remember having ever seen before. "I hope you are right."

A short while later, Elizabeth said her goodbyes to the three cousins and the happy couple left for Gracechurch Street. The music room fell silent for a few moments as Georgiana, Fitzwilliam, and Anne sipped the remains of their lemonade.

Anne peered at her cousins over the rim of her glass. "Did you see his *hair*?"

CHAPTER 31

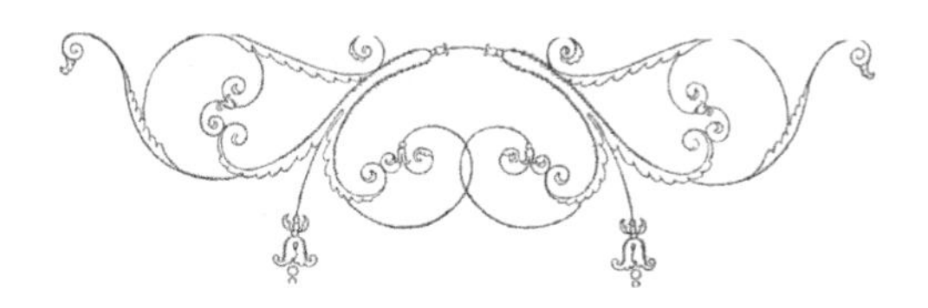

As Elizabeth was learning, with the love of her betrothed and the memory of her father's parting words, to come to terms with her sorrow and move toward her future with joy, the darkness of grief was settling over the inhabitants of Abbotsford Park. Or rather, most of the inhabitants.

Caroline entered the breakfast room to find serving dishes of food waiting on the sideboard, but the dining tables empty. Had everyone finished breakfast early? She made her selections and sat down at the table, idly curious as to the whereabouts of the rest of her company. The room overlooked the garden. Perhaps she should walk out there to see if her friends were enjoying the spring sunshine. She did not particularly enjoy walking outside, a thought which put her in mind of Miss Elizabeth Bennet—a wretched country chit whose only accomplishment was walking. She wondered whether Miss Eliza was enjoying her life as Mrs Collins. The thought of that lady being forced to tolerate that fat fool's marital attentions made her snigger so hard that tea came out of her nose. *Comme c'est amusant!* She must tell that joke to Mr Darcy this summer. And what of her elder sister, the so-called beauty? Caroline hoped she had found a comfortable spot on the shelf, poor dear.

Caroline made a quick search of the deserted garden, then checked the morning room, the drawing room, and Sophronia's favourite yellow parlour. She found no one. As she passed through a wide corridor, she heard the click of billiard balls. Lord Drayton and Lord Deerhurst were playing a desultory game in silence.

"My lords, can you tell me where I might find the ladies?"

Lord Deerhurst eyed her and answered flatly, "They are keeping Lady Riverton company as she sits with her husband."

"Oh." Caroline did not want to sit with the dying man. The last time she had seen him, he had looked so ghastly, she had quite lost her appetite. Still, it was a little too quiet in the house, so she went upstairs to find her friends. They were dull and solemn, and within a few minutes Caroline found herself quickly shown back out of the old baron's sitting room. Why was everyone being so tiresome? No one wanted to gossip, or even play cards.

As she made her way back to her rooms, she remembered that the baron's young successor was due to arrive that day. Perhaps he could offer some diversion. Perhaps she would flirt with him. There was some amusement to be found in the idea that he might fall to her charms. Goodness, she could even usurp Sophronia as the mistress of Abbotsford Park! Almost shocked by her own audacity, Caroline had a new thought. Mr Darcy had certainly missed her over the winter, and was likely anticipating their summer sojourn at

Pemberley as much as she was. Very well then. She would return to her rooms and have Bertha bathe her complexion with the distilled water of pineapples she had heard so much about.

SUPPORTED as Lady Riverton was by the friends—and her now unwelcome house-guest—who had gathered with her at her husband's estate, it was the arrival of Captain David Riverton, Baron Riverton's nephew and heir, from his posting in Egypt, that fully confirmed the baron's impending death.

Once the old baron had slipped into a deep sleep, his wife at his bedside, David left her to try to get some rest. Sophronia knew her husband had only hours, or a day at most, to live. He had been fevered and delirious, muttering and talking in his sleep to friends and family who had been in his life long before she was born. He was peaceful now, and his fever had broken. She looked over to the windows. Dawn was breaking.

Turning back to her husband, she found his eyes on her: clear, alert, and smiling. "Rupert," she said softly.

"I'm going now, my little Sophy," he whispered.

"I know," she said, unable to keep a tiny sob out of her voice.

"Do not worry about me, child. I am not afraid. I am happy to go on. I wish to see old friends and family again."

Sophronia forced a wobbly smile. "Tell Aunt Augusta that I love her."

He smiled slightly. "She already knows. She loves you too, as do I. Love goes on forever, you know." He paused and drew a rattling breath. "You will be all right, my dear. You are as strong and independent as Gussie was." The baron seemed to falter and his eyes closed. He opened them with a visible effort. "Listen, child. This is important. You must allow yourself to give up part of your independence to allow love into your life. Trust your heart. Trust Broughton."

Sophronia was looking at the floor. After a few moments, she said, "I might be too selfish to be a good wife. Or mother, for that matter."

"Nonsense, my dear, look at what good care you have taken of me. Please consider marriage again. A true marriage. I only wish I could be there to give you away." A whisper of a chuckle escaped him. "Would not that start the tongues wagging, eh?"

Sophronia had to laugh. She looked up at him again, but his eyes were closed. His breathing slowed, and he seemed to sink further into his bed. He murmured, barely audible, "*There* you are, my love." He exhaled one last time, and Sophronia heard a faint rattle.

"I love you, Rupert," she whispered, and sat, holding his hand until it cooled in hers. Then she rose and went to inform David and the others.

DARCY'S CARRIAGE pulled up to the Gardiners' town house just as Mr Gardiner and Mr Hurst were also arriving. The four walked in together, Darcy doing his best to inconspicuously catch Mr Gardiner's eye while Mr Hurst pretended not to notice.

"My wife has spent the afternoon here with your aunt, Miss Bennet," Hurst said kindly. "It seems they will be working their magic on our home once more. I do hope they have not chosen any bilious colours." He offered his arm to Elizabeth; she took it, casting a quick look behind her at her uncomfortable betrothed. Darcy glanced gratefully at Hurst's retreating form and then turned to Mr Gardiner, who was looking at him with an expectant gleam in his eye.

"Sir, I wonder if I might trouble you for a moment. I wish to speak privately with you."

Mr Gardiner led Darcy up a short flight of stairs to his study, where he invited him to take a seat. "May I offer you a glass of wine?" Mr Gardiner, unable to hide his smile, turned to busy himself with the decanter and glasses as the younger man fidgeted in the chair behind him.

Darcy took the proffered wine, sipped it, and then looked into Mr Gardiner's sympathetic face. "Sir, you have entrusted your niece into my care for several weeks now. I can never thank you enough for giving me your trust." He hesitated. "I told you when I asked you permission to spend time with your niece that I wished to help her recover her spirits. I must now admit to you that I also had a more selfish motive. Miss Bennet and I have come to an understanding, and I now come to beg your blessing upon our betrothal."

Mr Gardiner pulled a long and serious face, though there was humour in his eyes. "So you have skipped courting her completely. That seems to be the mode these days. That is exactly what your future brother Mr Bingley did!"

Darcy frowned before it dawned on him that Mr Gardiner was roasting him. "My future brother…" he repeated, looking at the older man.

"Yes, son. You have my heartfelt blessing. Mrs Gardiner and I have been witness to the tender care you have taken of our niece and have come to have deep respect and regard for you. I think I can say with certainty that my sister will happily and noisily give her blessing"—at that, he rolled his eyes—"and that my brother Bennet would have just as happily given his."

As they entered the parlour, Elizabeth's eyes met Darcy's and he smiled, stepping over to sit next to her on the sofa.

"With your permission, Mr Darcy?" Gardiner asked, and that gentleman nodded, his smile widening to a broad grin. "If I may have everyone's attention, I have some happy news. It gives me great joy to announce the betrothal of my niece Elizabeth to Mr Darcy."

A chorus of delighted exclamations and cheers rang out, and the couple was enveloped by embraces, hearty handshakes and claps on the back. After they all drank a toast to the health and felicity of the flushed and radiant couple, Elizabeth and Darcy outlined their preliminary plans. Almost an hour later, Darcy took his leave, intending to go next to the Matlocks. Elizabeth bade him a private farewell, while the Hursts and Gardiners made their own goodbyes.

"Two pieces of good news, today, Louisa!" Mrs Gardiner said *sotto voce* to her friend. "Will you tell him tonight?"

"Yes, after dinner," came the quiet reply. "I am so happy!"

They squeezed each other's hands and joined their husbands. "I shall have to do some thinking as to where to put all of our relations when they arrive for the wedding," mused Mrs Gardiner.

"Jane and Charles must stay with us, of course," said Hurst. "And—"

"And with Caroline still away," his wife finished his thought, "we have room for all of the girls!"

"Are you certain? That will make quite a house full for you!" exclaimed Mrs Gardiner.

"I am sure we can cope," Hurst assured her. "Charles and I will barricade ourselves in my study while the ladies control the rest of the house."

Laughing, the friends parted.

DARCY RODE alone in the carriage, his joy turning to trepidation the nearer he came to Matlock House. He relived the horrible scene months before when he and Caroline had talked Bingley out of courting Jane. *Such insufferable, prideful fools we were!*

What if his relations dared to disapprove and demonstrate such misplaced prejudice against Elizabeth? He desired their blessing, for Elizabeth's sake, but their opinion mattered little. Elizabeth was the only woman he could ever possibly marry, and he was going to have her. *It did not matter.*

Nevertheless, the corners of his mouth were sinking into a ferocious frown at the thought.

He hoped that Fitzwilliam and Anne had arrived before him. Would he need their support? He disliked making visits uninvited, but perhaps the news of his betrothal would be enough of an excuse. Upon arriving he was ushered in by the butler, who did a double take at his by now scowling face. He led him to the parlour. "My lord, my lady…Mr Darcy," the butler intoned sonorously, as he bowed out of the room.

Lord Matlock rose to shake his nephew's hand. "Good to see you." Darcy moved to his aunt and bowed over her hand.

"Darcy! Richard said you might be visiting us this evening." The countess peered at his face. "Are you well, dear?" she asked.

Though gestured to a chair, Darcy did not sit. Standing stiffly, he got abruptly to the point.

"Aunt, Uncle, I have asked Miss Elizabeth Bennet for her hand in marriage. She has accepted me, and we plan to marry as soon as her family can travel to town from Hertfordshire. I wanted to inform you of our plans," he said, nearly glowering at them, daring them to argue.

Lord and Lady Matlock stared at him, and the earl's face became stern.

"Miss Bennet, eh? Well…you are of age, my boy, so I cannot stop you. But it is a terrible misalliance any way you look at it," he grumbled.

Here we go. Darcy stiffened, staring at his feet, his face hardening.

"Your aunt, your cousins, and your sister have all sung Miss Bennet's praises. To be truthful, boy, I think she may be entirely too good for you."

Darcy's head snapped up, his eyes wide. The earl was smirking, and the countess had fixed an amused but disapproving stare on her husband.

"So, Darcy, why did you glare at us so fiercely? I assume that you expected some resistance?" The earl smiled sympathetically at his nephew. "There are some of your relatives that will no doubt be angry with you, but I am not one of them. You have always shown great loyalty to family, my boy, but in choosing your bride, you must please yourself. Your aunt has given Miss Bennet her complete approval, and that is good enough for me." The smirk reappeared on the older man's face. "That, and it will make my sister furious! That alone is reason enough!"

Darcy dropped into the nearest chair with an ungraceful thump. His betrothal with Elizabeth had never been in doubt, but all the same, relief overwhelmed him.

"Now our dinner party can be a small engagement celebration," smiled Lady Matlock, clasping her hands. "No engagement ball, of course, for a family still in mourning. I daresay you would never have enjoyed that kind of a fuss, even if that was not the case."

"That is correct, Aunt, and Elizabeth shares this opinion. We wish only a small wedding, as soon as her family can travel from Hertfordshire. Mr Gardiner will send an express to Netherfield tomorrow, and I will obtain a common licence. I daresay we can be wed and off to Pemberley in a week."

"A week?" exclaimed Lady Matlock. "Oh, dear! I understand that you would like nothing better than to whisk your bride off to Derbyshire where you can have her all to yourself, but consider your families. Can we not take a few days to make it a lovely, joyful occasion, especially for a family that has endured such sadness? Can we not at least have a special gown made for her?"

Darcy blinked, confounded. He had fallen back into his old habit of taking control without regard for anyone else. "I am sorry, Aunt. You are right, of course." He shook his head ruefully.

"Let me speak with Miss Bennet and Mrs Gardiner tomorrow." A martial gleam appeared in her eyes. "We will make our plans, and you will not have to worry about a thing. I believe we can have a small, beautiful wedding for you in ten days!"

Ten days! Darcy wanted to be married in one day. "All right, you know best, of course," he conceded.

He rose. "The hour grows late. I must go." He looked at his aunt and uncle. "Thank you for your support. I would marry Elizabeth even if you had disapproved, but your blessing means everything to me. I confess I am surprised, however, that you have no concern about what others of the *ton* will think."

Lord Matlock opened his mouth to answer, but his wife interjected. "Your uncle does not suffer from the excessive pride of the Fitzwilliam family because he had the good sense to marry the fourth daughter of an impoverished and insignificant baronet." She smiled affectionately at her husband, reaching over to squeeze his arm. "He knows a thing or two about defying family and society and marrying for love."

Blushing slightly, Lord Matlock eyed his wife and then turned to his nephew. "I could not have expressed it better, and I have nothing to add except to urge you to let the ladies handle it all. They will have everything their way in the end, no matter what you do. Now goodnight, my boy. We shall see you soon, I daresay."

Darcy went home, emotionally drained and oddly grateful that all he had to do was get the licence. For once, he would let others take care of everything. His only worry was how often he would be able to see Elizabeth in the ensuing rush of wedding planning. He resolved to call on her first thing in the morning, before she was swept away by his aunt.

THE HURSTS RODE home in amiable silence, each deep in thought.

"Another wedding in the family! Two unhappy people have found joy together!" Hurst mused aloud. He took his wife's hand. "I am glad to find that our prediction that Darcy would never overcome his pride was wrong. I only hope they find as much happiness as we have, my love."

His wife leaned her head against his shoulder and sighed, exhausted by the excitement of the day.

Upon arriving home, they partook of a light supper and then went to sit before the fire in the parlour. Hurst had noticed his wife's fatigue over the dining table.

"You are pale and weary, and you ate but little of your supper. Are you well?"

She smiled and turned towards him. "I am well, my dear. I have some more happy news for you." She took his hand and gently placed it on her slightly rounded belly. "I am increasing. We may expect our child to be born sometime in November."

There was only silence. His eyes were wide, staring at her.

"A baby...*our* baby..." He was silent for a moment. "Are you quite sure? Do you need to lie down? Shall I put you to bed? What—"

She put a finger against his lips, silencing him. "You can *take* me to bed, Gilbert. I feel marvellous, my love. I am perfectly healthy. There is no reason why I cannot enjoy all of our usual activities with as much enthusiasm as ever, at least for the time being," she said, waggling her eyebrows.

Hurst pulled her onto his lap and covered her face with kisses. "You have made me so truly happy. I do not know that I can ever tell you how much."

"Then show me," she sighed, melting into him.

"Every day, for the rest of my life, my darling." He rose and carried her to her bedchamber, where he spent much of the night expressing his love and joy.

CHAPTER 32

Elizabeth rose early and had just finished dressing when a maid brought her a note. Her heart leapt when she recognised the handwriting. She read it and closed her eyes briefly, savouring the lightness of heart that washed over her. One more glance at the mirror, and then, grabbing her bonnet and shawl, she left her room and moved swiftly down the stairs.

Darcy was waiting by the front door, already looking up the stairs for her. The smile that lit up his face made her weak in the knees. Gripping the railing, she instead quickened her pace, and upon reaching the bottom step impulsively launched herself into his arms. His panicked expression was priceless, and though momentarily stunned, Darcy rallied and whirled her around, his deep chuckle in her ear. "I can see that my reflexes will have to improve if I am to be your husband!"

Elizabeth, now embarrassed by her behaviour, hid her face in his shoulder. "I do not know what could have made me do such a ridiculous thing, except that I am so happy and surprised to see you this early."

"I remembered once hearing that you are an early riser, Elizabeth, so I ventured to see if you would go walking with me this morning before our aunts conspire to take you away from me."

He set her down, and taking her bonnet from her hand, settled it on her head and bent to tie the ribbons under her chin.

Elizabeth looked askance at him. "Take me away? Where?"

"After I left you yesterday, I visited my aunt and uncle Matlock to inform them of our engagement. They have given us their whole-hearted blessing, and my aunt particularly wishes to assist you and Mrs Gardiner to prepare for our wedding. She has been the closest thing to a mother to me, has no daughter of her own, and she loves to plan and organise events. My uncle often says that Fitzwilliam owes his success in the army to inheriting his mother's gift for command. A note will no doubt soon arrive inviting you both to Matlock House today."

He looked at her apologetically. "I did not even think to ask if you wished a new gown for the occasion, or flowers, or what your mother and sisters may require. I was foolish enough to assume that we could simply get a licence, go to the church, and be married. My aunt is of the opinion that a little more preparation is in order."

Elizabeth blinked. "I had given no thought to wedding preparations either! Oh, dear! Lady Matlock will not overrule our wish for a small wedding?"

"No, but she would like us to think about taking a little more time with our plans, making our small wedding beautiful, and sharing our joy with our families for a few days. She is correct, of course." He sighed. "The only idea I had was marrying immediately and sweeping you off to Pemberley right after the ceremony, but I understand that that plan will not be acceptable for everybody."

"It is acceptable to *me*," said Elizabeth.

Quickly glancing around the hall, he pulled her into his arms, and she stood on her toes to wrap her arms around his neck. He kissed her forehead, and then worked his way to her eyes, her nose, finally taking her lips. She met his kiss, tightening her arms around him.

"Dearest," she breathed into his ear, "only think that we will soon be able to start every day like this!"

She looked at him curiously as he closed his eyes and swallowed. His idea of starting every day began with them naked in his bed.

"Perhaps we had better get started, my love, before the wedding authorities catch up with us." He moved his hands to her waist, and then regretfully let go of her, taking a step back.

"Oh! I need to inform my aunt that we are going walking!" She turned towards the hall to seek out Mrs Gardiner.

"Too late, Elizabeth! I asked her permission before I gave the maid your note. Shall we go to the little park where we took our first walk together?"

Elizabeth beamed her assent, and they stepped out into the early morning sunshine.

They walked around the tiny park, her arm wound around his, their fingers discreetly entwined. Stopping to look over a collection of peonies, Elizabeth leaned her head against his arm and closed her eyes, inhaling their fragrance. She felt him release her arm only to take her left hand in his right and opened her eyes.

He was tugging at her glove one finger at a time, his

expression intent, his head tilted at an angle. "Have you taken a dislike to my gloves?" she teased.

He smiled. "Only the left one." He finally freed her hand, and then removed his own gloves. Reaching into his inner coat pocket, he extracted a small box, and opened it. She caught her breath. It was an exquisite ring, with a sparkling deep blue sapphire surrounded by diamonds set in warm gold. "It was my mother's," he said as he slipped it on her finger. "It has been waiting for you for years, my dearest."

"Oh," she gasped. "It is beautiful! I have never seen anything like it!"

She stared at the ring, beginning to comprehend that her life as Mrs Fitzwilliam Darcy of Pemberley would be quite different from her life as Elizabeth Bennet of Longbourn. She raised her eyes to his and was caught in the tenderness of his gaze, his heart in his eyes. *I shall do whatever it takes to deserve this man*, she vowed. Only the voices of an approaching nursemaid and her charges kept her from kissing him then and there.

While they were out, the anticipated note arrived from Matlock House. Darcy returned Elizabeth to the Gardiners' home and kissed her quickly before her aunt entered the hall. With a bow, he bid them both good day, and rode his horse back to Darcy House, scheming as to when he could next get his beloved alone.

AFTER BREAKFAST and some time with the children, Elizabeth and her aunt took the carriage to Matlock House. Lady Matlock welcomed them into a small sitting room that contained silk-cushioned chairs positioned around an elegantly carved round table. She smiled at her guests, and her eyes fell on the sapphire gracing Elizabeth's finger.

She took Elizabeth's hand. "I have not seen that ring these fifteen years or more." Lady Matlock blinked quickly, then squeezed her hand and let it go. "It looks as if it was made for you, my dear."

"Thank you, my lady," said Elizabeth softly, as the countess settled in at the table.

"Mrs Gardiner, Miss Bennet, I hope you do not think it too forward of me to insert myself into plans that you may want to keep within your own family. Just say the word, and I will leave you to it."

Aunt Gardiner looked searchingly at her niece and patted her hand. "It is your wedding, Elizabeth. What say you?"

Elizabeth met the gaze of the distinguished lady who was soon to be her aunt and smiled a little bashfully at her. "I would value your opinion. Mr Darcy and I agree with your idea of a small celebration for our families. While we would both be happy with a quiet event like the recent wedding of my elder sister, we would like our families to share our joy. We are still in a state of mourning, however, and need to plan accordingly."

"How will your mother feel at not having a say in these preparations?" asked the countess.

Elizabeth and her aunt exchanged a glance before Mrs Gardiner spoke. "Mrs Bennet will be realistic. She is still bereaved, and while she is recovering, has not quite regained her bearings. Not to mention, she is unfamiliar with the merchants and tradesmen here in London. Perhaps we can leave some tasks for her when she arrives in town."

Elizabeth had a guilty sense of relief that her mother was not present, but she was sorely missing her elder sister. She and Jane had oftentimes discussed weddings in their late-night conversations, Elizabeth mostly listening. She would have so loved to have Jane with her.

She pushed away her still-conflicted feelings about her mother. “When my father was alive, my mother liked nothing better than to host dinner parties with many courses. They were always wonderfully planned and beautifully executed.” A shadow flitted over her face as she recalled her father sitting at the head of the dining table at Longbourn, puckish smile and arched eyebrow in place. She blinked furiously for a second, then swallowed and looked at her aunt. “Perhaps when she arrives, she could be in charge of the wedding breakfast.”

Lady Matlock, unable to miss the fleeting expression of sorrow on Elizabeth’s face, quickly agreed. “That makes perfect sense, dear. If it is something she has always enjoyed, she will feel more comfortable, more within her own element I daresay.”

A short discussion settled them on the breakfast at the Gardiners’ home, with an offer from Lady Matlock to send over servants to assist.

“We need invite only family and a few close friends. I should like to invite Sir William Lucas and his family, and possibly their married daughter, Mrs Collins. Mr and Mrs Hurst are family now, and have been such good and generous friends.”

Lady Matlock sat back in her chair, her eyebrows high. “Hurst? Do you mean Bingley’s brother? That choleric man and his mousy little wife? Are you well acquainted with them, Mrs Gardiner?”

“Yes, we are. Our acquaintance with Mr and Mrs Hurst began only a few months ago, and I have never known them to be anything but warm and cordial. We count them as particular friends.” Mrs Gardiner smiled slightly and exchanged a glance with her niece. “I admit, however, that Elizabeth has depicted them to me as she knew them last year when they first visited Hertfordshire, and your description would have been apt at the time. I believe they have been much happier, and thus more comfortable in society, since their sister, Miss Caroline Bingley, moved out of their home."

"Oh! Well! That would explain quite a *lot*!" Lady Matlock shuddered slightly and leaned forward, speaking with particular emphasis. "I am acquainted with Miss Bingley, and *well* acquainted with her ambition to wed my nephew. I do not know if I can express how relieved I am at her failure."

THE FOLLOWING EVENING, they all gathered again at Matlock House for the countess's previously planned dinner. Out of sheer curiosity, Lady Matlock had at the last minute extended her invitation to Mr and Mrs Hurst.

As the dinner progressed, toasts were drunk to the betrothed couple. Mr Hurst, sitting on Lady Matlock's left, rose to propose a toast.

"Little did we know, last October, when we visited Hertfordshire, that we were witnessing the beginnings of a love story. Although," he turned and winked at his wife. "Louisa and I did have an inkling." Louisa winked back amid general chuckling as her husband continued. "We are both thrilled that our speculations turned out to be accurate. To Mr Fitzwilliam Darcy, our old friend, and to Miss Elizabeth Bennet, our new sister, we drink to your now and future happiness."

The assembled company cheered, clinked their glasses and drank. Lady Matlock observed him thoughtfully as he sat down. She leaned over and said quietly, "Well done, Mr Hurst."

LADY CATHERINE DE BOURGH, chin in the air, was watching with narrowed, critical eyes as a footman buttered toast to her specifications. A stack of correspondence lay on a small tray next to her plate. She ignored it at first, entertained as she was with an idea of bypassing the dean and going straight to the bishop in Rochester in her search for a satisfactory candidate for the Hunsford living. Finally, her breakfast prepared to her liking, she took a letter from the stack, opened it, and choked on a piece of ham.

Purple-faced and spluttering, she jumped to her feet as the hapless footman stood paralysed with indecision. "You! Call for my carriage! Dawson! Dawson! Prepare my trunk! We are to London!" she bellowed. Clutching the crumpled, twisted letter in her hand, she hurried toward her chambers, growling through gritted teeth, "This is not to be borne!"

Later that day, once she had reached London, Lady Catherine's dudgeon was even higher. A frenzied pounding at the large front doors of Matlock House brought the butler hurrying across the wide expanse of polished marble tiles to open it. He was knocked back on his heels as Lady Catherine pushed quickly past him.

"Where is she?" she cried. "My daughter, where is she? Bring her to me immediately!"

The butler sedately adjusted his coat and bowed. "My lady, Miss de Bourgh is not here at present. I will tell Lord Matlock that you are here. If you would wait in the blue parlour, refreshments will be brought and my lord will receive you." He showed her to the parlour, offered her a seat, and went in search of his master and mistress, closing the door behind him.

Lady Catherine paced agitatedly back and forth. Her journey to London had done little to blunt the edges of her anger. Her own daughter, a traitress! *How sharper than a serpent's tooth it is to have a thankless child!* After all she had done for Anne, the child went behind her back and corresponded with the diocese!

As she paced and fumed and waited for the earl, the muted sounds of the busy household reached her ears. Footsteps and muffled voices of servants made for unintelligible background noise until her ear caught the word 'wedding'. Lady Catherine halted. Whose wedding? She moved to the door, pressing her ear against it. She could hear the voices of two young females, obviously maids going about their business. She could just make out the words 'Mr Darcy' and 'wedding'.

Darcy's wedding? With Anne staying in London, had he finally come to the point? This intelligence should have pleased her, but her sense of being ill-used only intensified. Why had she not been told? Were they going to marry in London? Not if she had anything to say about it, and Lady Catherine determined to have *everything* to say about it. Nothing would do but a grand wedding at Rosings. Her proud visage darkened. Had *Darcy* been the one to trespass on her authority to fill the living at Hunsford? Hah! He would hear about that! It could not have been Anne's doing after all!

She opened the door a crack and stood very still, listening for any further titbits of gossip. The maids' voices were farther away now, but with the door slightly open, she heard the unthinkable. "I like Miss Bennet, she's so kind," said one girl to the other. "'Tis like a fairy tale, it is, her and Mr Darcy getting married…" and the voices faded completely.

Lady Catherine froze. Bennet, Bennet, where had she heard that name? It did not matter. She threw open the door to the parlour and stomped furiously back across the shining floor to the front entrance, her walking stick tapping an agitated counterpoint to her heavy footfalls. A footman hurriedly opened the doors for her as she exited. Her carriage had not left, and without even pausing to be handed up, she scrambled inside, shouting, "Darcy House! Take me to Darcy House!"

THOUGH THE WEDDING was only days away, the preparations were well in hand. Darcy and Georgiana had invited Anne and Elizabeth to spend a quiet afternoon prior to the Bennet family's arrival.

They had been enjoying tales of each other's childhoods. Darcy, in particular, had been teasing Anne and Georgiana with his remembrances of childish foibles, when the sound of slamming doors and raised voices penetrated to the music room where they were seated. Darcy and Georgiana had both begun to rise when the door burst open with such force that it bounced off the wall. Lady Catherine rushed in, her walking stick raised as if she were leading a charge.

"Mother!" gasped Anne, rising.

"Quiet! I will deal with you shortly," Lady Catherine snarled. Brushing her daughter away, she turned to Darcy, but the little woman persisted. "Mother, what brings you to London?"

"I have received a letter of a most alarming nature. You have gone behind my back in regards to the appointment of the new rector, so you will understand the reason of my journey hither. Such treachery will not be tolerated!"

"As owner of Rosings estate, it is my prerogative to—" Anne began.

"I will not be interrupted! Hear me in silence!" thundered the older woman, who was turning again to Darcy when her eyes fell on Elizabeth. Lady Catherine stared at her, her lip curling into a sneer, her narrowed eyes raking the younger lady's appearance.

"This…creature…must be the jezebel who has distracted you from your duty, Darcy," she growled as Georgiana gasped and moved immediately to sit next to her new sister, grasping

Elizabeth's hand. The older lady stared at Elizabeth. "Bennet. I know where I have heard of you. You are the tart who refused your cousin's offer of marriage. Trying to catch a bigger fish all along, were you? You have failed. He will never marry you! He has been destined from birth to marry *my* daughter! Any connexion to you would disgrace my nephew in society; he would be censured and despised, ruined because of your paltry arts and allurements! You will be cast out, your name never mentioned by any of us!"

Darcy, pale and rigid with rage, hissed, "Miss Bennet is a *lady*, and she is the only lady I will ever consider marrying." He stepped toward his aunt. "How dare you…" he was saying, his voice rising as a further commotion was heard outside the music room. The earl rushed into the room.

"Catherine, are you mad?" he began, but his sister was oblivious to him, focussed completely on her nephew.

"Are you so lost to propriety, to honour, to all reason; that you would consider an alliance to a chit with such low connexions? She is nothing but a fortune huntress!" Understanding that she was getting nowhere, Lady Catherine tried a placating tone. "Your sense of pity for your inferiors overcomes you. No one of our rank will censure you if you take her under your protection, give her carte blanche, have your bit of muslin on the side, but you must marry *Anne*!"

Elizabeth stood abruptly, her bearing straight, her chin high, her face pale but composed. She opened her mouth to speak, but it was Darcy whose voice was heard, hard, icy, and controlled.

"Lady Catherine, the only betrothal between myself and my cousin exists solely in your own fevered imagination. I will marry Miss Bennet, and only Miss Bennet, if she will still have me after your little performance. I would happily, nay gratefully, renounce my place in society, but this will not come to pass. My betrothed will be received and admired wherever she goes.

"You, on the other hand, will leave this house immediately. You will never be received here, at Pemberley, or at any of my other properties again. Henceforth neither I, nor any of my family, will know you. Our connexion is broken forever. Now, I shall escort you out for the last time."

"I can do that, nephew." Lord Matlock stepped to his side. "Catherine, you have really done it this time. Not only have you been breaking the law by keeping Anne's inheritance from her, but you have disgraced us all, the entire Fitzwilliam family, with your behaviour. I should have you committed. I can do that, you know."

Anne, having quietly retreated and busied herself at a small table, quickly came forward with a note sealed with wax. She moved to the door and handed it to a footman. "Please have this sent express immediately."

She watched the footman go, then turned to fully meet Lady Catherine's glare. Chin in the air, Anne walked slowly to her mother, holding her gaze. "That was a note to Mr Kendrick. I have authorised him, and Mr Houston, along with the servants of Rosings, to remove all your personal belongings to the dower house. Any servants who refuse to comply will lose their positions. While I will not cut ties with you, at least not at this time, our relationship will be on a different footing in the future. Now, Uncle, please excuse me if I do not leave with you."

All colour had drained from Lady Catherine's face, but she braced to resist being moved until the earl said in her ear, "*Bedlam*, Catherine. Do not think I will not follow my words with deeds. Do I need to employ Darcy's footmen to get you out the door?"

As they turned away, another voice, as yet unheard, softly

and calmly broke the taut silence. "My lady, you have insulted me in every possible method. Yet I am sorry for your distress. You bring it upon yourself. You were born into a loving family of excellent, noble people, yet you bully and abuse them. You have a strong, intelligent, delightful daughter whom you should love just as she is; yet you kept her from the world, thinking only of how you can use her in your schemes. I am extremely happy to marry Mr Darcy, who is the very best of men, and deeply honoured to be accepted into this family." Elizabeth was visibly trembling, but her voice was steady and clear. "You have no cause to repine, yet you dwell only upon your discontent. You cannot see what is before your own eyes. I pity you, Lady Catherine."

The older lady's eyes flamed, but the earl, flanked by two strong footmen, gripped her arm tightly and pulled her from the room.

Elizabeth dropped to her chair, still shaking, wrung out by her emotions. Darcy dropped to his knees before her as, unnoticed, Anne and Georgiana quickly exchanged a glance and silently left the room, closing the door behind them.

He took her hands a little desperately. "Elizabeth," he began, but words failed him as they too often did when his emotions ran high. Finally, he stammered, "I…I am sorry, more than I can say, for my aunt's behaviour. It is especially hurtful, knowing that I demonstrated such arrogance in the past, such selfish disdain for others…but I never…what I once was…please do not leave me!" he blurted, his forehead dropping upon her knee.

"No, Fitzwilliam." He raised his eyes to hers. Her smile was weary but the warmth in her eyes reassured him. "Even at your worst, you were never like Lady Catherine. You never could be."

In a trice, he lifted her into his arms, whirled and seated

himself in the chair, Elizabeth in his lap. Clutching her to his chest, he kissed her once, twice, and then buried his face against her neck, murmuring hoarsely, "At times I fear I will forever be begging your forgiveness."

"And I will be begging yours, many times, to be sure. We share a tendency towards willfulness, you and I," she countered gently. She put her arms around his neck. "We are in our preferred posture for conversation are we not?"

He laughed ruefully. "Perhaps this will always be the way we share what is in our hearts. I love you so, Elizabeth."

"And I love you. You are *mine*, my dear man. You will not be rid of me, over this or anything else." She kissed him soundly. "Besides, we cannot let her win, can we?"

EVEN WITH THE happy anticipation of marriage, the prospect of her mother's arrival had Elizabeth on tenterhooks. She did not wish to be under the same roof as her mother, could think of nothing to say to her, yet could see no way out. Shortly before the Bennet carriage was to arrive, Darcy was ushered into the Gardiners' sitting room where Elizabeth had been waiting anxiously. Relief flooded through her.

"Thank you for coming today," Elizabeth said, as he sat down next to her and took both of her hands in his. She met his eye sheepishly. "I am being such a goose about this!"

"Your mother caused you a considerable amount of pain in an already dire situation. It is only natural that you would feel anxious about encountering her again." Darcy glanced quickly at the door and then wrapped his arm around Elizabeth's shoulder, pulling her close. He kissed her temple and then met her eyes.

"I do not know your mother well, but if I were to hazard a

guess, I would say that Mrs Bennet will treat you as her current favourite."

Elizabeth leaned away, regarding him with a sceptical eye. "I was never her favourite—even at the best of times."

Darcy smiled at her dubious expression. "My love, you last saw your mother less than a fortnight after your father's death. Since that time, her worries have vanished. She has one daughter married and another betrothed. Her remaining daughters will be educated and prepared to come out in society. She will always have a comfortable place to live and servants to care for her. She no longer has anything to fear. She may have even forgotten her antipathy towards you."

He cocked his head to one side, looking down at her with concern. "Do you think you can stay here with her, Elizabeth? If not, my aunt would gladly offer you her hospitality."

"That is generous of her." Sighing, she went on, "I do wish to know Lady Matlock better. But I cannot leave my uncle's house. They are as dear to me as my own parents, in some ways even more. When I leave to begin my new life, it will be from this house. I must think on my future happiness while enduring the sometimes unpleasant present," she said, rolling her eyes. Darcy squeezed her shoulder and leaned in for a light kiss. "That is my brave girl."

They heard Mrs Gardiner's quick step in the hall and Darcy deftly pulled his arm back to his side and shifted away from Elizabeth. Mrs Gardiner came into the room, slightly breathless. "They are here, Lizzy. Will you be all right?"

"Yes, Aunt," she replied firmly, her chin rising slightly, "I will be." She smiled up at Darcy and they rose together, his fingertips skimming lightly down her back before he stepped away to the other side of the room.

Mrs Gardiner hurried towards the front door, and within

minutes they could hear the excited voices of the Bennet family as they entered the house, all talking at once. Their enthusiasm increased in volume until the ladies burst into the sitting room.

"Lizzy!" they cried as one, and then Elizabeth was swept into a series of hugs, first by Lydia, then Kitty, and finally into a gentle embrace by Mary.

"We have missed you so, Sister," Mary whispered to her before stepping back and holding Elizabeth at arm's length. "You look so happy! Is all of this Mr Darcy's doing?"

"Yes, mostly." Elizabeth smiled into her sister's eyes and said softly, "He is such a good man, Mary. I love him."

Mary glanced sideways at her new brother. "And he loves you, that is obvious."

Elizabeth glimpsed movement out of the corner of her eye and turned to see her mother bearing down on her. Tensing, she moved to meet her, then felt a strong, warm hand cup her elbow.

"Oh, Lizzy! Two daughters married! I shall go distracted —" began Mrs Bennet, when she glanced up and her voice faded.

"Good afternoon, Mrs Bennet," said Mr Darcy, with a slight bow, his countenance serious, but not unkind.

"Oh...Good afternoon to you, Mr Darcy, I am sure. I…I must thank you again for your visit to us at Netherfield." Mrs Bennet seemed to be at a loss for words.

"It was my pleasure, madam, and indeed it is a pleasure to see you again today. I am greatly anticipating your guiding hand on the preparations for our wedding breakfast."

Mrs Bennet relaxed and smiled slightly. "Thank you, sir. You must give me a list of your favourite dishes, and those of Miss Darcy." She turned again to Elizabeth. "Oh, Lizzy, how rich and grand you will be…such carriages and jewels…and how kind he is…" She began to sniffle. "And your father would be so happy!"

Mrs Gardiner appeared at her side. "Dear Fanny, you must be exhausted. Let me to take you to your room." The two ladies left the room, and Elizabeth exhaled and sat down.

"That went well," commented Lydia brightly.

Kitty closed her eyes. "Lydia…"

"I must agree with Lydia," said Mary quietly. Her eyes moved to her youngest sister. "Although perhaps not aloud."

Elizabeth stared at them, her eyes moving from her sisters' faces to that of her betrothed, who was smirking at her. She looked at him, then her sisters, and began to laugh. "I have missed you all so much!"

CHAPTER 33

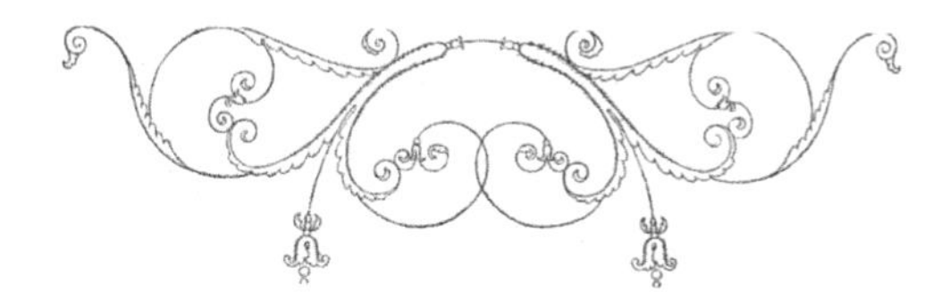

Georgiana, even at the tender age of seventeen, was far more comfortable navigating London's shops than its society. At the behest of her brother, she took charge of her new sister's wardrobe and led Elizabeth through a bewildering series of visits to drapers, milliners, and mantua-makers. Her head spinning, Elizabeth's protests were in vain. "Do not quibble," insisted Georgiana. "My brother wishes to pamper and spoil you a little. Not to mention, once we remove to Pemberley, you might not get back to town for months!"

WHILE HIS SISTER, Elizabeth, and all her relations busied themselves with shopping and wedding preparations, Darcy was growing restive. Besides the endless fittings, there were gatherings of one kind or another almost every day at Darcy House, the Hursts' in Grosvenor Square, in Gracechurch Street or at the earl's residence. In the whirlwind of preparation, sometimes an entire day would go by when he was not able to have Elizabeth to himself, even for a moment. It was all he could do not to abduct her from her uncle's house, throw her in his carriage and drive off as fast as his horses could run. He chided himself. Elizabeth deserved a beautiful wedding, surrounded by family and friends, with all the preparations that would entail. He would have her by his side for the rest of his life.

It was Bingley who first took note of Darcy's discomfiture. As the days ticked by, a small conspiracy formed to allow the lovers some time alone. Their friends and relations—even Mary—pretended to be oblivious as Darcy occasionally pulled Elizabeth away from the group and into darkened halls or alcoves for whispered conversations and stolen kisses. Mrs Collins joined the silent collaboration when she arrived two days prior to the wedding.

BARON RIVERTON'S earthly remains lay in state for three days, as neighbours, tenants, and old friends came to pay their respects. Though most of his contemporaries were long dead, a number of titled gentlemen travelled down from London for the funeral service. Since ladies could not attend funeral services (though she had considered attending and daring anyone to complain), Sophronia welcomed the work of planning the service and hosting her guests as a distraction from her grief. The shoulder feast, in particular, would be a tribute to him, a remembrance among friends, with the ladies included.

David, her childhood companion to whom the baron had been a de facto father when his own parents had perished, supported her in her planning. Broughton, along with her other friends, watched her carefully, ready to offer comfort when needed. Others, namely the guest who would not leave, had other motivations for remaining during this saddest of times.

Caroline Bingley's maid had packed several black day gowns and a few black evening gowns once she understood why her mistress's party was removing to Abbotsford Park. In her chamber, Caroline studied the options Bertha had laid out before her. She had also studied the list of guests staying after the funeral service. They included among their number several powerful gentlemen of distinguished rank and fortune. A marquis, heir to a duke no less, was among them. None of them were *her* intended gentleman; he was, of course, still at Pemberley, and besides, had not known the old baron well. Still, it would not hurt to show herself to advantage before these men of the first circles. Their admiration of her would further reinforce her advantage in Darcy's esteem.

The occasion would require full dress of course, with great attention to detail. As Caroline chose her gown, headdress, slippers and accessories, Bertha groaned inwardly. It was going to be one of *those* evenings.

HEAVY, roiling, black clouds had thundered over Abbotsford Park in the early morning. By midday a heavy, steady rain was falling from low, grey clouds, and the many lit candles did little to dispel the gloom. The afternoon was dark, reflecting the mood of the assembled company.

The funeral service over, the gentlemen guests returned to the manor house, gathering in the drawing room to proceed into the expansive dining room for the feast.

Lord Drayton came to his wife's side and spoke quietly. "Miss Bingley has not come downstairs. I will wait for her and take her in to dinner. Sophy and David should go on and lead their guests into the dining room. Dashed rude of the chit to keep us waiting."

Nearly everyone was seated when Drayton, red-faced and clearly mortified, brought Caroline in to dinner. One glance at the lady was explanation enough.

Caroline well understood the impact of a grand entrance. She clutched a handkerchief trimmed with black rosettes and dabbed at her dry eyes whenever she remembered. Her mourning frock, though black, was anything but subdued. It was profusely adorned with black velvet ribbons, black lace, and jet beads. The barely-there bodice was just shy of scandalous. She wore a black headdress decorated with feathers and a beaded veil that came down to her collarbones. The combination of dark fabric and pale exposed skin in the murky light gave the impression of a pair of bosoms floating around under their own power.

At her entrance, conversation stopped, cutlery clattered onto porcelain plates, and a footman overfilled a goblet.

SOPHRONIA, at one end of the long table, her face ashen, stared at the spectacle, frozen in her revulsion and fury. Her husband, her rock, her oldest and dearest friend, was dead, and Caroline Bingley was callously using the occasion to draw attention to herself. She made as if to rise when a gentle hand on her forearm stopped her. It was the marquis, who as the highest-ranking guest was seated to the right of his hostess.

"Before you draw even more attention to that *woman*, for she is no lady, think instead of what your late husband would have done in this situation."

Sophronia stared at him for a long moment. "He would have laughed," she finally answered. The anger faded from her countenance. She swallowed and offered up a watery smile. "He is probably laughing right now."

"Just so," said the marquis. "Let us think on the baron's amusement and pay no more attention to *her.*"

After dinner, the ladies retired to the drawing room in silence, with the exception of Miss Bingley, who rattled on about the most distinguished of the mourners who had been present. *As if it were some sort of party*, marvelled Lady Drayton, shocked to her core. She and Judith walked on either side of Sophronia, watching for any indications of distress, but the widow was calm and self-possessed.

As they reached the drawing room, Sophronia turned to the other ladies. "If you will excuse me, I will retire to my room. I need some time to collect my thoughts."

Lady Drayton's arm encircled her friend's shoulders. "Send for us if you wish some company," she whispered.

CHAPTER 34

Matlock House glittered on the eve of the wedding. Though an engagement ball had been out of the question, Lady Matlock had spared no effort for her small celebration. The magnificent home was alight with candles, marble and silver gleamed, polished wood glowed, and as always, there were flowers in profusion.

Mr and Mrs Hurst had been recent guests, as had the Gardiners, and Mr Bingley was also acquainted with the well-appointed home; however, the Bennets, the Philipses, and the Lucases were unaccustomed to such luxury. As Elizabeth's family was led through the magnificent hall, all conversation ceased, jaws dropped, and heads swivelled. Charlotte Collins, by now accustomed to great houses through her familiarity with Rosings, prodded Kitty and Lydia gently and they closed their mouths. Sir William and Lady Lucas walked slowly, intent as they were in memorising every detail to share with their neighbours in Meryton.

After almost an hour of introductions and conversation, the butler announced dinner. Lady Matlock had seated Mrs Bennet at her right. Elizabeth exchanged a worried glance with her betrothed, but he only smiled and gave an almost imperceptible shake of his head. Mrs Bennet looked nervous and fragile as she smiled tentatively and was seated.

"Mrs Bennet, your daughter has described to me the wonderful dinners you have hosted. I must confess I am looking forward to the wedding breakfast almost as much as the wedding!" said Lady Matlock kindly.

Mrs Bennet perked up. "Oh! My lady! Thank you!" she replied breathlessly. She launched into an enthusiastic and detailed description of the courses planned for the meal until Lady Matlock's head positively spun. As Mrs Bennet paused to draw a breath, a voice from her other side interrupted.

"Mrs Bennet, how does your cook like her new kitchen?" It was Hurst, endeavouring to draw her attention from the countess. He was successful, for which he earned a grateful look from her ladyship.

The dinner, with many courses, drew to a close. The men lingered briefly for cigars and brandy, and then joined the ladies in the large drawing room, where the assembled company broke into small groups and settled into chairs.

"Jane and I will return to Netherfield after the wedding, but we have decided to purchase a house in town before the next Season," said Bingley. He was sitting with Darcy and Fitzwilliam, the older gentlemen having joined in a discussion on the finer points of the law concerning land disputes, a subject on which Mr Philips was an expert.

"How about Netherfield? Have you found the estate you were looking for?" asked Fitzwilliam.

Bingley tugged at his neckcloth, his mouth quirking up on one side. "My wife and I have discovered that there is such a thing as being a little too close to family, as dear as they are to us. We have decided together to move into town when the lease to Netherfield expires, and to begin the search anew for an estate."

"I have heard of a small estate not thirty miles from Pemberley that may go on the market," put in Darcy. "Shall I make an enquiry?"

Bingley scoffed and punched him gently in the arm. "As a newly married man myself, Darcy, I will be astonished if you can spare attention for anything but your beautiful bride. Later, when you have the time and inclination, I would be most happy to learn more about it."

He frowned slightly. "There remains the question of where our mother-in-law will live after September, when the lease expires."

Darcy blinked. He had had every intention of handling that, but had forgotten it in the round of wedding plans. "Pray, let me take responsibility for that, Bingley. You have already done so much for the family, and I have contributed embarrassingly little. I will speak with Mr Philips and Mr Gardiner about finding a suitable house. Of course, we will need to ascertain if Mrs Bennet is desirous of staying in Meryton."

The two gentlemen met each other's eyes gravely. There remained the possibility that Mrs Bennet might wish to live with one of her married daughters, a sobering prospect indeed. Bingley heaved a sigh. "Let us not think about that today. Only happy thoughts on this occasion, *Brother*."

Darcy grinned. "Indeed, *Brother*."

"You do realise that I have sacrificed my wife's company tonight, Darcy. For the sake of your marital bliss, that is."

"Yes, Elizabeth told me that Jane is staying with her at the Gardiners' home this evening," smiled Darcy. After a pause, he said reflectively, "They have missed each other."

After another pause, Bingley nodded pensively. "We are lucky men."

The conversation had grown rather too serious for Fitzwilliam; as the only unattached man in the room, he endeavoured to lighten the mood.

"Darcy! I have just had an idea! Shall Bingley and I keep you company tonight? We can hold your hand and try to assuage your delicate sensibilities," he cooed solicitously. Darcy snorted and pretended to glare at his cousin, while Bingley roared with laughter.

"My only fear is that I may not be able to sleep a wink," Darcy replied, doing his best not to smile. "So if you would like to attend me and either ply me with brandy, or hit me over the head with a mallet, you may do so."

AS THE COUPLES mixed and mingled in conversation, the unmarried ladies sat together and chatted. Georgiana had pinned what she hoped was a calm smile on her face, hoping her nervousness among so many strangers was not obvious, when she encountered Mary Bennet's quiet gaze.

"How go your duets with Lizzy, Miss Darcy?" she asked.

"Oh, we had just begun to practise one piece when my brother proposed, and in the ensuing preparations, we have not had time to work on it. I suppose it will have to wait until we are together at Pemberley again. Not that I would have it any other way, of course," Georgiana added quickly.

"Will you be traveling to Pemberley with your brother and Lizzy?"

She smiled wryly. "No. They have invited me, but I shall stay with my aunt while they are at Darcy House and for a week afterward before travelling to Derbyshire."

"I shall also be staying in London," Mary replied, her

voice warming with excitement. "My aunt is hiring a music master for me, and perhaps some other tutors as well."

Georgiana's countenance brightened, her reticence forgotten. "Oh, I know just who your aunt should engage for your music lessons. And I can suggest a drawing master as well."

The two young ladies fell into deeper conversation, their heads together, and within a few minutes were headed for Lady Matlock's music room.

The remaining ladies drifted into conversation about the weather and their shared relief to be enjoying such a fine spring.

"We were almost completely housebound," said Kitty. "I have never seen the snow so deep, and the wind! How was it in Kent, Miss de Bourgh?"

"I would say we were fortunate, do you not agree, Mrs Collins? We did have snowstorms, but it was more likely sleet or freezing rain. We did have storms of ice, that broke off many branches from the trees. Nothing to compare to Hertfordshire, or Derbyshire for that matter. They were completely snowed in at Pemberley for months!"

Charlotte looked at Kitty. "My father told me that your farmhands were unable to make their way back to Longbourn after Christmas. Who helped Emmons with the horses and livestock?"

"Our footmen stepped in, but they also had duties in the house. Lizzy also did some of the chores, but she was much occupied with house matters and caring for my father, so Lydia took over most of them."

"Bravo, Miss Lydia!" said Anne.

Lydia blushed happily and chattered, "I am the tallest, and the strongest. Poor Lizzy had enough to do. I was glad to be helpful. All my sisters were working so hard." Her eyes lit up. "Lizzy said I was an Amazon! Of course, I am not really an

Amazon. I have both my bos...oh…oh. Well," she trailed off awkwardly.

"Lydia…" moaned Kitty, her head in her hands.

Charlotte, blushing madly, said soothingly, "I am sure that you were a great help, Lydia."

Miss de Bourgh's eyebrows had nearly reached her hairline. "Do not worry on my account, Miss Catherine. I think you were all very brave."

The ladies heard coughing and looked up. Colonel Fitzwilliam had approached them unnoticed while they were talking and was standing behind Lydia. He was beet red and appeared to have broken into a sweat.

"Are you well, Cousin?" Miss de Bourgh asked, biting her lip.

"Shall I pat you on the back?" asked Lydia helpfully.

The colonel regained his voice and rasped, "Thank you, Miss Lydia, I am quite all right. I simply need a glass of water. Cold water." He excused himself and headed for the refreshment tables.

His cousin, beaming, looked again at Lydia. "This is such fun," she said. "I do not believe I have ever seen Fitzwilliam turn quite that colour before. I do hope you will visit me at Rosings someday, ladies."

THE HOUR GREW LATE, and the guests prepared to leave. Anne had reluctantly retired early, and the others were now saying their goodbyes. Elizabeth stepped into the corridor to seek out Georgiana when a long arm shot out and pulled her into a darkened room. Her surprised laughter was stilled by a pair of lips descending on her own, at first gently, but then more demanding as her lips parted. The kiss deepened and their embrace tightened until they loosened their hold to gasp for air. She laid her head against his chest as he whispered, "My wife. My dearest wife. After tomorrow we will never have to be parted again."

Elizabeth slid her hands under his coat and stroked his back, feeling his body respond. Too overcome for words, all she could do was blink back her tears and kiss his neck. Upon hearing footsteps in the corridor, they broke apart. He leaned his forehead against hers. "Tomorrow," he said hoarsely. "Tomorrow," she whispered. He glanced at the door. "You had better go," he whispered, propelling her towards the door. With a lingering gaze at him, she stepped back out into the corridor.

AN HOUR LATER, Jane and Elizabeth were stretched out on Elizabeth's bed. Their aunt had offered to keep their mother occupied so that she would not remember to deliver *the talk* to her second daughter on the eve of her wedding.

"Before Charles and I were married, Mama was too distracted to talk to me, so Aunt Gardiner explained what men and women do together, for which I am eternally grateful," said Jane, her cheeks still pink, after she had gently explained the basics to her sister.

"Were you frightened?"

Jane took Elizabeth's hand. "I was nervous, to be sure. But I could never be frightened of Charles. Never. He is so good and caring, sometimes I think he is just made of love. Charles even told me he could wait, since it was so soon after Papa died. But I did not want to put it off, in spite of everything else. It just made me feel even closer to him." She paused. "Are you frightened?"

Elizabeth shook her head. "I am not afraid of Darcy.

"He loves you very deeply."

"I know. And I love him. I trust him. I trust him completely." She was lost in thought for a minute. "I am not afraid of Darcy," she repeated. "I am afraid of being vulnerable. But I feel such desire for him, I can hardly keep from touching him. I cannot wait to see him naked. Do not laugh at me, Jane."

The two sisters dissolved into giggles, their faces scarlet. "Who would have thought we would ever be talking about this!" exclaimed Elizabeth. Their giggles subsiding, Jane reached over to Elizabeth and raised her chin so that they were looking into each other's eyes.

"Lizzy," she said earnestly, "You and Mr Darcy have overcome so much to find each other. When you are together, giving each other pleasure, it is the physical embodiment of your love. You become one in every sense of the word. It is as if you discover you had never been whole before, and now you are."

"It is natural to be nervous. I do not think you will be so for long, my sister. Just trust your husband and follow your instincts."

They heard a light tap, and Mrs Gardiner put her head around the door. "Come in, Aunt," said Elizabeth.

Her aunt entered and sat down on the bed between her nieces, wrapping her arms around their shoulders. "All is well?"

"Yes," said Elizabeth firmly. "And thank you. Thank you, thank you."

Her aunt kissed her cheek. "Just be happy, Lizzy. That is all the thanks we could wish for."

CHAPTER 35

The wedding day of Fitzwilliam Darcy and Elizabeth Bennet dawned bright and clear. Sun shone throughout the brief ceremony, dappling the chapel floor with jewel-like colours as the bride and groom stood face to face and spoke their vows, each lost in the eyes of the other. By late morning, as the new Mr and Mrs Darcy climbed into their carriage for the short ride to the Gardiners' home, the sky still held few clouds to mar the perfect day.

They gazed at each other from across the carriage. "May we not sit next to one another?" Elizabeth asked, her head slightly tilted, her eyes alight, a small smile curving her lips.

He tore his gaze away from her for a moment and opened the window. "Take the long way, Jennings."

Darcy closed the window and turned to his wife.

"In answer to your question, Elizabeth, we may," he said, moving gingerly across the moving vehicle to take his place beside her. "But I cannot guarantee the survival of your exquisite coiffure." He took her in his arms. "At last," he breathed, and kissed her.

By the time the carriage pulled up to Gracechurch Street, all the guests had arrived, and the tables were laden with food. With flushed cheeks and rumpled hair, they entered to a chorus of cheers.

Mrs Bennet, with the help of Mrs Hill, Mrs Jenks, the Gardiners' kitchen servants, and one of the countess's under-cooks, had outdone herself. The wedding breakfast rivalled any offering of the best houses in London in elegance, variety, and sheer delectability. Course after delicious course arrived at the tables.

At last, the centrepiece of the meal was brought out. As their special wedding gift, Longbourn's own servants had lovingly prepared the bride's pie.

"Oh, Mrs Hill," Elizabeth said warmly. "And Mrs Jenks. Thank you."

Mr Darcy rose and bowed to them, then shook their hands.

"You take good care of her now," sniffled Mrs Hill.

"I promise, madam," he replied.

The pace of consumption finally slowed as the guests were sated. All present were relaxed and convivial, the smallest ones full of sweets. Little Henry Gardiner had eaten all the cake he could manage and had availed himself of every lap in the room, even the earl's.

Lord Matlock leaned back in his chair with a groan. "Mrs Bennet," he rose laboriously to his feet and raised a glass. "My sincere compliments, madam."

Mrs Bennet beamed, looking happier than she had been in months. An *earl*, for heaven's sake, had complimented her. She wished her husband was there to see. Her smile wilted a bit, and her eyes filled. Mary and Kitty appeared at her side.

"It is all right, Mama," Kitty whispered.

"Yes. Yes, it is. Thank you, girls," she answered, somewhat shakily, and took her seat.

THE AFTERNOON WAS DRAWING to a close when the bride and groom bid their loved ones adieu and boarded the carriage for Darcy House.

"My wife," said Darcy, pulling Elizabeth onto his lap for a deep, lingering kiss. Lifting his head, he sighed. "I am glad my aunt urged us to have a real wedding, Lizzy. It was beautiful. *You* are beautiful. But I was beginning to wonder if I would ever have you all to myself for more than a few minutes at a time again."

Elizabeth leaned her head on his shoulder. "It was just right, was not it? I would have never wanted it any other way, even if my family had not been in mourning. And now I can have *you* all to myself."

They kissed again and again, long, languorous kisses, lost to time until the carriage stopped in front of Darcy House. Darcy regretfully let go of her and alighted, handing his bride down only to lift her into his arms and carry her over the threshold.

He set her down, her coiffure listing perilously to one side, and they turned to greet the butler and housekeeper, who offered their welcome, asked if there was anything they required, and then discreetly vanished. As had, seemingly, all their servants, careful to give their master and new mistress their privacy, though Darcy knew they were there whenever wanted. The vast hall and wide corridors felt strangely deserted, as if they were the only two people in the world.

Blushing, Elizabeth embraced her husband and buried her face in his chest. He wrapped his arms around her.

"We are home, my dearest heart. Do you wish any refreshment? A glass of wine, perhaps?"

"Perhaps a maid? To…to help me prepare for..."

"*Bed*, Mrs Darcy?" he whispered in her ear. "We do need to hire a proper lady's maid for you. But until then..." He kissed her again, moving from her lips down to the curve of her neck. "Is there anything *I* might do to assist you?"

"Well, I might need assistance with buttons," she gasped. "And there are ribbons and...my hair."

"I can untie laces. I can remove hairpins." He swept her up in his arms and strode across the hall to the magnificent curving stairs and up, taking them two at a time, kicking the door of his room shut behind them.

He set her down on her feet, taking her mouth for a lingering kiss before turning her and setting to work on the tiny buttons of her gown. He worked intently, pausing occasionally to kiss her neck and shoulders. Elizabeth could feel his hair tickling the skin between her shoulder blades and shivered. As her gown loosened, she shrugged her shoulders clear of it and turned to face him, her delicate skin flushed. Their eyes met for a moment, then she reached up and began untying his cravat. When it fell to the floor, she unbuttoned his waistcoat as he set upon the ties of her corset.

He lowered his head and again tasted her lips, and then moved his mouth slowly along her jawline, lightly nipping, searching for the pulse point below her ear, the fragment of a dream flitting through his mind. *I wonder...* He reached it, and feathered kisses against it.

Elizabeth gasped, her eyes flying wide open only to flutter closed again as she captured his mouth with hers.

His coat dropped to the floor, followed by gown, waistcoat, shirt, breeches…and finally, her fine, delicate silk chemise floated gently to the floor.

"Do you trust me, Elizabeth?" he asked, pulling her flush against his body. "Yes," she sighed, relaxing against him. "Yes. With all my heart."

DARCY'S EYELIDS fluttered and opened. Light from the three-quarter moon streamed through the windows. He lay on his back, completely at ease, Elizabeth in his arms. She was asleep, her hair spread across his chest and shoulders, their legs intertwined. Her skin was smooth and warm under his touch, her hair silky, tangled in his fingers.

Was this a dream, like so many he had had before? He felt as if he were floating, as if they were drifting together in moonlight. He had so often imagined making love to Elizabeth, but nothing, *nothing* could have prepared him for the sensation of his palms sliding along her curves, her fingertips drifting over him, her body rising to meet his, her voice gasping his name. She shifted slightly, nuzzling and then kissing his chest.

"Darling," she whispered, and then sighing, relaxed back into sleep. He closed his eyes as deep waves of peace and joy overwhelmed him. *Can you die of happiness?* His heart swelled and his throat tightened. He breathed in deeply and let himself slide back into slumber.

LATER, Elizabeth stirred, warm and drowsy. The sky outside was beginning to lighten. Strong arms encircled her from the back, a large hand curved possessively around her waist. She turned in her beloved's arms and met his warm gaze.

He tightened his hold on her. "Did you sleep well, love? You were dreaming, were you not?"

She chuckled, slightly embarrassed. "Was it that obvious? I *was* dreaming." A faint pink blush began to bloom across her cheeks. "It was terribly strange. We were at Longbourn. We were…" The blush deepened. "We were...together…on my bed in my room." She buried her face in the hollow of his shoulder. "I would swear I was in my own bed with my head on my own pillow. I could even smell my perfume on it. But the beds and bedlinens remained at Longbourn when my family moved out. I have not seen them in months."

Elizabeth stole a sheepish glance at him. To her surprise, Darcy looked uncomfortable. His eyes moved involuntarily to the head of his enormous bed and she followed his gaze with her own. Her eyes widened.

"Is that...that is...*my pillow*?" she cried, rolling onto her belly and propping herself up on one elbow. She reached for it. "It is!"

Elizabeth sat up with the pillow in her hands, staring at it, and then turned to look at her husband. "How did you get my pillow?" She looked at it again in amazement. "Did you *steal* my pillow?"

Darcy, his cheeks red, was by now clearly embarrassed. "I did not steal it, Elizabeth! I have never stolen anything in my life!" He smiled sheepishly. "Although I will confess to *almost* stealing it. It was quite tempting at the time." He lay on his back, propped his arms behind his head and related the whole story to her. "I have since wondered if I have a fairy godmother," he concluded.

"A fairy godmother named Mrs Hill, I suspect," laughed Elizabeth. "She could move through the house without making a sound. I do not know that I could even count the number of times she caught me in the midst of some childish prank."

"At any rate, it is mine now, Elizabeth. I refuse to give it back to you. It has gotten me through many a lonely night." Darcy said, rising on one elbow and wrapping his other arm around her waist from behind. He began to plant soft kisses up her spine. A soft moan escaped her, and she sank back into his arms.

"I will not fight you over it, my dearest," she said, nestling against him. "I certainly would not wish to provoke you. I still shudder at the memory of your anger at me at Netherfield." She ran her fingers over his shoulder and rolled back onto his chest.

Darcy looked dumbfounded. "I have never been angry with you, Elizabeth." A corner of his mouth quirked up. "Frustrated, bewitched, discomfited, but never angry."

"But you must have been. At the ball when I pestered you about...about Wickham. It was inexcusably rude. I *know* you were angry. Your face was so flushed…truly, you went scarlet to the roots of your hair…"

"Elizabeth," he interrupted her. "My face was flushed because while I was chastising myself for having feelings for you, all the while I was..." he paused, and she felt his deep sigh as his chest rose and fell beneath her.

"You were what?"

His head flopped back onto his pillow and he closed his eyes. "I was...oh, God, Elizabeth, forgive me. I was thinking of you...imagining you…unclothed."

Elizabeth's head shot up and she stared at him in shock. "You were *what*?"

He tensed and opened his eyes, bracing himself for the revulsion and censure that was sure to be on her face. Instead, he watched, transfixed, as her expression transformed from wide-eyed amazement to mischievous delight.

"Really?" she breathed slowly, looking into his face, her

lips turning up at the corners, her eyes dancing. "I shall have to do the same, just to get even with you, my dearest." She kissed his chest, her hands moving down his flanks. "I shall imagine you in just such a state when we are walking in the park." Another kiss, on his shoulder. "Or when you are working in your study." A lingering kiss on his throat, her fingertips brushing his lower belly. "Or at dinner." She kissed his mouth, her tongue swirling lightly between his lips. He felt her body begin to quiver against his chest, laughter bubbling up in her throat. "Or on your horse."

"Elizabeth," he groaned, rolling her, still laughing, onto her back. "Enough, woman! You are driving me mad." His lips took hers, as passion overtook them once more.

CHAPTER 36

Caroline's return from Abbotsford Park was accomplished more quickly than the journey thither. It had been decided among the friends that Sophronia and Broughton would stay at Abbotsford for the time being, and everyone else would return to London or disperse to other house parties in the countryside. Caroline had been quiet, sulking because the onset of Lady Riverton's mourning marked the end of her own gambol, but she brightened at the idea of returning to town. Perhaps there were still some society events for her to be seen attending.

The Draytons and Spurlocks were weary of her company and now that the need for disguise was over, they hurried her back to Grosvenor Square as quickly as possible. With promises to deliver her remaining belongings from Riverton House, Caroline and Bertha were packed into Lord Drayton's carriage and dispatched as soon as their party reached town.

The carriage came to a halt in front of the Hursts' home.

Caroline pouted at the prospect of again taking up residence in the shabby town house. The driver got down and handed out first Bertha, then Miss Bingley. They turned to face the darkened house, only to see that the knocker was off the front door. Not the grand reception she had envisioned.

"Bertha," snapped Caroline, "Go to the tradesmen's entrance." Several minutes later, the front door opened and footmen emerged to unload her belongings. Caroline, with her trunks and bandboxes, swept into the house.

Once inside, she turned to speak to the housekeeper and then stopped, becoming aware of her surroundings. Her mouth still open, she turned slowly in a circle. The great hall was shining, elegant, sparkling. The marble floor shone, the deep colours in the fine antique Persian rug glowed, the chandelier glittered. Obviously there had been some changes.

Belatedly, she realised that the housekeeper was speaking to her.

"Miss, the master and mistress have gone to Somerleigh. They have no definite plans to return to town. I shall have your room made ready."

Caroline, perplexed and unsettled, wandered through the silent house. She wandered into the beautiful drawing room and gasped. What had transpired while she had been luxuriating in the highest ranks of the *ton*?

Why are Hurst and Louisa at Somerleigh? Where is Charles? When are we travelling to Pemberley?

Caroline, who never had a moment of doubt in her life, shivered with foreboding. She vaguely remembered receiving letters. Perhaps there was some explanation. Within the hour, her trunks arrived from Riverton House and she directed Bertha to go through them and search for any correspondence.

After a fraught half an hour, the maid brought a tray to Caroline. On it was a bundle of letters inscribed in Louisa's elegant handwriting. All had been delivered to her and left unopened on the salver on the dressing table at Riverton House. Caroline snatched them up, ripping them apart one by one.

An invitation for Christmas. Invitations for dinner. For shopping. An invitation to see the remodelled drawing room. A note from Louisa after seeing her at the ball.

Caroline's head snapped up. The emeralds! *Where* had Louisa gotten those emeralds? Had she taken them with her?

She began to snatch the missives up, faster and faster, almost shredding them in her haste.

Another dinner invitation. A note informing her that they were leaving for Netherfield. *Netherfield? Nooo!* Caroline snarled and kept reading.

Another note. Charles had married Jane Bennet. Caroline screamed with vexation. Now she would be forced to keep company with that horrible family. Another note. Louisa is with child? *Disgusting.* A letter announcing their intentions of spending the summer at Somerleigh.

One letter left.

She hesitated, tentatively took the missive between her forefinger and thumb, and opened it slowly.

Darcy was married. To Eliza Bennet.

She set the letter down slowly, took a long, deep breath, and howled in fury.

A cook's assistant in the kitchens froze, up to her elbows in dough, and shivered at the sound of the long, unearthly wail. A footman dropped a glass pitcher, and it shattered on the marble floor of the butler's pantry. A hackney driver shuddered as he drove past the house and spread the word amongst his customers that the place was haunted.

MISS BINGLEY'S FURY NOTWITHSTANDING, events had transpired just as Mr Bennet himself might have wished—happily resolved with little effort on his part. His two eldest and most deserving daughters had blissful marriages that he had blessed himself. His three silliest daughters had much improved prospects for the future. A pretty cottage in Meryton was provided for Mrs Bennet, where she would find society, gossip, and fashionable bonnets for many years to come. The Collinses were at Longbourn and, well, as the old philosopher himself might have said, with a sip of his wine: one could not have everything.

But those, such as Gilbert Hurst and Fitzwilliam Darcy, who decided to choose love and show kindness, did indeed have everything. Their decisions and actions led them to find joy and inspired others to do the same. Their network of family and friends lay scattered about the country like bright jewels connected by a chain of letters and visits; connexions of true affection that endured over many years and into the next generations.

The End

ACKNOWLEDGMENTS

Writing fanfiction is one thing and the publication process is quite another. My profound and unending appreciation to my editors Jan Ashton and Debra Anne Watson for patiently leading the greenest of greenhorns through this process instead of throwing up their hands in surrender. Thank you also to Quills & Quartos Publishing and their crew. I was a fan long before I ever thought of submitting a story, and I am honored to be included.

To my four grown children and four children-by-marriage, thank you for your love and encouragement and for reading the manuscript as it went through changes. Your genuine support goes far beyond relief that Gran has found Something To Do.

Thanks also to my library friends and colleagues, who didn't laugh when I told them I was writing fanfiction, and who actively encourage and support readers becoming writers.

Finally, to Mrs Lee, the elderly school librarian at the tiny rural K-12 school I attended, whose face lit up like a Christmas tree when I pulled a dusty, neglected copy of *Pride & Prejudice* off the shelves, somewhere around fifty years ago. Dear Mrs Lee, this is all your fault.

ABOUT THE AUTHOR

Nan Harrison is a happily retired librarian who spent many years in public libraries large and small, urban and rural, digital and analog. She earned degrees in anthropology and library/information science but they are so old they were inscribed on clay tablets. She raised a family and is thrilled that her children grew up to be people she would want to hang out with anyway. She spends as much time as possible traveling and visits libraries (also thrift shops and used bookstores) wherever she goes. She loves reading, especially any type of genre fiction, and putting a warp on her loom to see what turns out. She still thinks like an anthropologist and believes that libraries are the last bastion of civilization. She is an excellent walker.

Any Fair Interference is Nan's first book.

Made in the USA
Monee, IL
18 February 2022